THE PEDLOCKS

"This powerful novel considers a Jewish family in direct and collateral lines from the Civil War to the Nineteen Forties. Stemming from Joseph Pedlock, source and perpetual inspiration, the characters have a bond with reality as sure as that of daily newspapers. Their questings for ultimate validities give the core of real life to all the outward emotions.

"Portrayals vary over wide compass. There is Ralph, the almost-renegade, who falters a lifetime between loyalty to family and tradition, and escape into expediency. There is Egon, the esthete, who has neuroses enough to pose his own rather pretentious notion of art, who has soul enough to operate a small asylum for children of tragedy, and courage enough to strike at a Nazi general. There is rugged Uncle Louis, who makes himself overconspicuous in Western boots and cattleman manners even in Paris . . .

"In his many-sided ventures the author has not always been this successful. It is quite apparent that he is the Peter Perry of this novel; and very probable that Peter's unfinished diary, of which the reader is given a glimpse, is in fact a carefully finished diary kept by Stephen Longstreet over many years."

—New York *Times Book Review*
April 29, 1951

Selected novels by Stephen Longstreet

THE PEDLOCKS

A NOVEL BY
STEPHEN LONGSTREET

DONALD I. FINE, INC.
New York

Library of Congress Cataloging-Publication Data
Longstreet, Stephen, 1907-
    The Pedlocks.
    I. Title.
PS3523.0486P43   1987   813'.54   87-81548
ISBN: 1-55611-047-2
Manufactured in the United States of America
10 9 8 7 6 5 4 3 2 1

Dear Joan and Harry,

You have both been wanting to read this novel for a long time. Now it is ready. It is not really the kind of book that needs a lot of family trees and charts to pick out its characters. But for those that like to trace family lines there is a family tree* with all the leaves marked and dated.

In case you should want to take your bearing from time to time, after you are in the book, I am listing below some of the important people of our story. As yet their names mean nothing to you, so wait until you know them a little better.

I have invented very little. Most of the people and most of the things here told happened in a just gone past. But I have changed everything just a little and developed the people as is only fitting in the novel; for to create printed life one must, in my books anyway, mould and reshape in the way a man like Cézanne refits nature onto his canvas, into a series of forms just a little clearer than life itself.

So in this journey you will meet, mostly, these:

JOSEPH PEDLOCK
REBECCA, his wife
SAM ⎫
RALPH ⎬ his sons
EGON ⎭
SELMA, his daughter
SARA KAHN-WASSERMAN, married to Sam
JACOB KOZLOFF, married to Selma
ALICE PENTLAND, married to Ralph
PETER and NICOLE, the children of Ralph and Alice
MIKE, the son of Selma and Jacob
TANTE STRASSER, the sister of Joseph
BELLA, the sister of Jacob Kozloff

* PUBLISHER'S NOTE: A chart showing the complete family history of the Pedlocks, the Manderscheids, and the Sontags will be found on pages viii and ix.

AARON and SIMON MANDERSCHEID, the brothers of Rebecca
LOUIS (THE COLONEL), Simon's son
ELIMELICH SONTAG, a cousin of the Manderscheids
EDWARD, his grandson, married to
ETTA
IKE and ROSE, their children

You will find they have the faults and some of the virtues of people we know, and a great deal of the fun and sorrow and troubles and pleasures.

Your Old Man
STEPHEN LONGSTREET

Beverly Hills
California

Was du ererbt von deinen Vatern hast
Erwirb es um es zu besitzen.

What you have inherited from your fathers
You must earn in order to possess.

—GOETHE

The Pedlocks

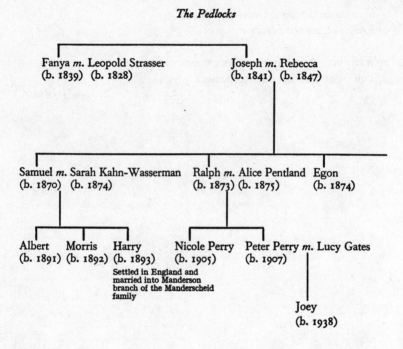

Fanya *m.* Leopold Strasser
(b. 1839)   (b. 1828)

Joseph *m.* Rebecca
(b. 1841)   (b. 1847)

Samuel *m.* Sarah Kahn-Wasserman
(b. 1870)   (b. 1874)

Ralph *m.* Alice Pentland   Egon
(b. 1873) (b. 1875)   (b. 1874)

Albert   Morris   Harry
(b. 1891) (b. 1892) (b. 1893)

**Settled in England and
married into Manderson
branch of the Manderscheid
family**

Nicole Perry   Peter Perry *m.* Lucy Gates
(b. 1905)   (b. 1907)

Joey
(b. 1938)

A Family

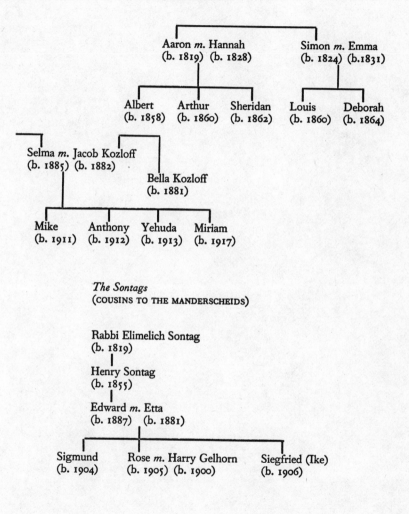

The Manderscheids

Aaron *m.* Hannah (b. 1819) (b. 1828)   Simon *m.* Emma (b. 1824) (b.1831)

Albert (b. 1858)   Arthur (b. 1860)   Sheridan (b. 1862)   Louis (b. 1860)   Deborah (b. 1864)

Selma *m.* Jacob Kozloff (b. 1885) (b. 1882)   Bella Kozloff (b. 1881)

Mike (b. 1911)   Anthony (b. 1912)   Yehuda (b. 1913)   Miriam (b. 1917)

The Sontags
(COUSINS TO THE MANDERSCHEIDS)

Rabbi Elimelich Sontag (b. 1819)

Henry Sontag (b. 1855)

Edward *m.* Etta (b. 1887)   (b. 1881)

Sigmund (b. 1904)   Rose *m.* Harry Gelhorn (b. 1905) (b. 1900)   Siegfried (Ike) (b. 1906)

BOOK ONE

CHAPTER I

On a rainy day, Peter Manderson Perry and his small son Joey left Paradise. The place was no longer called that. The billboard had read

PARADISE ESTATES
The Best of Westchester

but with the sale of the last lot, the sign had come down.

"Paradise," said Peter very low, as the wipers whimpered and raced across the windshield. He remembered and quoted some old school text. *The place in which the souls of the righteous abide after death in a state of bliss.*

"What, Dad?" asked Joey.

"Will you be happy to see Grandpa?"

"You bet. Aren't we coming back?"

"I don't think so, Joey."

"Ma *sick* again?" The little boy gave the word *sick* their private, secret meaning.

Peter nodded. "Yes. You mustn't think about it."

As he turned off onto the highway and went through the ornate stone gates of the "estates", the shadow came down on him again and all the fear and conjecture took shapes and hovered over him. He looked out. The swirling muttering of trees, the wet geometric shapes of Paradise were no longer idyllic. The rain grew bolder, flashing and blinding his vision as he drove.

He was finished with his home in that rather good development on the fringe of Larchmont, in Westchester County; finished with his wife Lucy, and alone with his son Joey. He was drained tired as if from a family service held for one lately dead.

That night Peter sat by Joey's bed in the little upstairs room of his father's house and thought back to his past and hunted in it the thing that had hurt him so much that day. He hunted a long time. . . .

At last Peter Manderson Perry, a tight bundle of outward composure and inward vexation, turned his thought to the Pedlocks. He had always been aware of the depth of his feeling for them, but his life, as he grew older, existed on several levels (like a well-worked coal mine, he felt, with many half-forgotten shafts). He had for a long time not thought of them fully and in detail. Now, with the rain on the roof shakes, he thought deeply of all the Pedlocks.

And as he thought of them he began—as always—to think of them as a small boy would think of them. For that was how he first met them. He was rather puzzled that the small boy—his melted-away past—was tonight such a feeble stranger to him. For as he sat there he seemed to feel warmer and closer to the Pedlocks than to the small boy, who was like a blurred flickering image in an old film that still had sections of its surfaces clear and full of detail. And had other damaged parts that were speeded up and blurred and fading, and turning the rust-brown of age.

It had been a fine thing, naturally, to be born Peter Manderson Perry. And live on a wedge of wooded land called Perry Point.

Joey looked up at his father from the bed.

"It's still raining."

"Yes, you don't mind, do you, Joey?"

"I like the rain and the sound of rain."

"When I was a boy, I used to like it too. I haven't listened much to it, not for a long time."

"Did you live here?"

"No. We lived at Perry Point. It was very grand in those days. Of course we kids, Nicole and myself, didn't know it was very grand. We just felt this is the way it should be."

"Tell me about the boats again."

"Some other time, Joey. It's been a big day."

"Just about *The Glory*."

It was an old story and Joey liked to hear it just before he fell asleep.

"*The Glory* was fifty feet long, she was a ketch and had sails of imported cotton and my father was the Captain. I wore a sailor suit. . . ."

"A real suit," Joey added, "with no fly in front, but rows of buttons on the side, like the real stuff."

"That's right, no fly in front, with buttons on the side. We used to sail to Newport with a lot of guests and one night there was a storm and I slept right through it and my father said, 'Peter, you're a born sailor. Some day you'll command a ship of your own. The Pentlands, your grandmother's family, sailed the first clipper ships.'"

But Joey was already asleep.

*   *   *

2

Perry Point on Long Island. On green acres facing the scribbles of distant smoke and the Sound, and the bobbling yachts. With the white turn of keels far out, seen across a well-clipped lawn. It was good to be a little boy called Peter Manderson Perry and to have an English brick house with real ivy, and ramblers climbing its walls like a well-kept pink beard. To have a sister called Nicole. And a shaggy pony of one's own. And a serious sort of father who smoked long polished pipes and wore tweed shooting jackets, and kept a kennel of long-eared braying hound dogs. There was Mother, who was all golden and tanned and rode a black stallion astride. She could smell so delightfully of fields and winds and the wool of her hunting pink. How "the Jews" entered into all this was a puzzle to the boy Peter.

Once a month Katie, their kind and wonderful Irish governess, with the Son of God banging his silver image between her bobbing breasts, would take Peter and Nicole up into the big bathroom paved with Dutch tiles showing windmills turning. She would scrub their ears very hard and comb their hair, the golden hair of their mother and father, until it curled and flashed and gave off sparks. They were dressed in stiff fine linen and Katie would inspect them carefully, smiling her kind smile, and finger her silver Lord with approval and say, "I guess we can go now to see the Jews."

Mother and Father never went. Just Peter and Nicole, with Katie. By a very exciting train that made little hooting sounds and darted under bridges, and across a river full of dull red tugs. Past naked boys making very obscene gestures as they dived into the brown garbage-filled waters. They came at last to the station, with its booming echoes. Semmel, the Pedlock coachman, would be waiting for them. At first it was with what Katie called "a spanking pair of bays" and a wide, fast carriage, but later, around 1912, the first of those wonderful stinking monsters with a red running gear, a Packard. The redstone house fronts they passed were very clean, then they would turn into the Hudson River streets. At last they always came to Riverside Drive. Peter and Nicole would lean out to see the sailors and the battleships on the river, when there were battleships. Semmel would chew a brown cud and tell them about the time he and Peter's uncles, Louis and Sam, had fought in Cuba, with old Teddy-Four-Eyes.

"Teddy could have won the war single-handed."

"Did you and Uncle Louis kill anybody?" Peter often asked. Uncle Louis was from the West and always carried a gun.

"Slews of people. Kill, kill all day, and sometimes all night."

Katie would say with a happy, mocking gesture, "Moskeetos."

"Was Uncle Sam very brave?"

"Bravest man I ever knew. He ate the condemned beef they fed us U.S. soldiers. We fought that war in our bellies."

"That will do, Semmel," said Katie primly. She didn't care for family histories. Or to have the children hear too much of the family's turmoils and laments. It sounded so Jewish!

Riverside Drive was always beautiful, with the green trees like those feathery blops in that painting by someone called Renoir that Uncle Egon had brought back from Paris. And the apartment houses with all the fancy grillwork and the doormen looking like heroes in old wars, standing there at the curbs—twirling moustaches that were at least six inches from end to end. Peter wondered how he would look some day in a long blond guardsman's moustache. And upstairs were "the Jews".

The Pedlocks lived in a white apartment, on top of the twelve-storey house called grandly "The Naples", perhaps because two white Italian urns in front of the doors had once bloomed, but now held only dying pine trees with stray string and candy wrappers tangled on their thin branches.

It was always fun to go up in the slow, sighing iron cage driven by the blackest boy in the reddest uniform. The pit of your stomach stretching tautly and Nicole wanting to cat. At last they came to the fumed oak door with the knocker in the shape of a naked man (with his private parts carefully carved in small, perfect detail). It was his big, bearded head that one took hold of and banged to attract attention. It was a rule; Peter and Nicole each took one ear and banged the knocker together.

The door would open and there would be the Pedlocks. It was a fearful, exciting time. Those wonderful animated people who seemed wound up and ready for all kinds of fun. Who lived often on a level of excitement not at all in keeping with the calm dignity of life on a Long Island point. After all, their mother was a Boston Pentland and Father and Grandfather were bankers on Wall Street.

First there came to the children the sharp smell, mouth-watering, of dinner cooking and seeping through dozens of tall white doors into the glass-walled sky apartment. Spices and odd sauces that burned the appetite and opened the mouth. Such food the children loved and ate with great relish and polite greed. The whole place was big and crowded with wonderful things. The furniture was heavy and solid and inlaid and highly waxed. The pictures were not dead game, or flowers, or Hudson River landscapes wrapped in mist. "Some of the ladies," Nicole said, "show their belly-buttons."

"You often see them in pictures," Peter told her.

4

Over the carved Spanish fireplace hung, in those days, the famous John Singer Sargent painting of Joseph Pedlock, and his wife, and their sons, Sam, Ralph, and Egon—all small boys in naked knees and velvet pants with big blue bows on their Eton collars. Joseph Pedlock with a dark beard then, holding a live cigar (it glowed beautifully, painted in two tones of pink, in the half dusk just before dinner). Flanking this huge picture was a long line of stiffly posed beards and female wigs and wing collars and genuine gold chains and stern Talmudic faces. They had the grace of features and beauty of things one saw sometimes dug up from the desert thousands of years after they were made. And oddly, Peter thought, wigs and three-cornered hats out of George Washington's time—family faces signed Copley and Stuart.

Over the big, wind-shaken windows that framed the river below (and as much of New Jersey as one cared to see) was hung Uncle Egon's entire estate; pictures that he traded for cash or jewels when he came back often from Monte or Paris, broke and laughing. Two of the famous Renoirs, and something green and full of dots by Pissarro. Men playing cards in wonderful colours which Uncle Egon never let them dust, or move, because it was by Mr. Cézanne of whom no one had ever heard.

The ballet girl pictures and the green, gas-lit dance halls of Degas and Lautrec pleased everyone much more. But Uncle Sam, who said, "I know what I like," never hung anything but Remingtons or faked Corots and bearskins in the library. All this, the children knew, had to be taken in with a gulping glance for soon the place would be filled with people coming for the monthly dinner of the family. Between the sliding doors the servants, big, plump, Rumanian immigrant girls, could be seen, still rushing food and silver and crystal to the long table with its crisp damask cloth in which one could still see the folded squares of its closet life. The Pedlocks were having dreadful business troubles but it didn't show.

Uncle Sam and Aunt Sara were usually in the living room, Uncle Sam brushing back the little hair he had left and bravely shaking off cigar ash without thinking of what it would do to the rug.

"Here they are," Uncle Sam would say, extending a hard red fist on which a ring with a red stone loaded down a bent, hairy pinky finger. "You sure look good, kids. How are things on Long Island?"

"Very well, thank you, Uncle Sam," Nicole would say as Katie removed her leggings, and fluffed up her yellow hair.

5

"Hungry?" asked Aunt Sara. "A glass of milk perhaps? And a cookie . . . the currant ones with walnuts chopped in?"

"No thank you," Peter always said, as he had been coached, "it would spoil my dinner."

"Not mine," Nicole said anyway.

Aunt Sara, who was tall and graceful with a large head of brown curled hair and the most beautiful dark eyes in the world, would agree and send a maid for the milk and the cookies. If Uncle Egon were back in America—"to get money for a season of gambling at the spas"—he never missed a family dinner. Uncle Egon was a real swell. A pale polite blue vest and spotted ties around high wing collars and flashing teeth in a round moon of a face. With a few red wisps of hair left to him combed well forward, "so that at times I give the impression I have a full head of hair". Uncle Egon spoke French very well and was always in need of money. He gambled a lot at a place called Monte and had a system in a little black book full of numbers. He knew horse racing and impressionism and Vienna Herr Doktors.

He made his own cigarettes with "a little machine I bought in Budapest while broke and a waiter in a café there". And Peter and Nicole loved to hand him the thinnest of cigarette papers, and the fine, sliced, curly Turkish tobacco, and he placed them in the little machine, pressed a lever, and out came a finished cigarette. When Uncle Egon really got started manufacturing, Peter and Nicole would make hundreds of cigarettes in an afternoon with him.

If there was time they would fill his collection of cigarette cases, big jewelled and golden cases that folded very flat and had things written on the metal in many languages (also tiny pawn brokers' markings).

All of this nonsense stopped when Sam's and Egon's father, Joseph Pedlock, and his sister Tante Strasser (rumour was that she was almost a hundred years old) came through from the next apartment, through a special door, "that had cost a thousand dollars to cut through solid brick walls". They came in just before dinner. A dignified respect always greeted them, but it didn't last long. Everyone liked to talk and laugh, and exchange remarks, and by the time dinner was served it was really a pleasure to sit down and eat the wonderful, spicy food served in huge Spode plates holding a great deal of everything. And you could ask for all you wanted as dear, kind Katie was busy gorging herself, because she was always hungry at Perry Point with its scientific, tasteless cooking.

It was several years before Peter and Nicole could get everyone in

6

his proper relationship at the Pedlocks' and remember all the cousins and the aunts (who weren't at all like the characters of the same name in the Gilbert and Sullivan song). Peter at first tried hard to remember them all, but after awhile he gave it up and just took them as they came.

Joseph Pedlock always sat at the head of the table, with Aunt Strasser on his right, and any stray European or South American or Chinese *lantzman*—translated as 'townsman or friend'—scattered among the family. The English Pedlocks were helping in building a modern European business section in Shanghai and Peter always expected the Chinese Pedlocks to have yellow skins or slant eyes. But they looked just like anybody else. "They might even ride at the Point fox hunt," as Uncle Egon often said, "if the shape of their grandmothers' noses were in order."

The dinners began by a quick swallow of amber-coloured, old brandy in very small glasses, with only Joseph Pedlock taking a Polish *slivovitz*, a white fire in a blue bottle. After which everyone was served a beautiful still life; a plate that contained a heaping portion of pickled French mushrooms, spiced artichokes, and chopped chicken livers; always a favourite made by Sara herself.

The table talk made little sense to Peter and Nicole.

Joseph Pedlock would look up from his hors d'œuvres and ask Uncle Sam, "How did Copper do today, Samuel?"

"Bad, the Guggenheims are fixing something fancy with the stock. We're taking a beating again."

Tante Strasser, eating very fast (before they stopped her), said, "Such small servings."

Joseph laughed into his square-cut beard and patted her arm with pleased affection. "Sara, are you opening the house at Lakewood this year?"

"We're going to Rome. After Baden-Baden, Sam's back is killing him."

"Last year we met the Kaiser. You could see his left arm was much shorter, even if he held it on his sword all the time."

"Kimberley isn't going to last for ever, then what will you diamond cutters do in Amsterdam, go kiss the British behind to discover a new field?"

"We're planning fifty thousand orange trees this year all along the coast from Gaza to Acre. And a hospital on the Mount of Olives."

"Just the best place the Arabs can burn it down," Joseph said. *"Kennst du das Land wo die Zitronen blühen?"*

"Tante, please save your strength for the rest of the food."

7

"I'm not going to live much longer. Let me eat my own way. You dieting again, Sara?"

At which point they brought in the soup. Peter was not too busy eating to listen to the table talk, which went from charity to business, art to fashions; to relatives all over the world; from famous fiddle players and honoured guests to the voices of noted cantors; and the habits of female actresses with which one lusty branch of the family was always involved.

Wine appeared. Dusty bottles in linen shrouds and red caps, and even Peter and Nicole had a few drops in tall Italian crystal glasses. Everyone but the very young had coffee.

Uncle Egon spoke best after coffee. "We buy the popular new mysticism, metaphysics and philosophies at bargain rates these days."

"Oh, shut up," said Uncle Sam, winking at Peter. "Don't take everything apart so. It's un-American."

By the time the coffee came Joseph had warmed into life and was looking around the table with a little sparkle and colour in his faded blue eyes. It was time to ask for small favours in hard times or report family troubles. If one laughed loud enough at Joseph's little jokes, everything would go very well.

"What do you think of the dinner, Peter? And you, Nicole?"

"It's better than Thanksgiving, Grandfather. Really it is."

"More?"

"I'm very full, thank you."

"Let's all go next door while the men smoke their cigars. Sam, please have the windows opened."

Peter felt really one of them. Yet no one ever called him and Nicole Jews.

He remembered how everyone rose slowly from the table and the women and children went through the passage and door into the apartment of Tante Strasser and Joseph Pedlock. Joseph hadn't contributed too much to the place, he admitted. Over a beautiful marble fireplace full of fat, sassy and naked angels hung two paintings, one of Judah P. Benjamin, the Confederate Secretary of the Treasury, and a dramatic picture of J. E. B. ("*not* Jeb, you Yankee!") Stuart, the dashing Rebel horseman, painted in a plumed hat and his beard cut as square as Joseph cut his own. There was a cabinet of mineral samples from the rich old days when the Pedlock Corporations were organized as the first copper and silver combines and things looked bright and hopeful. On one wall was a painting of Joseph's dead wife, Rebecca Manderscheid, as a young girl, by some popular London hack. And facing it, a Copley painting of her great-great-grandfather, Moses

8

Manderscheid, as he must have really looked in Philadelphia, in 1762. He was a bright, alert little man with beautiful eyes and a thin little mouth, wearing his three-cornered hat and frilled neck cloth with a daintiness and crispness that the great painter had rendered with remarkable craftsmanship and understanding.

"He's a hero," Peter used to tell Nicole.

"Did he know George Washington?" Nicole once asked after a big dinner that left her short of breath.

"Very well," said Joseph, sucking his black burning stogie into smoking life. "One of the apple trees at Mount Vernon was a present from Manderscheid to the General. They still grow those apples there. Big, fat, yellow fellows with freckles on them."

Nicole had eaten too much, alas, and was feeling ready to toss her dinner, and to save herself from that impoliteness, she pointed to a dark painting with many yellow varnishes on it.

"That man scares me."

"He scared a lot of people. The Duke of Escalona. He was the Viceroy of Mexico, in 1640, by Royal Appointment."

"He looks like Uncle Egon in a black beard."

Joseph peered down at his glowing cigar end ironically and said, "There is a family connection. The Duke's full name gives away his ancestry. Don Diego Lopez *Levi* Pacheco Cabrera y Bobadilla."

Peter put his elbow gently in Nicole's ribs. It was their private signal when a subject was not to be carried any further at the Pedlocks'. The Jewish and non-Jewish sides of the family treated each other with care. It was very apparent that the Duke of Escalona was "a New Christian, like Father" (oh, dear, the secret was out), and a subject not for the moment or the place.

Tante Strasser had done the apartment over to her own taste. It was a sort of upper-middle-class, Vienna interior. Blood-red hangings. Off-red walls and heavy gilt, like golden whipped cream, over everything.

The drapes let in a little light, just enough to show the family and their guests sitting around in the tall chairs digesting their meal. Everyone talked freely until Joseph went out for his after-dinner walk along the windy Drive. It was a walk he liked to take alone. Carrying a heavy blackwood cane that he had cut in a Virginia wood, the day Lee surrendered to Grant, and Joseph, his bad leg festering and puffy, sat at a muddy crossroads and watched the long soiled lines of Union troops, bayonets slanting in a cold wind, marching past, singing: "When This Long Cruel War is Over."

It was always some *lantzman* or "Chinese" Pedlock who would

9

look at the military paintings over the fireplace and ask, "What war are those from?"

"This family has been in many wars. It's been fighting wars, it seems," said Uncle Egon, the brandy filtering deep and mellow in his stomach, "since the destruction of the Temple."

Peter said to Nicole, "The one with the plumes is J. E. B. Stuart. The greatest sonofabitch that ever got on a horse."

No one corrected him as he was merely quoting Joseph, who always spoke in such an admiring manner concerning his old commander. "We've fought our country's wars a lot."

Uncle Sam would laugh and rattle his watch chain and say, "Papa at twenty-five, mind you, he held the lines after Stonewall Jackson fell, and held on until J. E. B. Stuart took command at eleven p.m. on the night of the second of May . . . so that when the main battle . . ."

"Enough of wars," Tante Strasser would say, and watch the silver candy dish being pushed beyond her reach, and she would close her mouth very tight and scowl down on poor Peter. Not caring very much about the excitement of a small boy, who had a grandfather who had lain with a shattered leg on the battlefield of Chancellorsville, a dead horse across the burning limb, a black tongue moaning for water, and the battle dying away in the brush and timber of those fields. Peter had seen war often on the floor of his father's library in the many leather-bound volumes of the *Photographic History of the Civil War*. Heavy volumes filled with bearded men in dusty uniforms fighting a bitter war in little caps and soiled boots and cavalry sabres so long ago. And that his grandfather was an old Jew now with a limp, and a short beard cut square across, as with a sword slash, and turning white, that spoiled it only a little.

There was an old photograph on an end table—turned pale brown around the edges, set in a small brass frame, but with the lens detail still clear and sharp. Taken in camp just before First Manassas. "Which the damn Yankees," the old man said, "called Bull Run." It showed a proud young man in Rebel gray, with the gold trimming the soldiers called "chicken guts" on the cuffs, and a proper cap with a black patent leather peak, and all the fine fit of real Richmond tailoring, "Judah P. Benjamin's own tailor". The face was calm and unlined, and the arms ended in long leather gauntlets folded proudly on the full chest. That was Captain Joseph Pedlock, C.S.A., Captain at twenty-three of Confederate horse. "A long way from the bloody shirt tails and the loose bowels," he often said, "and the leg shattered by a Sharps' rifle, the torn mouth and the stink of defeat. That's taken in front of a clean tent, ten o'clock in the morning, by a travelling photographer with a box camera and a glass plate, and a time exposure of one full minute. I was a jim dandy then."

Yes, the Captain was—standing there so calm. Just a little brown around the edges.

Peter used to study the picture in its brass frame, and when he was tall enough to look directly into the proud laughing eyes of his grandfather's silver nitrate image, he wondered why that bright and handsome boy should become the tall thin figure wrapped in a bearskin robe, with a dragging leg, and the lined face with the red-rimmed eyes. And wrinkles like gullies torn by time into once-green fields. Why should he have become such an old man? And would he, Peter, ever become that old?

And too soon it was time to go back to Perry Point.

Now night in the city was really coming down over the Drive and the gas globes were turned up higher in the carved ceiling. Dear kind Katie would appear with wraps and hats and leggings and begin to bundle and button and tie them up in a hurry.

"That's the last fast train. Now hurry, we just have time."

"I ate too much, Katie."

"Don't you dare toss it up, my fine lady!"

Bundled, buttoned, and trussed, the wrinkles smoothed out, Peter and Nicole would make their bows, and kiss the aunts and be kissed in turn. The uncles always shook hands politely. Joseph would pat their heads.

"Enough to eat? That's fine. Wrapped up warm? Good."

"Good night, and thank you for everything, Grandfather."

"Good to have you. See you next month."

"Something to eat on the way?" asked Aunt Sara.

Katie shook her head. "They're so stuffed to bursting right now, Mrs. Pedlock, their eyes are hanging out on stems."

They would leave all the laughter and the gay talk and the wonderful amusing relatives and "Chinese" visitors, and go out into the cold. Semmel was ready with big, warm buffalo robes. Away they would drive with millions of lights going on all over the city. Usually they had to stop for Nicole to lean over the gutter, while Katie held her head firmly and they all waited until her delicate stomach was relieved. She smelled a little sour and was very sleepy all the rest of the way home. But even that didn't spoil the most wonderful day of the month, the day they went to "the Jews".

As the train wheels click-clicked and the blue polite shadows of Long Island night crept closer around the train windows Peter would breathe against them. With his finger he drew cold wide pictures of nameless subjects until he too fell asleep, leaning against the soft, warm bulk of the kind, obliging Katie.

Joey tossed in his sleep and opened his eyes.

"You there, Pop?"

"I'm here, Joey. Don't worry, I'm here. I've been sitting here thinking when I was a little boy myself," Peter said.

"Was it fun?"

"Some of it. Most of it."

"Mom going away again?"

"Yes, yes, suppose so. For a long time."

"She *sick* again?"

Peter looked down on the boy and patted his cheek. "You go get some shut-eye if we're going out to the boats in the morning."

"You're not going to the office?"

"No, not to the office. Sleep, Joey."

Joey yawned, showing a space where the baby teeth had come out.

"It's good sleeping with the rain on the roof and the little light on and you sittin' there, Pop, and . . ."

By that time Joey was already asleep. Peter pulled the blankets higher and went back to sit in the old leather chair, a chair he used to know very well.

Sitting there, the questions came crowding into his mind. How did I happen? Almost childish nonsense like where did I come from, Mother dear? Are babies found under cabbage leaves?

How did Joseph Pedlock find himself a wife and have three sons called Sam and Ralph and Egon? And have a grandson called Peter, sitting now in a small room watching his own son Joey sleep?

How had Joseph Pedlock met the Manderscheids? Peter remembered his college days and his visits to an old house in Philadelphia.

CHAPTER II

An aged Philadelphia brick house near Kennett Square.

A house that had once been a station in the underground railroad that smuggled escaped slaves into Canada, in the 1850's. In this house Peter, as a very young man, had found many old letters and journals.

Weekends, Peter—thinking himself the perfect F. Scott Fitzgerald hero—used to come down from Princeton, carrying a small leather case that contained his dress suit and dancing slippers of patent leather. He wore his raccoon coat and a bowler hat as fitting to the time and era, and carried a silver hip flask full of a dreadful booze made by a college janitor. It was only ten years since Fitzgerald ("the great Scottie") himself had been at Princeton and no one, in those days, was trying to forget him.

Peter used to attend the polite dances in old homes in Chester County and wonder at the houses with their projecting eaves and small, diamond-shaped panes that gave so little light or air.

He stayed at the old Manderscheid house in Philadelphia because he was fascinated by the place, and because Aunt Ann—his grandmother's sister—was one of the last of the direct Manderscheid line. She was a crisp, witty old girl with big dark eyes and wide shoulders, somewhat of a bluestocking, and proud of the Manderscheid family portraits hung on the winding staircase. Good, solid Manderscheid faces by Hesselius and Matthew Pratt, and of course, the famous Gilbert Stuarts and Copleys; men and women and children in three-cornered hats and brocades, wigs, hair buckled in papillotes, knee buckles, and attending items such as gold snuff boxes and bound volumes later to be presented to the Philosophical Society, or Peale's Museum.

Aunt Ann looked like a warrior Quakeress in her grey bonnet, read Mary Wollstonecraft's *Rights of Women* as if it were a contemporary best-seller, had a morbid, shrill sense of humour. She had bought her coffin at an early age—after a Spanish-American War romance—and used it, meanwhile, as a trough for mixing bread in her little prim kitchen. A fine kitchen, Peter thought, its bricks painted with a red water paint and its fireplace scoured weekly with another brick.

13

She liked to have Peter there, so young and handsome and so popular with the Main Line families and in the big houses on the stone road
to Lancaster. She would brew a too strong oolong tea in her undamaged
Wedgwood and tell him of when Talleyrand was a guest in the house.
And how Joseph Pedlock courted Rebecca.

She did not mind when Peter did not go to the dances on rainy
weekends but preferred to go up to the sloping attic and rummage in
the huge, nail-head trunks smelling of fennel and mice dung and faded
Cherokee roses. There were thousands of old letters and tattered
ledgers and account books. Even journals written in a faded black ink
with great scrolls. And garden lists of old farms and hothouses where
someone had raised exotic plants; tobacco, figs, Oriental melons and
pomegranates. All collected by a Doctor Simon Manderscheid—as an
aid to his unfinished history of a family.

Peter came down from the attic one rainy weekend, mice dust on his
hands and a box of old journals under his arm. Aunt Ann sat at the
kitchen table, her face high-coloured, and a bottle of popular "stomach
bitters" at her elbow.

"Digging, Peter? Digging in the past?"

"I've found the journals of the first Manderscheids. They go back
to Jamestown and Captain John Smith!"

She poured a glassful of "stomach bitters" and drank it off quickly.
Peter tried not to see. Aunt Ann was a solitary drinker, and that was
why she lived alone and was not too popular with the respectable
members of the family. Aunt Ann laughed.

"Beat not the bones of the buried, Peter; when they lived they
were men. I've misquoted somebody, but you know what I mean."

"Of course."

"Don't look—look so foolish, Peter. Of course I'm drunk. Philadelphia is dreadful enough without having a secret vice. I used to
have another. A fine Christian lover who died in Cuba, a long time
ago."

"Don't you think you better lie down?"

"No. Let's look over the past. Let's turn the dry pages of men long
dead. They made me and some made you, Peter."

"They seem so real in these pages."

Aunt Ann found another bottle of "stomach bitters" in the closet
and opened it and nodded. "Little details bring them back. Like what
they ate, what they wore."

"And what they planted."

"Escape the family, Peter, or they'll ruin you."

14

"Oh, I doubt that. How did Joseph Pedlock get into the family?"

"There is such a thing as too much family. Leave 'em, Peter, and all their plants and their journals. Joseph Pedlock? You'll find some letters of his around."

Peter found the one he wanted, one day, folded into an old medical text. It was like a curtain rising on a badly remembered play. And the first words bringing it all back again. He had heard the story as a child.

Charleston, December 18, 1865

Dear Doctor Simon Manderscheid:

I do not know if you feel able to treat a member of the late enemy forces. I suffer from a neglected leg wound that has never healed; complications of the lower bones of my right leg.

I have not been able to get any relief for this injury, and you have been spoken of as the major bone specialist in America. If it is not against your principles to treat the late enemy, I would like to visit you professionally in the near future.

Yours truly,
Joseph Pedlock
Major, disbanded, C.S.A.

Philadelphia in the late 1860's had style and it was cool in the big ornate room fronting the narrow stone street, during those warm summer days when the heat came blazing across New Jersey and crossed the historic river. The street boys used to pick the warm, soft tar from between the cobblestones and chew it. Doctor Simon Manderscheid stood in his big bay of discreetly curtained windows and peered out at the boys and wished he were with his family at the shore cottage at Cape May, fishing. He relished the planked white flesh of sea life.

Late in the afternoon the patients had dribbled away, and above him the house was silent, all the rooms wrapped in white linen for the summer. The boys at last went screaming down the street to head for the river and naked bathing. It was very still again and the horse car was blocks away, but in his imagination, he could already hear its hoofs, and grind of brake, and he felt suddenly trapped and tired and bored.

Vienna of his medical studies was far away and so was the medical school in Rome where the students played tricks on each other with the dissecting subjects and put odd ears and toes in the pockets of lady students, whom one took on Sundays to the Protestant Cemetery to watch them weep over the grave of Keats, and later . . . later . . .

Simon was growing middle-aged and fat and just a little too famous for his own good, he felt. He smiled, and was about to turn away, to pull down the shades and lock out the summer heat, when he saw a large man cross the street and look up at the house. A white planter's hat, an object of age and much wear, was pulled over the face; all that Doctor Simon could see was the end of a smoldering stogie. That and a lean body and wide, unpressed grey trousers, and a blackwood cane. The man limped badly. He crossed the street, and then the bell rang in the wainscoting and Doctor Simon went to answer it. Doctor Nelson, his assistant, had already left, and the servants were all at Cape May.

The tall man stood there—too erect, as if with effort—beating his thigh with the cane. He had a lean, tired face, a face slightly yellow that had once been tanned, and a body beginning to gain muscles and strength again, as if leaving some long illness behind. Doctor Simon was just a little too proud of quickly guessing medical histories and he knew it and guarded against it. This fast look at people and running through their medical histories, past and future, and watching their amazed faces when he called the turns, was too much a game.

"Doctor Manderscheid in?" asked the tall man.

"He is. I am. Come in."

The lean man tossed his stogie into the street and limped into the dark hall. "Joseph Pedlock. I wrote to you."

"Pedlock?"

"Major Pedlock at one time, the late lamented Confederacy. You said you didn't mind."

The personal system of memory that Doctor Simon practised began to move quickly, like his hands during an operation. "Of course. The unhealed wound, the lower fibula."

"Correct."

"Please come in."

He sat Joseph down on the black leather couch with the groaning inner springs and had him put his damaged leg on a small oak stool. "Care for a drink?"

"I'm Bourbon-lined."

"Ever drink Scotch whisky?"

"In England . . . years ago."

Doctor Simon poured a small, silver-bound tumbler full, handed it to Joseph and smiled. It was a bond; they had both been in England once. "Here, you'll need it while I poke around in the leg. Give me its history."

Joseph held the glass in his long, tanned hand while Doctor Simon exposed the leg. Joseph began to talk, his knuckles tight and white around the glass. As he talked he felt a sickness and pain inside him, all the sterile futility of war, all the gallant nothingness of brave men gone and the dead come back. He gulped his heather-tasting whisky, and the leg was on fire again.

Doctor Simon looked at the mangled wound—the angry welts of scar tissue—and told Joseph to go on with his medical history. He half heard it; one part of his mind filed away all the facts . . . another part of him smelled the Scotch and looked up at the late Major of Confederate Horse, who had also once been in England.

It was perhaps, he felt, the late hour, the panting summer heat outside, the lean face of his visitor, but again Doctor Simon felt everything in life rushing past him too fast. As he gently flexed the wounded leg he remembered the pub. The Elephant and Castle near the hospital where he had interned and then those gay, careless years in Rome. It was dangerous to leave him alone on warm, dull days.

He had been a fat, foolish boy, suddenly romantic and in love at sixteen with his mother's Polish maid. He used to creep into her bed on the third-floor attic every night and weep on her large beautiful breasts and recite to her the poems of Shelley. She had been a beautiful, stupid girl, sensual as a brood mare, and when he had asked her to marry him, she had in horror told his mother, the little dragon of a woman who had flogged him at sixteen and locked him in his room. "Thank God the Polish girl isn't pregnant," his brother Aaron had said, and shipped him off to Europe to study medicine.

"Were you long in England?" he asked Joseph.

"A few years."

"Wonderful country. Next to Rome, I loved it best."

Joseph bit his lower lip as the pain surged through his leg. "Rome? I was there as a boy, with a cargo of Hungarian horses for a circus. A mangy, glorious place."

Yes, yes, thought Doctor Simon, those dirty, flea-bitten, little circuses, with those wonderful gipsy women who danced without underwear and tried to steal your watch when they held you close and read your palm. *"Beware of a passionate woman with green eyes. You will be very rich and have a long life."*

Rome, the Rome of a fat, ugly little medical student who drank too much and adored beautiful women, standing in the Sistine Chapel and brooding because he didn't have the beautiful body of one of those giants painted on the great ceiling. Those mobs on saints' days singing and drinking wine and shouting *"A noi,"* and so much local, cheap *chianti* of the medical students, and good middle-class *amontillado*.

("I don't like the stiff scar tissue, Major.")

It had been a romantic life with the heavy hairy monks smelling of damp cells and *strega* and garlic, and everyone smiling, *"fortunatissimo"*, and the waiters lisping, *"Si, eccellenza"* as they put down the *bel paese* cheese.

("It's a very neglected wound, Major. Military doctoring at its worst.")

Yes, he had become a Roman, had loved its streets and loud talk and sudden angers. And in Rome he was going to stay to grow old and fatter and most likely even uglier. But his brother Aaron had ordered him home, and home he had come, after a tearful night in a narrow iron bed with Nina cursing him and digging her dirty fingernails into his face and into his already balding scalp. He was a weak,

18

little man, and all he was good for was to do wonderful things with the broken bones of people he didn't care much about. He had even given up drinking.

("I'm sorry, Major—just a little longer.")

Ah, he could still be drinking his *asti spumante* in front of the shabby church with the pink tower, and Nina, or one of Nina's cousins (there were so many of those big-eyed, dark-haired girls in those days), would be with him, and bite and hit him and laugh and drink with him. But he had come home, and they, the family, had found Emma for him, Emma from a fine family and already a warm, happy woman. They had been married and there were children, nice, fine, fat children, very good to see, and hug, but still some wild, foolish, romantic part of him had died. Well, almost died.

("Major, you're an interesting and fearful bone case.")

He looked up at Joseph's face.

"I've hurt you."

"I don't deny it, Doctor."

Joseph had never seen such skilled fingers; how they bathed and probed and moved and flexed and turned and touched. When at last the little plump doctor looked up at him, the sweat on Joseph's upper lip stood out like a crystal scarring.

"It's bad, Major . . . very bad."

"Let's leave the Major out of it. How bad?"

"Neglect, very bad neglect, a lot of bone crushed, still splintering off, much too much weight for the leg . . . Perhaps . . . well . . ."

"Perhaps I should have it off, and get rid of the festering devil? Wear a wooden peg?" Joseph laughed, his teeth together in a tight intake of air.

"Have another drink."

"Thank you, Doctor. Join me?"

"No, thank you."

Doctor Simon took off his heat-fogged glasses and wiped them and put them on again. "Pedlock, I'd like to try something. Silver. Yes—silver wires and screws to bind up and pull the bones together. I want to get you off the leg, clean it up and trim it into shape, and put in the silver screws and wires."

"I'm in the metal business myself—not silver, however. Mostly old iron and copper in Charleston. You think it will work?"

"Don't know. Tried it on my sister Rebecca's collie dog two years ago. A coal dray crushed his shoulder bone."

"How is the dog?"

"In fine shape. I'd show him to you, but he's away with the family for the summer."

Joseph set down the empty whisky glass. "I'm game. If you are, Doctor. Oh," he stopped and wiped his face with a red silk handkerchief now frayed and faded, but clean. The doctor noticed how worn everything the tall man had was. "Doctor, I'm kind of land poor at the moment, that is, if I still have any land. As I said, I'm in the iron business. But my holdings are in legal trouble. You know what has happened in the South. Frankly, I'm up against a real shortage of cash." He smiled. "You wouldn't care to take a few thousand acres of Tennessee land for this silver-doctoring of yours?"

"You don't understand, Pedlock. You're an experiment to me. I couldn't charge you for this."

"That suits me fine. Oh, Doctor, could you tell me where there is a synagogue? I'm just off the Baltimore stage an hour ago."

Doctor Simon smiled. "A *schul?*"

The tall man nodded, almost ironically. "You see, before the war when I was young and had two good legs, I resigned from the Jews. I'm thinking of changing my mind."

"Why want readmission again to a very unpopular club?"

"Before I came here, I had a letter from Vienna. My father is dead. I want to say the prayer for the dead."

"I'll take you down there myself."

"I don't want you to think, Doctor, that I'm only an experiment and a bother."

"Nonsense. I'm all alone in town. Where are you staying?"

"Can you also throw in the name of a good, cheap rooming house? Very cheap."

"That wouldn't do. I need to have you near me for observation. This house is empty. You'll stay with me, here. I want to see that leg every day after I get the wires in. And the hospital is full of fever. So here you stay."

Joseph stood up and reached for his cane. "Only a fool would turn that offer down."

"And how long is it since you had a real home-cooked meal? I mean a real Friday night meal with *cholla* and some chopped liver and *gefüllte* fish, seasoned with real spices?"

"Longer than you think."

"Good. My brother Aaron is a little crazy on the subject of orthodoxy, so tonight I'll be able to bring him the guest for the Sabbath every home should have."

Joseph grinned and tenderly and carefully put his hurt leg on the

20

rug. "Doctor, I like you too much to stick you with any of that damn Tennessee land."

It had been a long time, not since his boyhood, when he had been badgered to attend, that Joseph had been in a synagogue. He had always, as a rational idealist, liked to make his own terms with God, and had felt that he and God could do their business alone, as two hairy males, without the ritual and the garb and the texts of organised religion. Therefore he had been rather surprised, himself, when he had blurted out a request to say the *Kaddish*, a son's prayer for a dead parent, to Dr. Simon. Some perverse chemistry inside him had made him do it. He had no use for dogma or rites or ceremonies, yet his father's death called for some gesture.

Joseph knew it was some sort of return to the stern God of his people that had prompted him. His father had been a Voltairian in the Vienna of the Hapsburg-Lothringen—a sort of agnostic with poetic edges—and Joseph himself had carried on his father's sceptical common sense a little further in America. But he knew now that what he was doing was the only proper gesture of respect available to his father; it was the only way that the lamp of Israel, that burned deep in him, could express itself with a full-felt theatrical gesture. And also, it would mark an unexpected reunion with his blood and kind. For he had come through peril and the shadow of death.

The watery-eyed old men who made up the *minyan*, the quorum necessary for holding public worship, looked up from their tangled ritual *tallis*, and saw and heard the tall, lean man in the crumpled planter's hat recite the *Kaddish*. It seemed to several of them that the Hebrew words were perhaps tainted by a slight Southern drawl.

"Yisgadal v'Yiskadash Schmei Rabo . . ."

CHAPTER IV

Aaron Manderscheid, brother of Doctor Simon Manderscheid, was a man of God, and a man of business. His household lived according to the Law. His doorways had tacked up on them little brass containers, *mezuzahs*, talismans against evil, that held a holy prayer from the Sixth Book of Deuteronomy. His wife Hannah put on a head shawl at dusk on Fridays and said a prayer as she lit the seven-branched candlestick. Aaron's male children wore little black caps, the *yarmelkas*, at table, and said a prayer for the meal and the fruit before they touched it. They were routed out by shouts and blows at dawn and, sleepy and yawning, had to don the winding black prayer boxes and straps—the *tefillin*—around their brows and arm and recite a long, droning prayer.

It was a large, happy household grumbling under ritual overtones. Aaron, even in cold October, built a leaf-roofed arbour in the garden and celebrated the feast of *Succos*. But when he went too far, Hannah said no, and that was that. She refused to use the local *mikva*, the ritual public bath for women, a steamy, filthy place where the orthodox bathed and exchanged germs, and she would not cut off her proud, heavy head of brown hair and put on a wig. Also, Hannah would not permit Aaron in their bed when he anointed himself with a ritual oil and claimed to be living from the holy books. For Hannah, whose own family was to be tainted with Christian Science and a hatless Reform *schul*, always felt "enough was enough".

Aaron, in his middle forties at the time, was a solid, round little man, very firm of flesh, red-faced, and muscled with stone arms and legs. In business he was fair, direct and cold. An ordered energy, a frenzy of purpose seized him every morning and kept him jumping all day. How good to be an American Jew! He could not delegate duty to others. He cried easily, and music of the Italian operas was his passion. He was very much in love with his wife, and thought women were frail, wonderful, foolish creatures to be protected and cherished. He loved to sit back in his big chair after dinner and lead people on, to talk and jest with them, and then turn on them and with laughter and loud, gay talk, his keen mind working at high speed, take apart their arguments and their ideas. A deeply religious man, he liked to feed old rabbis and moth-eaten old scholars and *Yeshiva-bochers*—young

22

students—and travellers from Palestine rattling their tin boxes for charity. And after he had fed them, he would laugh pleasantly and tell them that they were a lot of old frauds, and their yelling and lamenting and scratching were a disgrace to the true, sacred principles of Israel.

"Simon is bringing a friend to dinner, Hannah," he told his wife.

"One of his drinking friends who goes with loose women?"

"He wouldn't dare."

"Aaron, I hope not."

"By holy writ I am any man's host."

"Never mind the holy writ, go see if the wine is cooling right, and if Simon's guest isn't respectable I'm not coming down to dinner."

"Simon has reformed, Hannah."

"Then let him stop pinching the maid's leg."

"He's a great doctor. A student of bones and muscles."

"So the maid told me."

Doctor Simon and Joseph gave their hats to the smiling Polish maid, and she said the family and guests were all in the dining room. The Manderscheids imported dozens of these Polish girls, and several generations of them had served in their houses. Usually helped by the family, they had been married to coachmen, horse-car drivers, or packing-house workers. They often came back in a year or so, usually with a yawning, half-Polish child to show their old mistress how fast they were becoming Americans and replenishing the earth.

A large dining room panelled in a polished chestnut wood beautifully carved and well waxed. The long table surrounded by tall tapestry-backed chairs already loaded with cut-glass dishes and decanters of wine and spirits, trays of nuts, and silver platters of braided *cholla*, polished with egg white before baking until it gleamed like the mast of a yacht painted with spar varnish. Imbedded in this varnish were mohn seeds, little black seeds that played havoc in one's teeth. "Yet no Friday night *cholla* would be really *cholla*," Aaron said, "without these sweet-tasting, infernal seeds."

Aaron came towards the door and Doctor Simon made the introductions as they entered the dining room.

"My brother, Aaron Manderscheid. Aaron, may I present Major Joseph Pedlock, of the late-lamented war. I'm treating his leg and you're feeding him tonight."

"Good to have you. Whose side were you on?"

"The other".

Aaron smiled and showed Joseph to a chair by his side. The table was crowded with family and guests. "Well, that still entitles you to a Sabbath meal. The three grinning devils there are my sons, Albert, Arthur, *and* Sheridan. The General looked very impressive in the early days of the war, now the boy is stuck with the name. The two old fellows at the foot of the table with the rancid beards can hardly speak any English. Beautiful, aren't they? They're professional beggars who go around the world collecting money to keep a lot of old endowed loafers leaning against the Wailing Wall in Palestine." To the two old men he said in Hebrew, "*Shalom, shalom,* tonight, my *tzaddikim*—wonder workers—you will eat a wonderful *tzimmes*—*such* a dessert dish." Turning back to Joseph, he went on, "The two overgrown boys with the ringlets over their ears and the wide hats are from Poland. Their village was wiped out in a pogrom of the Tsar's Cossacks. I'm going to get them haircuts and make them into pioneer Americans. The tall, proud man leaning back in his chair on his elbow is my cousin and our local rabbi, Reb Sontag, may I present Major Pedlock."

The rabbi was a handsome, pink-cheeked El Greco painting. Cleanshaven except for a long thin beard in the manner of Napoleon III, his carefully tendered fingernails seemed to take pleasure in the good damask tablecloth they were stroking with almost a lover's touch.

"Ah, Major, a Jew at war? We are a peaceful people."

Joseph took the little black cap Aaron handed him, and sat down, careful of his hurt leg, before he answered the rabbi.

"Not in the Old Testament. The slaughter and killing and burnings and battles and throat-cuttings of the old Jews surpass anything you will find in any other era of history, almost. The Jew was always a great heroic warrior, but we are ashamed to admit it."

"He's made his point there," said Aaron.

The rabbi shrugged his well-tailored shoulders and sighed. "It is not easy to be a Jew. Besides, only the Jews made a literature out of it—and so left a bad record."

Doctor Simon looked at the bottles of wine reflecting the yellow gaslight from the overhanging glass fixtures. "Not easy to be a Jew. Not even on four thousand dollars a year, Rabbi?"

Aaron said sternly, "Simon, you look tired."

Hannah Manderscheid came in from the kitchen with a dish of ground horse-radish coloured with red beet juice. She was a large, beautiful, warm woman, much too large for Aaron, a blonde-brown beauty, almost a Saxon type, but for her dark, soulful eyes, with a witty mouth and a little pointed chin that showed, Joseph felt, just a little too much character.

When she was introduced to Joseph she smiled, showing little

24

girl's teeth, and a small bit of pink tongue, and said, "You are most welcome. . . . Rabbi, if you please."

The rabbi looked down at the tablecloth and said a beautiful-sounding prayer, ringing out his words as if only fitting to a dashing Philadelphia rabbi whose grandfather had died in the War of 1812. "It's a sad trial," he said now, "to be a fashionable rabbi going soft and lazy in my warm berth." He would have preferred, he admitted, "to stand in rags at the site of the Temple, in the city we Jews call *Yerushalaim*, the Romans called *Hierosolyma*, the Moslems *El Quds*, the Canaanites *Urusalim*, and the Christians, Jerusalem".

One of the beautiful old Jews pulled on his long grey beard and said to his friend in Yiddish, "Who the devil is this *goy*, this gentile?"

"He is their rabbi," the other answered, and he recited a prayer of his own. "*Kol Mekadesh Shevee'ee . . .*"

"I still say he's a *goy*."

"So here in this golden land a *goy* can become a rabbi—*nu*."

The meal began with everyone taking a slice of *cholla*, and the Polish girls coming in with a great tray of chopped chicken livers, and some *Königsberger Klops*, a small, spiced meatball made in the German style. This was followed almost at once by a big silver tray holding a whole *gefüllte* fish; a great carp chopped (not ground) and spiced, and replaced in his skin and covered with an aspic of his own juices studded with carrots and spices. All served cold, of course. There were also little sweetbreads and other dainties like beef tongue stewed with nuts and raisins, of course a noodle soup, steaming yellow, and the noodle, Simon whispered to Joseph, "cut by Hannah herself with a very sharp knife very thin and narrow". Good Rhine and Moselle wines were served, and Aaron kept filling Joseph's glass and pushing Doctor Simon's away empty. Joseph felt stuffed, but now in came platters of roast chicken, baked duck, and buckwheat-stuffed doves, a dish the holy men ate with relish, for it was permitted by ritual and kosher law. There was also a mountain of a side dish of *Kreplach*, small pockets of dough filled with spiced chopped meat, and gleaming yellow as gold from the chicken broth they had been well cooked in. The paupers, holy men, students ate each for three and sighed for more.

"Eat," said Aaron. "Don't insult us by saying you're full. After all, if God hadn't meant us to eat, he wouldn't have given us a stomach." He looked at the old men as if asking an important question.

"It follows," said one of the old men, his mouth full of chicken, his eyes shut tight in pleasure, "it follows as *Purim* follows *Ta'nis Esther*."

"A very fine wine," said Rabbi Sontag, twirling his glass in the light. He ate little but with a slow-mannered ease.

The two young men from Poland with the pale faces of an underdone roll, their ringlets dancing around their ears, were drinking *slivovitz* and giggling, and the fire-filled Warsaw plum brandy was going to do them no good. Aaron motioned for the bottle to be removed, but it was too late. Their eyes rolled like blue marbles in their heads.

Joseph turned to Hannah. "It's an amazing thing, how good this cooking is after all these years. My mother was not much of a cook, but somehow, for Friday night she managed to do herself real proud."

Aaron said, "We've just begun to eat. I want everybody to leave this table with the skin of his belly stretched tight."

"Belly? Please, Aaron."

The three sons of the house grinned, and their mother shook her head at them. Joseph felt warm and well packed and leaned back and looked up at the mass of hissing gaslights. A warm yellow glow filled the room.

"I like a big meal in this house. An overloaded table," Aaron said, "I suppose these Friday night dinners are my way of making up for the hunger, the bitter years of the war the family went through during the Revolution."

"The War of the Rebellion," said Rabbi Sontag in his best voice. "The birth of our country."

"Washington wasn't ashamed to write to my great-grandfather, and call it the Revolution," Aaron said. "It was hard those years. The family was living in the open fields in the northern part of New Jersey. My great-grandfather Moses Samuel and his brothers were off someplace trying to get enough money together to buy shoes and beans for the army at Valley Forge. It wasn't a mere name on a scroll of honour then. Things were at low ebb, I can tell you. In the old family papers there is written the story of a Passover they lived through up there. They made matzos out of some grey flour that had to be sifted for maggots, they ate ground corn that tore their insides out, and some turnips frozen and refrozen and turning black. It was a sad Passover. That night one of the children died of a lung sickness, and the old grandmother wandered off and was found with her mind gone. She thought the Red Sea had frozen up and the Egyptians were near. The next years they were all apart. One of the brothers was in a British prison hulk in New York Harbour. Two of the sons were dead, not in a real battle, just from marching and freezing and thawing out and

26

starving and eating acorns and marching. It was a long time before the family could eat a decently cooked meal."

Simon looked up at Copley's painting of Moses Manderscheid. "He was a proud old boy. I remember my grandfather talking about him. He was ruined, broken by the loans he had made to continue the war. Congress didn't pay back what they had borrowed. But as he said, 'They didn't have much of anything to pay back.' He was given a land grant in the western part of Virginia for his part in the Revolution, but something happened to it. He was, I hear, a neat old man, poor then, and he dressed neatly with clean, well-worn clothes. Once a year he used to go down to the poorhouse."

"The night before Yom Kippur," Aaron said, "and bring home a dozen old men. If he couldn't find Jews, he took what they had. He felt, he said, a meal did a man good, with or without ritual reasons. They didn't have much, but every year he had a big goose." Aaron stopped to wipe his mouth with a napkin, and he shook his head. "Goose is a little too rich for me, Major. I'm sorry to keep talking about war when you've just come from one. You seem to have come out of it all right."

"Your brother is going to rebuild a leg for me."

Aaron looked at his brother, his true pride in him on his face, and nodded, "He can do it."

"I can try," said Doctor Simon watching the ringlets drink the drops of *slivovitz* left in their glasses.

One of the old men said, "In the *Midrash Rabo*, it is said . . . or is it in the *Ein Yakov*? Anyway . . ."

"Those old volumes are very valuable literature," said Rabbi Sontag.

Great bowls of stewed fruit, a *kugel*, a steaming pudding like a fire, a suet pudding cooked with raisins and currents and spices, all came in the strong arms of the Polish girls. Also fine crystal bottles of schnapps, kümmel and kirschwasser.

The two ringlets were now far gone and turning green with too much food and *slivovitz*. Hannah hurried them out into the kitchen. Rabbi Sontag had reached for his cigar case of rare Havannas before he remembered it was Friday and he did not carry them on this night. The two beautiful old men were crooning to themselves, shaking themselves in some ecstasy as they gave the proper Hebrew prayer at the end of the meal. They looked up as more dishes were brought in, groaned and fell to again. For it is written someplace—in the *Midrash* —the exegetical literature, perhaps—there it is written, Joseph remembered, an excuse for almost any fine action as satisfying as eating.

Aaron ate little and forced his guests to take more on their plates. Hannah came back to report grimly that the ringlets were being sick in the garden. Then she shushed the three giggling sons of the house away from the table, and upstairs.

Rabbi Sontag removed one tiny crumb from his tailored bosom and said in his booming theatre voice, "Manderscheid, you are spoiling us."

"Thank you, Rabbi. And you, Major?"

"It's all been very fine."

Rabbi Sontag nodded. "You are staying on here in Philadelphia, Major Pedlock?"

"I am staying as long as my doctor wants me and the leg."

"You must attend our services tomorrow. We have imported a cantor who once studied for the Royal Russian Opera. Such high notes you have never heard. He's got a golden lark in his throat. The timbers of the ark shake. Ah, what he could do to Mozart—if he weren't so holy. . . ."

One of the old men turned to the rabbi. "Do you think it right to shave the upper part of your face?"

"One must live with one's people and perhaps we have to change certain minor customs to fit our needs."

The old man pulled on his bushy eyebrows. "And you don't kiss your holy fringes after prayer?"

"I don't wear the holy fringes any more. It's just a ritual gesture that is not needed any more."

The old man's expression did not change. "Tell me, Reb Sontag, are you still circumcised?"

It was at this point that Aaron suddenly said they had sat enough for one night at table.

The repairing of the leg of Joseph Pedlock was a tormentingly slow and painful process. He spent many agonizing hours on a sheet-covered table in the small upstairs room where Doctor Simon was now privately operating under a method that caused other doctors, when they heard of it, to shake their heads and laugh.

"God," they said, "didn't mean for us to tamper with the old tried and true methods."

Simon was full of some new germ theory on wound infection and he operated dressed in white rubber, the patient covered with waterproof mats because carbolic sprays filled the small room with a mist. Doctor Nelson, a dry, witty, blond Yankee, who served as his assistant, could only take about ten minutes of this carbolic fog before he had to run out into the street, to stand there weeping and breathing hard, a shocking sight to decent Philadelphia.

"Do we have to have these sprays going?" Doctor Nelson would ask, his nose and eyes running, his breath whistling like a bad pump. "It's like swimming under water all the time."

Doctor Simon, bent way over Joseph's leg, would grin and nod, "I tell you, Major, you don't know what a help to the advancement of real science you are. These carbolic sprays may look foolish, but I got them out of a great paper just published by a professor of surgery at the University at Glasgow. Am I hurting you, Joseph?"

"Yes, damn it, you're hurting me!"

"Lister, that's the Scotch professor's name, he says we doctors should wash our tools in boiling water before we use them, *not* after."

Doctor Nelson sneezed.

"Don't sneeze!" screamed Doctor Simon, turning up the carbolic sprays until a grey rain seemed to fill the little room. "Sneezing is full of wound-infecting material. All air is."

"Oh, my sainted aunt," said Doctor Nelson and ran out again to weep and wheeze in the street.

Doctor Simon went on. "Tomorrow I'll put in the first silver wires. I hope the Confederate Army didn't object to the use of chloroform?"

Joseph groaned, "Not when they could get it."

"I remember when Queen Victoria accepted chloroform for the delivery of her seventh child, Prince Leopold. In 1853. How the

Church and the blue-noses screamed. I made it popular in Rome when I called it *anesthése à la reine*, after the Queen. It was a great city, Rome, then, and I was younger, and . . ."

Doctor Simon looked down at Joseph's twisted face suddenly and went over and turned down the carbolic sprays. "This is enough for one day. More than enough."

Joseph said weakly, "Don't expect me to beg you to go on. You've even ruined my stogies. . . . They all smell of that goddamned carbolic."

"It's pickled your scar tissue nice and pink. Like smoked salmon."

In slow and painful stages the leg was treated and the silver wires and screws put into agonizing place. The shattered bones, held tight, grew together. The shiny scars looked healthy and were wrapped in diluted carbolic baths, and in time the scar tissue pleased Doctor Simon. "Such beautiful scars! I'm proud of them. They glow like holy wounds on an idol!"

Joseph spent most of his time in the upper front bedroom, a girlish kind of room, with a blond, polished bed, and gay rugs, and little flower prints on the striped old-rose wallpaper.

Lying in the bed so much of the time he would think of the future. Was there any use in going back to Charleston and trying to get the metal business going again? Everything was in ruins, everything was a long, hard job down there, now. Should he stay up here and become of the North?

He remembered the South as he had known it in his first years in the country. Young, handsome, well-off, he had had a fine life in those days. . . . Ever-ready pitchers of hot toddy, the games of billiards and piquet and loo, the happy company of raconteurs, horse talkers and the old half-Huguenot society among the peacock hens screaming on a well-trimmed lawn. They led a patriarchal plantation life among the scrub-palmetto and myrtle and sometimes went on wildcat hunts off Port Royal Sound. He had attended the St. Cecilia Society concerts of Mozart and Haydn. He had attended dances and parties, hunted in the sea marshes, and ridden along old trails after the yipping hounds. Their love of dogs and horses was amazing, and that, and their pride, were the things that amazed Joseph most. They seemed to live a life cut off by barriers of their own making from the real, bustling world beyond their plantations.

In time he had touched the South's deeper inner life behind the gardens of Cherokee roses; a life a little grimmer than the full glory of a spring sun and blooded horses and yapping hounds; he felt the gap-toothed skull beneath the healthy skin.

The best people accepted Joseph in great, white houses scattered over the low, damp, fertile land, houses placed along winding rivers and peopling the knolls and hilltops. Houses white and wide such as he had never seen. A great hedge of boxwood in front and then a lawn with a great bluestone drive circling to the wide steps, with columns out of Greek mythology, standing blandly in the blond sun. Always the slaves, running, or sleeping, or bending the knee, or laughing, wide red mouth with good ivory, smiling. And of course the dogs of all kinds.

And being young and a sensual male, he remembered his life in Charleston in full detail.

The markets were gay with a raw, dazzling colour and the thick, ropy laughter of the barefooted Negroes. The waiting buzzards would swoop down often for the scraps. The long, arcaded sheds were dripping with sea life and Joseph liked to buy dozens of lobsters and give small wild parties to the town bloods and help them drink his wines and brandies. He liked to hear the market cries of the yellow girls with baskets on their strong, turbaned heads, calling: "Veg-etub-bles! Guinea squash! Tomat-tuhs! Sibby beans! Hard-head cabbage! York cabbage!"

Oh, yellow girls—that fine, local, nocturnal product!

Joseph got a smiling pleasure out of seeing these high yellows walking in their thin, faded print frocks under the white Charleston sun. He used to bring a limber yellow girl called My My Betsy to his house, and on her body find a few moments of savage pleasure. She was a happy, laughing girl with gourd-shaped breasts, very pointed and hard, and her tapering thighs and legs ended in long, large ugly feet that he tried never to notice. There was no perfection in his life and he was wandering yet, so no woman could mean very much to him except as beauty and a sated moment. Every week Betsy, beautiful My My Betsy with the large naked feet, would leave the house in the bend of Church Street, a five-dollar gold coin in her mouth, shaking her behind at George, the coloured butler, and sassing the indoor "niggers" who hated her as they hated all field-hand people.

Often lying with her in the hot silent heat of an afternoon, he would suddenly hear the cries of street peddlers: "Oystyuhs! She crab! Raw shrimp! Raw! Raw! RAW!"

"Them damn niggahs shoutin'," said My My Betsy, turning over in bed, a golden object of soft yielding flesh.

"They're your people, My My."

"Ah hates 'em. Ah likes the gentry."

"Am I gentry?"

"Ho ho . . . you sure am. Mighty gentry."

He held her in his arms and he looked down at her and she grinned and wriggled. When she wriggled it was good and when he took her it was almost there. Afterwards again they lay side by side in the big bed and the sun slatting in under the wooden forms and marking their bodies with stripes of white and dark.

"Oh, you man," said My My Betsy. "You got the thing bad and take a lot of it. You sure do."

"I'm fond of you, Betsy. Very fond of you."

"Ho ho, don't tell no big-footed yella gal that. You got it and want it bad but you just keep thinkin', thinkin' of that them other ones."

"You crazy, Betsy? Who's been gossiping?"

"Just about every house niggah in this ole town. Just everybody knows all them white ladies just sets and waits for you and looks at you and you is still drawin' back. Black Pronto, their fiddle leader he just about split his sides laffin' at you making out you ain't wantin' any. Ah bet they all goes ridin' them big he horses just for the same reason you keep grabbin' little My My like you was goin' to never git it just right and just there. Ho, ho!"

"Oh, shut up, Betsy,"

"Now Ah done it. Ah said it wrong."

"It's all right, Betsy."

"No it hain't. Ah done spoiled it today fer you."

Then he was so tender to My My Betsy. Felt for her and himself a pity at the brevity and cruelty of life; felt a great sorrow for this black people in bondage, as he had felt for himself—the Jew—in this Charleston society. Looking at sprawled Betsy enjoying the soft bed and the clean linen and eating ripe peaches with the juice dripping down between the hard, pointed breasts, he would lean over and rub her soft, naked stomach and she would swallow peach and laugh and look at him in a puzzled, puppy manner, and sing a field-hand tune:

> *"All de doctors you can try*
> *All de medicine you can buy*
> *Yet you gotta lay down some day and die. . . ."*

He drove off the vision of Charleston and My My Betsy and he was again lying chastely in a Philadelphia bedroom. It was the room of Doctor Simon's sister Rebecca, and Joseph wondered if polite society would object to his occupying it, the bed of a young girl, used day and night by the heavy, wounded body of a male soldier. In mild, mocking tones he and Doctor Simon referred to her as the Fair Maiden.

Joseph spent most of the day propped up by pillows, his stogies going, a bottle of Bourbon, of which he had discovered a supply in town, on the night table by his side. He had not gotten to like Scotch, which tasted to him too much like that damn carbolic. It was pleasant, after years of war and pain, to just rest and let the sun come through the slanted slats in the window-blind and mark the white sheets whiter, and feel the pale, yolk-coloured warmth creep in lazy moments along his arms and face. He was not much of a popular-reading man, but one day Hannah and Aaron Manderscheid came to see him with a huge basket of hothouse fruit, and some novels. Hannah said he would like the very popular *Vanity Fair*.

He surprised himself by liking it very much. Of course, he considered it only one of those popular things of the moment with no lasting claim to literary fame, but very amusing. Joseph prided himself in his judgment of books. All his life he was to consider the novel a frivolous literary form of little value.

Afternoons when he wasn't being tormented by Doctor Simon, he sat in the small girlish bed and read of Becky Sharp. There was a great deal of England in it as he remembered it, and a great deal that he never suspected. He missed the full flavour, the ironic essence of *Vanity Fair* and the other social novels of the period that were just beginning to portray the horror of industrialization, replacing older social forms. Joseph Pedlock, a young man reading Thackeray and Dickens in bed in Philadelphia, in 1867, read only to pass the time, and to drug his mind while his leg healed and the level in the Bourbon bottles sank with the sun at dusk.

He was dozing one afternoon, with the first Indian summer colours of the trees outside carefully curtained from the small room, when there was a brisk, direct knock on the door. Joseph came half-way out of sleep and said, "Yes?"

"Care for some company?" someone asked.

"Don't mind if I do." He pushed back his disordered hair and wondered if he should hide the bottle. Aaron Manderscheid came in leading his son, young Sheridan, by the hand.

"I couldn't think of you cooped up here alone, Major. How's the leg?" the little man asked, crossing to the bed and sitting down.

"It's coming along, I hear."

"You've met my youngest son, Sheridan. He came to see your sword."

Sheridan asked shrilly, "Did you cut heads off with it?"

Joseph got up on one elbow. "Maybe I did. You know how it is when you're in a battle, you don't pay too much attention."

"Could I see the sword, Major?"

Joseph laughed. "It's in a Richmond pawnshop. Soldiers get hungry, and besides it always got between my legs and tripped me flat on my face. I kill best with a Bowie knife."

The child went bug-eyed.

Aaron put a box of cigars on the bed and patted Sheridan on his velvet-clad rump. The child, Joseph noticed, was dressed in the tight-fitting, English fashion of the period; he was having trouble breathing in his tight, fancy company pants and jacket.

34

"All right, Sheridan, go play on the sidewalk."

"Yes, papa."

Sheridan went and Joseph opened the cedarwood cigar box and sniffed at the pale, green-leaved shapes. "Too damn good for me, Mr. Manderscheid. I smoke horse dung and black pepper."

"Call me Aaron, Major."

"If you'll change the Major to Joseph. These are the first cigars I've had that didn't smell like your brother."

Aaron leaned all over the bed to hold a match to the cigar. "Simon's a good doctor, isn't he? A fine hand. So steady, did you notice?"

"When I have time."

"We've had our trouble with him. He used to drink like an Irish stable boy."

"Pardon me," said Joseph, putting the Bourbon bottle on the floor. "The Irish are overrated as drinkers."

"I mean he just couldn't control himself. Women, too. He was always in trouble. With *such* women, too. Maids, shop girls, waitresses, dance-hall creatures in tights. He has—I don't know why I say all this to you, but you're like family to us—he has very low tastes, and we must watch him for his own good."

"I don't believe in reforming anybody. I'm not much of an object to admire myself."

"Simon thinks a lot of you. He's been happy lately, since treating you. We've all noticed it."

"Why don't you let him drink, and chase and lift petticoats? It's a normal male procedure. Some men enjoy it."

"You're an odd Jew, Joseph. The family is important to us people. Our work is important. Simon is a great doctor. Why should we trade that for a drunkard and worse? Joseph, perhaps you've got the same problem in a lesser degree, but you have character."

"Aaron, people don't like to have people tell them what's good or bad for them. I'm that way myself. Leave Simon enjoy himself."

Aaron laughed. "And me? Always I've carried the problems of the family, since I was fourteen, when my father dropped dead, *olov hasholem* on the grain-exchange floor. Now it's leaning out and bothering strangers. To change the subject, Joseph, what do you know about copper?"

"I suppose a little more than most."

"It's the coming metal, I keep saying that, and so is steel. The telegraph, it's knotting together the world. Millions and millions of miles of copper wire. And for alloys, copper is a good metal. They're going to need a lot of bronze to harden steels and cast into engine parts. It's a big, wonderful country we're going to have. Joseph, this country has been using copper since the Indians but no one has really done anything impressive with it. Carnegie and Morgan are beginning to do it with steel, and Rockefeller with lamp oil. But they're rogues—they don't give a damn for the country. I'd like to keep copper away from them."

"American copper-smelting processes are behind Europe's," said Joseph. "Even so, all existing processes aren't much good."

"You don't see a future in it?"

"Never thought of it. I'm going back into iron and maybe coal."

"I want to make you an offer, Joseph. Some years ago we got involved with the Vanderbilt steamboat people in New York and almost were wiped out by the old pirates. We had to sell out quick, or be ruined, and the best offer we got was paid off in part, by copper lands in Michigan."

"I heard there was copper up there."

"Joseph, could you go up there for us, when you can travel, and see if there's anything big in it?"

Joseph shook his head. "I'm sorry, Aaron, but as soon as I get on my feet, I'm going back south. If I can keep title to my Tennessee holding, I'm in iron for a while."

"What are you going to use—pardon me—for cash?"

Joseph reached and lifted the bottle. "Don't know yet. Can I offer you the heel of the bottle, Aaron?"

"I'm not a drinking man. But go ahead. *L'chayim.*"

Joseph filled his glass and looked at it. "Yes, it's all in a good, cheap, smelting process. Try and get some bright young man to invent one for you. Well, here's looking at you. And as soon as I can, I'll send for that sword for Sheridan."

"Can you come to dinner tonight?"

"I'm resting the leg. Doctor Simon and I are going down to Cape May for the weekend to be with his family."

"If you like fishing, it's fine."

"Don't you, Aaron?"

"I can't sit still that long, wriggling a pole and drowning worms. So get well quick and we'll hang the sword on the wall where it will annoy Rabbi Sontag the most."

They were celebrating the success of the silver wires. Simon had found someplace two large girls with huge breasts, a taste for flashy outfits and a real love of whisky. The apartment was done in yellow drapes with tall pictures of fat actresses in tights, on the walls. The girls were

36

called Doll and Marie. Marie was sitting on Simon's lap pouring whisky into his hair and rubbing it in. Doll was the refined one. She lifted her pinkie to drink and would only take two puffs on Joseph's cigar, sucking the fat tobacco roll skilfully.

"Love soldiers, Major, love 'em to death."

"Just spare my leg, the rest of me doesn't mind."

"A toast!" said Simon. "Gotta drink for a reason."

"He's a card," said Doll, "Doc sure is a kind man. When my mother tripped over a cab horse last year, he set the leg and let her have a pint of gin a day. Good old Ma. She loves Doc, everybody loves Doc."

"He loves you too," Joseph said, putting aside the very wet cigar.

"He loves *it*. But they keep him tied down at home. Be a sport, Major, and refill my glass. You're beautiful I think with that beard, and that limp. It gives a gent dignity, I allus say, to have a limp."

"I'm pleased you're pleased, Doll."

"Oh, stop *that*!"

Simon took off his shirt and threw it over the little table covered with seashells. Marie started to save the seashells and the two fell onto the floor and rolled and laughed and Marie's legs kicked out showing the frilly drawers and the red garters. Simon made a stallion sound and said, "We'll operate at once. The patient will please lie still. Ah yes, very bad. How long have you had *this* condition?"

Doll put her face close to Joseph's and said, "Didn't I tell you he was a card, honey?"

Later in the rattling cab as they drove into the dawn, Simon groaned. "Wallow and roll, wallow and roll, that's me, Joseph, and I always hate myself in the morning for it."

"Why hate yourself in the morning? You go of your own free will and you should come back without a pack of self-pity. What time is it?"

"Marie got my watch. But it's late enough. We have to sober up and get out to the family for the weekend."

Joseph grinned, "Is there a good steam bath in town? I'll boil sin out of you and present you starched and clean to your family, you old lecher."

"Yes, take care of me, Joseph, I'm not to be trusted out alone. Did you give Doll your watch?"

"No, she had to be satisfied with simpler things."

Joseph needed sleep. He wished they were not going to Cape May.

The ocean-straddling pier cast sharp blue shadows in the sand, then ran away to sea, and above it was the guttural geek of sea gulls, and far out on the ocean a scribble of chalky clouds, and then the pencil smudge of a steamer's smoke as it headed south towards the Gulf Stream. The day steamed, the sun blinded, and the smell of livery stable and of horse-and-carriage polish was overpowering. Joseph closed his eyes as they drew near the pier. Back from the pier ran sand for a hundred feet, fine white sand that drifted across the hard-packed road, and ground with a brittle, glass-like sound under the steel tyres of the carriage.

There were cottages under wind-bent saplings, in ordered rows, and some attempt at gardens in the salt-and-sand world. Doctor Simon pointed to a rise and to a mottled, brick bungalow carrying a gaudy awning, surrounded by plants in pots. It was a very warm day and the cottage seemed crouched, as if cowed by the sun.

"That's our place. Rather Italian, isn't it?" Doctor Simon said.

Joseph nodded and got carefully out of the carriage. The leg was holding up fine. Doctor Simon blinked, his eyes were dissolved away by the sun on his glasses into two shiny black wheels. "I designed it myself from a little place I once stayed in at Capri. You could see the Blue Grotto rock from it.

Two young children came running down towards them, naked as young jaybirds, so tanned that their blond hair looked white. They were shrill and happy, and behind them ran a girl with a large, flapping towel, a towel that made, Joseph thought, sounds like distant rifle fire. A collie dog followed them, a lean-headed, friendly slob, all tongue and streaked golden hair.

The children came up to them fast, stopped and shouted. "Father!"

"Hello! Hello!"

"A crab bit Louis!"

"Oh dear—a crab?"

"You'll have to cut his toe off! Off! Off!"

"Well now——"

"We're naked, naked! We're all over naked!"

The girl with the towel caught up with the children and was dying of shame at this nude exhibit. Joseph could see the blood colouring her small, warm neck. She began to try to wrap the children in the towel as they danced and shouted, "We got belly-buttons—we got——"

"I'm sorry, Simon. They do this every chance they get. The neighbours are shocked."

"We're all over naked! Naked!"

Doctor Simon slapped a small, pink rump. "First one dressed gets his present first."

The children dropped the towel in the sand, the collie dog grinned, and they ran toward the house, their small heels kicking up flying gouts of sand as they ran. "Presents! Presents!"

Doctor Simon smiled at the girl and said, "Joseph, this is my sister, Rebecca. Becky, Joseph Pedlock. If you want him to make love to you, don't call him Major."

Joseph laughed. "I'm taking no part in these offers."

"You're such a fool, Simon," the girl said stiffly in confusion; then she blushed again and held a small hand out to Joseph. "It's good having you, Mr. Pedlock. Simon, I'm sorry I lost my temper, the children shouldn't go around naked."

"Peel the body and expose the soul? Well, it's good for them. How's Emma?"

"Fine. A little sick in the morning, but that's to be expected. After all." The girl coloured.

"Sixth month," said Simon to Joseph. "Emma doesn't have much trouble delivering the whelps. Good wide pelvis, and . . ."

"Please, Simon, no clinical details," said the girl. "Did you have a nice trip?"

"It's been a hot trip. Dogs sticking to the sidewalks in Philadelphia."

A woman in a large garden hat was waving to them from the scrubby front garden. She was plump and placid-looking, and she smiled in a thin, dainty way and had very blue eyes.

She stood waiting for them under a grape arbour to which a few strands of tired vines clung with no hope of getting any place in this sand and sun and salt air. She was wearing a large apron and she had her hands clasped under the apron, as if she were playing at hiding a small melon. Simon kissed her briskly on the cheek and introduced Joseph to his wife Emma.

"He's written about you, Major," Emma said. "His letters are full of you. It's good having you here. The sun will do your leg good."

"I feel better already." Joseph sniffed the air. "And if I am not mistaken, I smell a *cholent*."

39

"It's been potted and baked and simmered all night. And there is very good cold fried fish for Simon. He has a delicate stomach for *cholent*."

Joseph smiled at Rebecca. "I used to have the job of running around to the baker's in Vienna and bringing the baked *cholent* home Saturday morning. Once I dropped it when some dogs attacked me in the street, and there we were, rolling in the street, me and the dogs, all of us covered with the potted meat and vegetables."

Rebecca laughed a small, alert, amused laugh and he joined her as the children came out with some clothes put on in haste, and they began to dance around Simon.

"The presents, presents!"

Emma stepped between them. "Now, children, is this the way to greet a guest?"

The children examined Joseph closely for the first time. Louis cocked a blond head to one side and asked, "Did he bring presents, too?"

Joseph and Rebecca sat on the night sand and the moon was low enough to grab, almost. The sea wind had died down and it was warm again.

"Simon must have been bad in town. He's so kind to Emma."

"Men don't tell on each other, Miss Manderscheid."

"It's hateful."

"Yes, I suppose it is."

"Well, let's forget Simon. Shall we?"

"For a while, anyway. Do you like it here?"

"I love the sun and children. I love children. I hope to have a lot of them."

"The family doesn't seem to have much trouble producing them."

Rebecca tucked her skirt with care under her and looked out to sea. She was very frightened of this man. He came from far off, he was thin and had been ill, he didn't care about business, and he cheerfully admitted having been to the fearful fleshpots with Simon.

"Men do dreadful things."

"They don't do them alone."

"Those poor creatures can't help themselves."

Joseph looked at her earnestly. "I doubt if they are poor creatures. They seem to be out for a good time and a lot of pleasure. People are not all alike."

"I'd rather not talk about it any more."

"I didn't mean to. You seemed curious. Most good women are."

"What makes you think I'm a good woman!"

"Miss Manderscheid, I am sorry if I misjudged you."

They laughed and got up and dusted themselves and went slowly back to the house, both thinking very hard how to avoid being attracted to each other.

Peter found some details of the courtship in that Philadelphia attic as he went through the letters and journals in the old trunks. There were great gaps in the material, which he found could be maddeningly complete in other details.

There was, for instance, an old bill for fishing gear, with a pencil note in Doctor Simon's monk's Latin handwriting: "Louis ran an inch-long fishing hook into leg this morning. Sea bass running with the rip tide at five."

There was a yellowed boxed copy of the *Poems of Longfellow*, in which there was a loose sheet of paper: "Dear Miss Manderscheid; I cannot say I care much for these poems. Just a little too literary and cheerful. Life isn't always that heroic, or perfect, or simple. Nor as pretty and pastoral. I can't read Dante at all. I find him a great bore, even in Mr. Longfellow's simple translation. J. Pedlock." Things got better after that. The next book in the series was missing, but a short letter showed some progress had been made in the matter of names. "Dear Joseph: The Villon is, of course, rather good poetry, but don't you think somewhat coarse? Even in French I dislike that poem where he speaks of *what* he and Fat Margot do for a living, and *how* they live. As a modern woman [Peter was rather amazed to find anyone in 1870 thinking of herself as modern!] I do not shun a direct approach to life, but still there are certain things one does not put in print. We are all looking forward here to seeing you again next Monday. Louis caught a ten-pound flounder in a rain storm and has a bad cold, and Deborah has had me set her hair in curls for your visit. Cordially, Rebecca."

Aaron Manderscheid came back with Joseph for a weekend at the shore. He sat beside Joseph in the carriage as it moved slowly across the beach roads and he grinned when he looked at Joseph sucking on a long stogie.

Joseph smiled. "Do I look that foolish?"

Aaron waved a short, fat arm. "I was smiling at the change in you, for the better. Understand, I can say it now that I'm a friend, but you were a pretty bitter young man and in pain when you came to us."

"So I gather, Rebecca—that is, the people at the beach—seem to think I was rather a bore when I first came."

"Nonsense, just a little boiled out and thin in a war."

Joseph pulled the new hat lower over his eyes and shook fire off his stogie. "You've taken in a stranger and been kind to him."

"Joseph, why beat around the bush, we expect you to marry Rebecca. As head of the family, after all, if I can't say it, who can?"

"Well, there is always Rebecca to say no. I scare her."

"Oh, nonsense. All men scare young romantic girls. It's the way we bring 'em up. All flowers and tender mottoes and suddenly we expect them to be at home with a naked man smoking a cigar and full of ideas that don't fit a knight in armour."

"You paint a confusing picture, Aaron. Anyway, it's more than the girl not being sure she likes me. I'm pretty much a pauper at the moment."

"Post-war panic. You'll come out of it and anyway, I like to see you in trouble. I still have that copper holding that needs looking into."

Joseph mused to himself, but said out loud, "So, to you all, I'm a naked man with a cigar and no knight in a tin suit?"

The small boat with the sail furled was just far enough off shore for them to feel free of the people on the beach. Rebecca lay on the bottom of the boat and Joseph sat by her side and with delighted fingers outlined the blue piping of her sailor blouse.

"I never thought it would come to this, Joseph."

"You feared me?"

"You frightened me and yet I wanted you very much and then I felt indecent about it."

"I know, there is a rigid idea about all this in certain classes of society. But if kissing does no harm . . . why . . ."

"It does a great deal of harm, Joseph. I dream."

"So do I."

"Don't tell me about it."

"Of course not." He leaned over and kissed the tan valley of soft flesh between her breasts. She sank down even lower and put her lips together and she said very low, "Joseph, Joseph. I'm as bad as Simon. We're a tainted family."

"Oh, you're much worse. You're not weak like Simon and yet you go on having those dreams." Joseph smiled.

"What can I do?"

"Better stop reading poetry and seeing me alone."

"I can't accept those things as poems. Joseph, a poem should be something noble."

"Aren't our meetings noble?"

"They're taut and confusing."

"A good poem should be like that, too."

"Joseph, better put up the sail. And don't look at me. I don't know what's come over me."

She sat up, buried her face in her hands and wept.

Joseph groaned, then cheerfully steered for shore.

In the end she accepted even the lines from Herrick that Joseph sent her:

> *Fain would I kiss my Julia's dainty leg,*
> *Which is as white and hairless as an egg.*

Peter unfortunately, did not find many of their letters left. Filling in the gaps, however, was often simple. *Dear Rebecca* becomes *Darling Rebecca*, and *Yours cordially, Joseph*, and *Truly, Rebecca*, become *Your beloved Joseph*, and, *With all my heart, Rebecca*. There were opera programmes for an Italian touring company of *Faust*. Ticket stubs to some early, and then new, Gilbert and Sullivan. And a bill from Brill Brothers, "Jewellers to Baltimore", for a small locket and chain, eighteen-carat gold, engraved: R.M. from J.P., which showed the jewellery stage had been reached and that Joseph was travelling a bit that year, trying to get started in the iron business again. His success or failure was noted in a letter from the law firm of McCall and Baker, Nashville, Tennessee.

Dear Major Pedlock:

The matter of Pedlock and the Pedlock Land and Iron Company *vs* The Borey Combine and New York Refining Company has been postponed again by certain judges. I am sure that we can prove that your title is the legal one and that the carpetbagging rights brought by the Borey firm from—shall we say—an odd Land Claims Court, will be set aside.

This may of course take years with the present confused condition of the Reconstruction Courts and the thousands of similar cases on the dockets.

May we congratulate you on your coming marriage to Miss Manderscheid. We have often served the firm of Manderscheid and Sons, of course, but as personal friends of the family we want to extend our wishes for a long and happy married life. The small,

silver token we enclose as a wedding gift; may it ever shine bright
in your home.

Most cordially,
Charles J. Baker
Jackson C. McCall

Joseph sat very stiff in the parlour of Aaron Manderscheid, a glass of brandy held tight in his fist. He scowled up at Aaron pacing the rug, happy in doing family business of a romantic nature. Doctor Simon sat against the wall, his eyes following his brother's steps around the puce-and-green rug.

"All right," said Aaron with a purr. "You don't want a big wedding. Just a simple, legal wedding service. Can I have a few members of the family? Good. Just a few family is fine. For myself I just beg the duty of inviting a few business people I can't let down by not having them in my house. It just can't be done. So. If you have people, I must serve something. It's expected. Something cold, maybe hot, a row of serving tables. All right! All right! Sponge cake and wine, but some cole chicken. Something warm also?"

Joseph swallowed the brandy and looked at Simon, who sweated and wiped his face. Aaron walked around the rug again, placing one small foot in front of the other.

"A wedding needs a little joy," he said. "All right, some music. Nothing loud or vulgar. Some Hungarian fiddles, expanded by a piano or something like that. And I can't insult Reb Sontag. He's blood of my blood and flesh of my flesh, as he would say. He'll perform the services. He's a big man and he'll most likely bring a cantor to sing a prayer, and his best gold and red velvet canopy with the golden columns. I can't stop him."

Joseph stood up. "All right, have your goddamn society wedding!"

"Anything *you* want," said Aaron, "it's your wedding, Joseph."

Doctor Simon said, "We were sort of forgetting that."

Aaron folded his arms and smiled. "I'll use up every bottle in the wine cellar. A man doesn't get rid of a sister every day."

Joseph said, "It's a good thing *my* relatives aren't in this country."

Doctor Simon Manderscheid did not join in the gay feeling of celebration over the coming wedding. He sat at his desk in his little room called the "writing den" and held a thin ivory penholder in his hand, and sighed. It as late at night and in the street below the late hurry of a late cab, its iron tyres and its iron hoofs, made the only sound in the night. He felt sorry for Joseph, now to be warmly embraced, sucked up into the fat, smothering arms of the encircling family.

Poor Joseph, he would even be happy in the family and never brood over its protective grasp. Doctor Simon sighed again, wished there were some brandy in the house upstairs not under lock and key, and rolled the ivory penholder in his hand again.

He looked down on the sheets of folio paper before him. He was amazed how much he had written in the last few years. It had started as an interest in the medical history of those Manderscheids who had been doctors and healers. But, somehow, personal family history was creeping in. He must be careful or he would end by writing one of those dull family things of marriage and interbreeding and giving and taking of many sons and daughters in wedlock.

He picked up the thin, white, ivory penholder, dipped it into the silver inkpot that once belonged (or so the Fleet Street dealer had sworn) to Samuel Johnson, and began to write quickly, glancing, from time to time, at a batch of rat-eared notes.

The Manderscheids are an old English family going back beyond William the Conqueror and back beyond Alfred the King who burned the cakes [he wrote]. For they came out of the fog of un-recorded history, perhaps with the Roman Legions under Caesar, and had settled in the marshes among the blue-painted, native savages on the chalk cliffs.

What was known was that by 1290, in the Year of the Great Jew of the Gospels, they were living as doctors, healers, cattle gelders and potion makers within call of the Royal Court. They were, I have found it recorded, tall men in remarkable beards, with long, fur-trimmed coats, bearing themselves well with their long rods of office and their golden chains, living with a dignity and calm that made them the best doctors in Europe. And perhaps in the whole world. They gave—their notes are before me—the enema and the puke. They treated for the pox of Venus, that snake in the garden of love, which they kept at bay with mercury. They of course called it, in England, the French sickness, and in France the English sickness, and in Italy—what could they do?—the French sickness. They were wise enough to know that honest men can blame any-one mortal for anything and often hit the truth.

They mostly were famous in all the Christian countries for their operation for the great fistula, and had carved and sewed on most of the noble ends of the royal barons. The Arderne Manderscheid *Tractatus de Fistula in Ano* was published in Latin, and a copy still

46

exists in the Harvard Library, where I found it one day in 1869 and read with glee the listings of the Manderscheid-designed instruments for the operation: the *sequere me* or flexible probe; *acus rostrata* or grooved director; *tendiculum* or dilator; and the *siringa*. The anus of Europe, the book states flatly, was theirs.

And their white ointment, in modern form, was used in the British Navy up till the time of Nelson. I still read of its making in my editions of Ambroise Paré and the *Regimen Sanitatis Salernitanum*. It was made of powdered bole armenic, *sanguis dragonis* (or, frankly, "dragon's blood," most likely chicken gore), oil of roses, rosewater and gum arabic. More practically, the Manderscheids invented and sold at fairs "a sleeping ointment for people about to be cut and treated that left them without pain or sensation". Much needed, for the usual barber-surgeon or pig-physician of the period was little better than a blacksmith. The Manderscheids—good Jews—mixed the juice of henbane, mandragora, water hemlock, and equal parts of Thebaine opium and meconium, beaten, it *is* to be regretted, in fresh swine grease.

But none of this saved this English family when, in 1290, Edward the First, on All Saints' Day, expelled the Jews from England. Modernism of the worst sort, in the shape of the Crusades, had broken the centuries-old calm in England, and it was easier for many to turn out the Jews rather than go and fight the Turks in the Holy Land.

All sixteen thousand Jews were expelled, among them the tall doctors and their packets of herbs, their cutting knives, and their secret of treating the great fistula. The king let them go in peace, and when a few were killed by his pious sailors, he had the sailors hanged (two of whom became minor saints).

The Manderscheids found refuge in France, where they practised their trade and art and gave French knights a better seat in the saddle on their great war horses. In 1306, Philip the Fair (in hair) being in good health, and in need of money, confiscated the goods and wealth of the Jews and pushed them out of his country. Some went to Spain, to await the faggots of the Church. But the remaining Manderscheids split up, and went to Venice and to Amsterdam. They married into the Jewish families of the Villa Reals, the Medinas, and the Laras, who had been ennobled in the times of the Saracen States.

In exile they turned not to the study of the Torah and the Talmud. The Manderscheids remained doctors, or became merchants and shippers out of Dutch ports, and even sea captains and

47

sailors when they could. Jews were still not legally welcome in England until 1649, when the Puritans assumed Jewish names, and went hunting for the Lost Tribes. Petitions were presented "for the return of the beloved people of Israel", and Cromwell approved, and Charles the Second, between trouble with Samuel Pepys, and Nell Gwynn, and his little dogs, confirmed their return. But long before that, Manderscheid doctors and sailors were landing on the English coast for quick cures, and quicker bargains. And so three of them sailed for Jamestown. Two of them reached it, and one of them stayed on to found the American branch of the family. . . .

Doctor Simon stopped writing and put down his pen. Folding his arms, he fell asleep at his desk.

Joseph Pedlock and Rebecca Manderscheid were married at the end of May, 1871, under the marriage canopy erected in the home of Aaron. Joseph, failing to get his Tennessee land case through the panic and corruption of the Reconstruction period, was going out to survey the Manderscheid copper-land holdings, with his bride. A man must feed his wife, Aaron had explained.

Two items in the attic trunks brought back more or less relevant events concerning the wedding. One was a letter on fine rag paper:

Dear Aaron Manderscheid:

It is written in the book of the poet Habakkuk, in the part of the scroll that follows the Vision of Isaiah: "Write the vision and make it plain upon tables. . . ." And so I am penning this letter after much thought and much inner turmoil. The wedding was a beautiful thing. The uniting of two fine people in the glory that is God's. Among that glory are the men of Manderscheid, and their flocks and vineyards are overflowing, for they have lived the true life to their Lord and have prospered much in their time.

Therefore it is before you that I must put a simple fact. You have a place in the community, you are looked up to. You are the rich man, the king among us. I am returning your check for fifty dollars. No wedding, such as a Manderscheid wedding, can be dignified by less than two hundred dollars to the rabbi. For it is sadly written in Ecclesiastes, "Money answereth all things."

Glory in Israel,
Rev. J. Elimelech Sontag.

Peter also found a large yellowing sheet of paper headed "Department of Police" and written on it were the words "Confidential.

Report Officer J. J. Normans, May 23, 1871" "Suspecting [the part that is of interest to the family begins] that perhaps there had been foul play of some sort, after finding Doctor Simon's coat and gold watch and chain in the Robbins' ship supply shop, a search was made of two vessels about to sail. On board the Swedish ship *Karen Lenstrom*, in the sailors' quarters, we found Doctor Simon Manderscheid, in a stupor brought on by what appeared some drug to drink. The crew claimed he came aboard drunk. But it is our suspicion that he was drugged with knockout drops and taken aboard and stripped. We removed Doctor Manderscheid from the ship to the dock and, while waiting for a carriage, he kept repeating certain demands in his semi-drugged state. He refused to get into the carriage until we promised to get his brother-in-law, Major Joseph Pedlock, who he said was at the William Penn Hotel. An officer then went round to the hotel and awakened Mr. Pedlock, who dressed and came with us to the docks, when informed of what had occurred. It was only later that we learned this was Mr. Pedlock's wedding night. At the dock . . ."

Simon was lying on burlap bags and they smelled of dead oysters. The police had placed them over the wet planks of the dock. When Joseph came over to him, Simon looked up trying to focus his eyes, for he had somehow broken and lost his glasses. The thinning hair fell over his blue-white forehead, and his mouth was slack and open. He could only look up at Joseph, the big bulk of him so close up there as if cut from black tin, outlined in the smelling bull's-eye lantern held in the fist of the frowning policeman.

Joseph bent over into the beam of stabbing light and said, "Hello, Simon. Been out on the town?"

"I've been away. Far away. I've been going back—sailing away, Joseph. You see it was all so fine, but then the wedding. Oh yes— it's your wedding night, and I've taken you away from the bride, and I'm such a fool on your wedding night. Curse me, Joseph, and never speak to me again. The bridegroom shall not tarry."

"You need a bath, Simon, and a good clean bed, and lots of sleep."

"It was the wedding, I guess, that did it, Joseph. All the family there in their best bibs and pearls and the fiddle players and the hot, warm rooms full of the smell of roasting goose and the plum brandy in little goblets. With the smug face of the rabbi, and you stamping like a stallion on the wineglass, as it is ritual for the groom. And suddenly you know I felt you were trapped, too. You would be bedded and nailed into place. And become a repair man for broken knees and loose toes, or is it copper-mine holdings? And never again be wild and young and feel the lazy sun. Joseph, Joseph, come with me and we'll never set another leg."

"But I'm not a doctor, Simon. You are. Come on, try and get up. Emma is waiting for you. And Louis and Deborah and your new baby. Poor Louis, he got excited at the wedding and fell down stairs and chipped one of his teeth."

"Emma, Deborah, Louis, and the baby. Joseph, tell me again, what's happened to Louis? It's all too much for me. A respectable family and the problems of houses, and servants, and firing the cook, and the coachman has been stealing on the hay bills again. The new sewer-line rates, and those big, foolish dinners with Emma wearing the little diamond earrings, and all those contented pink faces. They don't know the futility of life, the shortness, the briefness of man's time on earth. Bounded by a dream, bounded. Rush, run, enjoy the little you want. Don't wear a collar, and, Joseph, please—is your leg hurting you when you carry me?"

Joseph set Simon down in the carriage and smiled.

"The leg is fine. Now sit here in the carriage and we'll soon be home. Get along, driver. Thank you, officer. Mr. Aaron will see you in the morning."

The carriage ran up the stone street. Simon swayed and sang.

"Clop, clop, clop, it's like the death wagon when the plague hit Naples, Joseph. All night picking up the dead, the dead who wanted to live, the living who saved and waited and were evil or good and dull, and waited. And now a priest building a salad of oil and ash and Latin on their head, and the lime pit called history, or eras, dynasties, civilizations, waiting. The plague in a town, the plague in the world, and the clop, clop of the death wagon."

"It's just the carriage horse, Simon. Philadelphia streets are built of stone."

"You don't know what a plague does to you when it hits a town. It makes you regret."

"I went through it in New Orleans in '59, when Yellow Jack hit."

"You're my strength, Joseph. I can face it now. The whole wide facet of my quiet desperation, as someone said. All its glowing shallowness and Emma, and poor Louis. Was it a front tooth? I'll be all right when I'm sober and have my gold watch and chain against my respectable stomach, and they say, there goes Doctor Simon, he can cure any bones but his own. . . . But his own. Go back to your bride, Joseph. What did they once beat into me in Hebrew as a child? *Yishar Koach*—May your strength increase."

"You're home, Simon."

"Home, home is where you hide your childhood. I'm Henry Longfellow Manderscheid tonight."

"Here he is, Emma."

Rebecca was standing by the big bay window, facing the dark street, when Joseph came back to the hotel suite. She turned quickly and her lace and silk nightdress of pale blue and gold whirled around her in curves and folds. Joseph thought, it's like a beautiful painting of some Madonna painted more for the flesh than for the spirit, more for the bed than for the manger.

"Joseph?" She was just a little frightened, but not enough to hide a stronger emotion.

"I'm here, dear." He took off his coat and dropped his hat and let the cane clatter to the floor as he turned the gaslight lower to an intense bud of fire.

"Is he all right?"

"He'll be fine in a few days. Too much wedding," Joseph laughed. "Almost too much for me. First Aaron told me it was going to be just a few of the family, then a few outside guests, then the important people. And the few fiddles grew into an orchestra, and before you knew it I had a wedding like a star."

"Did you mind, Joseph? Very much?"

"No, Rebecca, I didn't mind." He went to her and took her, with an urgent, brutal love, into his arms, and he kissed her directly and hard on the mouth. She giggled and said, "Oh, Joseph." Then she said it again but this time the "Oh, Joseph" was like escaping breath, as she was again gripped by a gout of sudden passion for this man.

"You're my lusty girl," said Joseph. "You're everything and all, and you're not ashamed of it, are you?"

"Joseph, Joseph, what have you done to me? I'm like you are. And I don't care and I don't mind."

He held her tight, little naked breasts in his hands—those mellow mounds tipped by blossoming pinks—and he rolled his great thumbs and he pressed against her, he thought, as the old scrolls said, to beget, beget, beget.

"I'm not Simon just doing my duty, darling. This is going to be a wonderful marriage."

And he turned the gaslight up to a blooming rose of fire.

BOOK TWO

CHAPTER I

"The frontier," Joseph used to say when Peter was a young man, "is a pretty romantic thing these days. The book stores never stop sending me copies of it with fancy-coloured jackets of women with huge breasts and lean, handsome men in buckskin. You ever smell or wear wet stinking buckskin? You ever shoot a horse at your door every winter and let the dogs feed over its frozen form till spring came? You ever see a frontier whore mangy and diseased, fat and puffy, reeking of bad whisky and worse teeth? You ever see the real frontier women? Lean as rakes and as ugly, coughing and spitting, dressed in rags, going mad in pine clearings? Women sick of the damn brat impregnated into them every year, sick of the men hairy and bitter, their birthright sold for a homestead and forest fires and blizzards and grasshoppers. No, the frontier wasn't romantic, sensual or clean. It was hard and dirty, and hard and dirty people made it."

"It made a great country," Peter used to say.

"Sure it did, Peter. But think of the mad women dying alone in sod huts, of brutes on two legs drowning at flooded river crossings, of the pain of black legs frozen off, of fires that burned out the clearings, of lawyers and land robbers and village bankers who swallowed it all in the end. It built a great country, but it swallowed up the best of us, when it didn't kill us. I gave my youth to a war and all my middle years to struggling on the frontier. And I did worse. I dragged Rebecca through the jumping-off places. It was like the children of Moses for us, years and years in the wilderness. I'm not going to talk about it."

"You were in Butte when the copper wars started, weren't you?"

"I'm not going to talk about it," the old man would say and lean back and close his eyes.

The children of Joseph and Rebecca never forgot it. It was the first railroad into Butte, Montana; the Utah Northern, that connected the town with Salt Lake City itself, and, naturally, with the world. The road had been promised by December 1881, and the night before the first train was due in, the children, Sam and Ralph and little Egon, couldn't sleep much, and were up in their attic bedroom in the cold dawn, talking about the railroad. Sam was nine, and Ralph was eight,

53

and Egon was less. When their father came clumping up to the attic bedroom, the two older boys were already dressed and waiting for him, their scuffed elkskin shoes polished, and the brimmed, black felt hats on the back of their uncombed heads. Joseph grinned when he saw them, their blue breath making vapour in the freezing attic.

"You're never in such a hurry to get up when there's wood to get in."

"The first train, Papa!" said Sam. "I wanta ride in it . . . just a block!"

"Well," said Joseph, "I'll speak to Condon and we'll see. Now down to wash and breakfast and bring the woollen scarfs for your ears. Lots of lost ears in this weather."

The boys laughed loud and long—as they always did when Joseph made a joke, for they thought him the most comic and wisest man in all Montana. Joseph, at forty-five, was already beginning to turn white at the top of his head and along the fringe of his beard. He was still tall and straight, and the planes of his face were harder, and full of character. His beard was trimmed a little carelessly now, and had lost some of its curl.

"Come on, train!" shouted Sam.

"Me, I'm goin' to be a steamboat man," said Ralph.

"And you, Egon?" asked Joseph, pulling the blanket off the youngest.

"I wanna sleep."

Sam grinned. "He just wants to go on wettin' the bed."

Ralph, the neatest, carefully tied on his scarf. "I'm goin' to wear diamond cuff links and smoke big cheroots and gamble for real gold coins. I'm goin' to carry a pistol like Papa and bang, bang. I'm goin' to . . ."

There was the knock of a broom handle on the ceiling.

Joseph nodded. "Mama is waiting. The town is waiting, and the train is due soon."

Sam shouted, "I want a ride on the engine! I want a ride!"

"We'll see."

The attic steamed with their breath until almost a fog filled the place. Egon got damply out of his reeking bed, escaped the knotted towel whips of his brothers, and stood weeping over the chilly wash basin in which ice had appeared in the night.

The boys cheerfully chattered, and their father looked at them and shook his head. All this life and animation and little minds running riot and he felt as far from being adult and sure of himself as he had ever been. Had the years since Philadelphia been good or bad? On the surface bad, but somehow, crude, and strongly etched, under it all some small satisfactions.

"Ouch!" yelped Egon as his brothers tormented him. Joseph came in to hand out a few brisk cuffs of his hands.

"A little order here!"

Standing there as they pulled their scarfs down from the rafters, Joseph warmed his hands over the iron floor drum that came up from the kitchen and was supposed to bring some of the cooking-stove heat up to the boys. Time and events had certainly run him into an odd corner. But here were the sons.

They were healthy-enough children, their clothes warm but worn, and Joseph wondered just where he had gone wrong. What had happened to his hopes of getting simple, dignified power and some satisfying comfort out of the metals of the earth? Had he failed some inner self?

Joseph was at this period puzzled by the reason for things. Like a non-theological mystic, he craved revelation. He looked not at the soul, but directly at nature, to open up—like a big eye—so that he could see directly the ultimate answer to life. That moment never came, but something almost comprehensible did—something on the edge of the unknown—and he drew back, sadly satisfied that only in clinging to nature's realities could he safely find firm ground for his life and family and his body. The exactitude of emotion in him was balanced, he now knew, toward the visible life and away from inner brooding.

His youth had gone quickly. He and Rebecca were middle-aged. Where had time and all those years slipped to? It had been a long time since he and his bride had left Philadelphia to develop copper lands in Michigan. The panic of '73 had been a fearful thing to live through. It had wiped out the old Manderscheid and Sons companies, it had ruined the copper holdings. And Rebecca, meantime (with his help, of course), had produced hungry sons for him. And often *so* pregnant. "Leave it to the Lord," Joseph had felt, "to overdo the plenty he gives a Jew."

"Are they going to drive a gold spike," asked Ralph, very blond, with a small button nose, shivering in the attic chill.

"Silver, maybe, we're a silver town," said Joseph as they climbed the split, mine-timber stairs down to the kitchen. Lee, the Chinese cook, whom the boys called General Lee, took over the feeding of Egon, who at seven still had to be fed his mush, which he hated. Lee pushed the big iron spoon in the little boy's freckled face.

"Come on, Egon, eat up the mush. . . . Papa take you see iron horse." Lee, born in San Francisco, did not, much to the boys' disappointment, speak like a Bret Harte Chink.

Egon rolled his big eyes and whimpered. "Hate mush."

"Eat it," said Joseph firmly, as Lee went to the stove and began to shovel fried eggs and fried mush onto plates. Joseph poured the black coffee into his big blue personal mug, and the boys drained their fresh cups of milk, a product they hated but which they were told would put hair on their chest. The Pedlocks kept two sad, thin cows, their teeth stained with copper from drinking mine-pump water.

Sam, his dark face shiny with excitement, swallowed his eggs and mush and waved his fork in the air. "The biggest g.d. engine in the West comin'. Wrapped in flags of all nations and firin' a cannon every ten miles. Hurray for the Utah Northern!"

"Hurray," said Egon, getting fried mush in his hair.

Ralph, the dude, combed his hair with a handful of fingers. "Nothing is as classy as steamboats."

Rebecca came out of the bedroom in her best blue dress, which was six years old, and a little old hat with red piping that Joseph remembered from their wedding day. He certainly had been a hell of a bad provider.

"Good morning," said Rebecca.

"Morning, Mom."

"Nobody washed well this morning. Lee, the soap and pan."

"Mama, it's *too* cold for real washing."

The wind came across the fields and slag piles and shook the warped, clapboard walls of the house. From the mills, smelters, and concentrators came, as usual, the deadly fumes of sulphur and arsenic from the open roasting pits of the silver ores. Joseph had built in open country beyond the town, but now the town was catching up and it had bridged the gully behind the Hotel de Mineral, filled it in and called it Hamilton Street, and soon it would push past his house.

"I washed, Mom. Honest, smell the soap on me."

"I washed, too."

"With spit. Step up here."

It had been a temporary sort of place where they had first come out after the panic, in '74. Joseph was going to build a regal brick house on one of the hills, above the dust and smoke and gas. Above the sound and the filth of the faro and roulette houses, yes, away from the dance halls and whorehouses. But somehow, the Condon and Pedlock Mines hadn't prospered.

"The ears, Sam, both of them."

"Serve you right if they freeze and drop off on me."

"Earless, earless," sang Egon.

Rebecca sat down and poured herself a cup of coffee with just a touch of milk and a speck of sugar. She sat drinking and smiling at the children, and listening while they excitedly talked of the railroad. Since her last pregnancies, Joseph noticed, she had slimmed down again, but, he sadly noted, her Philadelphia stylishness had left her. It had not been an easy thing to see one's simple, well-cared-for world fall apart. One's rich, cozy, stylish world. To see brothers and families and fortunes swept away, to feel life stirring in the womb, to bring into the world three sons in frontier cabins, with only the aid of the dirty hands of midwives, or defeated, backwoods medical men, too tired to care any more.

Joseph, growing harder, grimmer, needing her, had given her a purpose, a task. To make a home, to bring forth children, to come to his bed at night and help shake out the fury of his hopes, the defeats and mistakes, and the unrewarding turmoil of his efforts. To hide his face on her breasts, to press down and to feel the terrible, savage quiver that told her she was his one true harbour for hope. She remained for him in the one unchanging thing, the one real thing. Fragile, yet so strong, enduring and encouraging.

It needed no words of explaining—it existed.

Joseph put down his heavy coffee mug and wiped his rough beard with the back of his hand. "Lee, get the broncs into the buckboard, it's time we started." He looked at his big, silver railroad watch attached to a heavy brass chain (the golden one had paid for the year Rebecca and Ralph had been so ill). Joseph rose and took down his black felt hat and heavy belt with the grey-handled Colt revolver, from nails hammered into the timber wall. He had been wearing the Colt since the last rock slide had crushed two men in the lower shafts and there had been muttering that the cross timbers had been rotten. He suspected the Motherlode people of starting that untrue rumour. There was no telling when a drunken miner might offer to take a shot at him, "Street-corner murder is a frontier form of polo or tennis," he once told Aaron on a visit.

Rebecca wiped Egon's chin and wrapped a blue woollen band around him until he could hardly stir. "Do you have to wear the gun today, Joseph?"

"It helps keep me warm," Joseph said, and kissed Rebecca on the cheek. Egon stirred against his father, a bundle of blue wool. "Me, too."

"You too, Blue Bear."

Joseph picked him up, kissed him roughly with a mock growl, tucked him under his arm and went out to the frozen stables. The family followed, Sam screaming, "I'm the ole engineer . . . *toot toot.* Dead man's crossing ahead! Toot! Toot!"

Ralph ran and whirled around them on the frosty ground, pointing his fingers like guns, and said, "It's a stick-up mister! And my name is Jesse James. Just hand out them mailbags. The ladies—ma'am— can keep thar jewels. . . . But don't nobody git fancy and reach for thar shootin' irons, 'cause ole Jesse he don't never miss! Bang, bang!"

Rebecca said, "Joseph, Ralph's been reading penny dreadfuls again."

"They cost a dime, Mom," said Ralph respectfully.

The odour of frozen farm life and horses and cows filled the lean-to that served as the barn. Lee had the buckboard ready. Joseph had bought the broncs for forty dollars and a jug of squirrel whisky ("two toots—stranger—and you climb trees"). They were tough, evil little horses that had taken a lot of breaking and had twice wrecked the buckboard with its extra seats bolted on behind. But Gyp and Jim, as they had been named by the boys, when they left the barn, merely fought their harnesses and with Joseph at the reins, went along the dusty, frosty streets with a sliding side walk that threatened to become a bolt any minute, but didn't. The boys in the back tooted, hooted, and cheered.

The town was in celebration mood. The mills and stampers and smelters still poisoned the air, but everyone who could was making for the new depot, where the train from Salt Lake City was due to open the new railroad officially. Joseph, Rebecca at his side, held a firm grip on the broncs, and as the buckboard jolted and rattled in the almost brittle, cold air, he thought back on the years that had passed so quickly, and so many of his hopes with them. A rather ordinary human thought; true but trite, he felt.

The high hopes had left him and Rebecca when they first saw the copper lands of Michigan. But it would only be temporary, they had told themselves. The Manderscheid Michigan holdings were lean, and would take long, expensive engineering. Aaron had been willing to put up the money, then '73 had come and Manderscheid and Sons had been ruined in a bank failure and a Wall Street bear raid. The copper holdings had melted away to try to stem the tide of trouble. Rebecca's small personal fortune in rails and shipping had become worthless or thrown away to steady an unsteady market.

And so suddenly one morning Joseph woke up, lit a good Havana

58

cigar, and looked down at the big, blackwood double bed where Rebecca still slept, beautiful, mellow and warm, and beside her the naked head of a baby, Sam, his puckered mouth screwed up as he turned and blinked and waited for the great provider—the breast—to feed him.

"Rebecca, I guess it's all up here in Michigan."

"I don't want to go back to Philadelphia, Joseph. Things aren't what they once were. It wouldn't be pleasant."

"We're not going back. Condon wants me to go into silver with him."

"Silver? With Ira Condon?"

"Montana. It's a grim place. Rough, frontier. Very loose and hard. Not very ladylike."

"I'll go, Joseph."

"It's no place to raise up kids."

"It's where their mother and father are. A lot of children—if we have a lot—grow up on the frontier. They can, too, when they come."

Joseph held his cigar away from the bed and tickled his son under the chin. "So we're going to have more?"

"Oh, Joseph," said Rebecca, baring her breast and letting the open-mouthed Sam fall with a sucking, satisfied sound against it. "Didn't we say we'd have a dozen?"

"I suppose we can always afford children, even in Butte."

"Butte?" She closed her eyes and sucked her lower lip as Sam tugged and hurt her breast. She enjoyed the pain. He was such a fat, dark baby, with solid arms and legs, and even when he cried, it was, as Joseph admitted, "only to exhibit the full power of remarkable lungs".

"Tell me about Butte, Joseph."

"Butte. That's the big silver town in Montana. Condon has some worked-out gold holdings there that are showing signs of silver. He needs somebody who knows how to roast the ores. It's a hell of a job, to roast them with salt to eliminate the sulphur and arsenic, convert the silver to chloride, and produce the base metals at a profit."

"Yes, dear," said Rebecca yawning, as Sam, now fed and contented, closed his eyes and slept. "Anything you say."

Joseph put the now dead cigar in the chamber pot and went out to find Ira Condon.

Condon was a huge barrel of a man, a handsome, comic figure who chewed tobacco, drank his whisky neat, and had an odd love of excitement. Privately he was a man of some secret, black despair that didn't let him sleep. He spent most of his nights in wild and fearful orgies—or what passed for orgies on the frontier. He was a simple

59

man, happy or sad. Always gay in a parlour house, drinking, smoking, chewing, making the wild and unsanitary love of the mining towns. He was well liked and respected, for he never went back on his word or tried to make an unfair bargain. He and Joseph had both been ruined by the panic, but now Condon was again the cheerful drinker and shouter, and already he saw them, the Condon and Pedlock Mines, silver kings with private railroad cars and champagne for everybody. Alone at night, Joseph knew, Condon would sweat and turn and then if he dozed off, fearful images would awaken him. Fear and some morbid, depressive power filled his mind and warped his nerve ends until he screamed for release, for lights and gay women, and a great deal of whisky. Condon never carried firearms, for he knew—he said often—that in some dark moment he would use them on himself. "Too many ghost stories in my childhood," he explained with a grin.

To Joseph he tried to explain fully this darkness that closed him in when he was alone, for he knew no reason for it, no real reason why this futility, this fear of sleep should grip him so. He had, he admitted, "murdered a man once, a common horse thief; been married to a woman I caught with her lover, a groom; but I was never really unhappy about these things. Been rich several times. But the loss of it done nothing to me. I was born into the Church, but the faith was lost very early. Still, none of this matters much. What really gnaws me, I can't find or explain."

So he said it was his nurse's ghost stories told to a baby in Ireland. Years later, after Joseph had read Freud—he told Peter—perhaps it had been only the nurse's stories after all. But Peter said it was too simple.

Condon respected Joseph's knowledge of metals, and he enjoyed the home life, the children and Rebecca. He became a part of their life as soon as the Condon and Pedlock Mines went into operation in Butte.

They were not successful mines. At three hundred feet the silver was beginning to give out. Signs of copper appeared in '78, but they could not afford to build smelters for the costly process of refining the ore. They went on in hope that the rich veins of silver ore would be found before they had to sink deeper shafts and bring in whole forests, at a great price, from the mountains, to cut into mine timbers.

It had been a hard time and was getting no better. The giant combines around them were all in trouble but rich enough to talk of making copper king when silver failed, as gold had once failed and been replaced by silver. Labourers got three dollars a day, miners four dollars, timber men—and they were needing more and more of them —six dollars a day. Butte bragged of its thousands of men at work in the shafts and its payroll of millions a month. But Joseph and Condon had trouble meeting their share of it. They feared rock falls, or running into quicksand, or fire which would race through the underground shafts and burn out timbered crosscuts, drifts, winzes or races. Blasting powder was going up and Joseph brooded and spent his nights making plans and drawings for a cheap, effective, new way to smelt copper. But nothing had come of his planning. He was almost convinced that silver mining was over in Butte and Condon and Pedlock with it. No time for celebration, but he couldn't let the boys down.

There was no denying it, Joseph felt. He was forty-five years old and a failure, and had three small sons and a wife to support. He wrapped the reins around his rough leather-covered fists and shouted at the broncs, and the buckboard ran ahead, the damned broncs trying to tangle their leather legs in the loose harness.

In front of the Hotel de Mineral, a roaring, roaming crowd was already gathered, and their breath smoked in the cold air from the frost and the barroom whisky they had fortified themselves with. "The axe, the rifle, and corn whisky made America," Joseph often said. "It was a good job, but we haven't held on too tight."

Condon waved to them. His cheerful grinning face was under a white Stetson, and his high-heeled boots were polished and cruelly spurred (for a man who never mounted a horse). His red eyes showed that he had done little sleeping.

CHAPTER II

Condon climbed up beside Joseph and turned inside his bearskin to face the rest of the family. "Great day for Butte. Great day for everybody. How are you, Rebecca?"

"Fine, Ira, just fine. Sam, don't lean out so far."

"I'm holdin' on."

Joseph whipped up the broncs, scarring their buckskin legs. "Sam wants to ride in the engine cab."

Condon nodded and cheerfully slapped Sam on the knee. "I don't see why not. You stick close to your Uncle Ira. Pontdue owes me a little favour. I helped him get the chairmanship of this here celebration."

Joseph flapped the reins over the broncs' wrinkled rumps. "The less I have to do with Pontdue the better."

Condon grinned, "He's still offering to buy our mine for peanuts."

"Rotten peanuts."

"I see the depot! The depot!" sang out Egon.

A shifting, shivering mass of horsemen, carriages and riders was collected in front of a chilly blue line of rails. The line ran flat and even across the frosted land. Around the colourful point of celebration small fires had been built, and there shivering people stood or danced and talked. A flag-draped platform had been erected, on which sat some miserable, pink-coated musicians, dreading the moment their cracked lips would have to touch the freezing brass instruments in their red hands. Several men in cutaway coats, called "hammertails" locally, and wearing top hats perched on heads of hair oiled with bear grease or imported ointments, walked up and down the board platform. They looked at their large watches and shook their larded heads.

A large, square man with the upturned moustache of a Prussian officer, a great chest, large arms, and a round, dropping stomach held tightly in place by a white vest piped in German blue, had a pair of military field glasses to his eyes. He wore not a top hat, but a crisp army Stetson of a bright blue. His boots were long and came over his knees and had leather buckles that locked them tight around his heavy, over-muscled legs.

People called him "Herm," or "Mr. Pontdue." Several copies of a now rare booklet about him, printed in Virginia City in 1870, are extant. Called "Herm the Great" (author unknown), it is a slanderous attack on the man. However, it is the only information available on him.

Pontdue leaned over and looked at a telegraph clerk who was banging his brass key, screwed down to a freezing pine board in the stand.

"Well, Wilmer?"

"She's just passed West Lung Crossing, Mr. Pontdue, going like sixty. Due any minute."

"Twenty-three minutes late."

Pontdue fluffed back his moustache with the back of his short-nailed thumb in the military manner he had learned as a youth and closed his watch case with a snap. Herman Pontdue (according to the booklet) was one of those odd, strong men of the late American frontier, for whom there is no explaining—or too much explaining. He had once been a captain in a good, middle-class Prussian regiment, but a blond orderly found dead in the barracks stable one summer night had never been clearly or fully explained. Ex-Captain Pontdue appeared soon after that in Texas, with two Englishmen, to open a large cattle ranch that prospered until the partners drank up its success. He had served as U.S. Marshal in two states and killed six men, for he could handle any firearm with great skill. (The names of the dead are given in "Herm the Great".) He was now a very rich man, in his beefy prime, heavy, solid, and very formal and military. He still spoke with a Prussian bark, but he had no accent.

In the Congressional investigation of 1885 he is mentioned as an agent and a member of the board of directors of the Copper Combine, backed, it was hinted, by the banking giants of the East and West. Senator Hearst, the Morgan interests and their groups had formed a great combine and were buying up most of the Butte mine holdings, trying to weave them into a huge trust that would then be able to make its own ore and timber and railroad prices. Also get its smelters consolidated and ruin the independent mine owners who would not sell, by cutting them off from railroad rebates and smelter sources. All this is now over-exposed Americana.

Pontdue, on the splintered platform of celebration, nodded crisply at the Pedlocks and Condon and turned back to his field glasses and the cold, empty ribbons of blue rails. Sam and Ralph climbed high up on the platform poles. They suddenly shouted and pointed down the tracks.

"There she is!"

"Smoke! Black smoke! Jesus Priest, look at the smoke!"

Everyone saw it now and began to shout and crowd to the edge of the tracks. Far down against a pile of white winter sky, a soiling corkscrew of smudge grew into a puffing column of inky smoke. A high-flanged, snorting engine appeared, its driving wheels spinning and its driving rods pumping. And steam leaking from its many vents. The low, wide cowcatcher was crowded with people holding on at great danger to limbs and hats. The tall funnel stack blew smoke, fire, and cinders over its shoulder. Three passenger cars painted red and draped in bunting, a mail car, and a flatcar on which horses and some boxed mine machinery kept company made up the special Salt Lake City–Butte train. The boy Sam never forgot it. It came in screaming and *donging*, the cold steel rails and the polished wheels thudding and thumping together. Then sand ran onto the tracks and the engineer, grinning over his red bandanna, put on the brakes. With a skid and a hiss the gaily decorated engine groaned to a spine-shaking stop. The mob closed in around it, as if for a happy lynching.

Sam rushed toward the train with the people. Men poured off the cowcatcher, stamping out burning cinders from their hair and clothes. A dog, half red tongue, ran wildly down the street in howling fright as the Pedlock broncs kicked holes in space, and went completely insane. But, as they were securely tied to railroad timbers set deep in the frozen ground, they could only pant and roll great eyeballs and flap their pink nostrils open and shut like leather clam shells. Everyone cheered, and Condon lifted Sam up to meet the brave engineer.

Someone had champagne and someone was making a speech and the railroad hands were shooting off Winchesters into a cold, silver sky. The bell and siren of the engine were exploding all over the cold sharp day. Joseph lifted Egon on his shoulder and Rebecca held Ralph and clung to Joseph's arm. Condon was in the engine cab and he shouted and waved his big hat. The band put their reluctant lips to their cold tools; and music, frozen and coming out in jagged lumps, covered the celebration. Egon slid to the ground and, shaking with excitement, wet his pants.

There were many Indians. Condon, very gay, asked a fat squaw, "Your papoose a full-blood Injun?" She said, "Him part Injun," and pointed to the train, "part Injuneer."

Sam got his ride in the engine cab and several people, among them Pontdue, made short, frost-clouded speeches about progress, wealth, and Montana. At noon it began to snow and a blue twilight set in. Soon the whole wide world was blotted out and the broncs, aching with cold, turned homeward. The boys refused to sit near the steaming Egon. Condon sang for them an old song all the way home.

> *"Did you ever hear tell of Sweet Betsy from Pike*
> *Who crossed the wide prairies with her lover Ike.*
>
> *"Out on the prairie one bright starry night*
> *They broke out the whisky and Betsy got tight,*
>
> *"She sang and she shouted and danced o'er the plain*
> *And showed her bare ass to the whole waggon train!*

"(Forgot you were with us, Rebecca.)"

Later, after a heavy fried supper, the boys sat around the stove, trading marbles and talking over the day's event. General Lee played a one-stringed cigar-box fiddle of his own invention in his lean-to off the kitchen, singing a dull singsong tune with it. Condon and Joseph sat under the oil lamp, its reeking wick freshly trimmed, and outside the hail rang crisply against the clapboard walls, and made tiny, scratching sounds like baby fingernails on the window panes. Rebecca sat in shadow near the food chest, stitching together a pair of velvet pants for Egon. They were royal red, and she intended to add pearl buttons for decoration.

Condon rammed a blunt, discoloured thumb into a half-filled pipe. "I saw Pontdue at the bar of the hotel last night, Joseph."

"You'll drink with anyone, Ira."

"He's a mean squarehead, I admit, but he's got power."

"Still wants to buy us out?"

Condon nodded and put the pipe back in his mouth. "Only he's lowered the price. He says it's going to go down every time he makes the offer. And we can't afford to wait much longer, me boyo. The silver ore left in our pits isn't worth a harlot's hello—beggin' your pardon, Rebecca."

Joseph leaned over the table, his head in his hands, and looked up at Condon. "Do we crawl out of it all, Ira . . . leave it all behind, take a little cash and go looking for something else to try?"

"I'll do it your way, Joseph. What is your way?"

"Go into copper. I've been thinking a lot of a cheap new smelter process."

"Where can we raise the cash? We're windy and empty with good intentions. A smelter, even a cheap one, will cost at least seventy-five thousand, just to start."

"The Miners and Drivers Bank hasn't turned us down yet."

Condon shrugged his shoulders. "Not yet. I'll hate to walk in there some fine morning and find that first time. What are we doing in round figures a month?"

Joseph sat back and filled his own large briar pipe with a rough-cut shag. "I don't have to go into details, Ira. We're losing two thousand a month. We owe the bank sixty thousand dollars."

"And you think they'll give us seventy-five thousand more for a smelter? They'd rather invest their money in new privies, pardon me, Rebecca."

"This smelter, if I can design it, can be built cheap."

"I'm for taking Pontdue's offer and getting out."

"I'm not, Ira."

"How long will you stick?"

Joseph lit the pipe slowly, carefully, with a large kitchen match and looked over to where Rebecca was threading a big needle. He noticed she was having a little trouble threading. He took a deep draw on the pipe until it gurgled and sputtered and said, "Six months. June first. If it's still all bad news, we'll sell out."

"June first?"

Condon got up and stretched all over, his joints creaking so loud that the boys looked up from around the cherry-red stove to listen to the sound. "Joseph, we'll get the sticky end of the stick if we fail to take Pontdue's offer now, but I'll stay like the devil on a witch's rump till June first. . . . Have you heard the story of the old Irish woman who was asked if she were ever bedridden? 'Hundreds of times,' she answered, 'and once in a sled!'"

Rebecca held the needle up to the lamp-light and frowned.

"You look tired, Ira. Why don't you go up and sleep with the boys?" she said.

"No, there's a big shindig at the Casino, and some Englishmen have hired the private boxes at the Comique. . . . Anyway, I don't sleep much."

"Why go out into this storm? Stay the night."

"The mine drags are keeping the ore road open." Condon looked at the Swiss clock hung over the battered dish and china closet. "The big drag is due soon on the corner. I'll get back to the hotel on it. Good night, folks."

Condon got into the large bearskin coat that was one of the sights of the town, winked at the boys, pulled Egon's ear, and went out. letting in a blast of wind and a crisp shower of stinging hail.

Joseph turned to the boys. "Up to bed. No arguments."

But there was a short period of yawning protest, a kissing of small

66

faces, and then, at last, they were up in their low bunks with the hail coming through old cracks in the badly pitched roof.

Joseph came slowly downstairs, and sat down again at the table. He did not, as usual at night, take down the mine and smelter drawings and plans pinned to the wall. He turned towards Rebecca.

"I'm a fool, Rebecca. I can't battle the Combine. It's a big Wall Street fight for control of rails and timber and ores. I'm nothing to them. They don't even know I exist, except as so many feet of tunnel and shafts."

"You can get copper out of the mine, Joseph?"

"It's there. All the signs are there. The deep-water pumps bring it up. Green signs. When we spill the water down the hill it flows through a dump of old pots and pans."

He got up and took down a burlap bag hidden in the kitchen rafters. Out of it he took a tin can and a pot without a bottom.

"Look at these. The iron has been washed out and replaced by something else."

He held the objects to the light and a green metallic sheen could certainly be seen.

"What is it?"

"That's copper, pure copper!"

"Copper?"

"Yes. It's from the water pumped out of Number Three pit. And look at these."

He took some large teeth out of his vest pocket. "Got these from the butcher. Teeth of cows that have been grubbing the grass near the dump. Look, their teeth are copper-coated. It's even settled in the grass roots. It's every place—copper."

Rebecca tried to look at the big, yellow-green teeth plated in metal, but turned away. "I think I agree with Ira. The bank may not give us any more money."

"They have to. They're a miner bank. I'll give them part of the stock in the smelter. It's just business, Rebecca. They can't afford to close us up. We can't afford to sell at Pontdue's price! We'll get the smelter built, if I can design it."

He went over to the wall and took down the plans. He looked at them a long time, but did not work on them. Rebecca stitched the pearl buttons in place. Three on each leg, three alongside each pocket, and six more where she felt they would help. Joseph sat, the pipe dead in his hard, firm mouth, listening to the wind and hail howl around the shack. The timbers were groaning and the fire in the stove dying down as it gnawed through the last chuck in the firebox. Ashes dead and grey began to fall into the grate. It grew colder.

Joseph sat a long time, and he wondered why the hopes and plans of his youth had ended so badly. The Tennessee lands case had been settled at last. It was all practically legally his, *if* they hadn't yet sold it on him for back taxes and lawyer's fees. He could not spare a cent to develop it. Something had trapped him. Something he could not dislike. This woman sewing here—this marriage, those fine boys up under the roof-tree—it had been fine and honest and a real pleasure. Yet somehow the words of his brother-in-law, Doctor Simon, came back, "They've trapped you, too."

Thinking such nonsense, he put down the cold, acid pipe, went over, took Rebecca in his arms and kissed her tenderly. She looked up at him and he down at her. How tired and worn her face was. How coarse and weather-worn her once peach-bloom skin had become.

"What's happened to us?" he asked suddenly.

"Nothing has happened to us, Joseph."

"Too much, much too much. The dreams and ideas we had, remember?"

"We were very young."

"The damn poems we read. The love we made as if we had invented it all and there was nothing like it ever."

She put away the sewing and, grinning up at him, put up her hands and pulled on his crisp hair. It was a fetish of love-making between them, this pulling of his hair, and he grinned and put his arms around her, the breasts so slack and soft now, no longer the hard firmness of girlhood, and the face not smooth with youth and innocence.

"What damn fools we were."

"I don't think so, Joseph. I haven't changed. You haven't either."

"I worry more."

"That shows you've grown older."

"Don't you worry, Rebecca?"

"I'm too busy. The boys tearing their clothes. Egon wetting his bed. Lee spoiling the food. I can't find time to worry."

Joseph sighed, sat back in his chair and looked at her lying in his arms. "Here we are, the dashing Confederate officer, the daughter and sister of the Philadelphia Manderscheids, kicking pots in a leaking miner's shack in Butte. Your brother Aaron must think because we don't keep the rituals any more we've been punished."

"Don't say that. They admire you. You see, they're men of peace, good at business or doctoring, but you're action and war and outdoors to them. They have great respect for you."

68

"How the devil can they? I'm such a failure."

"What nonsense. It's still like the poems to me."

She smiled and, as always when emotion caught her, showed a sly, shy blush, and put her small, needle-pricked hand in his horn-hard palm.

"It's cold—let's go to bed."

They lay in the bed listening to the storm, and it was only when Joseph began to breathe hard through his nose, in that first crisp captivity of sleep, that Rebecca turned over and closed her eyes, and sighed, and went off toward sleep herself. The times of poems and long, romantic letters and little gallantries were really over. Still, a woman went on expecting them, even if she knew that other things fogged a man's mind. She thought (half in and half out of sleep), a woman never gets over expecting them and wanting them in greedy expectation. And she would have thought more on the subject, but she was already almost in a deep, undreaming sleep. Tomorrow she would try to get the washing done with Lee, and dry it into stiff, frozen ghosts in the lean-to . . .

General Lee did not feel or hear the storm. He was deep in his bunk, and the Yeng-Tsiang pipe was just right. He had rolled the little *gow hop* pill of opium, cooked it on the end of a pin over the little *ken-ten* lamp made of a sardine tin and put the sizzling, cooked pill in the pipe. There had been just enough for three strong draws to fill his lungs. It was his third pipe, and the best. Now he was far away in the *hutungs*, the lanes of familiar home places, and all the things that he didn't have, all the heavy, sensual dreams, the gay colour, smoking joss, and sacred things—all were coming to him. He was naked under a calfskin cover and the lean-to was cold as ice blocks, but he was eating out of celadon bowls. His round, drugged face had a thin smile, and as the last of the pill went into his lungs, the floating wick went out in the sardine tin, the thump of the bronc's heels against the barn wall was deep-etched in his mind. He heard the thump of the small bound feet of the little yellow girl with the great mass of black hair set into pagodas of design over the beautiful, calm, yet expectant face. . . .

Condon put the bottle back on the dark, oiled wood of the bar, and the woman in the tight red dress picked up her glass and drank it down quickly.

"Where you been these last few days?"

"Look, dear, I been busy, me and Joe Pedlock."

"Too busy for me?"

"I'll make up for it. Go sing me the song."

"Which one?"

Condon slapped her hard, with pleasure, on the wide, graceful behind. It made a beautiful, satisfying sound. "Look, hotheels, there is only one song."

"That damn 'Cowboy's Lament' gives me the colic. Why don't you like classics like Mr. Pontdue? 'My Mother Was a Lady,' or 'A Bird in a Gilded Cage'?"

"That krauthead!" Condon turned from the bar and held a whisky glass in each hand. The woman, already past her prime, had the ripeness that he liked; and older women were so damned grateful, too.

"The goddamn 'Cowboy's Lament'," she said to the piano player. Condon nodded. "You can keep opera."

A miner came in, his nose red, his ears purple. He looked at Condon. "Pontdue's boys just killed one of your machine hands. Over cards at the Crystal Hall. Christ, made cat's meat of 'em."

The piano keys danced under thin fingers.

"Copper," Joseph explained to Rebecca and his sons, "is a very odd and interesting metal. The common copper ore of Butte is mostly a sulphurated ore contaminated with arsenic and antimony. To get rid of the impurities it must be roasted."

"Like a duck?" asked Egon, looking up from the magazine picture he was cutting out with blunt scissors.

"Like a duck. After it's roasted it's smelted in a mixture of copper and iron sulphides to become copper *matte*. After a while you get a thing called copper sulphide, a pimple metal very impure and still full of iron."

"How do they get copper pennies, Papa?" asked Sam, closing his tattered stamp collection with a yawn.

"We'll come to that later. Blister copper is still full of stuff like lead, even zinc, nickel, or cobalt. Now, I remember when I was a boy in Europe, seeing them make bronze cannon in the Royal Vienna foundry, an old gun designer told me they got little batches of metal ready, say half a ton, by blowing air through it. That purified the coppers, and the impurities were driven off."

"Can I blow copper??" asked Sam.

"Let your father talk, boys."

"I'm going to make a big rolling vat of steel, lined with fire brick, and, through a big pipe attached to pumps, blow air through fifty tons of copper at once!"

"Will it work, Joseph?" asked Rebecca.

"I don't see why not. It's simpler than any process the Copper Combine has. Their refining is very bulky and very expensive. I'll patent the revolving Pedlock Vat and we're in business."

"And you can build a copper smelter plant?"

"We'll start as soon as the frost goes out of the ground."

Rebecca got up and took Egon in her arms. "It's been a very interesting lecture on copper. Now, boys, to bed."

The basic Pedlock Patent (as any lawyer knows) has now been in the courts almost seventy years. There are two hundred and twenty close-packed legal volumes of trial matter; three judges have died while trying the case. Hundreds of lawyers have grown rich, many dishonest, on the case's legal joy ride through the State and Federal Courts. Supereme Court judges groan when any part of this huge patent case comes up before them. It has been the major battleground of the great Copper Combine and independent copper men, and it has moved mountains and dug deep into the earth to pay for all this legal horseplay.

The basic patent idea has been—by now—much modified. The simple pipe and the revolving vat have been attached to electric power, to acid baths, and chemical processes. Most of the people who remember the first, shaky walls of the Condon–Pedlock Smelters are dead.

Old Mister Mont, of the Miners and Drivers Bank, a grand old man under his white whiskers, he of the large, old-fashioned shoes with the square toes, was very polite and kind to Ira and Joseph. They sat in his overheated office, under the elk horns, and watched him spit eating tobacco into a brass spittoon without getting a drop on his white linen suit; white suits he wore in winter or summer, against cold, heat, blizzard or smelter soot.

"This here bank isn't just a bank any more. We're part of a national jackass train carrying American credit on its back. I'll be as honest as a madam at a camp meetin', boys. We're a Copper Combine bank. They hold a lot of our stock and they're sittin' among our directors right now. Pontdue has just been elected to our board."

Joseph frowned and looked at his leaking boots. He had again forgotten to have them repaired. Rebecca would be very angry. "You'll not back our smelter? Even for twenty per cent of its stock? Hell, that's a banker's dream!"

Old Man Mont got rid of his old wad and refilled his cheek with fresh eating tobacco. He prodded and chewed the cud into shape and got it just right, tried a trial spit, and sat well forward in his chair.

"Gents, all I want to ask you is, have you got a real tight, bull-in-fly-time patent on this copper smelter process?"

Condon nodded. "I went to Washington myself with it."

"Good. And I hope you have a small lawyer pasted to every page of it. The Copper Combine has a process that uses air under pressure, and they now claim it outdates yours."

Joseph got up and folded his arms. "Maybe they want to make a fight of it, but we have the only refining process of this kind that will work."

Old Man Mont looked at them from under his bushy white eyebrows. "Well, good luck. Sorry about the loan."

Condon and Joseph left the bank. A wet, dirty spring wind, loaded with chills and damp with threats of rain storms, hit them. They crossed to the Dirty Shame Saloon and Café and leaned against the bar and looked sadly into thick shot glasses full of Bourbon. They nodded silently to each other and swallowed the whisky, waiting patiently for it to hit their livers.

"We're dead ducks," said Condon slowly.

"We have a valuable patent and we have a smelter going up."

"I guess the Combine will take the foundation and walls off our hands. We need vats and tracks and a million things."

"I'll bring out Rebecca's family from Philadelphia to help us. Nice people, the Manderscheids."

"Joseph, why don't you run down there yourself right away?"

Joseph refilled his glass and then refilled Condon's.

"Rebecca is pregnant again. I kind of see that as a change of luck. She always gets pregnant when my prospects are at low ebb and something always happens to change my luck. Yes—I feel things will work out, now Rebecca is pregnant again."

Condon grinned. "You're not recommending that for me?"

"No, Madam King, that jaybird, doesn't give that kind of service."

"Don't knock. Some of my best friends are madams."

They killed the bottle and stood against the bar thinking and making small, dull suggestions. At five, Pontdue came in—his boots polished, his moustache curled—and went to the other end of the bar and had a small glass of kümmel. Condon waved to him.

"Buy you a drink, Herm? You goddamn banker."

Pontdue came over to them, the kümmel glass in his fist. "I think I ought to buy, now that you've heard the news."

They had another round, Pontdue looked at them and rubbed his big round chin. "Naturally, I know about the bank loan you didn't get."

Joseph said, "You should, you voted against it."

"The day for small fringe mining is over, Pedlock. The Combine is going to run ore and metal in America. Why not come in on the ground floor?"

"We've got a floor," said Condon. "It's a beautiful floor."

"And that's all. I'll give you, in the name of the Combine, forty thousand dollars for all your holdings."

Condon said, "That's a real big drop from what you offered this winter, mister."

Joseph put down his shot glass. "What about our smelting patent?"

"Not worth the price of the paper the plans are drawn on. Our lawyers are going to prove that to you. But just to show I really want to make this deal, we'll work out a royalty deal for the patent."

"What kind of deal?" Joseph asked. He looked at the bar, not at Pontdue.

"Say something like this to start it: a dollar every thousand tons, dropping a bit every year, and at the end of twenty years, the patent belonging, without royalties, to the Copper Combine."

Joseph said calmly, "Go jump on yourself, Pontdue." At least that is what he said when he repeated the remark later in polite society. Actually he used a stronger word.

Pontdue grew white across his big fleshy nose, his fists closed, and he set down his glass. His voice when he spoke was very low. "You're lucky I'm not wearing my guns."

Condon leaned casually over the bar and spoke even lower than Pontdue. "If you were, you know where I'd put them? And I'd even find room for your big blue hat."

Joseph and Condon walked out of the saloon and the barmen put down their polishing cloths and looked at one another with tired smiles and someone began to hum an old tune. Pontdue stood at the bar, breathing hard, looking down at his empty glass. His eyes met no one's.

He put a five-dollar gold piece on the bar. The barman pushed it back at him. "They paid for all the drinks, Mr. Pontdue."

That night Joseph telegraphed a long message east and Condon put armed guards around the smelter grounds. The next day the firm of Shadrack and Sargent, Attorneys at Law, served legal papers on Joseph and Condon, in the patent suit, and two short-term bank loans against their mines were suddenly called in. Joseph brought home a box of shotgun shells.

A week later their log bridge, over which their ore cars crossed a gully, burned down, and one of their newest pumps went out with a cough and a sneeze and a deep shaft was flooded. The silver market fell, and even that, Joseph felt, showed somehow the long, long arm of the Copper Combine. Work on the smelter slowed down. Corey, their foreman, was fired on by unknown men and charged Joseph for a new Stetson.

The first, feeble, green weeds were seen on the lower fringes of the slag heaps, and the few, soot-covered trees tried life again with the first, weak buds of the season. Aaron Manderscheid and Doctor Simon, attended by Louis, now a tall young gentleman with a chipped front tooth, and a tight, stiff collar, appeared in Butte and put up at the Hotel de Mineral.

There was a small family dinner in one corner of the big hotel dining room for which Joseph trimmed his beard and put on his freshly repaired shoes.

Aaron and Doctor Simon had grown older, much older, Joseph felt, but of course he had aged in their eyes too, he was sure. Louis was a proper young man, thin and placid like a bored and happy puppy, and Doctor Simon kept asking him to eat more, as if he were stuffing a high-holiday goose.

"He doesn't do much, just sits around the house," Aaron said.

"He looks all right," said Rebecca. "You look fine, Louis.

"Thank you, Aunt Rebecca. I feel fine."

Aaron looked up from his plate of ranch beef and smiled at Joseph. "What's become of this old Jew here, eating unkosher food, in the Wild West?"

"Ranch beef is enough to make a man give up eating meat," said Joseph, "and eating it in Butte is enough to drive men from cities."

Aaron shook his head. "It's a lively place. I can't say I dislike it. Oh, I know it's been hard going, Joseph, but the boys look fine. And somehow, don't worry, we'll get that smelter up. I tell you, I feel it in my bones—it's the American century just ahead. We're going to show the world. We're going to make something fine out the progress of the times."

Doctor Simon smiled. "Aaron has never heard of William James' Bitch Goddess, Success. In his simple faith he still confuses mere speed with progress. Mind you, I don't see us failing as a great nation, but somehow I don't want us to take the path to power alone. Something can be lost, unless we are sure of what direction we take. But what kind of talk is this for a cheerful family dinner?"

Louis looked at his aunt and smiled, showing his chipped tooth; then he drifted off in some vague sort of brooding about something he saw on the stained ceiling.

The waiter came over and hovered like a hawk alighting, with two bottles of champagne in an ice bucket. "Mr. Condon sent these."

"Very nice of him," said Joseph. "Is he around?"

"At the bar." The waiter's head rolled around as if set in oil.

"Ask him to join us," said Rebecca.

Condon, when he came up to the table, was not yet fully loaded for the night. He was smiling, cheerful, and under control. He was introduced to the table, and held up his wine glass and looked over the tablecloth, every ounce of huge bulk full of a pleasure of the moment.

"Ah, the Philadelphians. Nothing like having family and lots of it. I've got nobody and nobody's got me. But it's no good. No sir, you gotta have roots, or you've got nothin'. Well, let's drink it down before the bubbles commit suicide in our glasses."

Aaron smiled and barely touched his lips with the glass. "Mr. Condon, it's good to know you. Joseph has written a lot about you, and I have a feeling that if anybody can get cheap copper out of Butte, you two can do it."

"We'll talk business later, much later. But I'm not so sure it's going to be very healthy work. Pontdue is bringing in bad hombres, gun tossers, and we're having trouble getting men to work for us."

Aaron said, "There's law and order out here, isn't there?"

"Oh, yes," said Joseph, lighting one of Doctor Simon's best cigars, "but it's a little different from Philadelphia law and order. The American pioneer loves his axe and his gun, and it will never be really taken away from him. This move of Pontdue's I don't like."

Louis brightened suddenly and sat up straight. "You mean there is going to be gunplay?"

Joseph shook his head. "I doubt it, Louis. Pontdue doesn't dare upset the backers of the Copper Combine. In the East they're all holy Joes and teach in Sunday schools. A new kind of pirate."

Aaron settled back in his chair. "Copper stocks are dropping. The Combine may be in a tight corner."

Condon nodded. "It's going to be a hell of a lot tighter for them when we put our cheap smelter process in operation. This town is really going to hum—like a squaw full of castor oil—in the next few years. Louis, I'd like to show you the town some night. You too, gents, if you're willing. Gay and exciting. Paris after dark, with spurs on, you might call it."

Aaron held up a small hand in protest, "You take Louis some night. But the Doctor and myself, we came just for the air, good, ripe mountain air."

Doctor Simon rubbed his mouth with a crisp napkin and didn't speak. He had grown very grey and bent and a little fatter and the eyes were the eyes, Joseph noticed, of a man at peace with himself. The peace of a fire that had been turned to calm, grey ashes. If Simon still thought of the youthful days in Europe, of the gay girls and the pleasures of the bottle, there was no sign of it. Perhaps he saved his memories for secret sessions—used them the way one took drugs—alone. He was just what he looked now, no doubt. An aging Jewish doctor with a reputation of greatness for something he had done in his youth, some process or method that medical science has long since caught up with the passed.

"I'm an old man now," he used to say, "pottering around with

76

rancid children in some river-front slum, running a Cheap John clinic, and begging the rich for a few dollars for healing salve for bedbug-bitten bodies. For young girls with budding breasts over chests full of germs that would strangle them and fill their pretty little mouths with blood."

He had accepted life. Even the quiet desperation seemed gone.

Rebecca lifted her head from her wine glass as the men lit fresh cigars, and said, "If you don't mind . . ." at which soft words the men sprang alertly up from their chairs, and Doctor Simon and Aaron rushed to their sister's side and helped her rise from her chair, gently lifting her to her feet. She was now visibly pregnant, and to the brothers it was always a sign of great fulfilment to see any of the daughters of Zion with child. They fluttered around her, and asked her if she were in pain, and said that they were brutes not to notice her discomfort. They broke the brown necks of their cigars in heavy silver ash trays. To the brothers, the replenishing of the earth, the ever-recurring miracle of family birth was the important thing in life. As Aaron said, "Our women in labour, their young broods growing, the full family life and its problems and manifestations, this to us is the true reason for existence on this earth."

Joseph felt a little distaste at the whole business. It made him feel neglectful when the brothers were gone. Joseph and Condon stood aside, their cigars behind their backs, and as they watched, Joseph saw that Doctor Simon had now (most likely without noticing it or knowing) caught the family spirit, thus herding and comforting the pregnant members of the tribe.

"Please," said Rebecca, in mild, pleased protest, "you men stay and talk over affairs. Louis can see me home."

"Sure," said Condon. "Sorry to keep you up this late, Rebecca. Louis, have the desk man get you the best hotel rig. And if he whips up the horses tell him I'll chew his nose off, in public."

"We can hold the meeting tomorrow," said Joseph.

Rebecca shook her head. "No, Joseph, you have a lot to do. Louis will do fine. And he can come right back. How handsome he is, and tall. Do you go with girls?"

"Not much, Aunt Rebecca."

"Not much?" said Condon, opening his eyes wide. "Listen, you either do or you don't go with girls. There is nothing as bad as just 'not much.' Eh, gents?"

The Manderscheid brothers felt this was not the proper tone to take before a very pregnant lady and they just shrugged, half amused, and watched Louis and Rebecca cross the lobby to the door. After which Condon ordered some brandy to be sent to his room, and they all went up to talk over the problems at hand. Condon, following the others, thought of them, in the great scarlet hotel rug, as still the followers of Moses crossing the Red Sea.

Condon's room was like the man. There was nothing on the surface there that showed the deep, solid truths about him. His living room was neat but rather worn and battered from too many brawls and nightly revels. The bedroom beyond was stark with a huge, dark walnut bed, an ocean of white bedding with many devices such as knee pads and scented pine-needle bags, special dim lighting, all supposed to bring sleep nearer, and always, as Condon admitted, failing.

He sat the men down, and later, when Louis came back, he gave him a book of mine photographs to look at.

When the woman in the red dress knocked on the door, he sent her away with a tickle and a promise.

CHAPTER IV

The men found seats that helped their digestion and after a while
got down, as if into a too warm bath, to the business at hand. "Things
have changed here and are changing fast," Condon said. "Joseph will
back me up in what I say. I'm not all blubber and laughter, and I
know mining. The facts are that the Copper Combine is secretly, and
not so secretly, pledged to take over the Butte mines and make them
one big company hill. We've been through every phase of fighting
them, and the one thing we can't do is sell out now at their prices.
One more very sinister thing has crept into the damn picture."

"What's that?" asked Aaron.

"They've been offering us—all year—less and less for our holding.
This week, suddenly, they've been offering us more and more. The
way I see it, we're about the last of the independents with any sizeable
holdings. Something big is brewing back on Wall Street. The market
is falling, which is all right for us at the moment; we're building. But
the Combine is rushing things. The gun slingers are a sign of it. Real
mean hombres out of the killer camps and cattle and sheep wars."

"There any danger to you and Joseph?"

"Nonsense," said Joseph. "We're in no shooting danger."

Condon shrugged his big shoulders and splashed whisky into some
tumblers. "I don't know. These killers get paid by the job. They may
be told to keep clear of us personally. But a man with a Colt ·45 for
hire isn't a household pet on the street corner. But back to our real
problem. We can finish this smelter if we have credit. We gotta get
credit. I've sold my last holdings in Michigan, for what they will
cash in. We still need a lot of money to get the smelter up. And more
when we get operating. How about it?"

Aaron sat well back in his chair and looked at his odd, blunt thumbs,
and when he spoke he spoke slowly and with a direct, cold logic in
his voice. "I think I see a way to do it. The family isn't rich enough
these days to take on the whole project, but I can arrange to start the
payments on the smelter as they come due. Simon is selling his holdings
in Philadelphia transit lines to help us. My wife's family is willing to
make a loan against Joseph's Tennessee lands. I can raise something
on the warehouses. The first fifty thousand in credit we can manage."

Joseph shaded his eyes from the overhead oil lights and stood up and walked to the window and looked down into the sooty street, then walked back and dropped a dead cigar in the polished, silver-plated spittoon. "I didn't know it would be such a personal thing, involving the family like this. But, Aaron, if you're willing and know the job ahead for what it is, and the chances, we can proceed. It will, in the end, cost several hundred thousand dollars before we're really in the clear. New pits, new machines, new timbering and rail lines. Chemicals to buy, vats to replace those that wear out, but I tell you we've got a smelter process that, once it gets working, will make copper available to every industry at an unbelievably low price."

Aaron nodded. "That's the way I feel. We'll keep getting the money somehow, and you'll get the smelter going, somehow."

Doctor Simon looked off to where Louis was stretched out asleep, the big book of mine photographs shading his eyes. "Now I think we better all get some sleep. Louis, wake up and try it on a bed."

Condon smiled. "You gentlemen sleep, and I'll drive Joseph home."

"Louis, wake up. The boy is always sleeping."

Doctor Simon shook Louis awake and for many years Louis remembered coming sharply out of a deep, warm sleep, and looking up and seeing the red, warm faces of the men, the oil light behind them, bent over him, grinning. The bigger men behind and his father and Uncle Aaron closer; and it seemed he had come back into a world warm and welcome, to men who saw life as struggle and battle, who were his people and friends of his people. Somehow, he remembered, he wondered why he could not yet be like them, rather than so placid and indifferent to most of what went on. He wasn't morbid, the way his father had been. Life was good and wonderful, and it was fine just to wait and watch it pass. Very pleasant . . . and he remembered the men pulling him to his feet, and him yawning, and the heavy book of mine photographs falling to the worn, dusty, old-rose rug. Oh, the good warm feeling of being part of a big man's world, it was with him until he was in the big hotel bed and saying, "Good night, Papa," to his father and falling asleep on his face at last without a struggle or a snore. Louis was a dainty sleeper. He never made a sound and did not toss or roll about.

Aaron and Doctor Simon left at the end of the week. The day before that, Doctor Simon came out to the smelter site and, walking over the broken, dust-filled ground, he came to the small weathered shack that served as office and planning room. Joseph was going over a batch of red-marked plans that he was scoring with scarlet crayon for Aaron to take back to Philadelphia. Doctor Simon waited until Joseph saw him and pushed aside the plans.

"Well, Simon, thinking of settling here and opening a hospital for the cure of the miner's Monday-morning hangover?"

"No, Joseph, the death rate is just as good in Philadelphia. You're looking tired."

"I am, I goddamn am. But that's just one of the things that always happens to a man who tries to raise a family and get a business running. Sit down."

"Joseph, how are things really with you?"

Joseph laughed and rubbed his bad leg. "I was afraid for a moment you were going to ask me if I am happy. I'd have had to say I don't know. But I'm living, the leg doesn't bother me much, and I'm in a peck of trouble. But I'm all right. And you, Simon?"

"I'm fine. With me it's the simple life. The new clinic. A few old books. Emma drags me to concerts. And I'm having an affair with Mozart. He wrote—for me—the most perfect music in the world and I'm beginning to understand all its little touches and nuances. Maybe you think that's sad, *nebbich*, a pity, that a rebel should settle for Mozart. But I think of the poor wretches who can't have Mozart, or the paintings of Turner, or the novels of Balzac. That's real empty living. Joseph, every man finds his drug in time. He calls it art, or literature, or charity, or beauty, but in the end he finds it, or he's a wandering, sterile soul, like that Condon."

"Just what bothers Condon? You've been watching him, I noticed."

"I don't know. Honestly I don't. What other doctor will give you such an honest answer? I've talked to him and gotten nothing I can explain. I'm just an old bone-setter and belly-rubber. I can't help Condon. Joseph, I really want to talk about Louis."

"Louis? He looks all right. A little uninterested in things, but you can't expect too much at his age. Fiddle music or fast horses might help."

"I've tried everything. We sent him to England for education. Then I wanted to interest him in medicine. He faints at the sight of blood from a boil. He doesn't read, he's indifferent to painting. Sometimes I think he's just a *schlemiel*. Then I wonder if he isn't just mocking us all behind that brooding calm of his. In the end, I think he's just lazy and rather happy about it. This puzzles me. Youth, I always felt, should be unhappy, moody, complex. He isn't. He's just Louis. I was wondering if living out here a few years might do something for him."

"Why not?" said Joseph grinning. "It's a fast, hard life and something always happening. I can't promise him the fake Wild West of the dime novels, but he's welcome to stay as long as he likes and take pot luck with us. Although our luck has been mostly pot with little in it. He can sleep with Egon if he can stand the smell of urine."

Doctor Simon took off his glasses and polished them. "You're very kind, Joseph. Louis wants to stay out here. If he's a bother, beat him over the head. I'm a modern doctor, a regular *maskil*, an intellectual, but I believe in a great deal of civilization coming to young people through the skin of their buttocks."

Joseph laughed and patted the little doctor on the arm. "Look, Louis is welcome to ride the broncs and enjoy the place as long as he wants. Tell me, Simon, how does Rebecca look to you?"

"Fine, fine. This time I hope it's a girl."

Joseph nodded and rubbed his greying beard. "Yes, a girl would be a good change. But I leave that to biology to decide. Boys are fine, but for Rebecca a girl would be company."

Doctor Simon put his glasses on again and pushed them hard against the bridge of his nose until he looked like a kindly, baffled owl. "You've changed, Joseph, a lot. Maybe it's only growing older, but I think there's a desperate quality about you that I never noticed before."

"Did you think that a man can remain the same when he has a family and big project on his hands that he can't ever let go of? Must grip it, hug it to him, till he dies? No, Simon, a war and battles and broken bones and all that romantic desperation is fine, all right, when you're young, and have no ties. Not children, and friends whose money and birthright you're about to spend on something that may never work out."

Joseph picked up the set of plans and threw them at Doctor Simon. "Give these to Aaron. He wanted a set of smelter plans."

Doctor Simon put his arm around Joseph's shoulder. "Between us, Joseph, there's a secret. A kind of secret that just isn't something you can put exactly into ordinary words."

"No?"

"No. The lousy-headed *Chassidim*, themselves, couldn't phrase it right even in Hebrew. It's like something we once shared, a feeling of being trapped, hemmed in, as if the wide, full adventure of just being had passed us by."

Joseph shook his head and looked through the dirty window to where a group of Irish and Chinese labourers were laying a concrete platform for his first Pedlock Vat. "I'll tell you something, Simon. I'm no mystic. This, now, what we are, and are doing, is the full, wide adventure. *These* are the good old days. Believe me, you'll see it that way some day. The rest? All nonsense. Youthful dreams, emotions we pampered and tickled our little prides with."

Simon rubbed the tip of his nose and rolled his head as if amused and perlexed by the thought. "Who knows? Spinoza says that on a high, philosophical level, such terms as *good*, or *bad*, *right* or *wrong*, are only words. I don't argue any more, Joseph."

"Don't look so damn tragic, Simon. I'll see you at supper."

"In Philadelphia we prefer to call it dinner, not supper, if you don't mind."

"I don't. It's still mine-town grub, cooked by a Chink."

Joseph sat a while and watched the little doctor skip across the broken ground and the brick piles. Odd, how much Yiddish and Hebrew Simon used now; the very fashionable, famous Doctor Manderscheid. He was trying to hold on to his unhappy past, ashamed of it now—like an opium habit—but Joseph suspected it was hard work. It had all slipped away—the past—was almost forgotten in a pleasant, routine present. Still Simon cherished it, when he had time for it. Joseph took his cane and beat some dried mud from his boots; he had torn the soles on the sharp rocks and would have to get them repaired again. Joseph wondered, as he crossed to the smelter site, if he were really unhappy. Perhaps when he had time for it, later on, he would think it out. Just now he had to put the fear of the devil into those Irish and Chinese labourers.

"Get their tails moving, Corey," he, shouted. "We're not building the Grand Pyramids of Egypt! I'll have Herdon send you more men from the mine."

Corey pulled at the red, loose curl of hair on his low damp brow and pushed back his new Stetson. "Hist them barrows, you sods! You miserable cattle, hump yerselves!"

"I didn't mean you to curse them out, Corey."

"Oh, it's all one or the other to 'em . . . seein' as they're all me relations. That is, all but the Chinks. Not that I'm denying Adam and Eve."

"When Herdon's men come, put them right to work. There's a lot to do."

Joseph turned to examine the vat platform. Corey was just a little bit too much the professional Irishman, and worked hard to get the proper, expected curses, wit, and Dublin tone into his manner. But he was a good, hard man with the labour gangs. Joseph looked at the vat platform and wondered how long it would really take to get the smelter working. He felt sad and worthless.

After Aaron and Doctor Simon left, the Pedlock household settled down to a roaring simmer again. Rebecca began to prepare for the Passover. No matter where the season found the Pedlocks, she always imported a package of matzos ("Hemstitched cardboard," Joseph growled, when they were put on the table) and the making of the *Seder*, the home holiday service recounting the full liberation from fearful Egyptian bondage. She celebrated ritually the first and second nights of Passover. Joseph, during the first years of their marriage, had shrugged and gone through with it. But now, he admitted, he was beginning to enjoy the rituals since he had children old enough to recite the Ceremonial Questions (in a faltering Hebrew Rebecca had taught them to repeat by ear).

Louis moved up into the attic with the boys and he slept with Egon, until Egon's bed-wetting drove him to a fresh-built private bunk. He was learning to roll tight cigarettes with brown paper and a vile black Mexican tobacco. And Condon was going to show him the night life of the town soon.

One such promised expedition had been delayed by the murder of the mine foreman, Herndon, by an out-of-town gunman on the sidewalk in front of the Dirty Shame Saloon and Café.

Louis had been very much impressed by the dime-novel murder and he had gone with Joseph and Condon, Joseph wearing his pistol belt, to the Sheriff's office to see the body. Louis had been a little sick when he saw the bloody horse blanket over the shape on the battered desk, with its muddy boots hanging stiffly over the edge.

Joseph had looked at the body and said to the Sheriff, curtly, "Well, you know Pontdue is behind this. This cuts my mine production again. I want a warrant for his arrest."

The fat Sheriff sighed and fanned himself with a tattered hat. "Now, Joseph, we don't know no such thing. The two Texans just hung around town loose and loud—and now they're gone. I've wired all along the line to have 'em picked up."

"Monkey nuts," said Condon. "I'm goin' to see Pontdue myself."

Joseph shook his head. "You don't carry a gun and can't use one. Talk isn't going to do much good."

"It will." He brushed past Joseph, heavy, warm, angry, and crossed to the Hotel de Mineral and had four fingers of Bourbon several times.

It was late that afternoon that Condon ran into Pontdue in front of the Miners and Drivers Bank. They faced each other on the loose, wooden planks of the sidewalk.

Pontdue was fluffing back his guardsman moustaches. Condon faced him very calm, and very polite, too polite. "Pontdue, I want to make a little speech. One little ole speech."

"Why not, Condon?" The wooden sidewalk creaked as they stood there, two heavy men in heavy clothing, both waiting.

"I know you had Herndon murdered this morning. Now I want to swear this, and mean it; if one more of our men is hurt or killed, I'm coming right to you and I'm going to kill you like a shoat in pig-sticking time."

Pontdue looked coldly at Condon, and his blue eyes and wide red nose did not seem real or alive. When he spoke he sounded emotionless, uninterested.

"This is Montana, in the Eighties, Condon. People don't talk like that any more."

Condon smiled simply, that charming barroom, brothel smile of his. "I'll kill you like a goddamn, fat, German pig, Pontdue. A pig that wriggles its hips like a dancing girl."

Pontdue walked suddenly off, his shoulders square and more military than ever. Several people had come out of the bank and they had heard Condon's last remark. They looked closely at Condon, as if he were already dead. But Condon merely nodded at them, and walked off whistling "Buffalo Gals." It would be a good night to show Louis the town and take him down the line. He knew Pontdue wouldn't dare kill him now; the Eastern board of directors wouldn't like it.

CHAPTER V

Rebecca and General Lee—rags tied around their heads, dusty and wet with soap suds—were washing down the house, carrying bread crumbs as if they were disease germs to the fire to be burned. Louis and the boys had been sent into the yard. The whole house was in cheerful, damp confusion. Rebecca had bought new tin pots and new china dishes for the Passover, and secretly she felt she should not have done it. Times were hard enough, without buying new pots and dishes for just a week's holiday. But her mother and all the family had always celebrated Passover in this way, and so she would do it now. "Thousands of dollars for a smelter, and worry over a few dollars' kitchen ware?" she told Joseph when he protested.

"Big holiday, madam?" asked General Lee, sneezing as he wrung out a soapy rug.

"Yes, and don't ever call me madam." Rebecca had picked up the frontier definition of "madam" and she frankly didn't like it. "To-morrow night is a big Jewish holiday."

"Like a Chinese New Year?"

"Yes, I suppose so, Lee, but no firecrackers. Now be sure no bread crumbs are left in any corners." She stood up to catch her breath and the child, big inside her, kicked at her ribs. She absorbed the pain with pride, took pleasure in the sweet agony.

"No worry over bread crumbs. Mice eat them all."

"Set traps for the mice. Remember, Lee, one bread crumb left around and Passover is ruined."

"Bread crumbs, even in mice, unholy for holiday?"

Rebecca gave up trying to explain anything sacred and ritual to Lee. "Go chop a lot of firewood, Lee. And don't leave the axe where the boys can get at it."

She began softly, tenderly, to sing a woman's kitchen song as she placed the new dishes on fresh-papered shelves.

> *"Of'n pripechuk brent a feirel,*
> *In der shtieb iz heiss. . . ."*
>
> (*In the oven burns a little flame,*
> *And in the room it's hot. . . .*)

Louis came in early, to dress up for his night out with Condon.

86

"Louis has been to Cambridge in England to be educated," Simon had told Joseph, "but except for bringing back a rolled umbrella and a new-fangled derby hat that sits too high on his head, the family wonders what good it has done him. He was sent to England with many letters of introduction and advice about the evils of loose women told to him in a low tone by me—Doctor Simon."

At Cambridge Louis took lodgings with a Mrs. Gliton at 19 Kings Parade, near Great Saint Mary's Church. Every morning Louis came out into the chill English sun and looked over the Kings College Chapel almost opposite, and the old University Library. He was very homesick. He wandered a lot along Lensfield and Huntington Roads. The village of Chesterton was out of bounds, but he played billiards at the inn there and had an innocent exchange of sidelooks with the head-scratching barmaid.

Louis yawned over the college's three-part curriculum: its Natural Philosophy, Theology and Moral Philosophy, and Belles-Lettres. Several copies of his books, his Paley's *Natural Theology*, Duncan's *Logic* and Newton's *Principia*, still exist, with ink drawings of tall, big-bottomed English girls carrying milkpails.

"He liked best the billiard tables, the races at New Market, the balls and hunts at Bury, Colchester, and Huntington," Doctor Simon said. "He fought, as expected, the canal bargees and got a lumpy ear, but he did not join the bloods for those sinister sexual adventures at Barnwell and Castle End."

"Did he study at all?" Joseph had asked.

"He did very well—within certain limits—with the social end of life at Cambridge. We're related, you know, to the English Mandersons, who have married one branch of their family into the pallid, spent branch of the Purcells, Ah, the Mandersons, who had been in England long before Alfred the cake-burner, who came with Caesar yet are proud to be—pardon the expression, I always say—connected with the Purcells, who were Anglo-Normans. Louis was always amused, he said, when he went to London, to visit his uncle, Henry Manderson, to hear the lean old Jewish head talk of his "forefathers" who entered England with the army of William the Conqueror, and crossed to Ireland with Henry II in 1172. Uncle Henry said he was, through his Purcell grandmother, a lineal descendant of the Barons of Loughmoe. The family was direct, Uncle Henry would say, to Louis from Monton, fourth Earl of Kildaire, the Earldom created by Edward II, in 1316. A picture of the first Lord Justice of Ireland in the family hangs in the dining room. The family once held much land in Suffolk, Lancashire, and Staffordshire, but that was long since gone.

Now the house of Manderson, in good old yellow lamplight, just faintly tinged, even Louis felt, with a staged, Charles Dickens glow, carried on the blending of the great blood lines of rabbis and earls and scholars; the Talmudists and Cabalists and robber captains, three-bottle squires, and wenching parsons. Uncle Henry used to complain to Louis, with almost a glow of pleasure, of the touch of gout in the big toe he had inherited from certain Regency bucks!"

The Philadelphia family felt Louis's education at Cambridge was a failure. He never studied, travelled, or read his books. He dreamed of huge, beautiful women, but was shy and collected pictures of the actor Macready instead. The only actual document that remains of his Cambridge days (his *Sturm und Drang*), beyond the drawings of milkmaids, is a jotting in his notebook of a trip to Bath. "Ordered for dinner a whiting, a beefsteak, and a glass of negus. Dinner 7s., glass of negus 2s., waiter 6d. Half a crown to coachman of London stage."

"After two years of this Louis was recalled to Philadelphia," said Doctor Simon, "and then it was decided that perhaps in Montana something could be done with the casual, cheerful boy. He had once, I remember, begun a collection of clippings of wood engravings of Dan'l Boone and Kit Carson from the pages of *Harper's Weekly*. Perhaps it was a sign, the family said. Joseph Pedlock would make a man of Louis, we all said."

"I'll try," Joseph had answered.

Louis was willing. Louis came alive in the West, Joseph noticed. Condon had promised his dreams of big women could come true. Condon felt it only proper that he show the town to Louis. It was the duty, he explained to Joseph, "of every citizen of Butte to take a gentleman down the line to see the girls and enjoy the pleasures of what is the toughest town this side of Amarillo, Texas. Louis says he sees nothing wrong with the idea."

"Don't tell Rebecca," said Joseph, grinning.

"Greatest little town in the world," Condon told Louis as they stood at the bar of the Hotel de Mineral, Louis's imported derby hung balanced on his long head. The chipped front tooth was showing as he smiled shyly at the happy, talking Condon.

"Fine town," said Louis, nodding.

"This town is a mile high, and a mile deep . . . yep, that much above sea level and that much dug out below ground. Fun all over the place. Gotta make the round of the saloons, boy. The Graveyard, Frozen Inn, and The Cesspool. Nothing like it, even in ole New York. Gotta take you down the line."

"Can I buy the next round, Ira?"

"Not tonight, Louis. Real fancy night, pink drawers, black lace, Louis. Nothing cheap for us like the grimy tars on Mercury Street. No, sirree, we'll go to Irene's. Classiest stuff this side of Denver, or the Everleigh Club in Chicago. Solid gold thunder mugs. Gals all colours, all sizes. Blown, reamed, and bottled. You'll say this is a great town. Going to get greater if we can keep the damned, giant, agglutinated corporations out. The damn Rockefellers and their stinkin' kerosene interests. The Clarks and the Dalys I can take, but the goddamn Copper Combine crowd . . . What do you like, Louis? Faro, roulette, dance halls?"

"Dance halls."

"Good. We'll get a box at the Comique, then go get our ashes hauled. Great little town, Louis. Full of pistols, bowie knives, broncs, niggers, Chinese and Indians. Never had an Indian girl myself. Ready to travel, Louis?"

Louis reset his derby squarely and said, "Ready." It was, he had to admit, quite a town. The screened, discreet box at the Comique led to an unbelievably evil circus at the Casino ("Oh, them daisy chains," said Condon); and he learned about faro from Silver John, who ate a long cigar and laid out the cards without looking at them. Condon was well liked, cheerfully greeted every place, and they had more drinks; and Louis, who had gotten a reputation as a beer drinker in Philadelphia and an ale punisher at Cambridge, was having a little trouble with his drinks, as if they had buttered his elbows and softened his bones.

At the White Elephant there was a dark girl who sat on Condon's lap and laughed very loud and could move muscles any place on her body. When they were in the street again, Condon said, "It's a great life, isn't it, Louis?"

"It's been very amusing so far, Ira."

Condon turned slowly—his eyes wide open—and looked at Louis, and took off Louis's derby and brushed its nap with his sleeve and put it back on Louis's head with a bang, and pulled his tie around under its stiff collar. He looked closely at Louis and said, "It's been 'amusing' so far! Well, how do you like that! I can see, son, ole Uncle Ira has got to bring on the grand and glorious climax, the splendid and remarkable establishment that is known as Irene's, and right now!"

"Unless you'd rather get some sleep."

"Sleep, me? I never sleep. Big black things creep around in my dreams. I just stay awake all the time. Irene is the greatest little sleep cure on the whole goddamn Great Divide."

It was a wide, tall, wooden house built in some strange, twisted style, but overdone and now sooted and soiled. The iron railing was stylish and strong. The heavy, red shades were down and one could just hear the sound of a piano, the rumble of its struck strings in a deep, mahogany belly.

Condon, now walking well back on his heels, led Louis (who was suddenly worried about his virginity) up the worn marble steps and stood him against the fumed oak doors. He smiled at Louis and listened, one ear on the door.

"We're real early, but the fun has started. Chicken, here we go."

Condon stabbed at the bell with a wavering thumb. A tall, handsome coloured woman in a short silk dress, with lovely legs in sheer silk, opened the door and smiled at them a mouth pure ivory.

"Evening, gentlemen."

"Hello, Bella. How's tricks tonight?" asked Condon, handing her his hat and Louis's derby and then shelling his body out of his coat.

"Miss Irene will be glad to see you all."

The two men walked softly, as if in some sacred service, into the great parlour. It was walled in red silk, there were many pictures of heavy, nude women, rubber plants, deep yellow-silk sofas and too many lamps with cut glass and feather shades A great Steinway piano of black walnut stood in one corner At the piano sat a thin, bald, young man with two huge front teeth, giving him the look of an evil, toy rabbit.

He waved to them and yelled, "Hey, Irene, company!"

His fingers moved skilfully over the ivory keys in some Chopin. The bead drapes parted and Irene walked in with a slow, boneless strut. She was wearing a tight, belted dressing gown and smoking a long cork tip. She closed the door carefully behind her, where drunken voices could be heard in mixed chatter, and the scream of a girl being tickled reached a breath-shattering intense pitch that hurt Louis's chest just to hear it.

"Hello. Nice to see you, Ira."

"Hello, Irene, how about a drink? This is Louis. Treat him well, and treat him often."

Irene smiled and sat down beside them. She kissed Condon on the brow and pulled a bell cord, one gesture flowing into the other.

"Certainly, honey. Had a hard day?"

"Hell, yes. Who's in?"

"All the girls," said Irene as Bella entered bearing a tray of wine bottles and glasses. "Get the ladies, Bella. We have a new guest."

The coloured woman smiled and went to the head of the stairs. "Company, girls!"

There was a flutter and a stirring above the stairs, a rustle of silk on Louis's ears, and then the hiss of slippers. Three big women came down slowly, smiling gaily and yawning. They wore open dressing gowns and nothing much else. They greeted Condon and said Louis was cute, and the professor at the piano broke into a cakewalk.

The tall blonde with the wet, slipping mouth, on Condon's lap, mussed his hair and whispered something in his ear. Condon roared and slapped her nude thigh. The blonde yelped and kicked her long legs into the air. She was the only girl wearing long, black stockings and pink garters. Condon leaned over and snapped a garter. The girl yelped again. Louis smiled and gulped the wine.

That started the party. A girl pouted and asked Louis if he wanted her to wear garters. He didn't. The place, the girl, excited him. He was no longer casual or placid.

A door opened behind the bead drapes, and Old Mister Mont came out. His shirt off and he carried a bottle under a white, naked arm. Three more men came out of the room. Condon waved to them. "Big Copper Combine muck-a-mucks," he told Louis. The piano never let up. The professor played on, his eyes closed, his two rabbit teeth shaking.

Now and then Irene would walk over to him and give the piano player a drink of raw whisky. The piano player would put down his glass and play sentimental music.

The girl said to Louis, "Would you like to go up, honey?"

"I don't mind."

"That's my boy! He don't mind," she said to Condon.

Condon stopped, with a bottle half tilted to pour, and nodded at Louis. "*He* don't mind. Take 'im up, Cherry, and if he yells for Mama you mother 'im. Wean 'im and treat 'im till he howls for mercy."

"You bet, dearie."

The stairs were very steep, Louis thought, and the upper halls not very well lit. The small room, the walls with the sickly, yellow plants struggling to escape from a red rug patterned full of flower petals and thorns. The girl lay back on the bed and lifted her naked legs high in the air and wriggled them at him from an animated, pubic base, and then she laughed. He had trouble with his belt but the rest just peeled off. When he was beside her, she leaned over all pink, all polished and smooth (as sin should be, Louis thought), and she turned the lamp way down. It was very pleasant. Then very difficult. The rest? Well, as he later told Condon, "it was just like mailing a letter".

Once the process began the thing was done, the postage spent, and afterwards in the small yellow room, and the girl stroking his hair, he buried his nose in her ear and snorted with glee.

"You tickle, Louis."

"I like you. I like everything tonight."

"You're just sweet as all hell, baby. Don't they ever call you Louie for short?"

"No, just Louis. But if you want to, Louie is all right."

"I like Louis better, and I like perfume. French perfume. I like everything sort of French, six dollars a bottle—don't you?"

"Well," said Louis, very amorous, "I'll buy you some perfume, French perfume tomorrow."

"Shall I put out the light?"

"Turn it way up. You're very wonderful, Cherry."

"You're a real treat, Chicken. Oh, so tender and all white meat."

The little room was cut off from the whole world. Someplace downstairs glass broke and a shrill laughter came up to them. But they were alone and travelling together in some sweet, desperate journey. The shadows on the yellow wallpaper stopped their patterned dance and it was so still that Louis had to breathe very hard to keep from the idea that he was spent and dead and that none of this could ever happen again. . . .

When they came downstairs Condon didn't say a mocking word. Condon was a card. He knew a dozen ways to make a girl scream. The music went madder. There was, to Louis's vision, a steady rising haze of flesh and tainted body powder and rugs and spilled wine and stale breathing. Silk tore, men grew red in the face, clawed and poured, went boldly in laughter up the stairs, pulling willing figures off the banisters, kept the coloured girl Bella grinning but beyond clutching range.

It was a night of battles and little wars to remember. Guests came and went. "Company, girls," became a war cry. Two rubber plants were uprooted. Irene herself stood above the fray, her black-rimmed eyes smiling, warding off the attention of all but a few special guests. Hard-looking men with pistols went into the back room. Old Mister Mont went to sleep, with a smile, in the middle of the rug, his naked, aged rump sadly exposed to cigar ash.

The smoke of tobacco thickened. The wine grew viler, the music sadder and higher-pitched.

A man fell asleep, open-mouthed, against a wide, red-haired girl, and they undressed him, painted him with mustard and wine lees, and dressed him in obscene hot-water bottles and crepe paper. The big muck-a-mucks told Combine secrets, and the call, "Company, girls," went on.

Beyond the closed red drapes the dawn was almost ready to break— but the foul musk and air of the red living room was dank with sodden armpits and wine-breaths and all the old, frenzied odours that the house walls held.

Limbs, torsos, moved in tired patterns, rhythms before Louis's glazing eyes. Then everyone settled down to slower, less-active graces. Faces were lined, teeth coated, eyes bloodshot. A dry, baffling sterility seemed to come over everyone. They tried to fight it with odder schemes and projects, with louder talk, with deeper, stronger drinking. Just before morning everyone left but Condon, Louis, and someone in the back room. The beast-pit odour grew and grew on Louis until he felt his yellowing eyeballs pop. The piano music never stopped and seemed to pump bile into his stomach.

Condon looked up. Over him stood Irene saying something, something he couldn't understand at first.

"Come on, clear your head, Ira. A gentleman in the next room," she winked at him, "wants to talk to you." She leaned over and whispered into his ear. Condon blinded his eyes, than an amused look came over his face.

"You sure, Irene?"

"Hell, yes. Go ask him. The guy in the long underwear."

Condon got to his feet, brushing himself free slowly from a nude sleeping arm. He looked at Louis, also asleep on the sofa, and went, with an unsteady step, into the back room.

Corey, the labour-gang foreman, drove up in the chill dawn and stopped in the dirt-packed yard as Joseph, the frost white on his boots, came out of the steaming barn. He had been feeding oats to the broncs.

"Mr. Pedlock," Corey said, not getting off the buckboard, his horses nervous in the cold morning. "Just a minute."

Joseph put down the oat bucket. "What's the matter, Corey?"

"Mr. Condon. He's dead. Killed an hour ago . . . mercy on his soul . . . at Irene's place."

Joseph stared, stood still, then slowly rubbed the palms of his hands together. A few grains of oats fell from his hard, square fingers. "What happened?"

"Big brawl. Someone—may he burn eternal—called him into the back room and let 'im have it. Three times right between the eyes. With a navy Colt. One of Pontdue's out-of-town guns, they say."

"Who says?"

"Irene. She's screamin' and scratchin' and kickin' all over the place. Condon was a favourite customer." Corey looked straight ahead and went on talking in an even, earnest voice. "Your nephew Louis was there, all through it."

"He hurt?"

"Passed out. I left him sleeping it off—sweet as an angel—at the hotel. Irene sent for me soon as she could stop screamin'. Sure now it's the devil's business has been done tonight." Corey couldn't resist the proper Irish touch.

"Where's the bo—Condon now?"

"At Irene's. Didn't want to do anythin' until I spoke to you."

Joseph went back to the barn and came out with a battered double-barreled shotgun. It had once been a beautiful, handmade weapon, with silvered hammers and an embossed, black walnut stock. It had seen much rough usage since its manufacture for a sporting squire in England. Joseph slipped two heavy oiled cartridges into the barrels and clicked the gun shut. He climbed with a heavy grace up besids Corey, who kicked at a buffalo rug at his feet to reveal a Sharpe buffalo gun. "Not takin' any buggerin' chances, Mr. Pedlock. Pontdue is out to get us all."

"Keep this quiet, Corey. Tonight is Passover, don't want to upset the wife. Let's get back to town."

"You favour a shotgun?"

"I like damage when I shoot."

"Sure now, I'm a rifle man myself. Never could see much use in six shooters unless it's a barroom fight and no room to swing an elbow. A rifle is sure."

Joseph nodded, not really listening, and they drove fast down the road. Joseph was still numb with shock but the power and anger were rising in him now. It was going to be fast and wild—beyond restraint and peace—for a few days, but he knew now that he had reached a peak of purpose and cause from which he had to leap. Leap out once again wildly and tangle with death. There was no use cleaning out the town, making gang war or a sheep-and-cattlemen's battle of this. Pontdue was the key. He and Pontdue would add and subtract all this in their own way. If he could avoid being chopped down before he reached Pontdue. It had been a long time since he had killed a man with relish and skill. The sureness, the touch was stale and lost. He had never liked it the way some men liked it—killers who glowed and sweated with deep, secret pleasure as they shot down a man and stood over him and spit on him. Even in war Joseph hadn't liked it the way some did. He had never cared for the ideas of Nietzsche (the Philadelphia intellectuals among the Manderscheids, he remembered, who had never been to battle or tripped on the entrails of a mangled corpse, were taking Nietzsche up and making a cult of cozy danger in their stuffy living rooms). It was nonsense. He remembered Doctor Simon reciting lines from Nietzsche. "Man is a rope stretched between the animal and the Superman—a rope over an abyss." What of it? "All prejudices can be traced back to the intestines." Joseph felt nothing. Perhaps the tragedy of true tragedy is that there is no feeling of tragedy. Not even what he had felt that morning with J. E. B. Stuart, did he feel now. The Union guns so long ago in the brush and death nearer than he had ever seen it. Nietzsche again. "Life always gets harder towards the summit—the cold increases, responsibility increases." Joseph spit hard.

Corey, the reins wrapped around his big fist, looked at Joseph. He was a good, solid man to lead; Corey himself did not command or want to. "The hotel?"

"No, Irene's."

The places in night-town looked scabby and obscurely diseased in the daytime. The steps of Irene's place were dirty, the doors scarred

95

and cross-hatched by drunken fists. In the disordered parlour Irene sat at a small table eating ham and eggs out of a cracked, Wedgwood-blue dish. She had not slept and her eyes were rimmed in dark, unhealthy flesh. Upstairs it was very still. As Joseph came in she put down the fork and crossed her large legs.

"What's under your coat, mister?" she asked.

"Shotgun." Joseph took it out from under the coat and put it under his arm. So, he felt, King Solomon must have held the child while the mothers bickered. "Where's Ira?"

"Back there. The back room."

Joseph looked closely at her, his voice cut crystal clear. "You didn't know about it?"

She listlessly pushed the plate from her and did not clean her puffy egg-stained mouth. "I'm just a noble whore, with a heart of gold, like in the storybooks. I cry at sad songs, and I save my money. No, mister, I didn't know they were plannin' to kill Condon. I guess I like him better than anybody I've known in a long time. He wasn't just trade, mister. Not that I would have lifted a finger to help him if it meant trouble for me, but I wouldn't get him killed, not even if they paid for it, and I'm a girl who thinks of her old age."

"What happened to the man that did it?"

"He went out of the back window. Some hoodlum I don't know with a big mouth and lots of cash."

Joseph looked at her and she looked back at him, expressionless: it was a hard tired face, the eyes looking at him, not wavering and yet not entirely untouched by some personal sorrow she wasn't sharing with anybody. He felt she was feeling this thing as deeply as she could feel anything and it was shocking to think how deeply she must really feel it. After all, she was human. He had heard of sentimental whores but never met them. He turned toward the back room.

Condon's body was on the floor, on a rubber blanket, his head covered with a whorehouse towel. Three ·45 slugs at close range between the eyes do great damage and Joseph did not remove the towel. One big fly, a shiny, blue-bellied fly, was buzzing around the airless, warm room smelling of rancid flesh and stale body powder. It was early in the season for insects but the fly had already come out, scenting carrion, Joseph thought, already willing to do its duty—planned by nature—toward the dead in the scheme of things.

Joseph turned and walked out of the room; the lonely fly bumbled and battered its fat blue body against the white glass shade of the hanging oil lamp.

The plate of food had been removed from before the madam. Irene still sat. Louis, a shaking Louis, his nerveless fingers edging slowly around the brim of his derby, stood there now—looking at nothing. Then he glanced up at his uncle. Joseph noticed the boy's tight chin, the taut jaw muscles, the earnest, direct look. The boy was going to be all right. He was a little green, of course, and Joseph could imagine the horror and the hangover and repulsions going through the paper-white brow. Well, it was time Louis learned to suffer like the rest of us his uncle thought.

Louis did not speak. Joseph turned to Corey. "Have you located Pontdue?"

"He's been out of town for two days. Has a labour gang working on that spur line to their smelter at Watertown. Most likely he planned to be away when this happened. Smart hombre."

"Too smart," said Joseph. "I'll wait for 'im."

"The depot says his work train is due in at nine tonight."

Joseph turned to Irene. "Do me a favour."

"I might be able to. Sure, mister."

"You've kept this pretty quiet till now. Keep it all that way till tonight."

"I'll close the house, don't worry."

"Keep Condon here. I'll have him picked up late tonight."

She rose and walked, very steady and tall, toward the stairs. "I don't think he'll go away." She turned. "Mister, when you let Pontdue have it . . . give him just a little warnin'. They say that second or so before they're hit with slugs makes 'em really suffer, just before the blast. I'm a sentimental slob, so do this for little ole Irene."

Joseph shifted the shotgun to his other arm and then put it under his coat. "I hope he gives me a second or so. Come on, Louis. I'm borrowing your rig, Corey."

"Sure, Mr. Pedlock."

The sun was leaping high now across the slag and smelter soot and Louis was feeling very wretched. Joseph flicked the whip on a horse's rump and looked out over the slag heaps, the dying, cinder-filled poisoned grass. "Take a can of tomato pulp, Louis, put some tabasco sauce and a raw egg in it, and drink it. You'll feel better."

"I feel terrible."

"Louis, I want to say something serious to you. Tonight is the first night of Passover. Rebecca isn't too well. Her condition and all this getting ready for the holiday . . . you can understand. So not a word about Condon. I'll just explain you stayed over in town. At the

Seder ritual tonight, we'll act like always. I'll have to slip away later, but you make plenty of noise and chatter."

"You're going back to meet Pontdue's work train?"

"I'm going to try. Now listen hard to me, Louis. You're a man, a full-grown man, and I've no time to be fancy about this. If I'm hurt tonight, or even killed, you're in charge here. Telegraph Aaron at once to come right out. Get the doctor to take care of Rebecca."

"Killed?" Louis held his chest with both hands. His guts seemed suddenly to boil away into paste.

"That's right. I may be killed tonight. There isn't anything I can do about it. I can sit and wait at home or go out to meet 'em. They're out to get rid of me."

"Killed?"

Louis leaned over the side of the wagon and vomited for a long time into the moving roadbed. He turned at last, pale green, slobbery, and bleary-eyed, and said to his uncle, "I'm feeling a lot better, now."

"Sure you are. You're still too young to hate yourself in the morning."

Joseph smiled and whipped up the lagging horse. He was rather pleased Louis hadn't suggested that he leave town. Joseph was feeling suddenly cheerful, well *almost* cheerful. At least he again had that tight, eager feeling under a dark ceiling that he always had felt before a battle. In a way it all added up as usual, he felt. Whatever debt to death he failed to pay at First Manassas, at Chancellorsville, or Cold Harbour, maybe he was going to pay it now. Someone had once said, some poet of course, you pay that kind of debt sooner or later . . . but in the end you pay it, a few years more or less, one way or the other, doesn't matter.

They trotted smartly—the horses foaming—into the barnyard, and from the kitchen's leaning, tin chimney of pure rust came curling, black smoke, and even in the yard he could smell the frying *griebbenes*, those small, crisp pieces left from rendered poultry fat. Joseph had always eaten them as a delicacy, ever since boyhood, he remembered, as he carefully placed the loaded shotgun behind a pine rafter dripping rosin and covered with horsegear hung on wooden pegs driven into the timber.

Joseph's father (who had the crisp wit of Elisha ben Abuyai, the atheist of the Talmud, Joseph always said), when the rabbis of Vienna disapproved of his reading of alien books and called him an *Epikouros*, used to smile and quote a saying he once found in an old book: "If triangles were to make God, they would give him three sides." And so Joseph now felt about the Jews of Butte. For here, in the stink of the gases of the smelters, under the great marching hulks of slag heaps where the grass died and the trees gave up the struggle and the birds fled; here, the Jews, being Jews, made on Passover the Seder of the first night.

The over-polished brass candlesticks had been lit at the Pedlocks' and the white cloth crisply ironed, and now they sat around the table. A pillow was under Joseph's elbow so he could recline on it in the manner of the Egyptians, or was it the High Priest—Joseph had forgotten. The table was covered with many things hard to get in Butte. The battered silver trays (wedding gifts) filled with the pale, square matzos, memory of the unleavened bread and water they ate in the Sinai wilderness on their flight from the slave camps of the Pharaohs. There lay on the table the shank bone of lamb, charred on the open fire to remind them of the slaughtered lamb whose blood, smeared on the lintels of the houses of Jews, spared them from the punishment the Lord wreaked on the firstborn of the Egyptians. And the roast egg, the Temple offering, and the bitter herbs to remember the bitter years. All as called for by the Seder evening.

Joseph sat facing Louis, Louis with a little more colour in his drawn cheeks and sitting there trying not to look into Joseph's face. Rebecca came in from the kitchen, after they had tasted and said words over the ceremonial shank, and egg, and bitter herbs. Rebecca, with a tray of *gefüllte* fish. Fish glittering in its own, cold aspic. With it the red horseradish chopped in beet juice, and exploding in one's nose.

The matzo-ball soup was finished, that soup about which Joseph joked to his sons. "My mother made the matzo balls so hard that my father limped for weeks when he dropped one on his toes."

"Did they cut his leg off?" asked Egon eagerly, seated on two volumes of the engravings of Doré Bible pictures.

Joseph shook his head. "For a while we didn't know. But in the end he kept his foot. He danced at weddings till he was seventy."

Rebecca sat down and turned to Louis. "Did you read all the Questions?"

Joseph said, "What?"

Rebecca said, "Go ahead, Louis, finish reading."

Louis nodded and he opened a little red book and read out in a Philadelphia Hebrew the Questions of his race on this the night of Passover. "Why do we celebrate on this the night above all other nights?" . . . and so on down a long list of questions ending with the reason for the crossing of the Red Sea into the Promised Land. The last few questions and answers were recited by Sam and Ralph, and then all recited as best they could the Aramaic which had displaced

Hebrew and fell to eating and laughing and talking, for this was a holiday celebration.

"A little more chicken, Louis?"

"Just a little more, Uncle Joseph. I'm really full."

"I want bread," said Egon, pouting and banging his spoon.

"Bread!" Sam turned on him in shock. "On Passover night he wants bread!"

Ralph shrugged his shoulders. "It's all so silly and crazy. The Deegans don't do this sort of thing. Why should we?"

Joseph said calmly, "We don't dance jigs, Ralph, and eat roast pork at wakes, or hit each other over the head at Irish weddings with black canes, or kiss the fingers of priests. Every American has his own habits. This is ours."

Ralph filled his mouth with too much red horseradish sauce and began to suck in air. "I don't want to be different from the rest of the boys."

Joseph smiled. "You're not. You've got two legs and two hands. But no head, Ralph. I can see that, no head at all."

Louis reached for the wine glass. Joseph held up the thin blue bottle of Mount Carmel wine. "Sweet wine for a *Buba Yente*. Whoever saw such a sweet wine, this rabbi's piddle?"

"It's bottled in Palestine by old, holy Jews. It has the seal of David," said Rebecca primly. "It's the only wine permitted on Passover. Later you can have brandy."

"The things you do for God's endowed," said Joseph as he filled the wine glasses with the pale, red, womanish wine.

"Joseph!" said Rebecca, not really shocked, but just to impress the boys.

"Let us proceed with the ritual," reminded Joseph piously, winking at Rebecca.

"Ah, yes," said Louis, "Elijah's goblet."

Joseph took a battered, silver beaker—used usually to keep loose shirt buttons—and filled it to the top with the wine. "You see, boys, there is a legend that the prophet Elijah would return to the Jews on Passover night . . . and so every Jew fills a goblet and leaves it at an empty place at the table, so in case he should come to our door he could always find himself a good, stiff drink of this tiger's milk."

Rebecca protested, "Don't be ironic, Joseph, just historical."

"Egon, you go open the door," said Joseph.

Egon ran and opened the door. Outside the night shone and a chill ran around the room. Joseph went with the goblet to an empty place and set it down on the table. "And this is the first night of Seder."

He put a few drops of the tepid wine into the water glasses of his sons, and the faint pink water shone in the glowing yellow light of the candles. "Let us drink," said Joseph, calmly, looking at Louis, "to our freedom, our birthright."

They all drank, and Egon swallowed the wrong way and had to be pounded on the back until he wept and howled for mercy. Louis drank his wine quickly and the boys pounded walnuts with a horseshoe and ate the nutmeats and loaded their pockets for gambling the next day among themselves.

Joseph had not looked at his watch all evening, but now as the far-off whistle of a smelter came to their ears, he got up and took up Egon in his arms. Egon was already sleeping, his head in his arms, on the table. "I'll put him to bed, Rebecca."

"Elijah," said the sleeping child, "the door is open. . . ."

Egon awoke as they mounted the attic stairs and rubbed his half-closed eyes, from which forgotten tears still hung. "The Elijah," he said, "did he drink it, Papa?"

"Not yet, Egon." Joseph kissed the child's soft ear. "Elijah again hasn't come to us this year."

"I don't want to go to bed . . . he'll come when I'm asleep."

"If he does, I'll wake you, Egon. I promise."

"That's good," said Egon, falling asleep again in his father's arms. Joseph, in the attic, took off his clothes, got him to make water in the tin pot, and tucked him in. He sat there a little while—a little moment of full peace—looking at his sleeping son. He put the blanket close under the warm little neck and went down, his heavy shoes making a solid, satisfying sound on the stairs.

Sam and Ralph and Louis were singing softly and cheerfully a little song that Rebecca was teaching them, a song called "Raisins and Almonds."

> *"Unter Yidele's vigele*
> *Shteht a klor, a vais tsigele.*
> *Dos tsigele is geforen handlen,*
> *Dos vet zain dain beruf*
> *Rozhenkes mit mandlen. . . ."*

> *(Behind the cradle of the little Jew*
> *Stands a pure white kid.*
> *The kid went off to market,*
> *This will be your calling,*
> *Raisins and almonds. . . .)*

A silly little haunting song, Joseph remembered it from the hundred times he had heard it. His mother had sung his sister to sleep with it and then him, adding the line, "*Shlof Yidele, shlof. . . .*" (Sleep, little Jew, sleep. . . .)

Sam, his mouth full of nutmeats, said, "Sing it again, Ma, sing it again from the beginning."

Rebecca had a fine, small voice, full of feeling.

*"In a far corner of the Temple
The widow, the daughter of Zion, sits alone. . . ."*

Rebecca looked up suddenly—in mid-song—as Joseph pulled on
his long coat. "Joseph, you're not going out?"

"Yes, it can't be helped. Something that can't wait, in town."

"On Passover?"

"On Passover. I must." He leaned over and kissed her hard on
the mouth. "And sing something more cheerful. That's for graveyards."

"We like it," said Sam firmly.

Louis did not look up at Joseph. He said, "Let's sing the tailor
song."

Rebecca said, "Hurry back, Joseph."

"I'll try."

"The tailor song comes later."

Joseph nodded and looked at Louis with a hard scowl of warning
and went out quickly, closing the door tight behind him. As he har-
nessed the broncs, he heard the group in the house singing again. He
took the shotgun down and wrapped it in the grey horse blanket on
the floor of the buckboard. He took four extra cartridges with him.
As he drove briskly out onto the road he herd their voices, and saw
the orange square of window and the group around the table singing,
for one flashing moment.

"The widow, the daughter of Zion, sits alone," they sang.

He slapped hard at the rumps of the broncs in hard anger, jerking
the reins, and he put one firm foot on the wrapped shotgun to keep
it from rattling.

He avoided the busy streets, the moving groups of night-town, and
drove up to the back of the depot, across the gritty cinders. He tied
the broncs to a chipped rail and put the shotgun under his coat after
breaking it open and making sure the cartridges were in place. He
crossed slowly the cinders of the depot square, his bad leg dragging
less than usual. Avoiding the bright windows of the depot itself, he
went up past the sagging water tank and stood in the shadow of a
rotting pile of railroad ties. He stood tall and very still and at first
it was all a great cold silence. Then the telegraph key began to chatter
in the depot. That stopped after a while and far down the rails something sang. A vibration came along the steel ribbons and a telegraph
pole made an almost unnoticed booming sound, like a cricket on a
bass drum. The rails clicked as the work train clanged over a cross-

switch, miles down the roadbed. *Coming home, coming home*, said the rails.

Joseph opened his coat and put the shotgun across his hands. His finger just touched the worn triggers.

Standing in the shadow of the pile of railroad ties and the work train chugging in with the *jong jong* of its iron wheels on the steel rails, Joseph waited.

It was a short, heavy work train, with what they called a yard-pig for an engine, hooked on backwards for better traction, three dirty cars of work coaches, two of heavy timber and a repainted fancy coach that had once seen service in some crack Eastern line and had now been made into a travelling private car by the Copper Combine. Dignified by the fancy painted name of "Copper Queen", in sweeping, golden scrolls.

The green and red train lights had been lit. The workers were already clinging to the iron rails above the steps, ready to jump off as soon as the train slowed enough for a leap to the ground.

The train brakes hissed, the men poured off. A fat little man smoking a stub of cigar passed, carrying on his shoulders some surveying chains. Joseph stopped him by putting an arm on his shoulder and closing his fist.

"Just a minute, Reggen."

Reggen stopped and looked up at Joseph. His teeth juggled the cigar stub. There was just a little corner of worry to his wet wide mouth under the large ill-shaped moustache. "Why hello, Mr. Pedlock."

"Get back on the train. Tell Pontdue I'm waiting for him." Joseph lifted one end of the shotgun an inch or two in the air. Reggen gulped, nodded, threw away his cigar, swallowed, and went darting down the line till he caught the iron railing of the "Copper Queen" as it passed, just slowing down to a stop for the station. The train crews, and the workers were suddenly interested, and no one walked away now, but backed up against the depot and the water rank and waited, no one saying a word.

The train slowed even more, groaned, and stopped. The "Copper Queen" was about twenty feet from Joseph. He slowly moved his arms and the shotgun went up under his arm. He did not want this to be mere murder. Pontdue would have his chance and a damn good one. He should appear at least three feet above Joseph, and would be able to fire from a height. He would use, most likely, a bolt-action Winchester, much favoured by railroad crews. Pontdue had another advantage. He could exit from the cars four ways, by the two platforms at either end of the train, and he could get out into the scrub brush on the other side of the tracks. Joseph had no way of knowing, but he knew Pontdue would not bolt into the brush. This was the climax both men could not avoid, nor would want to now . . . .

Joseph stood still, the shotgun, almost casual now under his arm, waiting. There was, his mind said, only one split second that would count. That moment when they both faced each other and knew this was their climactic pinpoint of time. There were a few other dangers racing through Joseph's mind. The hired killers might be on the train or among the men now watching behind him at the depot and water tower. A shot from the rear would certainly expose him as a dozen kinds of goddamn fool. He took one quick glance behind him, and his expression didn't change. He felt better. Corey and several of the mine men were standing there, navy Colts strapped to their legs. Corey was all right. There was now no great danger from the hired gunmen. It might yet develop into a battle, if Pontdue and a group inside wanted to come out firing. But the odds were Pontdue had to come out alone, for self-respect.

The lights suddenly went out in the "Copper Queen"; the crash of glass was heard as something hit the oil lamps and they shattered. Joseph took one last look around, up and down the train. The engineer's white, staring face, the hiss and groan of steam dissolving with a sigh on the tracks, the green and red signal lamps still cutting out coloured butterflies in the night. He saw everything clear and sharp, his blood pumped, his hearted worked, he waited. . . .

A heel hit some bit of iron flooring on the car. Pontdue appeared, frock-coated, a blue hat well back on a round fat face. On the rear platform. He carried a Winchester. A cigar glowed, a cheerful, cherry colour, from one corner of the expressionless face.

He saw Joseph walking toward him, the shotgun now held in firing position. Pontdue lifted the Winchester and aimed. *That* was a gesture Joseph did not permit himself to follow. He had learned an important lesson in many battles. *Never* take time to aim at close quarters. Merely point the weapon without looking at it toward the object of the kill and press hard on the trigger. He did not throw the shotgun to his shoulders. He pushed it up toward Pontdue without looking at it, his eyes on the figure of Pontdue, and he pulled both triggers tight. Fire and explosion lit the night. Pontdue was a fragment of a moment behind him; the moment of aiming threw him off. The quick action spoiled his aim. The shotgun blew a great hole in the night, shattering and re-echoing in the stillness of the depot. When

Pontdue fired, his face was already gone. A double-barrelled shotgun loaded with heavy shells at close quarters is a bad thing to stop.

Joseph remained very still, only one hand reaching for new shells, as the smoke swirled past him, while the body of Pontdue stood firm, solid, a red, staring thing, and then it fell slowly, slowly, and crashed into the cinders with a thud and lay very still. Corey came up to Joseph and took the shotgun from his hands. The slug from the Winchester had gone through his neck and Joseph could not speak. His mouth and stomach began to fill with blood.

Joseph's daughter Selma was born that night, prematurely. They had carried Joseph into his house, his neck wrapped in bloody bandages, and when he tried to speak to Rebecca, his mouth was full of spilling gore. They laid him down and the doctor drugged him. Rebecca held on to the doctor's arm, and asked him to stay. She knew it was coming now, dragged into life by shock—right away. A beautiful girl.

The doctor held the wet baby like a skinned rabbit and whopped it twice hard across the buttocks. It wailed. Rebecca lifted a tired, wet head from the damp pillow.

"Joseph?"

"He's resting."

"Will he?"

"Don't worry about him, Mrs. Pedlock. I've sewed gunfighters up with sack thread and they've lived. Look at your daughter. Bigger than a new-born shoat. Howls just as loud."

"Joseph, he's . . ."

"Sleeping. Here, look at *this*. Miss, meet Maw."

"It's such a small one."

"Now drink this, and . . ."

The room spun, the hot water steamed. "Joseph, on Passover. Killing."

"Mrs. Pedlock. Here, feed this howler."

"Tell me the truth, Doctor."

"Look, he'll live, he'll be fine. Throat a little torn, but he's alive."

"Doctor, that face, the face of Joseph, it's not disfigured?"

"Missed the face. Take care of that baby. It's puny and should have stayed under cover another month or two."

"I'm tired, Doctor . . . so tired."

"Sure you're tired. So am I. It's been kind of a big night, all around."

Selma lifted her button nose from the flesh of her mother and wailed.

. . . Life in the open wasn't perhaps all she had expected.

* * *

Someone unseen by all had watched over Rebecca in her labours and at the birth of her daughter. From overhead in the attic. Egon could not move. For an hour he had crouched on the attic floor looking through the dusty crack in the board floor, into the room below. He shivered as if in fever and in his ears still rang the screams of his mother, his wonderful mother, who, big and clumsy, panting like an animal, had cursed and roared and pulled on knotted towels. And at last had projected from between her legs this scalding blot of bloody flesh that awoke to life and howled while his mother panted open-mouthed, and wept. His brothers had been sent to a neighbour—he was so alone.

The cruel pangs of this birth had cut deeper into Egon than into his mother. He felt her defiled and disgraced, bloodied and humiliated by this animal grunting, this hurting of the tender body he loved so well. It was with shame he had watched, not for himself, but for her. He had of course seen the beasts at play and making family, and had shouted in feeble mirth at the filth that the mine boys spoke. He knew of some of the lust that made the frontier livable, but he had never believed his mother was part of this rolling, tumbling and close embrace, this fertile growing and bellying out, and the final degrading drama of screams and sweat and bloody thighs.

Egon sobbed softly and promised himself that he would never speak to his mother of her degrading participation in that night's exposing and probing, the flowing and tossing, the dirty business of afterbirth. All for a clot of red flesh with a redder mouth and the evil face of an old woman that could only howl, or tear with blind face and gasping mouth at his mother's breast.

It was from that night that Egon's nerve ends were set in a pattern that he could not change. He could never himself impregnate a woman or go through the gestures of it. As if in him something had come to a certain stage, and the scenes between the crack of the attic floor had turned it into a solid crystal. He never spoke of it to anyone.

BOOK THREE

CHAPTER I

When his grandsons, pumped full of bad "Western" movies, would ask Joseph Pedlock about the great gunfighters of the West, he would snort and say, "The whole damn thing is a legend invented by Eastern frumps writing so-called 'Western' novels. The damn motion pictures have gone even further in their distortion of the simple, dirty, murderous morals of the West."

"There *were* two-gun men, Grandpa."

"Those slick trigger-men who draw and shoot from the hip and kill quickly at any distance? I tell you the pistol and revolver were all right if you were butchering a calf or a tired drunk at arm's length, but the serious shooting in the West was done with the Winchester and Sharps and the Remington. And with shotguns. And all those damn movies where unshaved boys in fancy tailoring fan the trigger with the palm of the hand. I never heard of such foolishness. . . . It's like drinking whisky through a hole bored in the bottom of the bottle. And those long, slow walks down a frontier street, two killers stalking each other, and meeting halfway to blow each other down! Hell and high water, a man would have to have his head examined to do anything as dramatic and foolish as that kid's horseplay. How did we kill? Well, we didn't, much. A lot of that nonsense of twenty-four-hour shootings is built up on the records of professional killers. A few mad, brutal men who shot mostly their own lousy kind. The cattle, the sheep, and the copper wars saw real shooting, sure—but it was rifle-work mostly. Ambush and dropping a man from horseback, or getting him as he stood in the light of his windows and drilling him quickly and leaving him on his front steps to bleed like a stuck pig. Nothing romantic or dainty. Me? Yes, I suppose I got mixed up in some killings. Doesn't make much of a story. I wasn't a Halliday or Hickok."

When she was a little girl Selma remembered the trips to the smelter and the great day when Montana territory was admitted to the Union, and Louis went off to the Oklahoma land rush, and came back with two horses he had won in a crap game, and half his moustache burned off. The first Pedlock copper came out of the vats, and there was even a telegram to Joseph Pedlock from President Grover Cleveland. Selma sat on Joseph's shoulder and pounded his head with her little fist and he grinned and shook her—he couldn't speak. It was years before his vocal cords healed enough for him to be operated on, for him to learn speaking all over again. He was a big, silent man, always heavily armed, surrounded by hard-looking men, his neck scarred and his voice gone.

The Copper Combine was cutting prices, buying judges and courts, but Joseph went on making copper. He and Louis. Louis was now a happy, Western figure with a long, ragged Buffalo Bill moustache, white Stetson and high-heeled boots. They went together to New Orleans and saw John L. Sullivan beat Jake Kilrain. Louis brought Selma back a doll house in sections. All the furniture in it was small and in perfect scale. Selma used to sit for hours on the floor and move the furniture around with the help of Egon, and her silent father would come in later and kiss them good night, and Mama would come in too, smelling of body powder. It was the fashion then, with long white gloves on naked arms. They were leaving in a few days for Chicago, where those dreadful murders by Doctor Cronin had taken place, those horrible killings that Sam used to read to them, going into all the details, the full gory evidence.

It was a fine, full girlhood, with Uncle Louis coming home from the timber and water rights they were fighting for, and Uncle Louis always had something for her from the fancy houses, as Mama sadly called them, that he had visited. Mama never let her keep the dolls and perfume and jet earrings. He was worse than his father, Mama said. Uncle Louis got caught in a washout and a tornado that year, and someone tried to kill him in a Kansas City hotel lobby, and he shot and buried the gent. The jury said, "A man ought to learn to draw fast before he tackled anybody from the Pedlock crowd."

They all went to Washington once when the Copper Combine lawsuits reached a court there, and Papa couldn't speak and wrote down a lot of words on a blackboard. They celebrated that night, and Papa put a drop of wine in her glass at the Willard Hotel, and added soda water. Louis came in drunk late at night and smelled terrible when she saw him in the morning asleep on the sofa, his cowboy boots on the cushions and a black lace-trimmed garter sticking out of his pocket. Mama said he was *much* worse than his father, and Papa laughed and hugged Mama very hard till she screamed, and Mama was very happy. For Papa had decided that the family would move to New York. Louis and Corey would remain in Butte to run the mines and smelters, and if they were lucky, they might make some money that year.

Egon had rejected much of the American life of the period. It was not for him. He read his tattered books and went for long walks across the hills and was happy in his personal dreams. He refused to listen to the filth of boy-talk, the normal chatter, the banter of sensual promise, of hopes of lust and a goatlike pleasure in young malehood. Always all this talk of clinging, wrassling men and women brought back to him the picture of his mother in sweat and blood bellowing in agony as they tore a child from between her legs. It was no use accepting this as a way of life, a way of replenishing the earth. All he could remember was his wonderful mother, her face scarred with sweat, her little teeth gripping her lips till they bled, the gasp and heave of her clumsy, bloated body and the issuing of the man-made lump of flesh that was to become a sister. Egon had resigned then and there such partnerships.

He should have been unhappy. He read many novels about unhappy childhood, about sensitive childhood tormented by evils and misunderstandings, but Egon managed to enjoy life very much. He liked the brilliant glitter of surfaces, the subtle tones of the colour of things, the pleasures of tasting and feeling, the excitement of travel, and the warm comfort of being part of the family group. Only to his mother could he or would he explain a little of what he felt.

Sam and Ralph respected his dreamlike state, his silences and his reading. Their friends did not accept Egon and would have hooted and knocked him down with dirty shouts, but Sam and Ralph would stand for no such nonsense. They had an excuse. "The kid has a delicate chest. He's really bright as hell."

Egon would grin when he heard this and go back to his book, gnawing on a big sandwich of his own invention—a huge, open white roll plastered in butter with a giant beef tomato mashed inside it.

There was the sad time Aaron Manderscheid sent for Joseph for the last time, before the doctors were able to make Joseph speak again. Joseph remembered the old Philadelphia house as it was when he had been a young man fresh from war. It was shabby now, business was bad, money hard to get. The big rooms were draped in covering linen, the paint was off the ceilings, and the panelled rooms dull and warped. But it was still a clean house and upstairs in the big black walnut bed, a small, thin, white version of Aaron lay and smiled up at Joseph as he came into the room.

"Good of you to come, Joseph. I wanted to see you before I went. Don't sigh and roll your eyes at an old man. I don't fool myself. They stick things into me and test my joints. But I know I'm going away, going to die. Sit down, close to me, Joseph."

Joseph sat down. The small, thin face, the bones already thrusting almost through the flesh as if not prepared to wait for liberty just a little way ahead. Aaron grinned, showing his little, yellow teeth.

"It's come to this, Joseph. I can only talk. All the hurry and all the running and all the business. What for? The old Jews of the scrolls were right. They wrote some place, in Ecclesiastes, all flesh is grass. Wealth is vanity and pleasure is vanity. The earth takes us back and we become the herbs of the fields and the sheep gnaw on us. All flesh is grass. A family is a little group of herbs, pleasant, beautiful herbs. A cluster of related plants in the night. A little circle of limbs held one in the other, and now I'm letting go. . . ."

Aaron began to cough. A nurse came in and gave him a drink and punched his pillow, and then he motioned her out and went on talking.

"Joseph, it's not too good, what I'm leaving behind me. The family is breaking up, the dignities, the good deeds we wanted to pile up haven't come to us yet. You're still fighting. Try and keep us together a little bit, after I'm gone. You don't know our history, do you? Hand me those papers there. Old journals my sister Ann hoards in her attic. It's an amazing family. Very amazing. But let's not talk about family pride. We have more than we can consume."

Joseph sat well back on his chair, held out a cigar, and Aaron nodded and Joseph lit it and puffed. He felt near tears and yet he could say not a word of comfort to the man in the bed. What good were words anyway when soon the spark would blow out, nothing would rush in, and it would all be over, for ever? He shivered at the idea of death being so powerful, so sure, and coming even to him now in a fistful of years. The vanity in Joseph hated the idea of being put away into nothing. All flesh *is* grass.

But the little man in the big bed was talking again. "Joseph, I've lived a long time and I would have liked a little more time with the sun on my face, but I don't bargain with upstairs. God isn't a business-man marking down lives and throwing in an extra yard because you tell him a hard-luck story. I wanted to see you, Joseph, because now it all passes to you. All of it. You're the family now. Simon, he isn't anything but a great doctor; Louis, he's a good solid brain and a habit of dressing up like for a masked ball because he wants to belong to something he likes. Your boys, they're fine. . . . My boys, they'll try and keep the Philadelphia end going. But beyond that, Joseph, we're part of this country . . . a lot of it. These papers. Let me read from them. Do you know where we came from . . . listen. . . ."

The little man on the bed coughed and Joseph bit hard into his cigar. His fists closed and he wanted to say, "It's all right, Aaron, it's terrible and all right. I'll watch out, I'll see what I can do." But all he could make known was a rattle in his throat of scar tissue.

"The first Manderscheid came to America with Captain John Smith —to Jamestown," Aaron began to read. "Jamestown was on the edge of a stagnant swamp, against Doctor Thomas Manderscheid's advice. They had to drink the brackish river water when the wells failed, and it was a long, long story of horror and dirt and disease. But by 1614 Thomas Manderscheid owned a thousand acres of sandy soil, was owed by the Virginia Company six hundred pounds for medical treatment to the colony, and had no seat in his pants. He was married to a bond-woman, Hannah Cohen, who had come out of a London slum carrying a rag bundle that held an extra shift. When Thomas first saw her, she had muddy feet and her red hair was knotted over a small, frightened, peaked face. She was not beautiful and just a shade inadequate.

"Thomas was lucky. His son David was forty before he married a Huguenot girl, the only member left of a huge family shipwrecked on the coast. Flung ashore naked, she was sheltered by the Manderscheids, and after a short, tight bereavement, she married David, the only one of the many children who had come alive through river fevers, storms, and Indian raids. It was the son of this Jewish-Huguenot merger, called Saul, who began the dynasty of us Philadelphia Manderscheids.

"Saul found that being a Jew, even one going back to the founding of Jamestown, was a hard task in Virginia. He tilled the family land and fished the river and found no one to marry. There were Indian squaws, true, revolting Catawbas, rather gamy in flavour.

"One day in a roadside ditch he found a young man stripped of his clothes, smeared with tar, and covered with hen feathers. He took him home, cleaned him, and found that the broken stranger was a Quaker, an object in the colonies to be hated and feared like the devil by all true followers of God.

"Saul poured bear grease into the whip wounds on the Quaker's back and the young man earnestly explained he had been preaching in the town square that one must worship God, not the Sabbath. And that all men must have the liberty to worship as they saw fit.

"Saul said there is no such place, and the Quaker said there was a place called Sylvania, up north. Settled by persecuted Quakers, to whom its Proprietor, William Penn, opened the colony, all were free to come there—all who were respectable men who wanted to till the soil and raise up a family and treat God in their own personal fashion. Saul was very excited and did not sleep that night on his husk bedding. He remained awake and thought of such a place—Sylvania! In the morning he went to question the young Quaker again but found that he had died during the night because of the loss of a great deal of his skin and heavy kicks in the stomach. Saul buried him in the potato patch, packed a deerskin with his few Hebrew books, some letters of his grandfather, and a bit of beef. Putting his musket under his arm and his wide-brimmed hat on his head, he went down to the sea to find transportation to Sylvania.

"It was three months later that a Swedish ship stood in a muddy creek just off the river and Saul was rowed ashore. The King of London, he found out, had liked the name Sylvania. He had put the name of the Propreietor's father—a loyal, old boozing sea dog—in front of it, and Pennsylvania it remained.

"That's how we came to Philadelphia, Joseph."

Doctor Simon came into the bedroom and shook his head. "You've been talking too much, Aaron. Much too much."

"Yes, I have. Such a pride and snobbery in our past. Forgive me, Joseph."

Joseph stood up and pressed the little man's hand and smiled, and Aaron said, "Good-bye, Joseph," and closed his eyes.

Joseph and Doctor Simon walked out of the room. Doctor Simon mopped his brow with a brown silk handkerchief.

"He isn't going to last much longer, Joseph. And he did want to see you."

Joseph nodded.

"I hope we'll have you talking again. It can be done and we'll start on you soon. It seems to me I'm always helping patch you up."

Joseph nodded and watched Doctor Simon pour two small glasses of brandy. Doctor Simon saw the glance and smiled.

"It doesn't matter any more. It doesn't burn inside as it used to. Nothing much does. I'm running down like a cheap clock. Not as fast as Aaron, but running down. Those notes and journals he's reading. I've been helping to collect them. Who knows, I may even publish a family history . . . the kind of dull book they sell by the pound in old bookstores. Well, here's to health and hope, Joseph."

They swallowed the brandy and Doctor Simon sighed.

"Ah, spirits, a wonderful thing. Joseph, I'm pleased with Louis, very pleased in most respects. But he's such a sensualist. I mean all these women of his . . . it's something that shocks even me."

Joseph smiled and took out a pad and short gold pencil and wrote: "It's just the way they used to talk about you, Simon. The sins of the fathers, et cetera . . . huh? Let's have another drink."

Aaron Manderscheid died two days later in his sleep. . . .

CHAPTER II

And all the time the boys and Selma were growing. New York was fun with Papa and Mama, Selma thought. First in the big hotel suite while they looked for a house. And the first home in New York was a Stanford White house on East Sixty-fifth Street with white marble steps, and Italian urns in front of it. Sam was away at school, some fancy prep school in New Jersey, but that didn't last long. He came home one night covered with road dirt, and happy and saying he had had enough of schooling. He went down to Papa's Tennessee land with some of the sons of Aaron Manderscheid. In a few years they had some coal and iron, producing it at only a small loss of a few thousand dollars a year. Joseph wrote on his little pad: "It's all right. The boy is learning something."

Papa and Mama had a lot more trouble with Egon as he grew up. Slim and blond, but already showing a plump chin, he went through Harvard in a fearful hurry. Begged a season in Paris and got into the Sorbonne somehow, and went into debt buying paintings at the Salon des Indépendents. Papa sent him to England to see about Pedlock patents on smelters being built there, but Egon complicated the whole thing and Uncle Louis had to be rushed over to untangle a fearful mess. Egon wrote very cheerful letters and was very amusing, and Papa at first worried he was going to become a writer or a painter. But Egon wrote back and said he had no talent at all in a creative way

It was fun those years the boys and Selma were growing up.

Even the scandal about Egon seemed very funny. Egon came back, a very young man with a cane and spats, and Mama had to talk to him.

"Really, Egon, I can't understand it."

"Just don't tell Papa."

"But two thousand dollars. We can hardly pay the lawyers."

Egon tapped his cane on the floor. "It seemed a good idea at the time. A little publishing house. But the woman who put up most of the money has followed me here."

"Let her."

Egon wiped his face. "She wants to marry me, and I just couldn't think of it. I look on the whole idea with dismay."

"You want to marry, don't you?"

"No."

"Really, Egon."

"Mama, I'll do anything, anything at all, but not get married. Let them send me to jail or Devil's Island. She's a big woman smelling of scent and wanting to mother people and lead causes."

"I see. I don't know how I'm going to tell Papa."

"But you can't."

So Egon went on a trip around the world. And in time the thing blew over and it was a family joke to say to Egon that a woman was looking at him with a wedding in her eye. Egon was not amused.

The family travelled a lot. Selma loved the journeys by car. Joseph wanted to travel now, to see the land as he remembered it. They went south one year in a big car and saw Charleston, all white and green with a tired, yellow sun. Joseph found it a strange city and he felt a stranger there. His early life was gone. Nothing was the same.

Later, when the funds and lawsuits would permit, there were trips to Saratoga, and Papa began to get his voice back slowly, and Mama was wearing those Gibson Girl hats. Even if all the time the Copper Combine lawsuits and stock-raids on the Pedlock Corporations kept them always on the fringe of bankruptcy, they lived in great expectations. And when Sam, big and wide, with a brilliant deal in iron and coal behind him, married Sara Wasserman, of the big German-Jewish tailoring family of Kahn-Wasserman, from Rochester, all the relatives came from every place to the wedding. All except Ralph, who was in California on a walking tour with some engineers from Stanford. Even Egon came back, full of small pearls for a necklace for Selma, and a lot more debt he wanted Papa to pay.

It was a fine wedding, and old Rabbi Sontag came up from Philadelphia, with his beard shaved off. He performed the ceremony all in English, and didn't even wear his hat. Papa's sister, Tante Strasser, was shocked. Papa had brought her over from Vienna to live with them. She was a crisp and firm old lady as befitted someone who had married a Strasser in her youth, but Herr Strasser was dead these many years, and so she had brought over her drapes and furniture. Papa admitted his sister was a handful, and that her bite was as bad as her bark.

Those were the happy years of Selma's girlhood, as the century drew to a close. Only later did she realize that the trouble with Ralph was beginning. Ralph never came home much any more. He had become a mining engineer and somehow avoided the family holidays and gatherings and even refused to come into the Pedlock Corporations. Papa was in his sixties now and had divided the companies and given all the sons an equal share of the stock. But it was years before they suspected that Ralph was ashamed of being a Jew, and that he called himself Perry, instead of Pedlock, out there in California.

Such were the years of Selma's girlhood and of young womanhood, and looking back, it seemed that Butte and the fearful memory of the time Papa was shot in the neck, and killed a man, were only a legend. The only thing that seemed always with them, never changing, never letting go, were the lawyers. There was trouble in the Tennessee lands that always showed a yearly loss, and the Pedlock Patents and the Copper Combine fought in the courts for years. The first words that Joseph said after they operated on his vocal cords, that Selma remembered were "those goddamn, blue-bellied lawyers!"

The second thing he said was, as he looked over the three babies Sam and Sara had produced in quick order, "The family is certainly spawning like salmon!"

Only Sam seemed to care for business, and love the job of getting metals out of the earth. Sam was fat and squat and often short of breath, but when he came back from the war in Cuba with a stomach spoiled for a long time, he lost weight and was white and weak. He could have been a sick man all the rest of his life, but Sam loved life and fun, and he took an interest in the metal business and kept office hours and learned to smoke his father's cigars. He hoped to make a good place for Ralph, and Ralph promised to study hard at engineering so he could help Uncle Louis in the field.

"Uncle Louis fools everybody until you get to know him well," Sam used to say. "That cowboy finish and the high boots and the Wild Bill Hickok moustache is just window-dressing. It makes Louis happy and it lures people in the copper business into thinking he's soft in the head. But sit across the table from him during a business deal and he's almost as good as Papa."

Uncle Louis didn't have much hope of Ralph or Egon going into copper. "Hell, I don't know why, but it's something they seem ashamed of. Ralph is a good boy with a fine mind, but now he's playing tennis. Only dudes play tennis and I hate to think old Joseph raised up any dudes. Of course Egon is pretty fancy, but on him it looks good. You don't mind Egon acting like a piano player in a parlour house. He carries it off. But Ralph, what he wants I don't know. Somethin's eatin' off 'im."

"Right now, he's eating off us," said Sam. "He's spending a lot of money getting educated."

"Educatin' costs money," said Uncle Louis, "even at poker."

CHAPTER III

"Mr. Perry. Mr. Perry, sir!"

Ralph came awake with a clouded vision and yawned and rubbed his face until the sounds of the polite knocking at the door of the bedroom focused fully in his ears.

"Mr. Perry, sir."

"Yes," he said, sitting up in the wide Colonial bed, and looking over the strange room he had been shown to the day before; its wallpaper, with scenes from Charles Dickens *Pickwick Papers*, the milkglass globe shades of old, brass oil lamps (cunningly converted to the use of electric power) and the curved and twisted and wormy original pieces of what was known as "Early American" furniture, most of it made for barns and poorhouse farms but now waxed and restored at great price as collector's items.

"Come in," added Ralph.

The thin coloured man of a yellow butter colour, the Ravel servant who came from Trinidad and spoke like an Oxford graduate, came in with a copy of the *New York Times* and some letters and turned to Ralph. "They were afraid, sir, that you would miss the hunt this morning."

"Oh," Ralph groaned and stood up and rubbed his right leg. "I guess I'll have to forget the hunt. I hurt my leg on the tennis courts yesterday. But I'll be down to see them off."

"Yes, sir, Mr. Perry."

Ralph nodded and stood there, the strong Long Island sunlight pouring in the windows, scratching his belly, his lean, brown belly. He was still not used to being called Perry, after having been Pedlock for so many years. Still, it was a good change, and Alice had liked it and her father had asked her if he were related to *the* Admiral Perry who had done something wonderful on one of the Great Lakes during the War of 1812.

There were three letters with *The New York Times* on the little table. They had been there a week waiting for him to arrive. One had the embossed seal of Stanford University—that daffy prof who wanted to turn sea water into drinking water as California expected some day to die of thirst with a huge increase of population; a catalogue from a dealer in rare books whom Ralph never encouraged by any order; and a heavy letter, with the Baden-Baden mail seal over large, crude Germanic postage stamps, showing a pregnant housewife wearing a sheet and a paper crown. The engineering office in California had merely added the word Perry to *Ralph Pedlock, Esq.*, and re-addressed it to Ravel House, Point Jefferson, Long Island.

Damn! That Oxford-sounding nigger was just a little too smooth and must, of course, have noticed it. Ralph tossed the letters unopened into his bag and went to the un-Colonial, bright bathroom. He brushed his teeth with violence, scowling at the slim, blonde young man reflected in the mirror The thin, handsome nose, the deep blue eyes ("like spoonfuls of star," said Alice), the narrow, wet mouth, all the face scowled back at him. He turned on the shower, very cold. It was a good habit, he was sure, these heavy, cold morning showers. It made him more of a Christian to have the habits of those who, in theory, took these chilled morning plunges under showers. Of course, poor Jews bathed in cold village pools—but it was different. . . .

The Ravel dining room was rimmed with solid buffets on which dozens of steaming silver trays and platters heated by little alcohol lamps simmered and politely boiled. Under the early landscapes of the Hudson River school, under the sporting prints of Stubbs and Morland, a score of well-dressed sporting gentry and their ladies moved and served themselves to plates of little pork sausages, spiced Virginia ham, the heavy clotted cream for the Ceylon tea in the Royal Doulton cups. The men were all in hunter's green, and sporting pink, their slim legs in black leather boots, and the women were in heavy riding skirts hooked over their arms. They looked out from under neat bowlers or romantic riding hats with long feathers sweeping necks tanned by the good outdoor life of a Long Island hunting set.

Mike Ravel, big, dark, glossy, sun-cooked and weathered by his duties in the duck blinds and horse shows and yachting races, leaned against a Tudor doorway, smoking a heavy briar pipe. His wife, in a green, smoked-velvet riding jacket and skirt came up to him and offered him a cup of tea. It was all too perfect.

"It's a good day for it, Mike."

"Hope so, dear; blasted rain may have made the back meadows a bit spongy."

"The hell with it, let's ride," said Bob Wexley. He was a balding stockbroker, a little man, very young, who rode huge black horses and broke a great many bones and was spoken of as a great polo player who gave too much time to his Wall Street offices to be really a top-goal man. "Of course, Mike, the mangy foxes you get out here aren't worth the chase. I remember a run with the Dorset hounds in Sussex now . . . and . . ."

Mike Ravel put down his teacup. "I've turned six foxes loose here this past spring; pairs I got from Virginia, from Washington's own, old hunting country, so, Bob, we'll have good foxes from now on."

Mrs. Ravel said, "It's about time to start. Ah, here comes Ralph. Ralph, darling, but you're not dressed for the hunt!"

Ralph, in hairy English tweeds, a dotted scarf knotted around his neck, came over and took Mrs. Ravel's arm. "I'm sorry, Helen, but this tennis knee is still bad. I couldn't insult your horses by riding them badly. I'll watch from the porch."

Mike Ravel shook his head. "Missing a great run, Ralph. Got a great day for it."

"I'll bear up, and welcome you home."

"Oh, Ralph," said Mrs. Ravel, "you know the Martin Bixbys, and this is Captain Roger Kaw, and Mrs. Max Mont; you must ask her to teach you that new dance step tonight. Oh, dear, it is getting late."

The names sounded like something out of a bad English novel to Ralph.

The hunting horn was sounding from the stables, and doves were suddenly flying from the cotes, and the bray of hounds, choking on their leads, was filling the front lawn.

Everyone moved slowly, excitedly outdoors. It was a pleasant scene full of the great hurry of the hunters as they put down their teacups and the men putting the brandy-filled, leather-covered flasks in their hip-pockets and gathering their short-braided whips; it was like a stage ballet. Ralph stood under the painting of the Ravels by John Singer Sargent and watched them pour out on to the lawn. He followed, limping slightly.

It was a beautiful, clear day of smoking horizons, with the lawn falling away on one side to the Long Island Sound, heaving and white-capped in the light chop of wind, and on the other side the two hundred acres, kept for the most part in their wooded and natural state, only slightly trimmed and tailored by the squads of Ravel gardeners. Old stone walls, weathered fences silvered by rain and wind, enclosed the meadows and wood, the little rises, the cheerful brooks, and the expensive, carefully tended wild flowers. "Not a damn foot of barbed wire on the place," Mike Ravel used to brag. "Unspoiled, that's Ravel House. General Cornwallis slept here."

The horses, high-strung, over-bred and excited, stood and twitched on the lawns, and the grooms, in green and white, helped the ladies up and placed their legs on the saddle horns as they took their position side-saddle. There were daring sets of hunters and riders, newly rich Westerners, who had moved near by, where their ladies rode astride and clasped their legs tight as lovers around both sides of the horse; but the Ravels were too formal for that kind of modern riding.

It was beautiful, exciting and colourful. The hounds, great ears and tongues flapping, toes dug into the turf; the handlers circling around; the horses being walked. The hunt master, attended by a man with a long French hunting horn, was looking at the sun and then off to the little woods down past the lawn.

A round little man, with sleep still in his eyes and a bushy, untrimmed moustache, came out of the huge, white porch and stood beside Ralph. He was dressed in a blue business suit with a lumberman's coloured checked shirt, and his bare feet were stuck into cracked leather bedroom slippers. He put a loose home-made cigarette to his hairy mouth and lit it carefully with a match in a cupped hand. Ralph expected the bush moustache to go up in smoke.

"Fine day," said Ralph.

"Farmers could use more rain," said the round little man. Ralph remembered meeting him last night. He was Ed Ravel, Mike's brother. "A sort of newspaper chap," Mike had said, making the brief introduction.

The hunting horn sounded; the hounds, suddenly loose, found their full voices, and with a clatter and bang, with a clop-clop and a rush, they were all off. The dogs were ahead, noses to turf, yelping and running with over-wound strides, whitish liver spots against the shaggy green of the ground. Then the riders, first in a massed clot of colour, then spreading out as the bolder spirits grew reckless. Then there was a rush as the main body followed, one by one—then two riders, arms sawing wood, were having trouble with their horses.

The hounds flowed like water over a low, stone wall. The first horses sailed over. A series of riders topped the stone wall and Ralph could see the sky, a wooded rise under their horses' bellies. Soon they were all climbing the meadow of short spring oats and heading for the winding brook. There was a greater braying and Ralph was thrilled.

"They've scented the fox!"

Ed Ravel nodded and sat down on the steps and drew on his cigarette and exhaled from wide, hairy nostrils. "If they had to eat the fox, they wouldn't be so damned earnest in their hunting of him."

Ralph said, "It is odd, I suppose, fox-hunting so close to New York City."

Ed Revel threw his cigarette into a clump of hydrangeas! "It's damn odd because it's just a big charade; all those Jews trying to act like eighteenth-century drunken Englishmen."

That stab of emotion that he always felt when something like this came up caught Ralph. He sat down on the top steps and caught his breath before he answered. "I don't see anything wrong in Mike and his friends hunting a fox. It's not a sport for only certain creeds. Lots of people do it."

"Sure they do," said Ed Ravel, "but they don't go in for it with such a religious fervour. They don't do it so perfectly, dress so well for it, go about it with such perfect ritual. The truth is, Pedlock ["Perry, Perry, you bastard!"—said Ralph to himself], the truth is Jews don't hunt. They've been hunted too long to get any real pleasure being on the other side. . . ."

"That's pretty narrow. You're enclosing yourself, making a mental ghetto of your mind."

Ed looked at him and laughed with a sing-song roar. When he laughed, he shook like jelly. He needed a shave and the blue business suit didn't fit well. It looked and was, most likely, one of the ready-made suits of his sister-in-law's family. *A Kahn-Wasserman Creation, Styled for American Manhood.* He didn't like Ed Ravel. He was a cynical, fat, little hairy Jew, the kind who made it a point, before you even asked him, of telling you he was a Jew and and and almost begging you to insult him and mock him. Ed kept smiling at Ralph.

"Pedlock, don't be such a horse's rump. I don't care if my brother Mike perfects a portable foreskin, or has my great-grandfather, a little watchmaker in Holland, suddenly been discovered by experts to have been an English admiral, by Gainsborough. And I don't mind these fox hunts, or the vicar in for dinner, or smoking their own hams—*oy*—in Virginia. It's just that they, we all of us, think we're fooling somebody. Well, we're not. Would you like some whisky?"

"Yes, I guess so."

"Hey, Charlie!" Ed called. The Oxford voice came out. "Some of the old Scotch, and, Charlie, you old fraud, bring the bottle."

Ralph got up. Ed grinned. "That's a smart shine, that Charlie. Him and his fake actor's accent."

"I just remembered," said Ralph, "I got a letter from my family. Must answer it."

"Sure," said Ed. Far off, the hunt suddenly became excited. The dogs stopped their barking for a moment; voices floated over the trees, and the clatter of horses out of control was heard, then a great splashing. Ed began to roll himself a fresh cigarette. He looked off across the trees. "The granddaughter of the Grand Rabbi of Kiev,

I would guess, just took an asser into the big brook. I noticed Mike gave her that balky bay. Mike's a real snob. He doesn't like the Russian Jews."

Ralph turned and went up to his room without answering. Ed, he felt, was the kind of Jew who made anti-Semites out of Jews.

My dear Ralph,

We are here, your mother and myself, at Baden, trying the waters. It has been a long time since we have heard from you, and I would not, at any other time, intrude on the privacy of whatever life you have made for yourself. . . .

(Ralph looked up from the letter and wiped his face with his hand and wished he had waited for the whisky.)

However, your mother is ill. Very ill. She has not asked me to write to you. She is a very proud woman, but I know that she would like to see you. I do not ask you to come; I order you to come. What you do with your life, how you handle it, what you want to make of it, in all that I will not interfere, but there is one last task you are not going to avoid, and that is seeing your mother, soon.

Perhaps I wrote too strongly above, but let it stand. It says what I feel, and you're young enough to be hit on the head by an old-fashioned father, and come through it. There is also some business matter we must take up, but I shall leave that for later. Louis has gone back to New York, to take care of what must be done. They need your help.

Ralph put down the letter on the bed and got up and looked out of the bay of windows. The hunt was far away, and very little sound came from it. A horse, without a rider, was coming across the lawn, and two grooms were walking carefully toward the horse, trying to catch him. He let them come very close before he tossed up his head and bolted away.

Ralph went back to the bed and picked up the letter. He turned over to the last few lines on the last page. The scrawl was wilder; the pen had sputtered.

My son, my son, what a fool you are and how I suffer for you. Do you think I didn't go through it all—the pain and lament, hurting myself and my family, doing the wrong things and inventing reasons for them?

Now all I know is that I sit here and something I love very

much and have neglected all my life is dying in the next room. How can I do it all over again, I think? How can I give up the worries and business and the rushing in and out of trouble, how can I make up for the neglect and pain I caused her? She gave me her life and I kept her around, and bred children, and took her to a wilderness, and set her among frontier savages. And then, when we were old, and I was ready to settle down and hold her hand. Suddenly, now, it's too late.

Forgive everything in this letter, the language, the way I talk to you, the way an old man writes a lot he feels and has no one else to tell it to. I expect you, of course, on the next boat.

Your father,
Joseph

He folded the letter carefully and put it away in the bag. His father didn't understand anything, of course. It was hard to believe that Joseph had ever been young or hot-blooded, passion-willed, or made mistakes. There was a German boat leaving in two days. He would borrow a motor-car from Mike Ravel, and go over and see Alice tonight, after phoning her. Pentland was twenty miles up the coast. Then he lay down and cried for ten minutes for his mother. Ed Ravel would have liked it. It was heavy, emotional, "Jewish" weeping.

Ralph borrowed Mike Ravel's chain-driven Simplex and, at dusk, drove over to Pentland. It was a heavy car, from the primitive age of motoring, with a stiff, brutal steering gear that was never actually scientific. Ralph had plenty of hard work on his hands tooling the heavy car around the bends in the dirt road that went eastward along Long Island. The car and road left him little time to think over his action in rushing like this onward toward asking Alice's father for permission to marry her.

He had met Alice in California at one of those tennis parties that are always being given in the lime-coloured sun under blue-blossomed Jacaranda trees of fashionable Santa Barbara. It was almost a coastal ritual among the well-to-do, this polite, hard-fought game, with its white flannels and sweaters twisted around tanned necks, and the soft sound of the polite "Well played. Your serve, I believe."

Ralph played a good, solid game with much forearm and a hard-to return backhand. Alice Pentland was tall, with taffy-coloured hair under a blue head-band—a marvellously put-together girl—in the crisp, white loose skirt of the period (right out of Charles Dana Gibson's drawings). Well, Ralph suddenly knew he was in love and that Alice was the girl he would "hope to marry". Any other romantic youth would have thought, "the girl I am going to marry", but Ralph had to go through more than just fight off some Yale rivals, the first oil kings, even perhaps the several sword duels and a revolution in a mythical kingdom (he didn't read the popular fiction of the day, but he had sucked up its contents in conversation). He was lucky, of course, to have no coloured blood, or come from a Mandarin family of old China; not to be either a Catholic or a Democrat. He was neither poor nor very rich—both classes, perhaps, being outside the pale of Pentland acceptance. He had gone to a good college and was neither a great student nor a dilettante—both things in his favour. Yet he knew the fight would be long and difficult against much insular composure.

He took Alice bicycling up the California coast, up among those bent and twisted pine trees over a postal-card blue sea dimpling in the eternal sun, and they sat on a cliff, and he held her hand. Alice was a young lady who had been to Saratoga, to Boston, visited relatives in Richmond, done the tour in Europe (in three months), attended Vassar, and been courted by Rhodes Scholars and one mangy English duke, and a few dozen mere Americans.

She was neither foolish nor stuffy, and had a good mind, a wonderful body, and a hope that some day she would marry someone a little like her father: Freud, in those days, was mostly incomprehensible incantations, so it was still all right for a girl to admire her father.

It was very pleasant to lie on a carriage robe under warped pines, and have a tanned, blond young man make love to her. He kissed with a fervour, ardent as the usual American male, and he was neither crude nor impolite yet had an intensely positive attitude. She had no intention of losing her virginity, or her composure, but when he asked her if she had ever thought of marrying and settling down, she sat up and pushed her hair back into place and she said it was getting late and they had to dress for dinner. At Santa Barbara one always dressed for dinner unless one lived in the native Mexican section of town, where shirt, pants, and reasonably clean feet were enough.

In the next few days Alice knew that she was falling deeply in love, or at least in the preliminary state known by a French novelist, then very much unread, a certain Stendhal, as the crystallization-of-love period, a process in which one puts one's emotions, like a small branch, into a vat of sugar water and, in time, crystals form on the branch that shines and has gleaming facets like diamonds. And the loaded, crystallized branch is the full growth of romantic love. "At least it was"—Egon used to say—"an interesting theory." But neither Ralph nor Alice had ever heard of it; yet, in some such way, they came together daily, lay quite decently in each other's arms, nights by the sea, and talked and talked in low whispers, and experimented with kisses and caresses. In a week they were in that state of acute suffering and pain that is ideal, civilized love.

"There is no explaining," Egon used to say to a small circle of friends, "why happy young people, and even people with worldly wisdom, should go into this agony, this painful thing—this trouble, this unhappy state of waiting, feeling, tormenting with all its inner lamentation." But it happened to almost everyone, and as the glum Ralph, one day, took a suffering Alice to the railroad station, they were certainly a couple that any fool could pick out as ardent lovers. They reeked of misery.

"You'll write?" said Ralph, the look of fever in his eyes.

"Really, Ralph, I wonder if it wouldn't be better if I didn't."

"You can't be that cruel, darling."

"Don't you see, perhaps a clean break, sudden, even if cruel . . . Oh, my darling, how foolish I am to even say it. Ralph, don't listen to me when I talk like this. Just love me, love me, no matter what happens."

"I'll be east as soon as I get out of this engineering contract. We'll work it out."

Alice sighed. Pain and suffering—the glandular adjustment of love —made her only more beautiful. "If you were only a Catholic or a Greek. My cousin Dotty married a sort of Egyptian Turk, and they eat a lot of lamb and rice, and have brown, fat babies—but, darling, why did you have to be born a Jew?"

"Your father will ask that, too, I suppose."

"Father, too, but don't worry. I'll have a talk with him. It isn't as if you had a long hook-nose and greasy black curls and spoke with a ghetto twang. Oh, Ralph, you're so beautiful, so precious and strong. I love you so much."

"It's worth all this suffering. We both know that."

She began to weep, and they walked through to the train and Ralph put the large box of chocolates, tied with its big red ribbon, on her lap, and the novel by Robert Chambers about a mythical kingdom. He kissed her and said, "Stout fella," something the tennis players were always saying at Santa Barbara, and Alice said, "My darling," and prepared herself for suffering across a continent.

After the first shock of recognition of their love, and its major problem, neither really understood the full struggle ahead, the reality and seriousness of what they were facing. Love had a numbing effect on them, like a dentist's drug, and while they could suffer for and with each other, they could not feel very strongly the real pressures of active society, family positions, or the impractical politics of marriages between creeds. "Nature in her mating processes"—Egon used to say —"had always been interested only in the reproducing of its species, not in maintaining special congregations, or breeding missionaries or builders of churches."

It was the raging blood, the normal and happy lusts of the young, the gradual crystallization of their love for each other's bodies, minds, manners, and beings that had attacked Ralph and Alice. And with all that done, nature had dumped them off to solve the mere society-made problems in their own way.

Ralph was not a deep thinker. He had a good mind, but he had skilfully trained himself not to abuse it, so that he would not appear like an outsider in the special layer of society he had picked out as the one to join.

His thoughts, as he steered the chain-driven Simplex around the Long Island dirt roads, were much simpler than the methods of nature, and a polite, entrenched society. He merely wanted Alice forever, he wanted to make love to her, cherish her, build a wall of easy pleasure and conservative contentment around her. To live by her class and her people; live with a fine, semi-cultured ease—nothing long-haired in either of them, thank God.

Good clubs, nice people, fine lawns and a collection of fairly old family furniture. To see her every day, to have wonderful, polite children, to face his equals (as Mr. Ralph Perry) across a bridge table, to say the normal things about the Republican Party, the German Kaiser, the painting of Frederic Remington, and the wonderful American holidays of Thanksgiving and Arbor Day. Egon would have been cynical to have felt all this. Ralph seriously prayed for it. Ralph could not say to himself that he wanted to be merely accepted. Rather, he felt that the problem was only the matter of being like those people he admired. Perhaps in his inner mind he hoped that after a while he would take on a protective colouration, like an innocent insect in an owl-haunted world, and merge with them, become one of them, and remain unnoticed. A man from a good college, a fine bird shot, a good party man. A drinker of just enough whisky, with features just blank and handsome enough never to be anything like a deep student of life or a great artist. Not one of those talented eccentrics who neither bathed nor combed their hair and often ate with their elbows on the table. He hoped to achieve a monochromatic entity.

The amazing courage that Ralph showed, at this time, was not entirely that of ignorance of the closed gates he faced. He had studied, as any good engineer would, the direct approach to the project, and he knew the angles of attack, the mound of rise, the steep cliffs ahead, and the already piling up of waters of bigotry and prejudice against him. But it was, to him, like building a dam, and he saw it as a set of practical plans in blueprint. But actually the courage really came because he was in love, romantically in love and full of a healthy desire for Alice that made the rest of life seem worthless and profitless and a thing of no value. The rest of his earnest, placid life almost never touched the courage and intensity of his courtship.

The ornate, stone gates of Pentland appeared in the brass glare of his gas pressure lamps. Headlights were lit in those days by a special kind of gas carried in a tank on the running-board (and today, even the running-board has disappeared!). Ralph felt that the gas headlights gave the whole place the look of a stage set. One of those foolish, happy plays that were laid in a Long Island drawing room, and everyone said the clever things that escaped one the moment after they were said. Ralph turned the car up the winding drive. The house—huge, gabled, slated, surrounded by boxwood hedges—an ivy, bastard Regency—loomed ahead. Ralph's hands gripped the great driving wheel; he cut the gas and put one hand outside of the car where the cloutch and brake fitted against a toothed checking device; he pulled back on the brake. The car stopped; the hot engine went silent like a big, angry heart dying. Ralph crossed to the front doors.

Nicole and Peter Perry, the children of Ralph and Alice, knew very little about the romance of their father and mother until rather late in life. By that time, Nicole was playing an amusing game of being one of the Lost Generation girls of the post-war world as presented by Scott Fitzgerald and *Flaming Youth* and other pictures of the time (while remaining a charming, witty, and beautiful girl). Nicole used to say, after she and Peter found out the facts, "It's got no suspense, that story, at all, you know. Mother did marry Father, and we were conceived, and christened in wedlock."

To Peter, the story of the mating of a Pentland and Pedlock-Perry was just a little more serious. In prep school, and later at Princeton, when some boy was not admitted to a secret society, or to a Philadelphia or New Haven weekend because he was a "Yid" or a "Hebe", Peter felt very sorry about it, and almost a little guilty. Not very guilty, because Mother had explained that the Pentlands were an old family and that the Perrys had come over at Jamestown, and that while there was perhaps a trace of Jewish blood in the Manderson-Perry stock, "there wasn't as much as one would think". All those pogroms, those big, handsome Cossacks and Hussars and Prussian officers. That's how it was all through history—rape, rape, rape. Peter didn't remember her saying it in just that way, or in those words, but somehow when he thought about it in prep school and college, that's how it seemed; the wonderful kindness of the Slavic and Saxon blondes, helping the willing and exciting women of the Lost Tribes brighten the stock, until it was like adding good English cream to dark Asiatic tea. And soon if you added enough cream, well, there you were— Father and Nicole and Peter.

But, actually, the evening Ralph stepped out of Mike Ravel's Simplex and was shown into the hall of Pentland, he was not a very brave young Cossack or Hussar; just a frightened Jew.

*   *   *

Alice had said over the phone that Father was expecting Ralph, but Ralph had hoped he could have a few minutes alone with Alice first To kiss her, hold that wonderful, tennis-trained body against his. Put his arms around her and drink in courage from her so close to him. To take on a fighting stance after looking at his darling, and knowing that she would—in the language of her set—stand by, hold the fort, keep the banner high, take it as they dealt it, and remain always the "stout fella".

But a large, flat-footed butler with a wen on his nose showed him into a dark, panelled room with great shelves of well-bound books, old globes of the world, and letters from Emerson, Carlyle, and Teddy Roosevelt hung on the walls. A large landscape so blackened by varnish and smoke that nothing but a yellowed, strained sunset was visible. Years later, when Peter had inherited it, it was cleaned and a valuable Turner would have been exposed, if the restorer had not destroyed it in the process.

Charles Pentland was looking into the cold ashes of the fireplace when Ralph was shown in. He was a tall man, with a brooding stoop, in a belted Norfolk jacket. His head was lean and beautiful, with a great shingle of a nose, white hair retreating into a noble baldness, and a triangle of moustache over a neat, character-curled mouth; not at all a weak mouth, but a mouth that carried few expressions and told no secrets either of strength or of weakness.

Charles Pentland and his kind have been presented to us for so many years as a caricature of the Boston gentleman that in time the light, competent novels of his kind of life have become accepted as truths.

Charles Pentland was not a caricature and certainly not a type. He was a kind, decent man, a very good Christian, a well-bred human being, born a little too late into a disintegrative society, who had been forced to go south, to enter business. Born a hundred years sooner, he would have drifted over Europe with the father of Henry and William James, have studied law or history, and perhaps have walked the streets of Rome talking of buildings and German lecture rooms. There was nothing of caricature about these older Americans, but so few are left that the surface is now accepted for the inner man, and the polish for a snobbish waxing that is supposed to wipe out the inner core of fine feeling and deep thinking. This was not true, and Charles Pentland, seen as such a type, would be untrue in the picture of life among the Pedlocks. That Ralph saw Charles Pentland as such a type and gave him a brief surface reading is not his fault. For Charles

Pentland was a fine play actor, and to protect himself he had taken on that expected aspic of coolness, that casual, easy way of speaking, that drawn-out voice that seemed to make him foolish, snobbish, and remote.

He hid his kindness, his warm heart, his gentle feeling toward the world, for the truth was, the modern world of wolf talk and big business frightened him.

But Ralph did not suspect any of this for many years. And Charles Pentland did not look upon Ralph as a brash young Jew poaching beyond his fences, but as a young man in love, in love just a little beyond his social means. So the calm, polished face that looked at Ralph was outwardly that of a hard-dealing Yankee trader. . . .

He held out a hand attached to a starched French cuff from which twinkled blue-stone cuff links.

"Ah, Mr. Perry. Or rather, Ralph. Welcome to Pentland."

"Thank you, Mr. Pentland."

"Sit down, my boy. A glass of Port? If not, some Scotch? I don't like it, but we have it."

"The Port will do very well."

"Good." They held up their ruby-tinted wine. Charles Pentland took a quick sip, like a clever bird drinking. Ralph wanted to gulp a full glass of courage, but he also took a small sip. They sat facing each other, looking up at the dark painting. Charles Pentland filled a long, tan-coloured pipe after running its bowl absent-mindedly against his huge nose. He filled the pipe from an oil-skin pouch with some Greek fraternity letters on it.

"Smoke, if you want to, Ralph. Cigarettes over there."

"Thank you." Ralph lit a stale, dried-out cigarette.

Charles Pentland looked at Ralph. "You're better than I expected. Much."

Ralph almost spilled his drink. He hurried it down on to the end table at his elbow. "Am I?"

"Fathers, you know, never think any young man good enough for their daughters. Never thought any young monkey good enough for Alice. Only daughter; smart, wonderful child. Read Shelley at six, could recite Scott, by the mile, Browning, too, all the long bits, at nine."

"I want to marry Alice."

The pipe needed cleaning and Charles Pentland worked a fuzzy cleaner in and out of the shank. "Ralph, you must understand that I am naturally expected to be a snob. It can't be helped. It's like having brown eyes. I was born that way and even if I weren't, there are dozens of uncles and aunts that would see I am kept in line. I am, Lord help me, the last of the direct male line. There isn't much for me to leave. Enough in pride and effort and loyalties to make it of value to a lot of people in Boston and Tuxedo Park, though, and to keep up my position as vice-president in the New Amsterdam–Manhattan Bank. You give me a tough problem: ethically, morally, and, I fear, socially."

"I know, but, Mr. Pentland——"

"If I may make my point, please. Thank you. I'm no bigot and I hold no holy vow to protect the sacred stock of the cod and the bean, but you see, I am important to the bank. But let us pass that by, even if I am of value to many old families. Another glass of Port? Ah, there, drink it down, my boy. Yes, let us pass the bank by. There is the matter of personal happiness. Oh, I know all young people are sure they can have it by the tail, permit me that indelicate phrase, but can you and Alice really be happy? Just let me finish. True, there is a great deal of society that will accept you both. I'm not saying that the part that will not is worth bothering with. Perhaps it's dying, like all good society. But will you both be happy? This race nonsense isn't very impressive, and, I've—well, I may say I've never voted against Jews in my clubs—the old guard insist they be kept out—but I refrain from casting a vote. A good club is only a club, but marriage, well——"

"We've been through it all, Alice and myself, and——"

"Oh, Alice has told me everything. At least, she has told me the essential facts. But frankly, my boy, speaking from my own past—I tell this for the first time—there was a girl when I was at Yale. Came from an Irish family, oh, no shanty or lace-curtain Irish. Rich, well-brought-up family. Rigid Catholics, of course. Very strict about it. Priests all over the place, and those bloody pictures of bleeding hearts and martyrs being done in, all over the place, and no decent chops on Friday. I used to go down there for weekends at their place at Nyack, on the Hudson. Yes, I was in love. Mollie was in love. We had also worked it out—Father Devlin and myself—over a bottle of Scotch. Nice people, Catholics. Solid and, well, not so bigoted as we expect. Just a little social inferiority, I suppose. The children, Father Devlin explained, to be raised by priests, a trust fund, and all that. On my side, Mollie to called herself Mildred. An uncle of mine insisted on that."

"Mr. Pentland, if I may say something."

"Of course. Just let me finish this. Give you an idea of these things. Bears on the issue at hand." Charles Pentland put down his pipe and folded his arms and looked into the cold fireplace. There among the ashes Ralph felt he was reliving this early romance, this past that he had perhaps forgotten or crowded into a corner of a mind filled with affairs of private clubs and the New Amsterdam–Manhattan Bank. His face had relaxed and he looked older, kinder, and rather a man to be admired.

"Yes, my boy, there we were, getting ready for the wedding. I wasn't to be converted. I was rather a feather in their bog-trotting cap. But a monk would marry us privately in a chapel, with the Archbishop, later, to come to the wedding reception. A big, fat, happy Irishman often dropping in and telling me what a hell of a fine fellow I was. And there were their relatives: little old men with crooked canes and wide old ladies who talked like a bad play at the Irish Theatre and smelled like a crowded morning Mass. They didn't call me a black Protestant bastard to my face, but I think they felt I had horns under my hair, and a spiked tail under my college tailoring. Narrow, honest people—a little dull.

"We parted, broke it up two days before the wedding. It was at the signing about the children to be raised by the Church. There they sat, a row of fine, red faces; peasants, ward-heelers, and Father Devlin droning on in Latin and a brogue of New York East Side English. I suddenly saw they felt I was outside of their good world. They were doing *me* the favour and I came awake. Mollie, Mollie, I couldn't do it. Not sign away my sons, or be married in a chapel by a monk, as if they were ashamed that I couldn't appear in St. Patrick's. It was rather hard. Mollie had a great crying spell, and they married her off next spring to a rising young Tammany boy who had street-paving contracts. They have ten children, all big and fat and red-faced, and none of the family ever missed a Mass. Even Mollie's husband, when he went to jail during a paving scandal, endowed a chapel at Sing Sing. Mollie was fun; she never became Mildred."

"How did you feel about it, Mr. Pentland?"

"Bad. After a while I stopped thinking about it. The pain passed. I thought I would never marry. Then, well, I met Alice's mother. I can't honestly say I had any trouble falling fully in love. It was very beautiful. But that isn't any part of this discussion, is it? Ralph, I've tried to keep this on a very polite, gentleman-to-gentleman level. I know you're a fine boy. Just looking at you is enough to see that your upbringing has been of the best. I believe in first impressions."

"Mr. Pentland——"

"And, of course, we know your father at the bank, and his people.

The Manderscheids, and your brothers, the Pedlocks. All fine people. Honest, and a delight to do business with."

Ralph wondered why Charles Pentland ground something guttural into the words *Manderscheid* and *Pedlock*. Would he have made it so heavy if he were saying: *Bunker Hill, Cabot, Washington?*

"About Alice and myself——"

Charles Pentland rose and came to Ralph's side and put an arm on his shoulder. "I want you to forget it, Ralph. I want you to get over it. I want Alice to get over it."

"Mr. Pentland, you don't mean that!"

"I certainly do. This hasn't been an easy evening to face. Believe me, Ralph, some day you'll thank me. You'll see it from my viewpoint, yes, even from Alice's viewpoint. When she comes out of this, she'll agree with her father."

"Comes out of it! I haven't been playing Svengali!" It was not a good choice, the name Svengali, Ralph thought as he said it. That popular idea of a Jewish villain feasting on a good Christian flesh in the form of the delectable Trilby. It had been a bad choice of phrasing.

"Ralph, I can't give you much hope, but suppose we have lunch some day and go into the subject further?"

"I'm leaving for Europe in two days. My mother is very ill."

"I am sorry."

"Could we have lunch before I leave?"

"Of course. Lunch tomorrow at the Bankers' Club."

"I still would like to feel, Mr. Pentland, it isn't hopeless. I still feel you'll understand us. It's been fine talking to you like this. I didn't expect all this kindness or understanding. I don't know what I expected, but I felt it was worth any fight. I still do, Mr. Pentland."

"Tomorrow, say, at one?"

Ralph took the hand and shook it. "Could I see Alice for just a few moments?"

"I am sorry. She went out at the last moment to her aunt's at Blue Point. I asked her to, frankly. I felt it was better, like this, just us two."

"Of course. Good night, Mr. Pentland."

"Good night, my boy. See you at lunch."

After Ralph had left, Charles Pentland sat a long time over his drink. He felt tired, drained. Had he been heavy enough, slick and in character? It was bad enough to keep the grim mask of snobbery on during banking hours. Well, it had to be done this way. And he stopped thinking of love and thought of the bank meeting in the morning. The pressure was on him and he didn't like it. But he was realist enough to know what was expected of him.

Ralph found himself with his hat, and the night air hitting his face. He walked slowly to the Simplex, primed it, spun the crank handle and the big motor roared into life. He got into the car and drove slowly out the winding drive onto the road, with a grind of chains. He was trying to think; he knew he had been outmatched in some subtle way by a shrewd brain. Yet he did not give up hope. The lunch. Of course, the lunch may have just been a polite gesture, an easy fall, something to break the journey down.

He dreamed that night that he was signing the wedding papers and Charles Pentland, dressed like an archbishop, kept saying "Of course, my boy, you understand that the *gefüllte* fish and the matzos must be raised as good Protestants, and that the children must change their name to Mollie." And Alice was dressed for tennis, and when his brother, Egon, dressed as a monk, asked her if she would have this Jew for a Cossack, all Alice kept answering was, "It's his serve. And do hurry up. We're playing in a doubles match in Pasadena tomorrow. It's his serve. It's his serve."

Toward dawn he slept and he did not dream—except for a moment before waking, and Alice was so kind and tender and wild and grateful.

The New Amsterdam–Manhattan Bank, and its neighbouring Chase, National City, and the other giants of banking, were all the banks of the oil and railroad and metal kings; of the houses of Morgan, Rockefeller, Vanderbilt, Gould and what a more worried generation was to call the Sixty Families, the Robber Barons. When Charles Pentland became one of the vice-presidents of the New Amsterdam–Manhattan Bank, the term "robber baron" had not yet been invented, the muckrakers were just starting to rake, and the trusts and combines were already being publicly whipped by one of their own, Teddy Roosevelt, who didn't lean too hard on the strap.

Ralph's son, Peter, as a child, used to be taken on Saturday mornings by his grandfather, Charles Pentland, to the great stone bank on Wall Street, and walk down the narrow street, holding his grandfather's hand until they came to an elaborate bronze and glass set of doors, and once past these and the Negroes in real admirals' uniforms, past great Roman tombs of marble and rare stone labelled *Cashier* and *Teller* (Peter used to wonder what a teller told) and *Notes* and *Accounts*.

Charles Pentland had a fine, pine-pannelled office full of sailing-ship models and animal heads and a stock-ticker which Peter rather feared as it used to leap suddenly into throbbing life and throw a long paper tongue into a huge waste-basket. His grandfather would read this paper tongue like a doctor, and frown, or smile, and then make phone calls to buy or sell or hold or deliver.

Peter thought of his grandfather, Charles Pentland, as a very important man. He was. Later, he was to discover that as a member of the Pentland family, he was delightful, noble, loyal, earnest, *and* grateful. For the Pentlands had come on hard times since they once owned clipper ships out of Salem, made the tea run to Canton, and (one must admit) had a hand in the deadly evil slave-trade off the Cameroons that wiped out entire tribes.

The main job of the New Amsterdam–Manhattan Bank was to focus the credits and monies and involved deals of the Copper Combine. Other banks were railroad or shipping or utility banks. The New Amsterdam–Manhattan was known as the metal and ores bank.

It took much pride in its great tombs designed as vaults and offices and business departments. It took pride in its old, Yankee names. Its faithful employees did not too often, as Charles Pentland joked, go off to Canada with a loose woman and a tightly packed bag. Its indoor employees were White, Protestant, Christian, and Satisfied. When, later, spoilsports and reformers remarked on this, two clerks named Kelly and Rosensweig were hired, and trotted out at the pressing of a button when someone hinted they did not employ anybody but good, pale Protestants.

This rigid loyalty did not, however, extend to avoiding business with one of the few brokerage houses of Jewish origin, Ravel, Melnick and Company, who had early organized railroads and metals, and had launched many major issues of great railroad and mining firms.

It was Ravel, Melnick and Company that helped the Copper Combine organize its raid on Pedlock Corporations. Old Melnick said it was something out of Balzac for one of the vice-presidents of the bank to have a daughter who had fallen in love with a son of the founder of the Pedlock Corporations.

Charles Pentland was seven minutes late for his appointment to lunch with Ralph at the Bankers' Club.

Ralph was waiting for him in the regal gloom and dulled good taste of the club fittings. He was standing under a mounted bull-moose head in the bar, listening to two bankers disagree on the proper ageing of Irish whisky.

"I am sorry, my boy," said Charles Pentland. "Bankers' hours have to be stretched a bit at times."

"That's all right, Mr. Pentland. It's a very impressive club. I was just getting up enough courage to order a drink."

"Of course." Charles Pentland waved at the white-haired coloured man behind the bar. "Two of my special Gibsons, Sam, not too dry."

"Yes, sah, Mr. Pentland."

"And have them brought to my table." He took Ralph's arm and steered him into the dim-lit dining room under its varnished rafters. He greeted a few men chewing chops over white tablecloths and showed Ralph to a small round table set against a screen full of furious Japanese warriors in desperate sword actions against each other.

"I don't say the club is the sort of place I would like to take you, but it's near the bank. And I did want to see you again. I like to have these things, relationships and all that, as man to man, brought to an understanding. Little enough tolerance and understanding in the world today, don't you think? Ah, the drinks. It's the little spiced onions that makes them. Yes . . . well, here's to you."

They drank and Charles Pentland recommended the T-bone steak, the hashed brown potatoes, the early tomatoes and red wine that the club bottled itself. "Fair, but imported, naturally."

"I'm not much of a drinker."

"Ralph, I was just talking about you this morning to Melnick, of Ravel, Melnick and Company. Melnick is always educating opera stars, or backing some artistic play from the Swedish, but he's a sound, foxy old Jew. I mean that, of course, as a compliment."

"My friend, Mike Ravel, is with the firm."

"Yes. His grandfather practically invented railroad stock sales. They think a lot of you, Ralph. We've been doing some business with them in the matter of forming a merger of all the big metal industries in this country. You don't know the chaos it's all in . . . but I guess you do."

Ralph pushed aside a fragment of steak, with the crested club fork. "I don't know too much. I'm not with my father's companies. I'm an engineer, as you know. Water projects and power utilities."

"That's the coming stuff. And if we can get the metal people together, this country would be, as it says in your Talmud—or is it Torah?—a land of milk and honey."

Ralph looked down at his plate and smiled. "It's also in your Bible, Mr. Pentland."

"Of course. The great Judaeo-Christian culture, all its ethics and moral code, is merely the flowing of one branch into another. Ah, my boy, you see I've been doing a great deal of thinking since last night. A man in my position . . . Yes—just let me finish what I want to say—sometimes, he doesn't always see himself clearly. That is . . . would you care for more wine?"

"No, thank you. I was thinking that——"

"Ralph, I've been overworked. This metal merger thing is one of the bank's big pet projects. It means a lot to me. Oh, not the usual material things in life, which naturally any sane man wants, but the idea of a good fight won, something done for his country, his friends. Now, you take iron ore or even copper."

Ralph looked up and began to count the Japanese warriors on the screen. *He had won Alice and knew it, now.* What the neat, dignified man was saying, across the table, what he explained in great detail, as they lit their cigars with the blue-and-gold club band on them—all that did not matter. The word "copper" was the magic omen, the talisman, the key to unlock the dilemma.

Ralph watched Charles Pentland carefully as he signed the club chit after adding up the figures twice. "Mr. Pentland, I'm sure I can't give you my answer right away, or that it will be the answer you want. My stock, while my own, is—well, part of the Pedlock Corporations family holdings."

"There is nothing I admire more than principle, family loyalty. Believe me, if this were a matter of a shrewd bit of trading, I would advise you against it. But damn it, man, I do feel strongly about this. A copper merger right now would make copper the biggest thing since the invention of the tin can. You would get new stock, two for one, in the Copper Combine, selling at a price higher than Pedlock is selling today. Am I right?"

"Yes, but it's under family control now. . . ."

"Of course it is. The family-controlled company was a fine thing, once, but I honestly can't recommend it any more. My boy, I shall be very frank. You have a great struggle to make. It must come from inside you. You are young, in love, have a way of life you want to follow. I may have shocked you by the bluntness of some of my statements, but I want my daughter to marry well. The Pedlock Corporations will be ruined in another year or so of expensive legal fighting. I can't give you my daughter, not on the salary of a water-pumping engineer. Also, I feel it only right—damn me, yes, only right—that my son-in-law be on my side. That is, if there is no harm done to anyone and you admit your stock will be worth four times what it now is in a year with the Copper Combine. I want you to see things from my viewpoint."

Ralph inhaled on his cigar. "No one in my family will ever understand my actions, if I vote my stock with the Combine's proxies."

"And if you don't? The Combine has Corey's stock to vote, and a great deal your brother Egon sold, and we're buying on the open market. We may still buy control into Pedlock without you and take it over, and you'd be nowhere. We're a proud family, Ralph. We aren't beholden, as my grandmother, Emerson's first cousin, used to say, to anyone. As my son-in-law, you'll have to act and think like a Pentland—see things our way."

A little thick, thought Ralph, but the honey was off it now. Charles Pentland was putting it on the table, in the open. Ralph could become a pretty good Christian, marry into a good family. The stockholders of Pedlock Corporations would gain millions in merger with the Copper Combine. Copper would be a tight trust, and prices would go up. Yes, he couldn't say that Charles Pentland offered a bad deal.

In the hall of the club, the coloured man in blue bowed and handed them their coats. Ralph and Charles Pentland walked out into the dusty Wall Street day. Dirty pigeons bummed along the curbs, among the hoodlum sparrows from Trinity Churchyard up the street. Ralph held out his hand.

"I'm leaving tomorrow for Europe. But you'll have my answer by noon. I used to know the full meaning of right and wrong but now I don't know. Everything was so black-and-white yesterday, and now it's all grey values, shifting and moving."

This was the longest speech Charles Pentland had permitted Ralph to make. He smiled, nodded briskly, and said, "I believe you're taking Alice to the opera tonight. What are they singing?"

"One of the Ring operas."

"Ah, well, I agree with Mark Twain, Wagner is better than he sounds. Good day, my boy."

Ralph stood at the curb, and the pigeons gathered around his feet, and he lifted his arm and shooed them; but they only fluttered their soiled wings and came trotting back to him on obscene pink toes. Slowly, Ralph walked up toward Broadway.

They sat late that night in a gleaming roof garden among many people in evening dress. They had not heard much of the opera; they had sat very close together and held hands and now they looked at each other and there was a taut understanding between them, a sudden feeling of the present moment, and the next day, and all the rest of their lives.

The waiter refilled the wine glasses. It was not a very good champagne, but they both gripped their glasses and Alice said, very low, earnestly, "We didn't make the world, Ralph, or plot all this conflict. We're just ourselves, the two of us. I've always felt that, since our meeting, nothing else would matter, and I still feel that way. I love you very much, Ralph."

"I know, Alice."

He stood up, took her hand, and said. "We're going to dance. And if I step on your feet, please forgive a poor engineer."

Neither one could talk in the beautiful poetry of lovers. Very few people can, or do. It did not matter to them.

They danced as close as the roof garden and polite society permitted. He took her home in an early flat-nosed motor cab, and he went back to his flat and had two very large whiskys and went to bed and slept like one dead.

In the morning he shaved, dressed, and was putting on his jacket when he remembered he had forgotten to take his cold morning shower. He paid his hotel bill, sent his baggage down to the Hamburg–American Line docks, and at eleven left for the boat.

Alice and Charles Pentland were there to see him off. It was a tall, high German ship with red funnels, named after some Teuton crown princess, and the sailors and stewards were very alert and helpful. He had a small cabin on B deck, and Charles Pentland stayed on deck while Alice went down to see it. Ralph held her in his arms and they kissed and then they went up on deck.

Charles Pentland, and Alice blowing her nose, shook his hand and they went down the gangplank and the little tugs seized the big ship and the dirty water appeared between the ship's steep side and the rough, wooden pier.

Colonel Louis Pedlock in Paris, later that week—on Saturday— appeared at Egon's at noon. He carried the Paris edition of the *New York Tribune*, opened at the Society Section. The Colonel said, "It's a damn funny place to announce stock market deals."

> Mr. Charles Pentland, of Pentland Village, announced this morning the engagement of his daughter, Alice Elizabeth, to Ralph Manderson Perry, of San Francisco, California. The Pentlands, a Long Island branch of the well-known Boston family, are . . .

"Perry?" questioned Egon.

The Colonel snorted, "Ralph Manderson Perry. It sounds like a name they put on things in a dog show!"

The family was not yet sure that Ralph was lost to them. But Louis knew how important it now was to have Egon hold on to his stock. And how sure were they of Egon?

The family always looked forward to seeing Egon. As the years passed, he became colourful and exciting to them, with his piped and fantastic, figured vests, his great, golden seal chains, his watches, his Greek and Egyptian finger rings. Even the cut of his too loose London tailoring helped to give his plump, round figure something of the colour of an exotic adventurer. His round moon-face, the thinning hair that clung to his baby-pink head, made him seem an odd, remote figure from the everyday events of American life.

Egon had gone boldly and bravely into the wilderness of impressionistic painting, the advance-guard poets, and the most interesting of the new novelists and writers. Egon was at home in Paris and London and Budapest, but like most Americans of the period who lived or travelled abroad, France and Italy were his special stamping grounds.

He was always starting a new magazine on the Left Bank, or supporting some movement in the *Revue Blanc* or *Figaro*, buying up the studio of a just-dead, impressionist painter, or ordering a new Italian car that cost more to keep up, with its motor troubles, its tyres, and murderous driver, than owning a full stable. He had an apartment in Paris just off the Champs Elysées and a villa above the hills of Florence that he never used, but which he kept because it was the proper thing for all young men who had read Pater to speak of their villa above Florence. He loaned it to Debussy or Gide or Valéry from time to time.

On the surface Egon gave the impression of a careless, witty, light young man, fluttering and listening to the great, near-great, the masters, frauds, and spongers of the early decades of the 1900's. He brooded over the crease of his trousers, the cut of his huge wing collar, the proper tone of his dove-coloured cravat, the tilt of his grey tophat. His Chinese dressing robes and his white Spode china tea-service were famous.

Two slim, rather badly bound books of French poems and Bonnard's lithographs for *Daphnis et Chloë* were dedicated to him. He was the hero of poor young men who could not get proper publishers.

He spoke of the "art of the dance", long before the Russians invaded Europe with their ballets. When they came he was there to greet them, to support them, to hire halls for them, to bicker and brawl with them and make up with loud, Slavic kisses, to travel with them and help untangle their involved personal and public lives.

"Dear Egon," said the second-best hostess in all Paris, "good of you to come."

"I had to come. I've brought two Americans."

"Those two there?"

"Yes, you mustn't frighten them. They're very brilliant. One is a novelist of promise," Egon said.

"And the other?"

"Oh, something important in the State Department. One of the bright young men."

The hostess tapped Egon on the arm with her fan; it was still a time when fans were a social weapon. "I would like a frontier type, Egon."

"I doubt if they are house-broken."

"Long hair, perhaps spurs. That will fix that Jewish duchess and her keeping Anatole France on a leash."

"Jews are coming back in fashion," said the dress designer standing behind Egon. "Young Proust is making a small splash."

Egon turned on the dress designer and looked directly through him. "I believe, madame, your tailor is here."

The Russians were much more fun and serious about their art. The ballet was in trouble and Egon went to a minor Rothschild.

"You understand it's the first sign of anything worth while out of Russia besides the novels," Egon said.

"I don't like Russians, Egon."

"I'm not asking you to like them, just given them money."

"I can see, young man, you aren't the business man your father is."

"Thank you, Baron Rothschild. This will see them through the season."

"Don't let them spend it foolishly."

"Of course not."

There is a photograph of Egon at Nice with the Russian Ballet. Egon in a summer straw—in white linen—and beside him, blinking in the morning sun, a row of pale faces doped with sleep and the remnants of a vodka orgy—Diaghilev, Bakst, Prince Volkonsky, Fokine, and Nijinsky.

That Egon knew Proust before his great book—*A la Recherche du temps perdu*—was of course something that the confessions of the period made clear, and the letters Marcel Proust wrote in his cork-lined room to Egon Pedlock will some day be published and give a clearer picture of what went into the great novel. Egon once owned the manuscript of *Du Côté de chez Swann*. Long before Gertrude and Leo Stein were "the famous free-lunch counters of Paris"—to quote Egon —Egon had bought an early Picasso. Leo once told Egon, "Gertrude is a *yente*, a rancid, Jewish shrew."

But there was another Egon, a secret Egon. This fat, good-natured dude and poet-feeder, this waltzing figure in the international art world, was a man of great integrity, and his tastes in art and literature were those of a great critic. His personal tragedy was that he himself knew he could never be a creative artist. He knew more about painting than Renoir or that wonderful Old Testament head, Pissarro. But he could not lift a brush to canvas. His mind was as keen as Proust's, his knowledge of the inner core of society, its little nuances, its secrets and habits and moods, was beyond that of any other European or American of his time. The true lives of Swann, Baron de Charlus, the Duchesse de Guermantes, he knew to the last detail. Yet he could not write a line of serious prose. Keener than his critical friend Roger Marx, he wrote nothing of value about painting. His letters are charming and full of petty details. His mind seemed to freeze to trivial things when he took pen in hand. Too fat to dance, too rich (only in credit, at times) to suffer for any art, not interested in his great love, he appeared to wander out his life in the fashionable hotels of Europe. He drank at the spas, served the best Chinese tea, made witty chatter and brilliant talk, and encouraged those lucky enough to suffer for a genuine art.

He awoke daily at noon, when he was in Paris, in his little white flat (he was greatly influenced at one time by Whistler's white period) full of discreet sunshine admitted, an inch at a time, by Eric, his valet. Eric was a former dancer who had broken his leg and now limped badly, a silent, blond shadow. He drew Egon's bath and rubbed the plump body for fifteen minutes to try to control its enlarging girth. Egon never ate breakfast. With his white gloves, swinging a slim cane, he went to lunch at some café, or to the Ritz, if there were Americans worth bothering with in town. Chez Larue saw him often. Small bistros, hidden little eating places, made their fortunes when he recommended them.

He loved Paris and only being a Jew kept him from shouting "*Vive le Roi!*" and joining the bigots and the Catholic Royalists. He liked to eat well. A simple white wine, a good red wine, and after-wards a crisp brandy to wash down the *sole Jonville*, or duck *Périgueux*,

and perhaps at the end, a sherbet *l'Ermitage*. He was an expert, everyone said, in the good vintage years for Motë and Chandon, and could
recommend a wine.

He wept easily. Even Mendelssohn's "Auf Flügeln des Gesanges"
would bring moisture to his eyes. He did not like Wagner's music, but
he went often to hear it, for all the best people paraded at the Ring
cycle and his friends liked to meet him in the lobby or go to a small
bar to have *café au lait* and *croissants*. His life was regular, settled, and
full of small pleasures, and he enjoyed many duties. He feared an early
death and was the victim of many doctors. His bowels bothered him
much more than his sexual problems and he had trouble sleeping. He
never went to bed before one or two in the morning. He had several
sure methods to bring on sleep; most of them did not work. But when
he slept he slept very hard. He had rare nightmares. When he did,
Eric would have to sit by the side of the bed bathing his head with
cold towels spiced with faint scents. He dreamed often that his mother
was dead and he could not find her grave, or that she was giving birth
to him in fearful agony and that his head was growing larger and
larger. . . . .

They were the two most fashionable doctors in Europe. A thin
German Jew and a fat French Jew. They sat Egon, naked, on the
white table and went into the next room.

The German poured two small glasses of a good wine. "Hot in
Paris for this late in the season."

The Frenchman looked at the wine to see if it was corked. "Nice is
very fine this time of the year."

"The North Sea yachting is more exciting. Tell me, are you getting
any results from the use of soda-water in colitis?"

"Fine results. I've bought two apartment houses. Ha, ha!"

They laughed again and drank their wine slowly. The German
polished his glass. "I'm buying paintings. It's a safe investment.
Nothing modern. Solid masters. Italians. Christs and saints being
tortured."

The Frenchman looked at his watch. "Dear me, I'm lecturing in
half an hour. After you, Herr Doktor."

They found Egon lying on the white table looking at the dusty
ceiling.

"Ah, Herr Pedlock. We've decided it's a serious matter."

"Most serious. You have a liver in a thousand."

"Bile ducts, remarkable, so large. But your nerves."

Egon nodded. "Yes, my nerves."

"Come back in three weeks. Bathe in tepid salt water, eat lightly, and no red wine. Please, no red wine."

"No red wine." Egon nodded.

Egon dressed and gave them a thousand francs each and walked carefully home holding his hand against his heart. He walked up the wide, white stairs very slowly. He told his valet to order a bag of salt.

"And get rid of the red wine."

"Was it the liver?"

"Yes, and bile ducts, and my nerves."

Egon, bathing in salt, felt youth leaving him and he knew that before he could catch himself and think it over he would be middle-aged. He thought often of death and came to the conclusion that it was something unfair, *and* rather vulgar.

He was part of a group of lost Americans, his friends said. Henry James in Sussex, Gertrude Stein on the rue de Fleuris, Whistler on Battersea Bridge. Later he was to be joined by T. S. Eliot and Ezra Pound and in the twenties by Hemingway, Tom Wolfe, by thousands of Americans at the bar of the Deux Magots.

Egon was always cheered up when the Colonel—Uncle Louis— came to Paris. He remembered him from his boyhood—Uncle Louis, who had been through the great troubles of the Pedlock Corporations, and now from Butte and San Francisco ran the mines and smelters of the family.

"The Colonel, my uncle, fought in Cuba with my brother Sam one of Teddy Roosevelt's Rough Riders and came out of it wilder and more Western than ever," Egon used to say. Middle age had filled out the Colonel's figure, chipped more of his teeth, and added to the length of his Buffalo Bill moustache. He never wore anything but suits made of heavy woollen checks by a Chinese tailor in San Francisco, cowboy boots, and a white Stetson. He was a famous figure in pre-war Europe (World War I), travelling fast, living high, surrounded by a bevy, a regular harem, of actresses, dancing girls, and ladies of the town. He laughed a great deal and talked with a Western twang, broke his grammar in the middle, and was proud of a red nose, a paunch in checked tweed, and an ability to drink anything or ride anything with four legs. Egon found it hard to remember that the Colonel had once been to Cambridge, had grown up in Philadelphia, and was a brilliant business man.

The Colonel always appeared in Paris suddenly, crossing on the Cunard ships in an enormous suite with sixteen boxes of his own cigars and a cloth bag of coffee beans. "The damn stuff them hombres drink in Europe and call Java isn't fit for a sheepherder's gut!"

He would appear at Egon's flat about ten in the morning, barge in past the shocked Eric, and shake Egon awake. "Get up, ole horse! It's the Colonel! Come to show you how to live good, clean American life!"

Egon was a low-vitality waker. At last he would focus his gummy eyes. And there the Colonel would be, cheroot sticking out under the Buffalo Bill moustache, his white Stetson flung across the room to hang on a Rodin group, and the loud clothes, the big man smiling at him, showing tobacco-yellowed, broken teeth. "Egon, you're gettin' fat. Must be eatin' high off the hog over here!"

"Colonel, I'm happy to see you!" And Egon always was.

"Very fancy place you have here. Looks like Liberty Hall in New Orleans, smells like it, too."

"I'll take your word for it, Colonel. How is everything with the family? How's Papa—and Mama?"

The Colonel set a fresh cheroot in his mouth and lit it with a wooden kitchen match that he ignited with a horny thumbnail. "Well, Egon, that's what I'm here to talk to you about. Things are in an uproar and gettin' worse. Ralph has us worried. Sam's comin' over here with his wife soon. Git out of that bed, boy, and let's go git some grub and whisky!"

"I'm gittin'," grinned Egon.

Eric was shocked, but Egon laughed and dressed in a hurry. Egon was no fool. He knew the worth of this theatrical figure, in its protective, regional costume, its hardness, integrity, and shrewdness. The Colonel was always fun; and while it meant for Egon the breaking of a few engagements, perhaps with the Duc d'Aumale, the Comtesse Diane de Beausacq, or Prince Roland Bonaparte, the stir he caused by escorting "an original" like the Colonel around added lustre to Egon's popularity. Egon might prefer Chateaubriand to Voltaire, or cause a season's laughter by saying, at Bayreuth, that Wagner was suffering from "Parsifalitis"; yet being the escort of the wild Colonel in his genuine Western tailoring and fittings was a good touch. Besides, the Colonel was fun, "even if a bit on the fleshpot side."

Egon and the Colonel had breakfast usually on a wide café terrace, and the Colonel had several big brandies, for, as he explained, "I like to sort of wash everything down with whisky. It's sure sanitary. Whisky kills germs. A Mex bronc breaker put me on the secret. A week after they buried that Mex, they had to take his liver out and beat it to death!"

"I always thought you drank because you liked it, Colonel," Egon said.

"I guess I do. But it's goddamn nice to have a medical reason for bendin' the elbow. Damn nice gals in Paris. My eyes been hangin' out on stems all mornin' just watchin' 'em wriggle their little rears. Too bad I'm a businessman or I'd devote my whole life to fun."

Egon coughed and politely changed the subject. "What's the matter with the Pedlock Corporations now?"

"Well now, son, as you know, the Copper Combine has been after us a long time. They've tried everything from burning our ore cars to getting freight rebates for themselves on every shipment *we* made on their railroads. Now they're getting ready to buy in on us. The ole game—if you can't lick 'em, join 'em!"

"But most of our stock is held by the family . . . or isn't it?" Egon felt a little panicky under his florid flowered vest; he had let a few shares escape him now and then. The time he had needed money to help the singers in St. Eustache Montmarte, or the little yachting trips among the islands of Greece with those fine chaps from Belgrave Square.

"Well, Egon—we're not sure Corey will vote his personal stock with us. He hasn't too much stock, but his Bishop has gotten hold of his soul and is pullin' it out of him and snappin' it back like a soft tongue, and scarin' him with fear of hell. And the Bishop is a friend of Ryan and Charles Pentland and the rest of the Copper Combine crowd. How's your shares, Egon?"

"Pretty bad, Colonel. But I've held on to voting control over most of it. I've loans against it, of course, and have sold a little outright—oh, say a third of it."

The Colonel's wise eyes rolled and he blew wind through his moustache and made rapid figures on the back of an old envelope. "Copper Combine is buyin' up everything on the open market. There's about twenty per cent of the stock sold to the public that nobody can really control. Our stuff in vaults and private family trusts. That leaves eighty per cent to fight over. If we can swing forty-five per cent of that, we remain in control. Yep."

"We've had—that is, the family has always had at least fifty-one per cent control of the stock."

"With Corey lost to us? And frankly, Egon, there's your brother Ralph."

"He wouldn't vote against the family, with the combine."

The Colonel tore up his envelope and threw the fragments onto the pile of small saucers in front of him. "That's what we'll find out. Ralph has kind of broken with the family. He's been huntin' in new pastures. Engaged to the Pentland gal."

Egon felt this a good chance to postpone talk of his own sales of some of his personal holdings. "Is that bad?"

"Don't rightly know, son. Joseph and the Philadelphia folk think he'll be all right. I'm a kind of sinful tough old bastard who has seen too many cards dealt from the bottom of the deck. I say we can't depend on Ralph. And if he should, well, vote with the Pentland bank and the Combine crowd . . . well, we'd be up S—— Creek with no paddle."

Egon shook his head. Business was such a dirty bother. "What does the Combine want?"

"They want a merger. One big, happy trust. Pure copper and all in one pile in their backyard. They'd pay us off two for one for our stock, and double its value in a year, I'm sure, and they promise to give us all fat, easy jobs on their board of directors. . . ."

"What's really so bad about that, Colonel?"

"I don't like trusts any more than Teddy Roosevelt! Also I don't like any strange brand on me. I like to git upon my hind legs and howl, a free critter and all my own range before me. I don't want to belong to any Wall Street mob, and jerk prices up, or use up the resources of the United States so somebody can buy up all them crumbly art treasures over here. And your father feels the way I do.

"I'm sure he does."

Egon felt a brandy wouldn't hurt him at this time. He sipped it and said, "Of course I wouldn't think of going against the family, and I don't think Ralph would either. Where is he?"

"Was on Long Island playing polo or tennis and actin' like he was a real native. Like one of those lousy Dutchmen that married the Barbary Coast whores and went society."

"Ralph will be all right."

148

"Somethin' eatin' off 'im."

"Nonsense. Can I show you anything in Paris, Colonel?"

The Colonel brightened and wet his lips. "Been here six times. Know everything this town has. Givin' a little cavortin' party tonight, with some real he-man folks I met on the boat. Little place near that big church full of them fancy *cocottes*. Whadda ya say?"

"Not tonight. I have to go to a concert."

"Great gals in that house. Taught me a song last time. Can't talk French but it sounds very good." The Colonel stood up suddenly and shouted, "*La ligne les bourgeois!*"

The waiters turned around, faces open; an Englishman ruffled his copy of *The* London *Times;* and a French family shook their heads and said something to each other about Americans. The Colonel shouted again, "*L'humanité je l'emmerde!*"

"Really, Colonel, it's too early to sing."

Egon felt it was a good thing it was so early and his friends were not about yet. He paid the bill and led the Colonel down toward the Ritz. "It's not really a song. I don't know what the girls thought they were teaching you, but it's pure filth."

The Colonel pulled on his Buffalo Bill moustache. "You sure of that? Smokehouse stuff, huh?"

"I'm afraid so."

The Colonel put his big thumbs under some of his longer watch chains. "Well, wash my mouth out and call me Cedric. A man sure learns things travellin' 'round."

Egon agreed and took him into a little place to buy emerald cuff links in heavy gold settings and a curved pipe with a gold band and an amber mouthpiece. Egon went home with a creeping headache and wondered how he was going to clear some of the loans on his stock in the Pedlock Corporations. The world was no place for a rational idealist, he felt.

The madam had a real military moustache and wore a small diamond cross around her fat neck. "You leave it to me. For Mr. Morgans' parties we once had a big pie baked and six girls, naked, put in it just before serving."

The Colonel sat back on the dusty sofa and nodded. "That's not bad, madam, but not naked. That's not classy. Just black stockings and garters and very high heels . . . eh?"

"The Colonel, I see, has taste."

"Make it ten girls. Redheads and blondes, and one with thick, curly, black hair."

"Ten it is. I'll have to hire extra porters to carry it in."

"Just put it on the bill." The Colonel got up and collected his Stetson hat and his heavy yellow pigskin gloves. At the door he turned. "And I'd be much obliged, ma'am, if you saw to it that the girls didn't have scratches on their behind."

"In my place, never!"

"Of course. Good day to you, ma'am."

After an orgy Louis was a dreadful sight for several days. He needed time and nature on his side before he again could walk and talk. But the morning after that night before, he came awake as he looked at a cable message pushed under his door; he drank much black coffee and cursed.

He wired Joseph at Baden-Baden to come to Paris. Joseph wired back he was coming with Rebecca, but they would have to go back to finish her cure. Besides, he felt sure Ralph would not sell them out to Pentland. He wrote a long, following letter in which he gave many reasons and Louis read it and figured stock lists on a small bit of paper and shook his head.

He wasn't at all sure he was right in his thinking. But Sam and his wife were on their way over. And Ralph was also on the high seas, it was hoped. Louis felt he could sit back and wait. Let Joseph talk turkey to Ralph. He got back into bed and ordered a guard to be kept on his door. He needed sleep. The world and Ralph and copper holdings and problems of business would have to wait till his head felt better. Was he getting too old for lots of things?

CHAPTER VIII

Shortly after the turn of the century, Sam and his wife came to Europe alone; the children were in a Berkshire summer camp with an invented Indian name, Winadu. Rebecca was ailing. She and Joseph were planning to return to Baden, where Rebecca could again take the waters. Joseph could try out his new-found voice among the birch trees and gravelled walks; among the *Grafen* and Russian gamblers and the stomach-rumbling health-seekers full of the ritual cant of German doctors and the reeking waters of the spa.

Joseph, with a sensitive perception of life, as his prime passed, was still a striking figure; the sharp, slashed beard of a Confederate horseman had been trimmed more into shape, but it still followed in style, Egon noticed, that painting of J. E. B. Stuart. The limp was easy and casual now to Joseph's walk, and the scars on the neck had sunken and taken on the colour of the rest of the skin. He was just a little above the battle now, a tight, fiery core of patience, still full of plans of fighting, full of ideas and counter-strokes to the Copper Combine. But Sam and the Colonel did the actual battle now.

Egon was shocked to see Rebecca in the Paris sunlight. Somehow she had always been to him the brisk, young frontier mother with no affectation or pomposity, yet active; bending over him, petting and scolding him, shaming him for his damp morning bed, so cold and reeking, tenderly taking him up in her warm arms, crooning to him in a happy, trancelike meditation the little songs of Jewish childhood, and protecting him and his little emotions from the glib attacks of his mocking brothers. Now Rebecca sat in the sun of a little Paris park near the Chinoiserie pavilion, her tired hands on her watered-silk dress, holding lightly to a sunshade, and her face, the face Egon loved beyond anything on earth, so traced with lines, that the thin, tender bones were almost thrusting through the nearly yielding skin. He was looking on death and knew it. No waters at a popular German spa would save his mother, and some glob of emotion singed his plump body with the numb desperation of new consciousness. He took her hand in his fat, healthy fingers, and everything that Egon felt filled his throat. A Sargasso Sea of secret feelings massed in his mind. No doctor had severed the invisible cord that led from his navel into the secret corners of her womb, this much-needed, cherished, still invisible cord. The cord that led to the only peace from the world he had ever felt, so long ago before his recorded life began. They two were infinity and eternity side by side.

Rebecca looked at him and saw his face twisted into the sad thinking of the giving and passing of life, the futility of all endeavour, the great book of the Jews had said. She pushed a finger into the pugnacious, of the giving and passing of life, the futility of all endeavor, the mockery of art and fashion. Vanity, all is vanity, the great book of the Jews had said. She pushed a finger into the pugnacious, melancholy face.

"Egon, how have you been?"

"I've been very well, Mama. A little too fat, a little too lazy, but then you don't expect me to build railroads or corner a wheat market."

"No, Egon, you be happy, you enjoy yourself."

"I'm so happy, I cry for joy. Mama, take care of yourself, don't take any grand tour. Just rest."

"I'm resting. And stop looking at me as if you want to put your head in my lap and cry."

As that was just what he felt like doing, Egon dug into the ground with his cane and watched his sister Selma come toward them, walking like a Renoir painting, her white-toed shoes turned in, the great flaring skirt of the period regulated and trimmed like the sails of a racing yacht. Selma was one of the "dark" Pedlocks. There were always "dark" Pedlocks and "light" Pedlocks. The dark ones, like Sam, showed the earnest Semitic blood, the curved faces of the Talmud students and the ghetto merchants and pleaders. The light Pedlocks were the genes of the farmers, the drovers, the adventurers and gatherers of all the breeds of passage; the ripening and mixing of many adventures among many races.

Selma, constituted of volatile stuff, was thinking of nothing like that, as young, graceful, her pretty face bent into a smile, she approached the bench on which sat her mother and her brother. There was an elegant fragility about Selma, hung on steel wires.

"I've met the most dreadful, wonderful man."

"Did he flirt with you?" asked Egon.

"He shouted at me. He's back in the hotel shouting at Papa and Sam and poor Sara. His name is Theodor Herzl and he wants us all to go to London with him. Sara is very impressed."

Egon frowned. "That damn Zionist nonsense."

"The Fourth Zionist Congress is being held in London." Selma was a great mimic, full of special nuances and images. She put her hands behind her back, took the stance of the black-bearded man, and in a deep voice said, "My dear Miss Pedlock, *Hierosolyma est perdita*, Jerusalem is lost, is only the cry of the mobs in the Dark Ages attcaking the ghettos. Nothing is ever lost. We Zionists are organizing Jewry for its coming destiny."

Egon shrugged his shoulders with debonair inconsequence. "These damn dreamers, stirring up trouble with their beards, acting more Jewish than the ancient Jews, wanting to go back to a broken Wailing Wall and a few dried-up Turkish acres. And then whining all around us—begging for money, so a lot of lazy old men can sit around in the ritual curls and prayer shawls, and make us different from our friends."

Selma mocked Egon with an attitude of audacity and sat down on the bench. "Oh, he's very impressive, and he doesn't beg. He commands."

"Like Moses asking the Red Sea to open, wider, please?"

Rebecca said, "Did Papa buy him lunch?"

Egon shook his head. "This is going to cost us a lot of money. We're Americans, why can't they leave us alone? The Irish in New York are badgered to help kick out the English. The poor, Hunkie slaughterhouse workers in the West have to send their pennies to get rid of a Tsar, the hungry Italians give candles and offerings so the Pope can have a new chair. I tell you, we Americans are being milked by every racial pleader and God-seller in the world."

Selma said to her mother, "Isn't it odd, Mama, how well-informed Egon is? I bet he's been studying the subject."

Rebecca lifted the shade to keep the direct, white sun from her eyes. "I've never seen you so worked up, Egon, unless it's over a painting."

"I can't help it. We've been a displaced, tribal people, and gone all over the world, and worked hard as Americans and Englishmen and Frenchmen, and been given freedom to do almost anything we want. Then these dark ones with the bearded rams' heads come around with their rancid Hebrew, and we're back with a pack of fear on our backs, running through some new political ghetto."

"The Russian Jews and the Rumanian Jews and Turkish Jews," said Rebecca. "For them a homeland would be a blessing. Nobody is sending a good American like you away from your beloved Paris."

"You're mocking me, Mama."

Selma laughed and stuck a finger in Egon's ribs. "Well, what kind of an American are you, living abroad all the time?"

"As good a one as Henry James in London, or Mark Twain in Vienna, or J. P. Morgan in his French castle. America can also be a state of mind. It doesn't have to be a little box of dirt like Chopin's

Poland. Anyway, Selma, what's a young girl like you doing with these damned Zionists?"

Rebecca said, "Egon dear, leave oaths to Louis."

"The Colonel," said Selma, "is certainly spreading his brand of Americanism high, wide, and handsome. He led a parade of cab drivers down past the American Embassy last night and offered to bring John L. Sullivan to Europe to meet all comers."

"Was Louis arrested?" asked Rebecca.

Selma grinned. "They are going to give him the Legion of Honour ribbon, I hear."

Egon, who had himself hoped for years to wear the sliver of red in his coat, said, "In return he can sear the mayor's rear with his cattle brand."

"We must go back from where we came," said the heavy face in its shrubbery of black beard, the great eyes flashing, the eyes of a domesticated leopard. It was a face with the beauty of long, flat bones and tight, austere nostrils on a polished, aquiline nose. "We belong in a land of our own, where the Jews can again live together as a people."

Joseph smiled and knocked ash off his cigar and looked at Sam and Sara keenly watching Theodor Herzl sitting across the table from them, with a close, direct attention. Joseph turned his deep, sculptured eye sockets and looked into the excited face of Herzl. "You forget that the world is made up of people, people with just labels on them. Take off the labels and they are really all alike."

Herzl shook his head. "We have been pushed aside, and are watched. They fear two things from us. The dreams of our brain, developed by the students in ghettos of the Dark Ages, and the power of our purse, which is all they permit us to fill."

Joseph leaned back and nodded. "They and we fear ourselves, and they and we look for someone to kick. But all we have to do is kick back. The world respects a proud dignity, an ability to fight. But a land, a special ghetto, some acres of sand with a Wailing Wall left over from some fragment of history, is not for me a great battle. I'm an American, my family is an American one. Me and my sons fought its wars, for they were our wars too."

"A special kind of American."

Sam said, his words pouring out, "So are the Irish a special kind of American, so are the Polish steelworkers, the Mexican field hands. You fall into the trap, Mr. Herzl—pardon me—of thinking England is all descended from Norman barons and Saxons; Americans, all family names who came to Jamestown and Plymouth."

Joseph shook his head. "My wife's great-great-great-grandfather helped settle Jamestown. Yet it doesn't matter *when*, but *how* we became Americans. Yes, Herzl, I'd like to see a place where the beaten, the starved, the oppressed Jews can have a little peace and safety. But I see it all like the Irish problem; all good Irish-Americans work like mad to free Ireland, but they're still good Americans. The Poles in Chicago support an idea of a free Poland and collect fortunes for it, but no one says they're bad Americans. They have died in American battles and done their duty as Americans. So you see, Herzl, I don't mind a Jewish homeland, but don't save any space for me. You can't even speak for the good of the Jews of the world. You must only answer for your own heart, your real pity for those who need refuge."

Sara looked up at her father-in-law with new respect. She had never expected such a speech from a man who just had gotten back the full power of his voice. Sam held her hand and grinned. Papa was in rare form.

Herzl made little balls with some bread crumbs and looked down at his dark, strong hands. "In the end you will be happy, even thankful we have made a homeland for you."

"In the end," said Joseph, "if I am to be pogromed or killed by bigotry, let it come in New York, in San Francisco, or Butte, or New Orleans. Let me go down fighting for the country of my own, free choice, and if it kills me, then, well, what difference is it, to die of intolerance in Kansas rather than in Jaffa? The Jewhater on the Mississippi can do as good a job as an Arab. You confuse values, Herzl, in your greatness of vision, your stern purpose. You don't see the problem clearly from all angles. You can't solve the Jewish problem by seeing only the Jews."

"I see that there is no real solution your way. Intermarriage will not work, for to work it must be accepted freely. It happens, but not often enough. The world opposes our assimilation.

Theodor Herzl was a little puzzled by Americans. He had been born Wolf Theodor Benjamin Zev Herzl in the Tabakgasse of Budapest. He was not amused when asked if the main product of the town was first acts (he shared the shame in the towns' weakness in second acts). He had been a student of law and had proudly left the Viennese *Burschenschaft* because of its anti-Semitic attitude.

But the law was cold and dishonest. Justice, what was it? But the richest nearest the judge; the loudest and the worst with the most influence. After all, he remembered Hungarians were supposed to be a nation of playwrights. Why not he? Berlin was as good a place as any to start. But he was only a fair playwright. The salt and spirit, the fun to be had with the bedroom and adultery (what else would you write a play about in Middle Europe?) were not for him. He became a writer of witty things in newspapers.

He went to work for the *Wiener Allgemeine Zeitung*—but continued writing plays. They did fairly well. Then came the Dreyfus case. His play *Das Neue Ghetto* was refused by all producers. "Give us the gay, tight-pants Hussars, the seductions in hayfields, Theodor, not the blasted Jewish question."

Playwriting could wait. He contacted Baron de Hirsch for a plan of political action. He started his masterwork, *Der Judenstaat* . . . "The Jewish State." He was a big, dark man with a cause now. Followers: Max Nordau, Zangwill, Baron Edmond Rothschild. . . . Mighty fine people. Rich, too, they could pay the way for his ideas. He must see the Sultan, the German Emperor, the Grand Duke of Baden. Get the order of Medjidie (third-class, of course) from the Grand Vizier. The First Zionist Congress at Basle. Busy. Hurry. A feeling he was going to drop dead in his tracks soon. Take time out to talk to rich Jews. Offer the Sultan a million and a half pounds for a charter to a colony in Palestine. Refused? Well, go on. . . . Raise more. See richer Jews. Joseph Chamberlain will help. Maybe the Belgian Congo will do? Approach King Leopold. A lot to do and his heart giving out. . . .

And here he was sitting in a café and Joseph Pedlock wasn't impressed. He listened to what Joseph was saying to him. His active brain was busy elsewhere. Thinking, planning. What had been done? What had still to be done? Rome. Audience with the Papal Secretary. The Pope. Nothing said one way or the other. Whichever way the wind blew Rome would take its time and follow. This new godhead in Rome, he thought, founded by the Jews. How new compared with the true Jews! The only race in the ancient times who had a real feeling for a true God. Letters to be sent off to Schiff. . . . And that ache in his chest. He would never see it now . . . *Der Judenstaat*.

He heard himself saying again, "The world opposes our assimilation."

"Why expect it?" asked Sam, the old man's son. "The American Indian, the Quaker isn't in such a hurry for assimilation. Your viewpoint, pardon me, Mr. Herzl, is European. America is big, wide, and rather new."

"We Zionists are a link between the ultra-modern Jew and the ultra-conservative Jew. It has never happened before. Zionism has done that. You see, our hope is to turn the Jewish question into something better

156

—the Zionist question. Zionism is a peaceful thing. But like all peaceful things, it is forced to fight. We suffer, therefore we are. We cannot be brushed aside because we stick out and bother the world."

"Ego! Ego!" said Joseph. "The Chinese in the hands of the Japs suffer more. The Hindus suffer more under the British, the intellectuals in Russia more than the Jews. The American Indians have been slaughtered like rats in a trap by clean, young Americans. Look at the centuries of blacks in the holds of the slave ships; look at the opium wars of England in their effort to drug half a world. Look at all the Irish burned, murdered, hanged, exploited. Hell, man!—pardon me, Sara—to say we Jews only stick up and bother the world is nonsense, because there are others. This isn't just a Jewish question; it's a world problem of why some people hurt other people. I remember seeing Chinese being buried alive in the railroad camps of the American West. I've seen dogs tear living Negroes apart. I've seen little children, eight years of age, in sainted New England cotton mills, dying young, their lungs full of lint. No, Herzl, I'm for you, but I'm for the whole world too. You can't cure blood-poisoning by treating just one leg."

"No genuine nationality can hide behind a strange mask. We are a nation—admit that much, Pedlock."

"We can be a nation, or, for those who want to be, merely a sect of American ram-horn blowers and Pass-over celebrators. I don't stop anyone being a Zionist, or an Elk, or a knight of Columbus, or a D.A.R. or a Bierverein Dutchman, but don't stick any fancy, peculiar labels on me and say you speak for me. I'll label myself."

"Palestine is of a peculiar nature. No spot on earth is like it."

"Bread is bread, no matter where it's made. A tired man will call a place where they let him rest, home. For the driven, the hunted, the tormented, Palestine is fine. If you can get it, some day. But I'm not going to worry over it for myself when I hold citizenship in something pretty wonderful. When my sons and their sons and their sons shall be able to point to their country's history and say we helped do this and this. We were peaceful, and we were warlike; we belong. Oh hell, I'm making speeches. But, Herzl, what you don't understand is that no one has an easy, fat time of it in this world—not even, I assure you, in America. They burned witches in Salem (all right, Sara, they only crushed them to death with stones), drove the Mormons west with fire and lynchings, slaughtered Mexicans, tarred and feathered thousands, stole from the Indians and from each other. So why should I feel they must respect me? I'm willing to fight, to work, to keep my own way of life and think my own ideas. All I ask is the room to strike back if I'm hurt, to be able to see a real jury decide things, and to re-member, no matter whatever comes, when bigotry and intolerance appear, that there is a Bill of Rights, even if sometimes they wink at it."

Herzl shook his head. "I am sure, Pedlock, that all who stand aside now and smile sadly at us demented ones will some day live in the beautiful houses we shall build."

"History is *anything* that can happen," Joseph said.

"You seem, Pedlock, pleased that you are tormented with the Irish and the Negroes and the Quakers and the Indians. It does little good to feel the whip is for everybody."

Sara suddenly found her voice for the first time. "There is no whip-thinking in America. A lot of good is being done."

"You will see bankruptcy of assimilation and soon the insolvency of philanthropy."

Joseph signalled the waiter for the bill. "You mean, Herzl, you'll stop taking my money?"

"What an insolvency is coming, for when the rich become bankrupt the losses are enormous. I am sorry if we appear full of arrogance, but philanthropic Jewish colonization, this talk of land in South America, South Africa, Lower California, it will all fail, but national Palestine colonization, that will succeed."

Joseph paid the bill and motioned another waiter with a box of cigars nearer. "You're a good man, Herzl. You talk of Jews as of Hindus or Eskimos. Mere labels. I talk of human beings. I'm sorry there is this labelling and that there is feeling that some labels are more evil or inferior to others. But still the best national colonization I know of is America. Even if some day, in the next hundred years, or thousand years, it fails. I shall be sorry, or rather my ghost will be sorry, but it will have been a great experiment. A cigar, Herzl? Sam?"

The dark man with the big black beard smiled at Joseph and shook his head. "Alms bind the lazy-rich to the lazy-poor. But looking at you, Pedlock, I see you were never lazy, so I know these two cate-gories do not represent all Jews. All I know is that I am right. It will come. Zion will be again. Even if not in my time. Wealth will not do it alone, for no one is rich enough to transport a race. An idea alone can do that."

"I like you, Herzl," Joseph said as the waiter lit the men's cigars. "There must always be men who think along certain, special lines, see clearly only one problem at a time. But this is a world of wolves. A world of great forces that will in time wreck—I think—what we call civilization. What if you get your little state? Can it stand up in the winds madly blowing in the world? Herzl, I think we must save *all* the world."

Herzl blew cigar smoke out of his powerful nose and smiled. "You said one problem at a time. I am not a unique man. I am just full of a purpose. There must be other men like me. In Ireland, in India, in Russia, in America. We can each save a little bit, and perhaps—who knows?—together we shall save the world. Thank you for the lunch, the charm of your company, and now good-bye."

He went off briskly across the dining-room floor, the big black head sitting firmly on the shoulders. Crisp, ringing steps showed the man was in a great hurry.

Joseph took Sara's arm. "It's a good thing there aren't twice as many Jews in the world. Poor Herzl would run twice as fast, talk twice as loud. Be twice as right, twice as wrong."

Sara asked, "Is he a great man?"

"A very great man," said Joseph. "He may even get his dream. It will be a good thing for a lot of people. But he doesn't see the whole picture. . . . You can't save a fragment, you must save the whole. But it's a good thing he doesn't see that, or nothing would ever get done in this world. Even that Jew, Christ, said on his cross, 'My Lord God, why have you forsaken me?' He knew."

"What did he mean?" asked Sara.

Sam took her arm. "He meant people aren't too helpful in saving themselves."

They walked down the street in the good, strong sunlight, the woman slim between the two large men, the hot city basking like a lizard. They passed a herd of English curates taking tea on a terrace and they looked in Charvet's windows on the Place Vendôme. Life flowed gently past them—they swam with lazy gestures against the stream.

Joseph smoked his cigar and said, "I hope I didn't give the impression to Herzl that my prejudices are hardening with my arteries."

A countenance of badly slacked rage passed them, muttering, "Zhid! Zhid!" It was, Joseph remembered, a time when the Dreyfus case still tormented France and all of Europe.

When Egon could not—or would not—show Sam and Sara a sensational side of Paris, the Colonel could. It was not the Paris that Egon was proudest of, but they enjoyed being taken, in the daytime, to the haunts of the *demimondaines*, to sit in cafés and drink a trinity, a tree-coloured, layered drink of *crème de menthe*, brandy, and gin. And one fearful night they went to the apache district near the rue de la Gaieté, a sorded, evil place, they were told, of brothel and café—a *chantant*—but nothing happened except that the Colonel lost his big gold watch.

Egon was talked into taking them to the *Cercle Russe*, a group of painters who held out in a cellar in Montmartre, where girls danced the *cancan* and the *gamines* wore tight skirts, bobbed hair, and no underwear. Egon took them to a *Sud-Américaine* dive and just before dawn, in another cellar, they heard *tziganes* play, and Sam and Sara felt they were part of the wickedest city in the world. They sent postal cards of churches to the boys in camp.

They finished the week with a trip to Medrano's Circus and had a brandy on the terrace of the Closerie des Lilas. Joseph came to see them off on the boat train. Rebecca was not feeling well enough to leave her room.

"Be sure you get Ralph to give you voting power on his stock holdings," Joseph said, waving his rolled umbrella.

"Don't you do no worryin'," said the Colonel. "You just go to Baden with Rebecca, and leave everything to Sam and me."

Sara was weeping on Sam's shoulder because she was so happy, and because she had seen the culture of Paris, and because it was such a beautiful day. And they were going to cross the Atlantic and see the children again. Sam was studying his cables from New York and brooding over the showing of Pedlock Corporations. It wasn't going to be fun to be back in a J. P. Morgan stock raid, and Joseph away at Baden.

"Don't worry, Father," he said, "we can always send for you if things get out of hand."

Joseph kissed his son on the cheek and his daughter-in-law on the mouth, and shook hands briskly—Western style—with the Colonel.

"Louis, you keep me informed."

"Bet your bottom ace on that"

Then they all waved and the French train made that silly little tooting sound all French trains make. Joseph was left standing in the great station under the iron beams and the glass roof. He walked out into the bright street and stood for a long time on the curb. He could go see Sarah Bernhardt that night at the Odéon, or eat at Le Duc, or go see the same damn pictures again at the galleries. Or join Egon at the rue Lepic and see that fellow's work, that one called Cézanne. But the idea of apples full of muscles, or even the sad paintings in blue tones by someone else didn't excite Joseph.

He saw himself in the passing mirror of a shop window. He stooped to look at the tall man, in the dark, baggy suit, the heavy, ageing face, the trim, greying beard, the rolled umbrella in the gloved hand with the coatsleeves too short for the starched shirt cuffs. Was this Joseph Pedlock? How did he get so old? And so tired-looking. It couldn't be that this was the wild boy from Vienna who had ridden in a circus, and fought as a Confederate Captain of Horse, and been full of wild juices and great fury and now had aged so. Where had the years gone to? So many years and nothing had seemed to happen. All that waiting in Michigan, all those years of fighting and turmoil in Butte. All those decades in law courts; he had accepted everything as merely periods of waiting until he could really live life fully, and with a fulfilment of culture and ease. Somehow, while waiting, old age had slipped onto his shoulders. It was hard to believe life could be so short.

He looked up at the crayon-blue sky, at the trees coming to lime-green bud, at the streets smelling of the best horses, and he went back to the hotel to sit with Rebecca. His children could have the full, easy, pleasant life he had missed.

Rebecca had found the hotel chair very low and comfortable. She sat in it much of the time. She was reading poetry again, a great deal of it. Joseph came in and just ran his hand over her face and kissed her cheek.

"You getting enough light for reading?"

"Yes, its just right. Leave the shade alone."

"They got off all right."

"Good. Let's have dinner sent up."

"I don't mind. What are you reading?"

"Poems, Joseph."

"We haven't done that since before we were married."

> "*Are they shadows that we see?*
> *And can shadows pleasure bring?*
> *Pleasures only shadows be,*
> *Cast by bodies we conceive,*
> *And are made the things we deem*
> *In those figures which they seem.*"

"Rebecca, that's plain morbid. I'll order a big dinner and cheer you up."

"Thank you, Joseph."

"Stop reading, the light is failing."

CHAPTER IX

They were back at Baden-Baden. The room, smelling of heavy German family life, was hushed, and the blood-red drapes drawn. The prints of Martin Luther and Prince Bismarck looked down from the rose-papered walls. Only the rattle of a carriage on its way to the fountains and the rustle of the fashionable people moving towards Mozart and Wagner in the bandstand of the town square were heard in the room. On the big bed lay Rebecca, and she neither moved nor groaned. Joseph had to make sure very often that she was still breathing. The big-bearded face bent over the bed and he made great efforts not to weep.

The doctor, that damn dandy from *Wien* with his *nein* and *ja*, with his spats and his little, blue beard, had been sure she would go slowly and painlessly. Addison's disease, *ja*, very painless, *nein*—what was there to do? But now she was sinking fast, and Egon and Selma were still in Paris and Ralph's boat still two days out of Brest. Joseph got up and crossed the room, sat down in the little balcony off the darkened chamber, and lit a stogie and pulled the blue smoke deep into his aching chest. The fine day, the first-cut flowers on the street corners, all the *Gemütlichkeit* of the spa seemed such an odd background for all this business of slowly slipping away from life. Rajahs, members of the Deutsche Bank, gamblers with faces from the *Kriminal Archiv*, all passed below the balcony and Joseph smoked his stogie. He was trying not to think, to weep, to brood, to feel the great pain inside himself. She was going—all else was sophistry and illusion.

Two fat, blond children passed with an English governess, all gnawing on *Bauernwürstl*, and cheerfully asking and answering each other's question's in traditional and prescribed phrases.

He tossed the stogie into the neat, Germanic patterns of the flower garden under the window. There was no doubt now it would soon. He had loved her (thinking already of her in the past tense!). He had loved her. Very much. He had been almost perfectly faithful to her. There had been a rare, frontier woman, and some casual tautness in sooty hotel rooms. A bigbosomed girl in Washington. But the truth was he had never cared for casual women or carnal adventures. Only Rebecca ever mattered. She was the only woman he could kneel to, could look into the eyes of, and feel that a bond, a spiritual and earthly bond, held them together. Always he had come to her in his troubles and doubts—to look into her eyes and take her into his arms and feel how foolish to look elsewhere. She was, he felt—thinking in Biblical language—the jewel of his life; she gave a glow and shine to his existence, and made the battling and the law courts and the frontier a fight for glory! Compared to other men, he had not known many women; he had never been a romantic sensualist, a wandering toucher of all available or eccentric flesh. He stuck pretty much close to home. It had been a delight, a satisfaction, and unlike many men, he had known for years what it would be like to lose her. The agony had come into his chest many times in the last few years when he saw her go limp, grown tired.

In the bandstand, by the fountains, the band was beginning a fragment of *Lohengrin*. Joseph could see the crowd from the balcony. The heavy, solid Germans, the visitors, the hikers with brown, bare knees—all gathered around, thinking, no doubt, of the music and the *Macht und Erde* it spoke of. Chewing *salmis de faisans* and drinking the *verdammte* water or dark *lager*. And on the fringe of the crowd were the invalids in their wheel chairs; paper-grey faces, lean and damp, the reeking breath of death already on them. They would scowl on the healthy walkers and drinkers and *Herren Studenten*. And over all poured the heavy music, and orders went out to the waiters, "*Bringen noch ein Glas Bier*." "*Und eine Zitronade*." "*Ein Käseschmarren*." And the dying in their wheel chairs no doubt would rumble the putrid spa water in their bellies and scowl again. Joseph turned away from looking at the bandstand. Life seemed dull and vulgar.

He went back into the room and pulled the heavy curtains closer.

"Joseph."

"Yes, dear."

He went over to the bed and looked down at the wasted face. The eyes were beautiful and the flesh had fallen away from them. There was little left to carry on the spark of life in her. He sat down and took the thin hand. The pulse was far away and only a ghostly thump.

"Joseph, I've been dreaming."

"Yes, Rebecca."

"It was Cape May and my brother, Simon, *olav hasholem*, had brought down a patient with a bad leg. A Confederate officer. What was his name?"

"Rebecca, shall I call the doctor?"

"It was you, darling . . . I remember now. . . . You were so handsome . . . and so tired and sick-looking. It was a sunny day and Louis

163

was a small boy who was always hurting himself. Oh, my heart, I love you so. *Ich bin ganz ab*," she added in German.

He leaned over and kissed the thin lips. "Joseph, what happens now?"

"Now?"

"Do we just blow out like a candle? Are we the flame, and the dance of the light is all there is to our life? Joseph, I'm cold."

He put another blanket on her. "I'll call the doctor."

"No, Joseph. It's good to be here alone. I wanted to see the children. But I've seen them so much and I love them so and they have wives and families and tender things of their own. . . . It's been a long time . . . since I held them to my breast. All I want now . . . Joseph, Joseph, are you there?"

"I'm here. See, I'm holding you in my arms."

"All I want now is you, Joseph. . . . All I can see now is that it's been a good life and we've been . . ." He wiped a little foam from the corners of her loose mouth. "When it all adds up . . . . I've been lucky. . . . Don't carry on and weep . . . just remember, Joseph . . . Joseph . . ."

"Yes?"

"I'm very tired . . . so tired. . . . Remember the Schiller we read: *Ich habe genossen das irdische Glück: Ich habe gelebt und geliebt.*"

Joseph repeated after her: " 'I have known earthly happiness: I have lived and loved.' Yes, yes, now, Rebecca—rest, rest."

"So very tired, a long time tired."

She sighed and turned her head and smiled and he felt her hand tighten in his. She had slipped away almost politely as if hoping not to make a fuss.

He could not move any part of his body for a while then he put her thin arm under the blanket and stood up and kissed her face and the tears scarred it as he wept over her, as a strong man weeps, silently, but heavy in his emotions. He did not call for anyone. There would be plenty of calling and rushing about and whispering in corners, but later, later.

Someone was singing Goethe's "Wanderer's Night Song" at the bandstand in the town square.

> *"Über Allen Gipfeln*
> *Ist Ruh*
> *In allen Wipfeln*
> *Spürest du . . ."*

He sat alone—very alone now—his face in his hands, and as the sun fell away and dusk came down suddenly, he began to word in his mind the cables he had to send.

The singer went on.

"Kaum einen Hauch;
Die Vögelein schweigen im Wald. . . ."

Joseph looked up and rubbed his face.

"Warte nur, bald
Ruhest du auch."

He must get an Embassy permit to bring her back to America, with the people she belonged to in that little Philadelphia cemetery. But first he had another duty. He found his hat in the hall and went out into the street. He must find a synagogue and a *minyan* of old men, to recite with them the prayer for the Jewish dead. He himself no longer believed in any Orthodox ritual or form of religion, but for her it could now do no harm. He needed the taste of Hebrew in his mouth and ears; otherwise he was a stranger alone with no one to mourn his dead with. . . .

It was a sad gathering of fragments of a family, in Paris—at Joseph's suite at a small hotel. Joseph, in black, the stern face under the beard now beginning to grow unkempt. The old man did not speak very much. He sat a great deal in a wide chair leaning on a heavy, black cane. Egon, also in black, a tailored black, his gay vests and strong-coloured ties gone, an Egon in pain and agony at the death of his mother, was also there. The cord had been cut at last. He was lost and adrift. The world seemed bigger, colder, and full of traps and shadows that he had never noticed before. He could not sit; he walked slowly from window to window in the suite, folding and unfolding a black-bordered handkerchief in his pink, fat hands.

Selma hovered over her father, her pretty face red with unfinished weeping, the ache still in her, but the maternal instinct, the care of her father and brothers, giving her something to do. She now brought in a glass of milk and went past Ralph and up to Joseph and handed him the glass. He did not protest. He took the glass and drank slowly, the rough-edged beard not moving as he swallowed.

Ralph watched him and sat very still on a thin, French chair with too much peeling hotel gilt on it. Of them all, he was the most nervous. He kept his tautness under control, but every word or thought showed

the shaking muscles under his skin. There were times he felt like screaming. He had been a great screamer as a boy. He would lie down, stiff
and enraged, on the floor, and close his fists and open his mouth wide
and scream. But there was no use in doing that now. Mama, for whom
he screamed best, was gone. There was no one now to scoop him up
and hold him close and wipe away his tears and tell him to please stop
screaming. "Please forgive Mama if she was wrong." So he sat, balanced
on a flimsy chair, waiting.

They looked at him often, all except Joseph, as if they wanted to
shout at him, speak to him in anger, as if ready to talk him out of
something they disapproved of. But their mutual sorrow kept a sort
of unspoken set of manners in operation on a certain subject concerning
Ralph. He was thankful for the respect one paid the dead.

Joseph put down the glass, and Selma wiped his beard, the corners
of which were stained with milk. "When are we sailing?"

"The twenty-third," said Egon, refolding the black-bordered handkerchief.

"Everything is taken care of?"

Selma nodded. "Yes, Papa, the permits have come through."

"Where is she?"

"On the way to the ship. We leave tomorrow afternoon on the
boat-train."

Egon mopped his brow and looked at his hankerchief. "It's dreadful, dreadful. More almost than a man can take. The futility of everything. The shortness—the brevity of happiness, of time."

"Put your handkerchief away, Egon," said Joseph, crisply, "and
spare me the prose passages. Take a drink if you need it."

"Later. . . ."

Ralph got up and went towards his father. "I would like to talk to
you, Papa, if I may."

Joseph looked up at his son. "Not now, Ralph. There is plenty of
time."

"I would like to say some things—something that has happened."

"Save it, Mr. Perry," said Egon curtly.

Selma turned toward Egon, in tones shockingly like her mother's.
"You stop that, Egon. There isn't going to be any baiting of Ralph.
Ralph is old enough to do what he feels is fit for himself. He's grown
up."

"And foolish."

Ralph shrugged his shoulders and went back to his chair. Joseph
pulled on his beard with strong, long fingers. "I'm sorry, Ralph, but
it's no use talking to me now. I'm numb. What is between you and

Sam and Louis—you settle to your own satisfaction. I can't take part in any business talks right now."

Ralph carefully turned on the creaking chair. "It's rather important, but if you'd rather wait——"

"Settle it with them. Louis and Sam know what to do."

Selma patted her father's shoulder. "I'm going to my room to lie down. You try and rest, too, Father. Please take some rest. It's very stormy out at sea this time of the year."

She went out. How like Mama she sounded! Egon began to pace slowly from window to window. He could hardly believe this was Paris, the old beloved Paris, down there in the windy street. The people, the cafés, the traffic, and the subtle odour of leaves burning, and fresh newspaper print, the river odours of hay barges, the smell of horse dung. The sound of carriages and buses, the clatter of vans, the murmur of waiters and the crystal laughter of women.

He had floated all his life in a world of petty pleasures; art studios, little books, poems, ballets, the over-refined pleasures of taste and culture. He had been happy in this world, balanced in it. Now he knew that the balance had been his mother at all times. A short trip and he could always be with her, sit by her side, hold her hand and tell her all the new, witty things and explain all the fresh, fashionable savours of life.

It was amazing what a confidence in life she had given him. He loved the family, but for his mother it was something stronger—something more primitive and almost, he supposed, dangerous. Some secret strength suckled from her. Some powerful spell that tied him to her because of the machinery of birth. Something distilled from knowing she was alive and on earth. That made him the gay, bouncing figure sure of himself and his world. Now, that was over. He would have to go on only with her memory. He reached for his handkerchief, but he had dropped it. As he turned to look for it, he saw Ralph staring at him. He had never seen anyone as frightened as Ralph was at that moment. He felt a sudden pity for his brother. After all, Egon was not the only one to suffer a deep loss. Joseph was dozing now, leaning on his cane. Egon crossed the room to Ralph's side.

He spoke very low. "Let's go for a walk."

"You think we——"

"Papa is dozing. Come on."

They tiptoed out of the suite and under new, black hats walked slowly out into the street and down past a row of young trees set in small circles on the concrete sidewalk.

"I'm going to get married," Ralph said, looking directly ahead.

"Yes. Very fine family, the Pentlands."

"Alice is a wonderful girl."

"They always are."

Ralph touched his brother's sleeve. "This isn't what you think— ordinary."

"I'm a little unstrung. Let's have a drink. I'm sure you see marriage properly. Sorry—forgive me."

They sat down outside a big gay café and a waiter with a slight limp brought them apple brandy. They drank and sat watching the people pass and the limping waiter pivot around the tables to spare his bad leg. He was very skilful at it.

But Egon was looking down into his drink. Ralph settled back in his chair, wallowing in his misery. He knew now how a soft-hearted criminal felt, even an undiscovered criminal. A great load that he could not put down, a great load crushing him on all sides. And no one wanted to know or cared if he put it down or not.

A blind man with a battered fiddle stood at the curb playing an addled tune; two little girls in white head-dresses and carrying their beads passed, followed by their parents in stiff, churchly black. It was certainly odd how life did not stop for anyone's personal tragedy.

Ralph's voice broke the texture of Egon's thoughts.

"I'm thinking seriously of turning Christian."

Egon looked up at his brother. Ralph could not be serious. "What are you talking about? You have a religion. God chose it himself and talked to his people about it. If you must have a religion."

"I believe we Jews can only be accepted if we go along with Christ. He was a Jew."

"Don't remind too many Christians of it, Ralph. Notice how Nordic his pictures have become? Besides, as Heine said, 'If reason offends you, become a Catholic.' "

Ralph became angry.

"That's very unfair to some very fine people, Egon. Besides, I'm inclined to the Episcopal Church. Now that Mama is gone, there isn't anyone that would be hurt."

"To you, I see Judaism is not a religion, but just bad luck. Well, I hope you're right in thinking a dip into baptism is a card of admission into certain society."

"Don't be witty, Egon. It's all pretty painful to me."

"You really should read Heine. It will save you a lot of brooding. 'To a thinking man, there are only two cultures with real roots. The Jewish and the Greek.' Christianity. I remember him once saying, was

Judaism run divinely mad, a fine religion but without a drainage system."

"I don't care to hear any more of *that* sort of thing!"

"It is a beautiful dream," Egon went on, "not attached to life, but a soul cut adrift from the body and sent floating through space, when it can at best be only a captive balloon. Of course, one shouldn't take one's ideas of Christianity from modern Christians. The Jewish mission, if you want one, is to really convert the Christians to the true teaching of Christ."

"I hate this kind of talk, Egon. You spoil something a lot of simple people need in their lives."

"And unsimple, too. Look, Ralph, when the world is ruled by justice, by kindness and by brotherhood, the Jews can shut up shop and become Holy Jumpers, Yogis or teacup readers. But, at the present time, there's no discharge in the war. You can't send your Godhead out, like the laundry, and want it back, tomorrow, dyed the new popular shade. You'll find that out if you become a Lutheran or a Jesuit. Or even if you become like the only truly great Christian since Christ, St. Francis."

"I can see now, Egon, you don't believe in anything."

"I do. I believe in the Something that made us. That gives us that beautiful thing—life. I am thankful for beauty, life, small pleasures, and eyes to see it all with. I have a code of decency, of morals. I am a man and this is my world. Everything around me is God. The good and perhaps the evil. The world is soaked in God. God is soaked in me. So, you see, I do believe. Not in pomp, ritual or ceremonial, pope or rabbi, but I believe in God."

Ralph stood up. "I don't think we should talk of it any more. We're miles apart. I shall make a good Christian. Do you think the family will forgive me?"

"I can only answer for God, not the family," said Egon. "When the great Jewish poet lay dying he said, '*Dieu me pardonnera. C'est son métier.*—God will forgive me. That's his business.' I hope Papa is as kind," said Egon, letting Ralph pay for the drinks—"I really hope so."

Eric, Egon's valet, was entertaining a friend in the kitchen. They sat at the plain table and ate and drank, smoking Egon's best Russian cigarettes. Eric's friend had red hair and large ears and wore a chipped moon-stone ring on his left hand. His nails were none too clean.

"I don't suppose you'll be going to Monte this year, Eric?"

"Worse luck, no."

"Have to put on weeds for the old lady, I suppose?"

"She was a good sort, ponied up when we needed it badly."

"Leave him anything?"

"A bit, I should think. Try this lobster tail."

"Too fishy for me. Well, losing a mother is pretty serious. Broke me all up for a year. Fred couldn't stand it at all. I suppose it was the worst time I ever had. That year."

"You still carry the fearfully ugly urn of her ashes with you?"

"No, lost them when I let the flat go. The Bishop was ordered to China you know, suddenly. The bottom just fell out of the world."

"Don't like China?"

"Too much rice for me."

"Fred and I liked it."

"*You* and Fred . . . *well* . . ."

CHAPTER X

The old man with the stern, square head was seventy years of age and just a little over. He had a bad cold and was drinking whisky—not for the cold but because he often, now, drank himself into a stupor. J. P. Morgan hadn't been down to 23 Wall Street for some time. He liked to sit in his red, velvet chair in his fifty-million-dollar library (he didn't care for books and read few of them) and play cards with himself under Madonnas in labour or suckling infants. J. P. Morgan sniffed down a tumbler of whisky, and played a few cards. He remembered he had once given the city a lying-in hospital, and he was amused at the talk that he had tried to fill it himself.

The year 1907 was a hell of a year to be in America, the old man felt. Europe was much more fun. Rome, Florence, Aix-les-Bains and the yacht *Corsair III* (the other two were gone now—like memories; the orgies and the women and the drink on them). He would always be thankful, anyway, he hadn't missed the Cowes Regatta.

Copper. Copper. The damn copper people were a pain but a good excuse for a panic. He shook his huge, diseased nose. The Copper Combine had been fighting for control and now needed his help. Some fools outside the Combine had tried to corner copper. One of the minor copper companies even had a bank of its own. How they all hated to be gobbled up!

He had been in Richmond, as an elder of the Protestant Episcopal Church, in its General Convention, when he was called back to untangle the copper mess. A run on a copper bank had started. The bank wanted clearing-house aid, which was the same as asking for Morgan, and the hell with it! Let it fail! *Let* the Copper Combine pick it up cheap. The panic was on. Let it whirl.

The butler opened the door and Charles Pentland came in and stood waiting for the old man to lay down a card. J. P. sniffed again and re-filled his glass. He appeared to be in a stupor; an old man with eyes like an eagle's, hooded and red. He did not ask Charles Pentland to sit down. Charles Pentland did not expect it.

J. P. Morgan growled himself into life.

"Well, Pentland?"

"The break has started."

"Everybody running for cover?"

"Yes. Investors, speculators, bank depositors."

"Panic?"

Charles Pentland looked at a hairy, goat-legged rape of a golden goddess on a Lefebvre Gobelin tapestry. He thought of the castle the old man had in France and his French mistresses, and all the gossip about his orgies. Yet he admired him. Morgan didn't cringe and try to salve himself into heaven by saying, "God gave me my money," as old John D. so coyly did. J. P. wouldn't let God run 23 Wall Street, he thought. God was good enough to make the heaven and the earth. But in the matter of stocks and trusts, God's heart wouldn't have been in it, Charles Pentland felt.

"Panic?" repeated the old man, sniffing.

Charles Pentland nodded. "It appears so. The Knickerbocker Bank is hard hit. It will go under unless we help it."

"Why should I? Let it sink. That damn Western copper crowd has been fighting the Combine long enough."

"There will be talk."

The old man grinned. "Let 'em talk."

"They'll have to close their doors at about two, tomorrow. The Secretary of the Treasury is coming up from Washington to look around."

"I'll see him. We've organized a committee of bankers. All have submitted to me. I'll have full control of all appropriations to save the banks."

Charles Pentland nodded. It was as simple as that. Not only was the old rip precipitating the panic, but he was going to kill off all rival banks, and consolidate anything he wanted to save into the Morgan orbit. And there he sat in a stupor of either whisky or old age, or the effects of a bad cold. He could hardly speak above a whisper. All the credit banking of America in 1907!

Charles Pentland said, "Westinghouse has failed. The Pittsburgh Stock Exchange has suspended. Western banks are pulling out their deposits from us."

"The New Amsterdam–Manhattan will come out all right," said the old man. "Bigger than ever."

"We may have to close the Stock Exchange. Shortage of funds."

"Never! Twenty-five millions will pull it through the day. Announce that I'm sending that over. I don't want it closed one minute before three today." He took out a paper cigar-holder and inserted one of his long, black cigars. Charles Pentland watched the old man puff the cigar into life. Then the smoke drifted up the red silk, damasked walls, patterned with the arms of the Chigi family of Rome. The polychrome ceiling sucked and whirled the smoke and blew it into the eyes of the fifteenth- and sixteenth-century Florentine paintings.

The old man came out of his stupor again and opened one eye, an eye with the inner lid of a hunting hawk. "U.S. Steel is going to get control of almost all the iron it can get in the South. The firms that handle that stock are failing, and we can get it if we give them credits. Judge Gary will have to move fast. They'll sign. I'll be there myself."

"One of our partners has been issuing statements that the *Times* carried. A statement in which he said, 'The sore point in the panic is the Trust Company of America.' A big run has started on the bank."

"Well, he can always deny it later, when it will do no good. Frick is in Washington hog-tying the President for us."

"He's breakfasted with the President. Mr. Roosevelt said to him he would, to quote his very words, 'interpose no objections' to the way you were handling the crisis."

The old man made a thin line of his mouth. "That goddamn Rough Rider has his uses." The old man threw away his cigar and his whisper tried to become shrill and banal, in some imitated tones— " 'Walk softly, but carry a big stick!' What side is he on? One day here, the next day there! Selling out his class one week, giving us his oily support the next!"

Charles Pentland nodded, but said nothing. The old man leaned back in the red velvet chair. The butler brought in a pot of coffee and poured a cup. There was no other cup. Charles Pentland had not expected there would be. He had not been offered a cigar, either. He was still standing.

The old man sipped the coffee. "And get the copper situation cleared up once and for all. This panic should be just what the Combine ordered."

"I think so."

The old man dismissed Charles Pentland with a roll of his head. When he was alone again, he put down the coffee cup and picked up the cards.

The ship carrying the Pedlocks home hit high seas the first day out. They screwed down portholes and strung life lines to the dining room and the salons and chartrooms. No one sat at ease on deck and drank eleven-o'clock soup from politely offered small bowls. Great green wings of water washed against the portholes, and the people who came to the dining room ate little, and held smelling salts to their noses or talked of special remedies for seasickness. A smell of spilled gastric juices filled the ship.

The Pedlocks ate, with a mere feeling of duty to their health, at a small table by themselves. Late at night, Ralph and Egon walked the decks with glowing cigars in their mouths, but during the day they just sat in the saloon and read or looked at old magazines and books that had made the trip too many times. Joseph leaned a little more over his cane. When Selma felt dizzy the second day out, he took her to her cabin and put cold towels on her brow and when she turned green and said she was dying, he held a huge, white enamel pail for her to vomit into. She felt the ship roll like something out of Genesis, drawn by Doré.

It was now Joseph's turn to take care of her and he dressed her and undressed her, and fed her with a spoon, and washed her when she was ill. He remembered her as a gay little girl in Washington, he and Rebecca walking behind her as they passed the White House. She had wanted to go in to see the President, because she wanted to see what room she would take when Joseph was President. She was a bright, alert child with a will of her own, and it had taken a lot of talk to keep her from invading the White House right then and there. We are the dreams of our past, he thought, and memory is where we hang our childhood.

He looked at her pale, green face and kissed her brow and the smell of her was like the little girl—long ago—ill in a hotel room, and the doctor talking about the infected ear. And Selma clinging to Joseph and shouting, "Don't let them cut off my ears, Papa! Don't let them cut my ears off!"

She looked up at him now. "Poor Papa. I'm all a mess."

"You'll get better. It's hard to believe but people always do, from seasickness."

"I feel so sticky and smelly."

"Just lean back, and I'll get you some hot soup."

"No more soup. No more anything, Papa, that can roll around inside you and splash."

"A little white of the chicken?"

"No food, please."

She put her arms around him and he held her close—the young girl flesh—and the miracle of reproduction overwhelmed him. He and Rebecca had done this, had created this young woman, had set free the generation of hoarded genes, had carried along the process of nature and had at last seen her reach womanhood. He and Rebecca had done it. Now his time was also growing shorter, shorter. Selma, in turn, would mate, bring forth nature's miracles and pass on, and the whole mysterious cycle would go on. The world growing older and older, almost before his eyes. He could smell and feel it. The sides of the ship were oxidizing into rust slowly but surely. The wood in the ceiling moulding was turning to dust, the paint was peeling. The whole cargo of people on board was decaying, developing illnesses; organs, limbs, arteries were aging, hardening. Germs were gnawing at them all. Everything was being destroyed by time. The great engines were wearing out slowly, a little bit each minute; the paper in the saloon magazines was turning yellower. The Captain's dog was so old now he could hardly walk. The flags on the masthead were losing their colour and flapping away into rags. All around was the sad process of decay and the dusting away of everything.

And far below, in a lead-sealed casket, was Rebecca—somewhere under rusting girders near the gurgle of the bilge and the rat tracks and the groan of sucking pumps. Some place deep in the cellars of the ship, packed with casks and boxes. Forgotten, merely an item of cargo: Rebecca. A skin of steel kept out the sea; a hull of weed and barnacles. Over her the engines beat time; the kitchens hissed and boiled for the messy process of digestion. Over her, the people would stop, would dance when the storm would clear. The busy stewards run with trays of drinks. Lovers would hug each other behind the lifeboat. Over her in warm, steamy cabins, men and women would get drunk and make love, would lie naked and close to each other, and gulp at pleasure. Other and more fearful things would happen in the layer upon layer of solitary little rooms, packed like beehives, over the lead-sealed casket that was Rebecca.

He could think no more along these morbid lines. He must stop this kind of brooding out of Jeremiah and Ezekiel. He went to the dripping washboard and wet a fresh towel and brought it back to the bunk and placed it around Selma's brow.

"I feel a little better, Papa."

On deck, there was a clatter. The deck stewards were opening up the deck chairs. The grey colour was gone from the sky. The sea had stopped clapping green fists across the screwed-down portholes. The storm was ending. . . .

They buried Rebecca in the little Philadelphia cemetery on a rainy afternoon, with a blooming of wet umbrellas over the brown clods of clay. The Philadelphia Manderscheids were there. The widow of Doctor Simon, her son Louis, and her daughter Deborah, and her many children. And Sam and Sara and their three boys. Off to one side stood

Ralph. And Alice Pentland under a fashionable brown veil, gloved hands, holding an umbrella. Joseph stood very tall, listening to a brash young rabbi, an earnest, red-faced young man with a pair of gold-rimmed glasses, as he read from a wet little book, with a slight mashing of his rolling R's.

Joseph leaned over on his cane when the gravediggers threw in the first shovel of clay; then he turned away and began to walk briskly towards the first carriage, where the wet horses were steaming in the drizzle.

He sat that night in Aaron's dining room, remembering his first visit there so many years ago; the thin, wounded officer with the bad leg, and those wonderful old Jews, the popular Rabbi Sontag with the stylish manners, and the gaiety of the evening. Now everything had grown old and dim. The house smelled old. The wallpaper had faded. They all ate in silence and, later, Sam and Louis spoke to him in the dimly lit living room. The old-fashioned gas fixtures overhead were like brass antlers of great metal deer.

They spoke in low voices a long time. Then they sat back and looked closely into Joseph's face.

"Where is Ralph now?" asked the old man.

"Gone back to New York with that *shiksa*."

"He's going to marry her, so be respectful to her, Louis."

"He's also voting his stock with the Combine crowd to help merge and destroy our companies," said Sam. "I can't understand it. Ralph doing this to us."

Joseph said, "This isn't the end of the Pedlock Corporations. He and Corey can leave us, but we'll buy on the open market. We'll keep control."

"We can't afford to buy a million shares on the open market. Everyone knows the Combine is after it."

"Louis, Sam, keep buying, mortgage everything, get loans. We'll beat off the Combine."

"We may ruin ourselves."

Joseph shook his head. "I never took a licking sitting down. We'll lick the Combine just once more."

"Look, Papa," said Sam, "if I found Ralph and talked to him . . ."

Joseph rose and took hold of his coat lapel. "I didn't tear my clothes—the way the old Jews did—to show my loss when Rebecca went. But it is our custom when one has a loss to tear one's garments." He took the lapel and ripped it with a brutal, tearing sound. "Now I have no son called Ralph."

BOOK FOUR

When Jacob Kozloff first saw Selma, the daughter of Joseph Pedlock, he thought of the Song of Songs, and said to himself, "Moshe Rabenau, what a girl!" He was not a man who made a study of literature. He ran a sweatshop on the top floor of a decaying old building on Division Street, New York City. The building was owned by a fine, fashionable uptown church, very busy with its missions in Africa, and therefore it could spare nothing to improve life on Division Street. In the cellar of the building, an old Polish witch mixed cucumbers and green tomatoes in rancid barrels full of vinegar and spices. She marinated, pickled, and smoked odd organs of cattle, imported fish, and was famous for a black, wrinkled olive called *maslinas*. On the ground floor, a jackleg plumber displayed a porcelain toilet bowl in a cracked window, and up above him there was a small, neat brothel and gambling house, run by an Italian, aided only by his wife and two nieces. Then came a floor of dark, windowless caves called railroad flats with many beds that were never cold; for two sets of boarders used them—a day shift and a night shift. And under a tin-and-tar roof, stained with pigeon dung, the hell known as "Jacob's Shop".

A large, dirty room with the obscene ribs of the lathing showing through the cracked plaster, a water paint of a dismal green fighting through the rain and bug stains. A series of swinging gas fixtures, rusty and badly crippled . . . a long platform at which Jacob and an Australian Jew called the "Starker Glitz" (the strong Galician), stripped down to their pants and dirty, long-armed underwear, swung huge, gas pressing irons, and in the steam and banging of their pressing boards, put creases into the ready-made "Classy Clan" garments of the great Kahn-Wesserman, clothing empire. Facing them was a rusting stove standing on a mound of cold ashes and bricks, and on top of the stove simmered and stank old pots boiling potatoes, tea cans, crusted lunch pans, and two sour nippled bottles of milk for Hannah the baster's baby, a ghastly, filthy child that lay on the floor on a bundle of lining trimming.

The windows were always nailed close to keep out the cold in winter and the heat and dust in summer. At some clattering over-repaired sewing machines, two men and two women ran a hard-fought race, sitting down, pedalling all day as they rushed the needles across the heavy garments of Kahn-Wasserman suits.

Jacob was a contractor—a small-fry, independent sweater. Twice a week he and the Starker Gitz loaded themselves like horses, under great bundles of finished suits, and went down to Canal Street, to the Kahn-Wasserman main plant, to collect the fees for sewing together the suits. Paid, after much figuring and lamenting and shouting, they staggered out under two fresh bundles to be sewed together and pressed into shape. Two desperate men staggering along past the Italian women, groping their way into Kahn-Wasserman with *their* bundles of jackets into which they had sewed those "handmade" buttonholes that the firm was so proud of.

Everyone—except Kahn-Wasserman—struggled. Times were hard. Mouths had to be fed. The ships were pouring in eager, hungry hordes. Jews, Italians, Hungarians, Slavs, and all the depressed, desperate peoples of Mittel-Europa. They would work for very little, they would bang their guts out, push 'em up and lay 'em down, go blind sewing buttonholes, dolls, flowers in their dark kitchens. Work night after night, struggle on icy streets under their miserable contracted bundles, happy to be given the chance to get a few mouthfuls of food, pay rent on their bedbugged, rotting, dark, insanitary hovels—listed in the rent-rolls of great real estate trusts uptown as "paying property".

The poor Russian Jews were the worst off. They did not dare lift their eyes level with the earlier-settled German Jews. They humbled themselves and bowed to the German Jews, who had come over as early as 1849, and fought in the Civil War, and spoke a good English, and ate pork "till the grease ran". And shaved every day. . . . Kahn-Wasserman was one of the giants of the ready-made clothing industry, but times were hard, credits tight, and many others were now in the business. So, naturally, they paid the least they could to their "sweater" contractors and made no effort to investigate the living and working conditions of this mass of hungry and rather dirty-immigrants that turned out the neat, cheap, two-pants suits of their popular labels . . . "Randall's Rage", "Style Sure", "Brumell Bond", and belted "King Kollege."

Jacob Kozloff had been pushed off a dirty Hamburg-American boat at Castle Garden with his sister, Bella. They had a silver dollar, a bundle of rags, and no great amount of shoe leather left. The dollar was taken from them the first night. They spent it in a barrack in an Orchard Street cellar, with the sticky damp coming through the insect-filled sacking they slept on. Men and women and soiled children all together, any one slapping the nearest howling child. In the morning, they went out to pick up some of the gold that grew on the sidewalks of New York.

Jacob and his sister Bella, young and earnest, were without food for three days, then German-Jewish charity gave them grey oatmeal, stale bread and a blue milk, and deloused their heads. Bella got a job stuffing dolls' bodies with straw. Jacob moved newly repainted, shoddy furniture on a pushcart across cobbled streets for a second-hand dealer in anything. "Cheap John Is My Name and Fame."

They moved from the cellar to a room without windows, but they got enough fresh air running daily to the toilet in the yard. Jacob got up at dawn, put on his prayer shawl and tied the little boxes of holy writ to his arm and brow and prayed, "Hear, O Israel, the Lord is our God. The Lord is One."

Bella, a large red-headed girl would curse him for waking her up and ask him when God was going to drop roast larks into their mouths. Jacob never answered her but went on with his morning prayers. He was God's true man and wanted no special favours, unless the Lord was in the mood.

"What are you thanking God for?"

"For his blessings."

"A fat lot of blessings he's given us. Sour bread and dirty herring, and not enough sleep in these bedbugged rooms to close one eye."

Jacob bent over and prayed louder.

"Enough making with the mouth. Let's think of some way of filling it better."

"In time."

"In time, he says! It's going to drop through the rotten ceiling!"

"We are lucky to be here."

"To you, Jacob, it's lucky. I wouldn't keep a rabbi's goat here".

"You want to go back, Bella?"

That closed Bella's mouth for a few moments. They had no desire to go back. Secretly they suffered and secretly they hoped to better their lot here. No Russian village could ever hold them again.

"Come on, *yente*," Jacob said as he kissed his prayer shawl and folded it. "We'll be late for work."

"Work! Everybody running, everybody whining, and everybody hoping to get rich. Oh, for a little peace and a little fun."

"Fun is for the rich."

"Why, where is it written that way, you rabbi?"

"So don't get rich, Bella."

"All I dream of is a pair of silk stockings and a man to admire them.

A drink of brandy, a little dance music, people happy. I'm human, Jacob. Who's going to live forever?"

"Not us, if we don't get to work."

Bella did not stuff dolls long. She put up her hair in the American fashion and dragged Jacob to a night school, mangled the English language, and got herself a job in an overall factory. Running a heavy, blue denim through a Singer sewing machine for the railroad gangs of Irishmen—herded like cattle—who were putting down the silver rails that were bringing the nation closer and closer to itself. Jacob became a presser. He stood in cloth-burning steam and ran a small, flaming battleship over wet cloth and then hammered in the steam with—beg pardon—a heavy wooden ham. He cursed, he sweated, he stood ten, twelve, sixteen hours a day during the season at the ironing board. He did not collapse or go insane. He suffered. He saved up a few dollars and on Sunday evenings he would fill a basket with cheap candies, balloons, Japanese fans, and climbing monkeys, and stand on the street corners of the East Side and peddle his trash for a profit of twenty-five cents or less. Thousands lived like him in an agonizing clot of misery: exploited, confused, yet hopeful.

In two years Bella was a mighty fine lady, making her eight dollars a week. She was smelling of cheap but powerful perfume, and her frame had filled out into alluring curves. She did not value herself, Jacob feared, beyond rubies; she was a laughing, sporting gal who went Sundays to Coney Island with the foreman and shop bosses. Drank beer at the popular German beer gardens and wept over the stage melodramas of the time. She could slap a man down or sing a popular ditty, and as she explained to Jacob, "Always the lady, you understand. Bella isn't going to live forever, so a little fun—what's the diff. I'm not a *tsaddik*—a saint—but I'm not dead yet either."

"Belle, this *meshuga'as*—madness—of yours, is it respectable? A girl, a good Jewish girl, should be married by now, not going around with sporting Yankee alrightniks."

"For the worms he wants me to save it!" Bella would shout to her mirror, pinning up her flaming hair, ready to go out for a night of beer, cards, and some Jewish Art Theatre. She loved *King Lear* on Third Avenue, with those pale Rumanian actors who appeared later in the evening in the cafés wearing makeup and fur-collared overcoats, and who spoke in deep, rumbling voices: "Max, another glass tea. And, if you please, one of those strudels, without flies this time."

And if they sported a gold tooth, Bella shook with passion.

In two years, Jacob and Bella had saved up two hundred and six dollars. They bought on credit, a credit and interest to break a *buba's* store teeth, four sewing machines, second-hand machines, repaired so often that the seller bragged, "On my mother's grave, there ain't no original part left in 'em. Like new, only better. Use 'em in good health."

They rented the Division Street loft, added some cracked board partitions, a cheap pressing table, some gas-fired pressing irons and made a deposit to have the gas turned on. Bella knew one of the sporting foremen at Kahn-Wasserman, maybe not a real, true-blue gentleman, with his pinching and groping, but they got two dozen suits to work on, their first week. From a flea-filled chicken market where he was plucking and tearing chicken guts, Jacob got the Starker Glitz. The Glitz was willing to starve for two weeks, "for free", to learn the pressing trade. "Who needs to eat, with free-lunch nickel beers?" Bella found two girls who could sew and baste. Hannah had a green baby and a husband in Colorado coughing up his lungs. Tessie had no teeth and you had to thread her machine for her, but she knew a million stories and would sew and mumble and talk and talk and come in Mondays drunk as a *goya* on St. Patrick's Day. But she didn't take full-scale pay either. The two old men were broken ghetto crumbs, leftovers from the days of independent and skilled craftsmen. Chaim was a strict old Jew who had left the cabinet and furniture business because he had to work on Saturdays. The Professor was a big, white-haired old man with a battered face, the nose flat as a *lotka* pancake, and two of his fingers were badly broken and twisted. He was the village atheist type, an earnest reader of Marx, Whitman, and Tolstoy. He had been beaten almost to death by troops in the Chicago Pullman strike. He mocked the high holidays and ate ham sandwiches in front of the *schuls* on Yom Kippur ("*Nu*, another beating, so what?"). He marched under big, noble-worded banners in May Day parades. He gave a lot of his pitiful earnings to widows of strike victims, and, at least twice a month, tried to organize the union in Jacob's shop.

The Professor was always being fired after one of his organizing periods, and in a few days, tired, hungry, desperate, and yet proud, he would come back to see if he could "please, Mr. Boss—to fill an old man's mouth—have my job back". With his union record, no other sweatshop operator would have him, and Jacob would wipe the steam from his face and give him one more chance. "But I tell you— one word of the brotherhood of man, out you go, you *paskudnick*!"

Life was hard. All day they ground the machines and pressed and sewed and basted, and all day the old house shook and the baby stank and the stove heated its sickening messes of food and drink into warm garbage. All day the sweat rolled off them, their limbs moved on automatically, their mouths went dry as cotton—and they poured unsweetened tea into themselves, rushed through short lunch periods of spoiled beef and sour pickles and heavy, soggy corn bread. They belched and groaned, turned white as the bellies of flounders from lack of sun, and went on.

In the season they worked through half the night—until the boarders under them would knock on the ceiling with broom handles, and the fat Irish cop would come up, his flat feet slapping the broken stairs, and Jacob would drop a soiled, folded dollar bills into his cupped red fist and tell him, "Pat, go buy yourself some good cigars, you *momzer*."

After the gas had burned a few hours, yellow and pale green, the machines would come to a stop. The men and women would stretch themselves and wipe the lint from their eyes and mouths and drink a last mouthful of cold tea, distasteful as horse urine. Hannah would diaper the baby and feed it from a thin, slack breast spotted with flea bites. Tessie would comb the lint deeper into her hair and flutter a shabby coat around her shoulders and go hurrying off to the saloon to sup off the free lunch, and have two whiskys and stand around hoping to be treated. Tessie was a disgrace to her race, everyone said. The Jews were not drunkards. A drinker, a guzzler, a *meshugvina* tank like Tessie was rare among them.

The Starker Glitz would blow wind through his steam-scalded mouth and fall asleep on the rag bundles in the back room. He had no home and was termed a "watchman" and slept on the bundles of lining trimmings that were saved for the junkman.

Bella and Jacob had a railroad flat two houses down. Two bedrooms and a cockroached kitchen.

When one turned up the light suddenly, the insects would be discovered holding a union meeting, and they would rush off, their antennae waving. Bella stood every night in a tub of warm water heated by a quarter-devouring gas-meter, and scrubbed herself and put on her "glad rags", as she called them, and was off someplace with her gents and sports. A large Rumanian actor who used a pale face powder, and had crisp, curly black hair, and owned a cane besides a fur-collared overcoat, was telling her she must play the Queen to his Hamlet, some day. When he laughed, two gold-jacketed teeth shone like the Temple in all its glory.

Jacob sometimes washed in what remained of the hot water. He tried to read a yellow journal, but before he knew it, he was usually grubbing with a small pencil stub on the newspaper margins, his head aching, troubles multiplying, and his shop ready to collapse at any minute. The panic of 1907 was in full fury over the land. The Morgan banks in their stock raids and the railroad battles had brought the country to its knees. It begged for mercy from the money king.

Jacob knew nothing of this, and if he had, would have cared less. In a foolish moment, after a good season's work, he had once bought two shares of stock, talked into it by a glib Lithuanian Jew, who had a cousin who had an uncle who was connected with a Wall Street firm. Jacob had bought a share of something called Coastway Gateways, and a share of Pedlock Corporations. Coastway Gateways had been a scheme to get gold from salt water. Pedlock Corporations had had an interesting history, Jacob found out, when the share fell away in value.

The Pedlocks, fighting the Copper Combine, had begun to buy up their stock in the open market, for control. At a loss, the Combine had let them buy thousands of shares and then they had started a huge selling panic. Pedlock fell to 60, 57, 43. Jacob sweated over his one share of stock. At 27, the Pedlocks, desperate now, figured that the stock was going to hit bottom, so they began to sell short thousands of shares, selling short stocks they no longer held. But the Combine merely started a huge bull market movement in Pedlock stocks. Up it boomed again . . . rising high. The Pedlocks could not cover or buy the thousands of shares at the new prices that they had sold at 27. It was now 82½ and rising. They were ruined. After two days, with their agents, Hodges and Clayton, waiting, hat in hand, in the outer offices of the New Amsterdam–Manhattan Bank, a settlement was made. The Copper Combine swallowed the Pedlock Corporations. The Pedlocks, ruined, escaped with their shirts, but little else.

There was a lot of scandal talk, and "conspiracy to control stock prices" was shouted in the yellow journal Jacob read, but he did not follow it. He had sold his share of stock as it sank past 37, taking his loss and promising never to listen to a Lithuanian Jew again. Bella said, "Everyone knows that in the old country, they lack pots and eat out of holes in the ground!"

The sewing machines were not paid for yet. A note for two hundred dollars was due on them, on the first. Two months' rent was past due and the fashionable, property-owning church uptown was pressing him to move. The brothel and gambling house on the second floor was expanding again and wanted to take over the entire building as a *pasta* factory. Kahn-Wasserman had cut the price on a finished dozen seven cents. Thousands of ghetto tailors were unemployed.

Jacob turned over on his bed and buried his head in his strong arms and groaned himself into a deep sleep. He awoke once when Bella came in, singing softly to herself, "I love my wife, but oh you kid!" He went back to sleep and got up early and remembered it was Saturday and that he did not run his shop on the Sabbath. He said his prayers, made a cup of coffee and left a cup of it at Bella's door, and went out to the store-front *schul*. A *minyan* of old prayer-sayers was already there, the dusty Torah open and the Portion of the week being read. He was called up and read his section, about Mount Sinai, "where God spoke to Moses".

CHAPTER II

Late in the afternoon, Jacob left the dusty *schul*, after exchanging greetings with Nathan, the mattress restuffer, a solid, bearded citizen who always ended all meetings, Jew or Christian, with *"L'shana haba' a b'Yerushalayim!* Next year in Jerusalem".

"L'shanah haba'a b'Yerushalayim," mumbled Jacob, even though he loved America and already had his first papers out and was going to found a dynasty here. For all his struggle and debt, he had no interest in Jerusalem. Not a hard-working American like himself. Let the Irish moan for Ireland. He liked it here.

In a dining room on Hester Street he had a bit of fried fish, good Jewish fried fish that is prepared for the Sabbath on Friday—fried just right and cooled overnight and served crisp and brown. "Pity the man whose wife couldn't fry fish," said Bella.

It was growing dark when he came out of the dining room. He walked slowly down to Canal Street and over to the Kahn-Wasserman plant. It was a huge, grimy, red-brick square, very grand. The solid, gilt, three-foot letters on the roof read: KAHN-WASSERMAN— *The Label for the Well-Dressed Man.* Mr. Gittelman, a sporting man who played cards well, had a waxed moustache, and a second-generation accent, was in charge of the local sweatshop contractors. He was seated at his desk, feet on the flat top, smoking a cigarette in a dark, amber holder.

"Ah, Kozloff, why the hell were ya two belts short in the last batch of tweed coats?"

"Maybe they weren't put in the bundle."

Gittelman did not remove his feet from the desk. "Damn ya greenhorns, the first thing ya learn to do is lie. I'm charging ya for those belts. Ten cents each."

Jacob looked down at his work-worn hands. "Mr. Gittelman, I can't keep going with all this taking off for this and for that. It isn't right. We don't lose things at the shop. Who's got room there to lose anything but the heart and lungs, sweating over your suits?"

"Oh, now we're sweating ya? Maybe ya don't like contractin' for us. Go to the *goyim*, then. Let Brooks Brothers or Finchley's or Wanamaker's give ya the stuff."

"I'm sorry, Mr. Gittelman. Things are bad for me—very bad for

185

me. Don't pay no attention to me, what I say. The price of two belts isn't gonna save me. I'm *kaput*—finished."

Gittelman threw away the cigarette. He looked up at Jacob and remembered his own father, his back permanently bent from the heavy bundles of women's dresses he carried all his life.

Gittelman was not a bad man. He was neither evil nor of too great an intellect. He took a little advantage of his power to give or keep work from these desperate immigrant Jews. Perhaps he barked too much, took a healthy, male advantage, a little, of their women. He was himself too close to them not to understand their agony, their brutal effort of survival.

He took his feet off the desk and turned towards Jacob.

"Bad season, huh?"

"Haven't paid the rent in two months."

Gittelman pointed to a huge bundle wrapped with white manila rope, in a corner. "Vests. Double-breasted. It's a fad. Piped edges. Some English actor brung the fashion over. Ten dozen. Fifty-two cents a dozen."

"Piping. It's like making an extra vest."

"You want it? Don't ya do us any favours, Kozloff."

"I can't ask the shop to work for that price. They gave ninety cents a dozen last year."

"That was last year. Don't bother. Finkel, the *krimmer*, will take it, and kiss his crooked fingers with pleasure."

Jacob went over to the bundle and tried to pick it up. It was very heavy. He braced his legs, with long practice, skilfully balanced himself and muscled the bundle onto his back.

Without speaking, he went to the door. Gittelman was refilling his amber cigarette-holder. "It's white piping. Keep it clean. What kind of pig farm ya running?"

Jacob went, bent over, down the hall and up to the front doors. He opened them slowly and let himself down the few steps to the sidewalk. He shifted the bundle a little bit and, suddenly off balance in his anger, he fell. The bundle rolled toward the curb and would have fallen into the gutter running with muddy water if two young ladies had not stopped it with their white, gloved hands. They had just come out of the richly decorated private offices of the firm.

"Thank you," he said. "It's heavy."

"Have you far to go?" said the dark, beautiful one.

"Up Division Street. A few blocks."

She turned and said to her companion, "Sara, doesn't your father deliver these things for them?"

"I don't know the procedure."

Jacob swallowed hard. A plague on his clumsiness. This must be old man Wasserman's daughter, who had married into that fancy uptown family. These German Jews didn't like the sweeping of Russian ghettos brushing against them. "I'm sorry, ladies. Thanks".

The dark one smiled again and held his arm. "The car is here. We're going uptown anyway. We'll drop you and your bundle. Mind, Sara?"

"Not at all." She seemed amused at the dark one's Lady Bountiful manner.

Sam Pedlock, at that time, was the owner of a Franklin, a rather top-heavy machine with leather seats and red running gear. A man with an Irish coachman's face, wearing a linen duster, got out of it now and put the bundle in the front seat and motioned Jacob in beside him, with a gesture that showed he thought Jacob smelled bad and belonged in a cage.

The two ladies got into the back of the car, and they all slowly started uptown. In the corner of the small mirror on the brass-bound windshield, Jacob could see the beautiful dark one looking at him.

Selma Pedlock saw a broadly built, young man, not as tall as he might have been, but solidly made. He had very curly brown hair, disordered now, and hanging in front of his eyes from the effort of struggling with the bundle. The face was even, regular, with a good, solid blade of a nose, a small, thin, good-natured mouth with little, even teeth. She liked him. A Russian Jew. Ignorant, dirty, and whining, and a beggar, most likely, like all of them. But behaving himself.

She had the proper prejudices of her class against these tattered Jews. They were not making it easy for the cultured and refined ones of the race; their huge, brawling broods of children, their odd and rather disgusting habits of clothes and worship. Very ritual and bearded, most of them. Really something out of the Middle Ages, like Shylock, or Dickens' Fagin.

The young man peering at her through the windshield mirror, of course, was not so bad. If he had been barbered, bathed, and neatly dressed, educated at Rutgers or Columbia, mannered, who knows— he might have made the grade. She might even . . .

"How far up Division Street?" asked the driver.

"The next corner. Thank you very much."

Jacob got out and dragged out his bundle, and nodded a thank-you to the ladies. The car went off uptown in a cloud of smoke. He stood

187

at the curb, the bundle at his feet. He had no idea who she was, but a relative of the Wassermans, no doubt.

And those who only saw a dirty, sweating, garment-district Jew were wrong. To his other worries, he could now add a bigger one. A fire had been lit inside him. Love. It was better—they all said—in the old country. You got a marriage broker and found out what man had a, cockeyed daughter, or someone even perhaps a little bit, just a touch. pregnant, and you made an agreement over the *nadin*, the dowry. In the end, you were a married man and raising children and loving them, and thanking God. But no, Jacob felt, as he shouldered the bundle, he, the fool, had to suddenly fall romantically in love with someone he didn't know the name of and would never see again. Like the time he made a fool of himself over those intellectuals in the Russian village, and almost killed himself. This was going to hurt, too, and a lot.

The next day, after the cursing and the protests over the piped vests and after a hot day pounding the pipings with the big, gas-pressing iron, he went down to the *schul* and found Mottke the *shadchen*, the fattest of all the marriage brokers, who seemed to boil his clothes in pure chicken fat.

"Mottke, what have you got in stock? Just asking, for a laugh—you and your brides."

"Business that bad?" asked Mottke, chewing on a match end.

"A man has to marry sometime. Maybe in five years I'll need you."

"In Rahway, there's a junk dealer. A millionaire, must be worth not a cent less than a hundred thousan'. Got a girl. Let's face it, thirty already, but a regular princess. Never put a hand in cold water. *Nadin* of five thousan' dollars. Half, almost, before the wedding."

Jacob thought of the dark beauty in the car and groaned inside. A fine time he had picked to tap his sensuality. "No, Mottke, too fancy, and a little too long on the vine. I'll wait for something practical and a good housekeeper."

"Long Island fruit stands and grocery stores. Fine people. *Glitz-yaners*—Galicians—with a girl that cooks and sews. Young, too, a little gimpy in one leg. Two thousan' dollars."

Jacob shook his head. "I'll talk to you again, Mottke, in a few years."

"A lively Magyar girl—gypsy blood, of course, but exciting, owns a tearoom on Sherman Square. Or a widow of forty in the Catskills, a fine hotel, real pine trees, kosher cooking, fine boarders—two grown daughters."

"Such bargains I *schenk* you!"

Jacob shook his head and went home and lay down on his bed. All he could see was the dark one. Jacob was a ghetto dreamer and didn't know it. His past had caught up with him.

Jacob Kozloff had not always been a sweatshop operator on Division Street. He had been born Yakov Kozloffsky in a mud village beyond the field of Kiev, a second-grade subject under a proud and ignorant Tsar. He was born in the Pale, that part of the country set aside as a Jewish ghetto. A boggy, stinking series of lanes, with leaning houses, and lamenting wives, and hungry children. And rickety old men and young men (yellow from lack of sun) sitting over their learned, tattered books, while their wives and mothers stood in the market-place with naked feet and sold fish and fragments of cloth. And screamed at one another and at their customers, the drunken, dirty peasants in their matted sheepskin coats, miserable creatures like themselves, living out a desperate existence.

Yakov remembered, as a boy, his first ritual fringes worn under his shirt and hearing the old men chant, "Hear, O Israel, the Lord is our God, the Lord is One." And Saturdays when the Sabbath *goy* came to light the straw under their pot of feeble soup—and the spiced dishes of the great holidays in the ghetto.

He often stood in the decaying little synagogue, his ritual ringlets growing long over his ears, himself wrapped in his long prayer shawl, and he sang out *Kadosh* three times consecutively in the mornings of the three festivals—Passover, Pentecost, and Tabernacles. He helped read the Portion of the week, for the five books of Moses were read through once a year. The Scroll was intoned by his neighbours, first by a man of Aaron, the High Priest (his uncle, Shmeral, who sold a fair, fat herring), then a Levite (either his father, or Fat Yankele), and then five ordinary Israelites (the peddlers, the butchers, or the *bat-agoles*, who drove the wagons into Kiev but who were not suspected of eating *treif*—unkosher). Yakov also liked the reading of the Prophets, those tortured, shouting men who thundered and cursed and ended on a note of sadness and a peal of exultation.

Three or four times a year, the Jews gathered, everyone and his family, and celebrated. Yakov helped dress the synagogue with flowers on the Feast of Pentecost. Roses, lilies, narcissi, and pansies (when they could bribe the royal forester and gardeners), oak and pine leaves and beautiful weed of the ditches when they couldn't. Then came the Feast of the Tabernacles, when wooden booths were erected in the dirty, packed courtyard of the synagogue, in commemoration of the days when the Jews lived in tents in the wilderness, true pioneers in all their glory. Green branches and fruit hung there, and on the last day, Yakov and the children were allowed to eat the grapes and the apples, if they could be afforded that year.

It was a time of the synagogue's being filled with palm branches, with the boughs of willow trees. All the men prayed and shook and pointed themselves like vessels of flesh and spirit, first east, then west and north and south, and then toward heaven, straight up past the rain-stained ceiling. As commanded in Leviticus, Yakov had a small wooden box lined with white wool, and in it nested a citron, that wonderful fruit of the Holy Land. On the Seventh Day, Yakov had a bundle of willow branches *Shaines*—with which he whipped the benches, and his sins fell away with the leaves as he shouted, "Hosanna save us now!" The Ninth Day of Tabernacles, when the very last Portion of the Pentateuch was finished, the boys scrambled for sweets and nuts on the synagogue floor, and Yakov led all the rest.

Yakov grew up loving and fearing his God, giving him the respect and the ardour of a good Jew. Outside the ghetto there might be blood-letting and men with broken heads. The Tsar, the Cossacks, the drunken peasants might kill and break them, but in the glow of the red, faded Torah covers, here Yakov felt one with the universe. God arched over him like a golden bowl. He coloured all life.

Purim came in time, the feast to celebrate Queen Esther's redemption of her people from the wicked Haman. The boy Yakov went around with a false red nose, in his mother's oldest rags. The fun contrasted with the celebration of Jewish redemption, Chanukah, or the Dedication. Candles were lit by the family—one on the first day, two on the second—until on the eighth night, eight candles were burning in front of the cracked windows. Yakov went hungry, fleas ate him, his feet froze, his bones ached, and they brought home his uncle spitting blood and one eye hanging out of its socket. (The Christians were celebrating the birth of their God.) His mother lost her stand in the market-place, and they sold the copper samovar and the two silver candlesticks for her to bribe the village Pope to get another stand. Winter killed the two youngest; his sister, Fanya, lay down and died of a great wound in her throat. But when the mud dried and the hungry horses had left enough of the village trees to bloom greenly in the spring, a great time came to Yakov. He became, in his thirteenth year, a son of the Jews—a full-grown Jew, permitted and expected to enjoy and suffer the lot of his creed.

He now would know his sins were his own and they would not fall on his father's thin shoulders. He would be part of the ten males who made a full unit, the *minyon*, needed to hold holy services. He had a full-length prayer shawl now, blue-striped, and phylacteries, by whose leather straps he bound little leather boxes full of holy writ, on his arm and head. He began to study his Portion to be read from the Sacred Scroll. His began, "And it was in the middle of the night . . ." He read it well, all the Hebrew without the vowel signs. A real little rabbi, they said. *Nu, mazel-tov*—congratulations.

Yakov went into the fields and dug the earth roots for his father, and his father and mother peddled them in season, and then he and his father went back and sat with the holy books and read and talked and rocked together. But outside was a world, a living, non-Jewish world, and it puzzled and attracted him.

And this one-time village lout dreamed now of love, and with an American-German Jewess. Jacob groaned.

The Pedlocks were living in an old brownstone house on East Sixty-third Street. It was a slightly run-down place of high-ceilinged rooms, large, sliding oak doors (that crept out of the walls at the pressure of a finger), and on the third floor there was a large, screened sun-room where parrots and ferns surrounded a bamboo-framed couch. Joseph liked to use it to take the sun, on those rare days when the winter and spring sun came over the city.

Sam and Sara, and their growing sons, Albert, Harry, and Morris, lived on the first floor, over the series of cellar kitchens and pantries. The boys were growing taller and wilder; they played baseball in the alley and went hunting small animal life in Central Park. When they raised a fuss at home, Joseph would beat his big black cane on the floor and so silence them for a few minutes. They feared the old man and yet were proud of his big sword hung over the fireplace. On the second floor, Joseph lived with his sister, Tante Strasser. Selma had the big back bedroom, a beautiful, bow-shaped room with a wedge of windows overlooking backyards and telegraph poles. For New Yorkers, it was a simple, comfortable way of life. All the Pedlocks felt the situation was only temporary. Things would change for the better.

Louis visited them often—either from Butte, where the family still owned a small and rather disastrous silver mine, or from Tennessee, where they were trying to get coal and timber from Joseph's old holdings. The Colonel would put up in the billiard room in the basement, on a huge, red-leather couch. Sam's boys believed the stories that he slept with his boots on in a true, Western tradition that a man liked to die fully shod.

The Tennessee lands were all that kept their heads above water, Joseph used to say. The boys wondered what danger there was of their drowning. Morris, the smallest, dreamed of the Hudson and East Rivers suddenly rising in the night, and he would wake up groaning and call for his mother.

The disaster that ruined the family in the merger fight with the Copper Combine and the aftermath of the panic of 1907 had left them strapped for cash, but had not broken their spirits. They carried the scars of many industrial battles, and could roll with the punches and defeats, and come back groggy but ready to go on. The deep reason the Copper Combine defeat really stung was the fact that Ralph had gone over to the enemy. They no longer did any banking with the New Amsterdam–Manhattan since Ralph, son-in-law to Charles Pentland, had been taken in as a minor officer of that bank.

Joseph, the family agreed, had somehow stopped ageing. It seemed that, at a certain moment, he had decided to stop growing older. For years the grandchildren remembered him as always the same. A lean figure, very tall, the beard still slashed across in a square mop of white hair, the heavy, black cane in his strong, brown hands, and the slight limp adding just a touch of mystery and adventure to a man they imagined had led the most wonderful, exciting life of all. A man who had seen General Lee plain, and been with Saint J. E. B. Stuart. "The mantle of sainthood is slowly settling over the Civil War and its figures," old Joseph used to say. "The dirt and grime and gore are being distilled into the precious and rather snobbish elixir of a mythical, golden past. Everything is to become twice life-size. The real images and the true facts are to be romantic fodder for the writers and worshippers of something they understand only dimly." Joseph hated this sainthood thrust upon the South; the Blue and the Grey—the dreamlike kneeling attitude of those who sank into and ached only of the past. He always stopped such talk, usually by calmly stating, "All I remember of the glory and the beauty of the Lost Cause (it's become damn capital letters very soon) is our wiping ourselves with our bloody shirt-tails at Cold Harbour."

"Oh, Father," Sara would say, and picking up a heavy, battered, old-fashioned flint-and-tinder lighter, she would set fire to her cigarette and then hold it up for the company to use. "Judah P. Benjamin gave it to Father. He was Jeff Davis' right-hand man. Secretary of War for the Confederacy, you know."

Joseph liked to lie in the sun on the third floor sun-porch and listen to the parrots that his sister raised from evil-looking eggs. The parrots spoke only German, Tante Strasser's Austrian-German, as no one ever bothered to teach them anything else.

Joseph spent a great deal of time in the sun-room, examining the maps of the Tennessee lands, and directing Sam and Louis in the field, where they were sinking coal shafts and trying to haul out timbers through the steep mountain trails. The parrots would drop empty seed hulls on his maps and shout, "*Liebchen! Das ist schön!*"

Selma always brought the old man his afternoon glass of hot milk, with nutmeg dusting floating on its boiled skin, and the old man would drink it and ask her what she had been doing.

"Been running up bills in Lord and Taylor's again?"

"Oh, just the usual ones, Papa. Drink it all. The best part is on the bottom."

"Don't teach an old gaffer like me how to drink."

"Sara and I had lunch at the Waldorf and then we went down to Canal Street to see her father, at their plant. Mr. Wasserman has been working too hard, and the doctors want him to rest."

Joseph put down the glass and let Selma wipe his beard dry. "What's so hard about getting rich making two-pants suits?"

"It's a big place and must be a godsend to those poor Jews that stagger in and out of it with those big bundles of cloth. How do the sweatshop contractors live on what they make?"

"Louis says they live by stealing from each other."

"The Colonel is ashamed of them. He wants them all to be ranchers and railroad presidents and members of the hunting club set. Nobody really seems to care about them. They struggle and suffer. They're just wonderful, with those big, patient faces, like those Rembrandt painted."

"*Liebchen*," said a parrot, "*die Zeit bringt Rosen.*"

Joseph looked up at his daughter and brushed seed hulls from his vest. "This is a sudden interest, Selma."

Selma turned and adjusted a parrot cage and pulled back her hand just in time to escape getting her fingers nipped. "I've been attending meetings."

"To tar and feather the immigrants when they get off their ships?"

"Remember Herzl, in Paris?"

"The old black-bearded pirate trying to scare us back into a desert ghetto of his own making? He's dead."

"There should be a place where Jews in flight, who have no place else to go, can live a life of their own."

Joseph smiled and took her hand. "I smell a Zionist."

Selma shook her head. "The American-Irish shout and parade for a Free Ireland for their people. And we've given money to the Polish-American Society to free Poland. Why, Papa, we even supported the Boers, helping the Germans collect money for them, when they were in British prison camps. I feel it's the job of every good American of Jewish descent to help settle the Russian and Polish Jews in Palestine."

"You don't agree with Herzl then, maybe they should save a place for us there?"

Selma laughed. "Not unless we give it all back to the Indians and you want to send the Cabots and Lodges back to Liverpool, the Vanderbilts and Morgans back to Germany."

"How much is this caprice going to cost me?"

"I'll let you know after the meeting tonight."

"*Liebchen!*" shouted a parrot, "*Geteilte Freud ist doppelt Freude! Das ist schön!*"

CHAPTER IV

Mrs. Edward R. Sontag—Etta to her friends—was an alert, rather wide young woman who had been to Smith College for four years, had studied for six months at Johns Hopkins with the idea of becoming a doctor, and had lived in France for a summer, taking vocal lessons. She once spent two days a week in the Henry Street Settlement House reading Robert Louis Stevenson to young louts who admired her breasts and wrote complimentary but dirty remarks about her sexual abilities in chalk on the sidewalks.

She had been thinking of devoting a great deal of her life to the blind, when she fell strongly in love with a young neurologist who was too shy to make a success of his abilities. She married him, made him spend a year in Vienna with Herr Doktor Freud, organized his office, hired a new nurse for him, put in a filing system, and got him a lot of rich, tired old German Jews who ate too much, as patients. The neurologist sometimes secretly felt he knew what the Sabine women had been through.

At thirty, her energy had produced some pale images of herself and husband, named Sigmund (naturally) and Siegfried (she was a passionate, *bravo*-shouting Wagnerite), and a beautiful daughter, Rose. She had just lately discovered Zionism, and was trying to break herself of a fondness for bacon and eggs.

Her son Siegfried began to call himself Ike.

She had been holding what she called "exploratory meetings", inviting a mixed group of Jews and part Jews (" My father, Captain Livingston, was half-Christian, you know"). There were also a few, rather odd people who were hunting the Ten Lost Tribes and trying to translate the Egyptian tomb carvings, and some New England ministers who had been painfully circumcised in middle age and were trying to grow beards.

Mrs. Sontag was a very serious, earnest person, and she was usually successful with any project she took over. "If Etta had only been a man . . ." all her friends said, after she shook charity checks and cash out of them.

Etta's living and dining rooms had been enlarged that evening by opening the sliding-doors and removing a great deal of the overstuffed furniture. It was a huge, white apartment overlooking Central Park West, the walls hung with a collection of now almost forgotten English painters of the Sixties and Eighties.

She knew what she liked. But she had real taste, and her Whistlers were of his best Thames River period.

A series of undertaker's folding chairs had been placed around the room and at the Steinway grand there were tall chairs and a small table, a pile of badly printed literature on Zionism in English and Hebrew, a crystal pitcher of water, and some glasses.

Up front sat a number of women in their summer best, chatting with Etta, and a few men who looked as if they had been dragged there. But the earnest Zionists, the converts and the merely curious were seated in the rear. Old Jews with beards and large shoes with elastic sides (oh, so comfortable!). There were also young garment workers in their blue shirts wearing new cheap ties, their hair plastered and combed with much water. Dark-eyed, sharp-nosed ghetto girls— "Firebrands," Etta had whispered proudly of them to her friends. Some older sweatshop workers, the factory lint still in their hair and their tired hands folded on their laps, a little too frightened at all this rich upper life to do more than peer about them. They were deeply awed by the solid, prosperous German Jews up front.

Jacob Kozloff wondered what he was doing here. He had no interest in Zionism. He wanted to make a living and be a good American and pay his debts. But the Starker Glitz had invited him to come and see "real class" and have his eyes opened at how well Jews did here. Jacob could no longer stand the empty evenings alone in his room. And if he were at home, Mottke, the marriage broker, would always drop in with his tainted bargains in marriage. So he had come to Etta's with the Starker Glitz, and sat now on a creaking undertaker's chair, watching Etta Sontag seat people and pat shoulders and make short, direct speeches into old, rather deaf ears.

Suddenly Jacob stiffened, and the marrow seemed drained from him and God's fire entered his veins. The dark beauty had come in and gone up to the hostess.

"You sick?" asked the Starker Glitz, loosening his pushcart necktie, which had been cutting off his breathing all evening.

Selma took Etta's arm and said, "It's a wonderful crowd, Etta."

"It's pretty good. Next time, perhaps, we'll have to hire a hall."

A tall, round-shouldered man with very large hands and a long straight nose came over and Etta grabbed his arm. "Meet my husband, Selma. Edward, this is Miss Pedlock. My husband, Doctor Sontag."

Doctor Sontag peered at her myopically, and smiled. "How do. My grandfather, I believe, knew the Pedlocks."

"Did he?"

"He was a Philadelphia rabbi. Now that I think of it, he was a relative and he married your mother and father. He was rather proud of it." The doctor grinned. "The old boy was rather a snob."

Etta said, "They wanted Edward to be a rabbi, too. But, after all, you know, a neurologist *is* a kind of modern rabbi."

"Not so loud," said Doctor Sontag, "those old beards back there wouldn't like to hear that."

Etta sighed and brightened, and a big smile of welcome came to her face as she looked toward the door. "Ah, the speaker!"

A well-tailored man approached them. He had a face like an anti-Semitic cartoon in a German newspaper—very bright eyes, a large-lipped, witty mouth, and a huge, eagle's nose that gleamed bravely under the electric lights.

Etta said to her husband and Selma, "May I introduce our speaker, Israel Zangwill."

The speaker shook several hands. Etta remembered he wrote well of the romantic poverty of the poor Jews—and the racial greatness of the rich Jews. He had given up hope of finding Christian virtues among the followers of the Great Jew and was now a Zionist. "A writer should really be read and not heard."

Etta introduced a large, elderly man with a moon face to the speaker. "Mr. Kolbar, one of our most ardent followers."

The fat man shook his head. "I just like to listen. I used to be a lawyer and now I'm a judge, so, Mr. Zangwill, I hope to do some good listening."

"That's rare—for a lawyer to listen."

"Even a rich lawyer must retire to silence sometimes."

The speaker nodded and smiled. "You have, I see, been dividing your time according to holy writ—between the Law and the profits."

The lawyer got the joke, but Etta frowned. These little jokes that writers made were not at all what she wanted at this time. Good, serious preaching, with much fist-pounding, and some dreadful quotations full of fire and death and trouble would do the trick, oh, much better.

Etta stood at the side of the piano as if ready to launch a battleship, and held up her arms.

"Attention, please. We are very happy to have here tonight a man who as a writer and a speaker has spoken often of us Jews, and has presented a picture of us to the world that is not only true, but is also literature. Without much further ado, then—may I present your speaker and mine, Mr. Israel Zangwill."

The speaker came up to Etta's side and nodded and smiled and shook his head.

"I can only wish I were as good a speaker as you deserve, or my message needs, but I shall do the best I can. As the King of the Schnorrers said to the rich man, 'Be careful of your clothes, don't soil them, they belong to me when you're through with them.' So I shall not try and spoil Zionism by fumbling it here tonight.

"When I first became interested in Zionism, I visited Herzl, in his Vienna home. He said about me, that I was a man who expends so much concern and thought on the care of his spirit that there remains nothing for externals. This annoyed my tailor, but I resolved to go out and meet people more, and here I am tonight, to speak to you of Zion."

The people had settled down and listened carefully to the speaker, as he outlined the plans and hopes of the movement. He spoke of his first disappointment, of then coming to see the problem as a whole and not as a part.

"There is really no Jewish problem. There is only a Christian problem. And one of the great problems of the Christians is the Jews. Having tortured, and been so long so un-Christian, to the Jew, they must now solve the problem. The problem they, not we, have created. However, to solve their problem, which in the end will mean that they will save their own souls, we must be able to present them with what we feel is right for us. And that is our problem; to save the souls of Christendom, to give them a chance to become true Christians, to undo their great wrong to their fellow man, to help them live as they hope to live, under the Golden Rule of their Saviour, the Great Jew."

Etta sighed. "Too clever in content, this speech," she felt, "for my earnest group." To grasp anti-Semitism and Zionism as a Christian problem was not, she felt, within the ability of anyone but an earnest, deep thinker.

"To be ready ourselves for Zion, we must go back to the words of the Midrash. It says there (I merely refresh your minds, I know), 'There is a wheel rolling in the world—not he who is rich today is rich tomorrow, but one he brings up and one he brings down.' So as a wheel turns, at one time or another, we shall all be equal, and all shall look, some day, toward that land which is ours, and which we shall again make ours. We can make just a state, but we must make a Holy State, not the mere rituals, but a state in which are the hopes of the best minds, and the commonest ideas of all of us. We are the first roots. Out of us as a people grew all ideas of God today . . . And so . . ."

"How he talks," said the Starker Glitz.

"Not so loud."

"When do we eat, Jacob?"

"This isn't a free lunch."

"Look at those *zaftig*, juicy girls."

"Be still."

"That dark one. A man could . . ."

"Shut up!"

"Don't push at me."

"Then keep still."

"I was only looking at the women. Can I help it if I love women? Some men love cards, or sea bathing; me, I love women."

"Not tonight, please."

Jacob felt that the speaker up front was a witty impassioned man who spoke well and to the point. He knew what he was talking about, and was driving his points home skilfully. But if anyone had asked Jacob what had really been said, he would not have been able to recall one point. He merely sat. And sweated. As if he didn't do enough of that in the shop.

The talking stopped at last, and the questions, too, and Etta asked everyone please to have some coffee and cake. Many newcomers had crowded into the back, so Jacob could not even break through and disappear. The Starker Glitz, who was always hungry, steered Jacob up to the tables that had suddenly appeared from behind screens placed against the walls.

"No *lox*," said the Starker Glitz, a lover of smoked salmon, eying the food.

Someone handed Jacob a coffee cup. Selma smiled at him. "I was going to say it's a small world," she said, "but I'll skip it. How are you?"

"Very well, thank you," said Jacob. "I didn't expect . . ."

"I didn't expect to find you here, either."

Etta swooped down on them and pushed close to Jacob. "And what does the workingman think of Zionism?"

Jacob rattled his cup. Selma put a hand on Jacob's arm and said, "Etta, this is . . . *is?*"

Jacob said, "Jacob Kozloff. It was very interesting. Of course, I'm new to all this."

Etta was off to hold the hand of an old, bearded man.

"She covers a lot of ground," Selma said.

"Thank you for giving me a lift with my bundle the other day."

"Let me get you some cake."

As she turned away, Jacob felt someone tug at his elbow. Mottke, the marriage broker, a mouth full of coffee tart, looked at him with love in his eyes. A dead sweat, cold and clammy, broke out on Jacob's brow. He turned away as if he didn't know Mottke, as if he were a Jew-hater.

Mottke rubbed his chin free of crumbs and whispered in Jacob's ear, *sotto voce*, "This is the right place for you. Fancy stuff here, and

I got something you'll like. Nothing like shooting high, my boy. You got the right ideas. Why not a German-Jewish maiden for you? Old Bromberg, of the fur family. They just brought over his sister. A fine woman, experienced in bed and kitchen. Not flighty and shy like a young girl. A little deaf, but you understand, who wants a chattery, back-talking wife. Now . . ."

"Go away, Mottke . . . before I brain you."

"All right. A niece of the Wolfs'. Lumber and roof supplies. Just back from Arizona, like brand new. Twenty thousan' dollars and a share of the business, Jacob."

Jacob was aware of Selma staring at him, a cake in one hand, and cup in the other. She was laughing.

Jacob put down his cup. Mottke seized his arm. Selma laughed again, seized his other arm. "I'm sorry, mister," she said, "but Mr. Kozloff and myself have a date. I think we can get along without your professional help."

Mottke shrugged his shoulders and reached for a business card in his vest, saw the look in Jacob's eyes, and slowly walked away. "Amateurs, the curse of every business!"

Jacob found himself in the hallway, Selma holding on to his hand, and then he was in the elevator, and out in the fresh air that hit him like a shock of ice-water in the face.

"I never believed they existed, these ghetto marriage brokers," she said as they crossed the street to the park. "I've heard of them, but fancy meeting one. Do you use him often? Give him all your trade?"

"It's nothing to joke about," said Jacob tragically. "They're like leeches. They never let go for a minute."

"His samples seem interesting. What are they like really?"

"I never go to see any of them. Believe me, it's all a big mistake."

They walked on, side by side, not touching.

"Would you mind walking me home, Mr. Kozloff? I live just across the park."

"I'll be very happy to."

"It seems odd that the Jews have such a fear of romantic love. How do all these arranged marriages turn out?"

"Believe me, I never tried them, Miss——?"

"Pedlock. Selma Pedlock."

"I once knew that name. Let me see . . ."

"It's been in the papers."

Jacob suddenly laughed. "The Corporations?"

202

"Yes, but . . .?"

Jacob stopped walking. "I once owned one share of the stock!"

"Think of us, we owned thousands at one time. We can't laugh over it."

Jacob felt much bolder. "Miss Pedlock, this sort of makes us less strangers. I mean, well . . ."

She took his arm and leaned on him. "All right. We're members of the same firm. But let's walk. I don't like these paths late at night."

"You don't have to worry."

She felt his hard, work-developed arm muscle through his jacket. "I don't scare easy. But hoodlums cause a lot of trouble here late at night. But I'm sure you'll protect me."

The faint mocking note in her voice escaped him. It was a clear night, and the glowing beads of the park lamps were making stars along the ground. They walked slowly, she holding his arm, talking now about Zionism in a formal way. They came out of the park and walked toward the brownstone house. A dim light burned behind the frosted front doors.

"Would you care to have a nightcap?" she said.

"Look, Miss Pedlock, I don't know much about it, how it is with a young lady from uptown. I don't know what to say or do, or accept."

"You'd better learn if you're going to meet all those endowed heiresses that marriage broker has for you."

"I'd rather not talk about that."

"All right, Jacob."

She had called him Jacob! "I think I better go now I'll watch you from here until they open the door."

"I have my own key Well, good night."

"Good night. Look, Miss Pedlock." He didn't dare say Selma.

"Yes?"

"Do you like the theatre? Plays and shows and things?"

"Sometimes."

"I don't suppose you care for the Yiddish stage?"

"Is there one?"

"On Second Avenue. I go, sometimes, Saturday nights. If you would care, that is, I would be very happy to take you. I don't know how it is for you. I like it. My taste isn't too good maybe, but . . ."

"Thank you, Jacob. Some other time. Good night."

"Good night."

She let herself in with her key and he walked away, downtown. It had been a glowing moment. No use thinking anything else about it. Only a fool would think more would happen.

In her room, Selma hung up her dress and brushed her hair. A very nice boy. Not at all the ghetto type she had expected. Well, whatever client of that broker got him, she would be lucky. It was pleasant to think that the new immigrants would not disgrace the established Jewish community. . . .

The shop looked more miserable than ever now to Jacob. The windows were dirtier, the ceiling sagged and fell in bigger bits on their heads. The lint and dust in the air caught in their throats and attacked and inflamed their breathing tissues. "You call this air? You call this health?" shouted the Professor, as he banged his machine into action and drove the needle with a skilled fury across the cloth. "Animals we are and animals we'll die! Our lungs all cotton dust, our breath stinking. Sand in our kidneys, and the mould in our stomach greener than a rancid sour pickle!"

Bella snapped the thread in her machine and fixed it quickly. "What's the matter, Professor—a policeman bit you? Or did you just find out Karl Marx is dead?"

"Marx Schmarx! I tell you this Gene Debs is the greatest American we've ever had, and they're going to kill that man. They don't know how great he is. What he's done for the workingman!"

"Never mind Debs," said Jacob, banging his pressing-iron down hard. "We've got to get these vests done tonight, not save the Union."

"Oy! Oy!" said Hannah, rising and going to the baby who was howling on his bundle of rags. "Scream, scream, *totelleh*" (little father), "what's so good in life that you should smile? That's right, get red in the face, shake your legs and turn inside out. Drive your mother crazy and the whole shop." She held the bundle to her and fed it a lean, freckled breast, and the tears fell away from the wide, staring blue eyes as the child grunted with pleasure. "That's right, darling. Eat your mother alive, you and the landlord and the butcher. Don't show me any mercy. Tug, tug! It's all free," and she began to rock and sing, "free, free, free."

The Starker Glitz banged his pressing-board down on a steaming vest. "Cheesecake, with real cheese it was made of. And such coffee they had at that Zionist meeting—heh, Jacob? Real coffee, black as a ward heeler's heart, and such silverware. So heavy, you could hardly get a spoon up to your mouth."

Tessie sniffed and blew her nose skilfully with her fingers and bent lower and lower over her machine. She played a game. She imagined she was riding a six-day bicycle race. Mile after mile she pedalled off, taking the curved end corners, never relaxing, never feeling anything but the mile after mile of racing the machine. All that mattered was that for this run she would be able to buy a night's supply of whisky and lie in some corner and feel nothing and feel good. Feel repaid for life's battering and daffy tumbles, its hardness and its indifferent cruelty. Yes, one paid for everything in this life, for whisky most of all. One rode this machine. God help her, she pedalled a long way on it. Maybe she'd better ride it in the country now. By noon, as she played her game, she figured she must be near Yonkers and as the day passed, she pedalled on up the Hudson . . . that beautiful river where once she had gone with Charlie, and they drank beer on deck and went later to the little cabin and Charlie took off his truss and his derby, and they banged it around, bathed in pools of sweat. Oh, Charlie was a real sport and certainly could set up the drinks, but he never would take off his long underwear. The shy type, but thank God, he took off his truss. A sport who never held the bottle away from her and said, "Tessie, you schnapps snatcher, you've had enough. Enough, enough. . . ." She pedalled on and passed the little river towns. Passed them all. Hell and Irish whisky, she must make this run to Albany every day, and when they worked overtime, there was time for a side trip to Troy. . . . Pedal, pedal, and her insides ached for whisky and she bent lower and pedalled on. Oh, she had the style and pace of a champ. Even, steady, eyes straight ahead. Road clear.

Jacob pushed aside the mop of hair that fell into his eyes and he looked over his shop, and his pride and joy in it were gone. What had he here What had he done these few years in America? Become an animal, become a slave-driver. He tortured people on machines, and if he didn't use them, they starved. This was penny-ante stuff. This was nothing. And he was going no place. Kahn-Wasserman made the money, and he, Jacob, had plenty of sweat. The sour infant (already doomed to bad lungs, boils, crooked legs), the women at the machines, and Hannah basting, putting together cloth, Tessie pedalling on, she must be near West Point by now (on the upgrade and never a muscle slacking never even stopping to mop her brow). Bella turning out the garments, a turban round her hair to keep the lint out. Her mind far off with her sports and actors, thinking of the fun ahead tonight. Sure of herself, and Bella, and never stepping out of her class. Bella could take on life and slap its face or laugh with it. She was big and full of health, and "what the hell, kid, you only live once".

Jacob wished he had Bella's direct, unthinking joy in life. Too many books and too much brooding over the Talmud had spoiled him

205

for the simple wallowing in life. It had to be refined now, beautifully dark, like . . . He banged the pressing iron down.

The man looked at him. The simple Starker and the two old men who broke out of their stiffening clay shrouds once in a while, but knew already that they were ready for the dust heap. Potter's Field for them—they knew it—if no Hebrew burial society took care of them.

"Oh, those German-Jew charities," said the Professor. "They like to bury old ghetto Jews. The more old Jews, tramps, and cripples they buried, the higher grew their own prestige. Bury them, hide them away underground." The Professor looked up. "What the devil is the matter with Jacob?" Had he heard about the meeting to help the strikers the Rockefellers were machine-gunning in Colorado? "What makes Jacob feel such a fellow club member with old J.D.?"

Jacob went to the stove and poured himself a tin cup of tepid black tea. He swallowed a mouthful and spit it out. Vile stuff. "Somebody been boiling eggs in this again?"

He looked out over the shop, scowling, as the door opened, and Tony, the boy who polished shoes and ran errands in the brothel and gambling house under the shop, came in.

"Hey, Mista Kozloff. Ya wanta on the telaphone downstairs."

The Bronzonis had a telephone, the only one in the building, the luxury of vice, everyone explained. Jacob gave its number to those big shops that sometimes needed a contractor in a hurry. He dusted himself and went down the sagging steps after the leaping Tony.

The Bonzoni flat was a place of luxury and sin. Its beaded glass curtains and its red-cloth-covered tables looked rich and promising in the half dark made by the heavy window curtains always kept drawn. The living room had blue-and-yellow murals of the Bay of Naples, and naked women dancing on grapes, or wriggling coyly in the hands of amorous males who were men to the hips and goat-legs below. The phone was hung on a wall under a small, chipped plaster statue of the Virgin, trying, it appeared (at first sight), to get her head out of the way of the flame from a copper cup of smouldering olive oil below.

Jacob picked up the phone.

"Hello, Jacob?"

"Yes, Jacob Kozzloff."

"It's Selma Pedlock. Remember?"

"Oh, yes, of course." He couldn't believe it. Here he was, standing in a hook shop smelling of wine and perfume and armpits and personal disinfectants, talking to Selma Pedlock! Overhead the sewing machines ground on, and he wondered vaguely if the machines helped the men and women who went to bed down here, if the vibrations drove them to madder furies and greater orgies, or to feeble, sated release.

"I didn't expect to hear from you," he said weakly.

"I always do the unexpected, Jacob. I called Kahn-Wasserman for your phone number. Does that theatre invitation still hold?"

"But of course. You seemed so sure, I mean set, against it. But, of course, I'd be happy, very happy to take you. It would be wonderful."

"Good. . . ."

The lecherous atmosphere, perhaps, made him bolder. He eyed a painted nude captured by a pair of goat's legs.

"Would you care, I mean, permit me to take you to dinner?"

He could hear her laughing at the other end of the buzzing wire. "Of course. You can take me to one of those little Hungarian places on Second Avenue. At seven, then, tomorrow night?"

"Yes. At seven, then."

He wanted to say more, but it ended with: "Goodbye, Jacob," and a click. He added weakly: " 'Bye," and hung up.

Bonzoni came into the room, carrying a tray of half-filled, stale wine glasses, smoking a long, black cigar. He went to a cabinet and took out some fresh packs of cards and poker chips.

"Ah, Mista Kozloff. *Fortunatissimo*. How'sa business?"

"Like everything else—just getting by."

"Itsa bada time. My galla bladda, shesa killa me. Why you don't come in some evening and try the cards?"

"I'm not much good with cards."

"Well, you don' have the fun enough. I alus say, a man is a man, not a stick. Yeah? Sure. You come down have some wine. Maybe one of my nieces, she please you, *Zaftig*, like you say. Very fine girls. Convent girls. Very good girls, no loose tramps like you pick 'em up in the saloons and geta the clap. You come down, Mista Kozloff, and I fix you up fine. Much fun. Wine, love, a plate of *pasta*. What is life, huh?—work, make love, and die? Then the galla bladda, itsa one hellofa joke life is, believe me."

"Thanks, Mr. Bonzoni, and thanks for taking my calls."

"Itsa pleasure. Look, you come down and tear off a piece anytime. And the wine—*Asti Spumante*—she is ona me. I stand the wine. The girls, that is up to you. They very fine girls and saving up to bring their sweethearts over from Italia. *A riverderci*."

Tony appeared from no place and Jacob put a nickel in his hand and went upstairs and into the shop. He felt drunk and unsteady and he picked up his pressing-iron and smiled. She was going out with him. The Starker Glitz made an obscene gesture with his hands, and laughed and winked and pointed downstairs. Jacob grinned back; if he only knew!

Selma Pedlock discovered with pleasure the Yiddish theatre in America, that hybrid that could have no children. It rose to its heights after the first wave of immigration at the end of the century. That gave it a huge, hungry audience that was still struggling with the English language, and looking back over its shoulder at what it had just left. This public was to die down to a small trickle when mass immigration was shut off, when the second and third generations migrated to Broadway and helped pull down whatever few, feeble traditions the American stage had left. Broadway never had the life, sparkle, and drive of the Yiddish theatre at its best.

Selma had never seen the Yiddish stage and she enjoyed it. It was a low-comedy farce, a diluted version of the popular middle-class European and American stages, with certain trimmings of its own. The comedy was fast and furious; but Selma, who knew very little Yiddish (that bastard German dialect), had only to watch Jacob's face to know when the lines were smoky and blue.

It was a gay, swift comedy of baffled immigrants with a rich uncle in the Bronx, a lost heiress, an orphaned girl who dressed as a boy, a witty, greedy rabbi. There was pratt-fall wit, and a chorus line of shrill, half-naked ladies of forty, who exposed their unshaved armpits and legs and swung more or less in order across the stage as they sang a Yiddish song that was half English in its words. The stage comic said, "They each have two behinds!"

The climax, as in most of these plays, was a wedding feast, with fast plotting under the marriage canopy, low comedy, tears, heart tugs, and a happy ending in a burst of song and an old-fashioned wedding dance that filled the stage with stomping feet.

Jacob was happy to get Selma out of the theatre. They went to a Rumanian place and drank coffee and talked. The Hungarian food before the theatre had been fine. Selma had enjoyed the show and she looked across the table at Jacob and smiled.

"It's all in a tradition I know nothing about. It's certainly spirited and as bawdy as the great Elizabethans."

"It isn't very high-class."

"A folk theatre never is. It only becomes art, my brother Egon says, when it's dead or dying."

"It's so vulgar," said Jacob. "I'm a little ashamed of it."

"Isn't life supposed to be vulgar and fun, Jacob?"

"I never used to think so. More coffee?"

"No, thank you. I'd better get back home."

"Of course."

They rode home in a taxi. Jacob's second taxi ride of his life. The first one came earlier in the evening, when he had called for her and she casually suggested a cab to the Hungarian eating place. It was only later, the next morning, that Jacob came out of his trance and figured out that the price of a bundle of sport jackets delivered at Kahn-Wasserman had gone into the evening. Bella and the shop would think him insane, but he didn't mind. Live dangerously, the village followers of Nietzsche had once told him.

The next time he took her out she wanted to talk about him.

"What's there to say?"

"Why did you come to America, what was it like in Russia?"

"I don't want to talk about it."

"A secret crime?"

"Please."

"All right, Jacob. But I do want to thank you, it's been real fun."

He looked at her—so fancy and such style! He was proud of her there in that cellar dive among all the fancy *allrightnicks* and builders and ladies' cloaks kings. In a way, this was coming up in the world, a little.

"A little bit more wine."

"All right, mystery man, a little more wine."

Jacob looked at her. "Don't think I'm hiding a crime."

"Oh, I'm sure you are. You tried to kill the Tsar?"

"No, but it was worse."

"Can it be worse?"

"If I tell you you'll promise you'll still see me?"

"None of us Pedlocks are too respectable."

"Don't joke."

"All right, Jacob."

"What happened to me was like dying and then . . . well, to begin at the beginning. My village was backward and holy. I was a holy boy. I did the rituals and I was a good Jew."

"I'm sure you were."

"Then I saw there was another, bigger world."

The waiter placed the fresh bottle of wine in front of them. Jacob told his story in a low, even voice, looking directly at her.

210

Something outside his boy world attracted him, he told her, something away from ghetto students and their little battles of what was said by whom and how. Men in furs and boots, big men smelling of plum brandy and the great cities and markets. There was talk of Moscow and Warsaw and Rome and London. There were thousands of Jews everywhere, he found out. "Not just a handful of ghetto prisoners in this Russian village." And he wanted to leave and see for himself. But he was in bond to his God and his rituals. He could not, he felt, leave the village Torahs and the old men at prayer, the glow of reciting and listening, of talking and comparing dogma.

He sat, shoeless, with the congregation on the ant-eaten floor of the synagogue during the Black Feast. And he wailed in memory of the destruction of Jerusalem. It was a fearful time and the groans rang out; and in stocking feet everyone tossed and bent and prayed.

Then there was the White Feast of the terrible Day of Atonement. There was a month-long season of prayer bringing in the New Year. This was the most sacred of all the holidays. One prayed for days and the most dreadful pealing of the ram's horn shook their bodies and souls.

Yakov leaned in a corner and the ram's horn rang out its angry and terrible call. It roared, it trembled, and then it wailed. Passionate bursts of prayer went with it. All knew it was a warning for the Day of Judgment, a time to repent and take stock of one's sins, to sort and rearrange one's life for the New Year. Yakov knew that "now for nine days, God judged the souls of the living and decided their fate for the year to come".

Yakov was satisfied with Pentateuch, its complex codex of a mere six hundred and thirteen precepts. He joined with pleasure in the talks and debates of its infinite ramifications. But outside, in the village, the season was advancing. The wheat sang as the wind ran through it. The women looked beautiful and desirable, and washed their feet. The animals mated and the peasants became drunker, and rutting and spawning ran through their lives. The Tsar's soldiers marched by, singing sadly along the street, their faces scarred with the whips of their officers. They sang soft, sorrowful songs and took time off to bang the doors of the Jews and spit in their faces and pull out white beards, hair by hair. Oh, those sad, damn, dark Russian souls, said Jews who had never read the great novelists.

Yakov discovered youths, intellectuals, at a club room, reading the forbidden books in Russian. They talked of a Duma, and of socialism, and of land in Palestine, of killing the Tsar, of going to South Africa, of draining the Dead Sea, of going to America, of Marx, and St.

Francis, of the holy rabbis, of becoming Christians, of anarchists. Of eating pork, or fornicating with *shiksas*—gentile girls. Of Sabbatai Zevi, the true Messiah, who at Smyrna had invited them all to take up the white turban of Islam and win the world. Worst of all, they read Spinoza (the excommunicated, the expelled, the cursed, the execrated Baruch Spinoza), read his infamous *Treatise on Religious and Political Philosophy* written so cleverly by that traitor to State and Church.

This was a new world to Yakov. Several new worlds for the simple student, Yakov Kozloffsky. For a little while, he fell from grace. He doubted the wisdom and greatness and awfulness of God. He doubted the Torah and the old wise men, the wisdom and power of the rabbis, the golden voice of the cantor, the effectiveness and lessons of good and bad, and evil and good, sin and forgiveness. He drank the raw plum brandy and read the forbidden books and ran with the inn girls.

His sister, Belka (only later did she become Bella), came to him. She was tall and yelled the loudest in the market-place, and went too often to the woods with the young men to pick the willow branches, and was shameless when she danced, and laughed at the stories of the grandmothers, and mocked them. But she had common sense and didn't care who knew it.

"Yakov," she said, "why waste your time with those Jewish intellectuals" (she spit at the word), "those bare-assed tramps and their French ways?"

"I'm lost. I've sinned and I've doubted."

"So do it in the dark. The rabbi doesn't like it. The *schul* is full of talk. They'll throw you out, curse you and your kind. Don't be a fool. Life is big and there is room for everything, so don't do anything the rabbi can curse you for. Don't stand up in the market and talk that socialist gabble, like a goose hissing."

"A man has to believe what he believes."

"What do you believe?" asked Belka, eating sunflower seeds. "A lot of talk with tea and lemon, a lot of cigarettes lit by a lot of young *goniffs*" (thieves) "too smart to work, too lazy to pray. Yakov, Yakov, don't be a fool."

"I'm confused, Belka."

"So be confused and be healthy till a hundred and twenty years. But don't talk against the rabbis."

"I'm only trying to explain to them."

"Explain! Better explain fainting to a cat!"

"It would be easier."

*   *   *

Jacob stopped talking and looked across at Selma.

"So far, Jacob, it isn't too bad."

"You want me to go on?"

"Yes, it's a world I never knew or heard of."

"It's a common enough story."

"Not to a Pedlock."

Jacob poured the wine and they drank and looked at each other. He had never told this story to anyone, but now he was telling it, it came easy. The dreadful part was yet to come. What could he do but go on?

"I lost my God. Then I was alone and I was afraid."

"What happened?"

"I had nothing."

So he decided to go back to the rabbi and his God (it was not easy, he explained to Selma). It was a small town. All the Jews were knit tight together against a world that killed and tortured them. And a man who tried to break away was cast out.

A great weight pressed on the mind of Yakov. He had lost his God. He had discarded his hope in the new books, the new learnings, the talk of social reform and post-Impressionism and Chinese causes. All had failed him. Of God he thought the most. It had been a stern and just God, and yet he had been happiest with that God. Now, Yakov had been tossed out into outer darkness. And unlike Job, as he sat broken and hurt, God did not even come down to argue it out with him. To even speak out against him. Yakov felt he was of no value to God. Yakov saw that for him the Torah, the prayers, the holidays and fasts were the true reason for existence. Without them, there was only the bottom of the dirty river.

So he came to the rabbis again over their tea and tattered books and he asked to be taken back into the fold.

"So the heretic wants forgiveness of the synagogue?" said Reb ben-Yosel.

"I want to be a full Jew again."

"We must devise a penance for this repentance." Reb ben-Yosel was a kind man. He played cheerfully on the floor with his grandchildren and looked wisely into the entrails of the chickens that old women brought him, and that were suspected of not being kosher. He loved God and was a wise old man who had suffered much and yet managed to have a full life; tea and snuff were his only sins. But with the heretic, he was always stern; with the pork-eaters, the youths who shaved off their ritual ear curls, who forgot their morning prayers, who fornicated with the daughters of Gentiles and brought forth *momzers.* With these, he was a stern man, like his awful and powerful God.

"Yes, yes—a penance. I shall think on it."

"I am ready for anything," said Yakov. And he went home, and Belka, his sister, shook her head as she combed her long, red hair and prepared to keep an appointment with a Jewish soldier from Minsk who was stationed in the town. "You're a fool, Yakov. What does it matter if the snuff-stained rabbi takes you back or not?"

"It matters to me."

"Go beat your head on the wall. . . . You'll feel just as good. And you don't have to do it in public."

"It's not to be that easy."

It was a day to remember, when Yakov Kozloffsky was brought back to his faith. The synagogue was packed with the town's Jews and those that had come for miles around. An atmosphere of brooding and sinister shadows filled the street and the synagogue. Yakov, the penitent, was led in, dressed in black gravecloth, and he held a long black candle of goat grease that sputtered and stank. He was walked between the oldest Jews to a raised platform and there read from the long scroll of recantation. He added, "I confess all my sins, my sins of the mind and the sins against the ritual! I confess my intellectual errors! I promise to live till I die a true Jew!"

The old men, the *Chacham*, stood around him and intoned, "For he remembered that they were but flesh, a wind that passes away and comes not again."

Then Yakov stripped himself naked to his hips and Reb ben-Yosel gave him thirty-nine well-placed lashes with a scourge of leather strands braided together to fit the hand. Yakov sat on the floor and the ban was solemnly removed. He put on his clothes and he was led to the threshold and he stretched himself across it and the whole congregation walked over his body, trampling it, digging its heels viciously into his groin, his face, his stomach, and his chest.

"But he, being full of compassion, forgave evil and destroyed them not!"

They passed over him—men, women and children. They spit down on him, they passed, some cried, some were frightened at the fearful punishment, some took pity on him. He sat up and wiped his face. He was alone. He stood up. The wind stirred the dust on the doorway. Some intellectuals across the street were grinning at him. The sharp shadows cut patterns of light and dark into his eyeballs. The intellectuals went to report what they had seen to the other godless Jews.

Belka came to him with a tattered sheepskin coat. She covered his aching shoulders and patted his aching head.

"Let's go home."

That Friday. Yakov went to pray in the *schul* and no one looked at him except when they thought he was not looking. But he no longer went with the scholars to talk of the fine points of the holy Law. He sat alone at home. The books had lost their savour. He tried to stand in the market but the insults of the drunken peasants, the bribing of the market overseer, all the small, sordid incidents of petty village life meant nothing to him.

Belka came to him one evening, as he sat in the doorway of their house, looking up at the dusty stars.

"Yakov, this town isn't for us."

"What can we do?"

"Let's go to America."

"America? As well wish for the moon stuffed with buckwheat."

"Yes, America. My soldier knows people who will smuggle us across the border. There are societies in Germany and Holland who will get us ship tickets."

"How will we live?"

"I can sew, and you can carry packs. Anything is better than to die here in this muddy village—a plague and curse on it. We're young, Yakov—full of juices. There's a big world out there. Yankel, my soldier, has been to Rotterdam. He says you wouldn't believe it, what's out there. And the streets of America, paved in gold, he swears!"

Yakov stood up and kicked the stool aside. "All right." He walked off down the lane toward the town square. The night before he and Balka left the village, he went down and threw a huge stone through the window of the intellectuals' club room.

The wine glasses were empty. Selma took Jacob's hand in hers.

"I've never heard anything like that, Jacob."

"I've never told it before."

"So that's your secret?"

"My big secret."

"I never suspected anything like this. We Pedlocks are Jews. But we don't carry it around with us. We don't follow the rituals or the rules. We blend, without making too much effort, into the American landscape. But it's easy for us. We've been here a long time. We've fought in the American wars and died in them. And we didn't go hungry very much."

"It isn't like that for a lot of us."

"I can see that. I wonder if my father knows all this."

"He didn't come from Russia."

"No. Jacob, I feel such a smug creature now. I've been full of cant. I've looked down on the ghettos as a place for a weak, dirty people. Thank you, Jacob, for telling me your story."

"I hope we'll go out again next week. They have a new show."

She stood up and let him put her coat around her shoulders. "Of course, Jacob."

He took Selma to the theatre once a week. They ate Rumanian, kosher, vegetarian, German, Litvak, and dairy. They saw tragic plays: *King Lear*, in a Yiddish that would have made the original author grind his teeth—and a series of musical comedies that followed a satisfactory formula and pattern. They saw good plays by Sholem Aleichem and fine productions of Ibsen and Hauptmann.

Jacob took out a loan on his sewing machines. In his madness, he borrowed at twenty per cent.

Bella could do nothing with him. She raved and threw dishes, waved her arms and screamed. She gave dramatic versions of household tragedy for him in her underwear.

"My millionaire! My *allrightnick*! Uptown ladies he is escorting around! Who are you? Diamond Jake Brady? Rockefeller? Now a new loan on the sewing machines! The machines, a black year on them, can hardly stand a touch and he hangs another loan on them! Have you lost your head—or has your brain been pickled like a sour tomato?"

"Don't chew at me, Bella. Get dressed."

"Chew! Chew! A fine talk, and you go off with your fine lady. Taxicabs! Flowers! Candy boxes with red ribbons! Poems you'll be writing her next!" Bella pulled a dress over her head.

"I'm not a poet."

"No. You're a——" Bella exploded into a full range of ghetto vulgarities, a torrent of obscenities. Jacob merely sat and listened and sighed. In an hour, he was meeting Selma for a concert. Bach, and some very fancy Russians: Borodin, Moussorgsky, Rimsky-Korsakoff. He had twenty dollars in his pocket. He had rented out a third of the miserable shop to a leather man, as storage space.

When Bella found that out, there was the devil to pay. Yet Jacob didn't care. Bella circled him like a wolf stalking a Russian sleigh.

"And what do you get out of it, you *schlemiel*—you oaf? Holding hands, not even a *top*" (a caress). "Your fine lady isn't giving anything. She's the talking kind."

"Please, Bella, no personalities."

"Personalities! Such a fine lady! Flies in her nose and goose feathers on her heels. Some high-class *mafka*!" (harlot). "I tell you, Jacob, this girl is going to ruin you, me, the shop, everything. And you sit there, a stupid pot on a stove, and sigh like a herring-eater for water! Bah! I'm disgusted with you! Go put your head in a hole in the ground and drown in your own bliss! And your *lady*," added Bella, finishing with a ghetto curse of great popularity, "it should only grow her a street-car in her *pupik*!" (navel).

Bella rushed out, tossing her cape over her shoulders, muttering curses to herself all the way down the creaking stairs.

Jacob stood up, looked in the mirror to see if he was shaved properly, pulled the handkerchief out an inch more in his bargain-basement jacket pocket, turned the gaslight low, to a pinpoint of colour, and went out.

He took the elevated train again uptown. No use hiring a taxi and wasting money until Selma was with him. He sat in the rattling train as it ground past second-story windows in which men in soiled under-wear sat smoking pipes or feeding birds; where fat, tired women leaned big breasts on pillows and shouted down to dirty-faced children to bring up "a penny plain" from the corner soda stand, and threw the pennies, wrapped in a corner of old newspaper, down to them. Some-times he saw young girls primping in their slips before mirrors, or pulling tight skirts over their heads. No one of the window occupants any longer noticed or cared about the elevated trains that rattled past the windows. "What can you see in a second?" And the riders had long since grown rather tired of the domestic window dramas they shot past. The old man praying in shawl and cap, the children torment-ing a cat, the couple at their meal in their shirtsleeves and wrapper, the sick or dying looking out with big eye-balls of pain and terror, the drunks fumbling, the taut lovers crouched and indifferent to the world. All this crowded life the train saw all day and night, and became bored with. Poverty—it's as hard to break, thought Jacob, as the drug habit.

Jacob stopped looking out at the windows and looked down at his shoes, shoes polished by Tony to a mirror gleam. It was time for him to continue thinking, and he had been thinking now for two days. The shop was ruined, finished, and about to wither away as so many ghetto shops did. He had kept it going a long time. Now he no longer cared. A plague on it! The heavy pressing-irons, the sour smell, the lint, the rancid odour of the tired people driving machines and pant-ing. It was nothing he wanted to go on with now.

He had observed, he had studied, and he had seen how business was done in this big city between its two polluted rivers. A great scheme was beginning to form, step by step, in his mind. He had, up till now, gone about it all with muscle, and not mind. Now he was thinking things out, thinking them out to the end. It was simple—he had to beat the German Jews at their own game.

Selma had been the cause of it. He saw now that he could not go on being a stupid animal of a sweater, a grinder of the few sewing machines, go on bowing to Kahn-Wasserman and their kind. It had to be something big and new. So that he could lay a victory at Selma's feet and take her in his arms and kiss her wildly, and . . . and . . . He had actually kissed her once after too much wine one evening. He had grabbed her badly off-balance at her front door. He had fumbled his arms around her slim hips and had kissed her on one corner of her mouth. A sliding, unsatisfactory kiss. She had said coolly, "Good night, Mr. Kozloff. I'll call you. . . ."

"Selma, please," but she was gone with a slamming of a door, and he was cold and his head ached with the echo of her bang.

She had not called him for two weeks, and then he had called her, and later, in a Russian café on Avenue A, over *pilmenis* and *pirozhoks* and *Zubravka* vodka, he promised never to repeat anything like that again.

They became very fond of the little Russian places and ate smoked salmon and mushrooms and *shashlik caucasien* and *kilki* and *bitki*. Jacob experimented with Kardanach wine and spent much more than he could afford. They sat close together in dark little places where often the faces of the Tsar and Teddy Roosevelt on the walls looked down at them. They walked, later, between ashcans and hurrying pushcarts. They moved past flares and fishmongers and the screaming buyers and sellers along the damp curbs. They waited for the great beer drays and their huge horses to pass, before crossing the streets. They stood in rain and snow, and sunlight on many corners, and they parted after each evening politely, as good friends. And it all ate into Jacob like acid. He knew the hour of retribution was near at hand, that he was a ruined man, and yet he did not care.

He wandered alone, later at night, down the dark East Side streets, the passing bums not bothering him, the lurking, congenital syphilitics in the doorways watching him with their staring idiocy. They were mean neighbourhoods, with hoodlums and drunkards and screaming women; and just before dawn, when he could not sleep in his box-like room, he would watch the man sloshing down the streets with great, black hoses spouting columns of water along the gutters, sailing the crushed cabbage leaves and old newspapers and little piles of wood ashes and the horse droppings down toward the sewer openings.

He could not understand Selma. Why did she not want love? Why did she come to him so often and leave it all so sterile and so empty?

Yet any move on his part, a slight gesture, a close touch, a moment's lingering as he put her coat over her shoulders, when they rode for fun the crosstown horsecars, and he would be reminded he had promised never to repeat anything like *that*; yet she had said she was very fond of him and was very grateful that he was showing her the city, this part of it. But of course he mustn't think that she cared for any of that sort of thing. She wasn't interested "in lovers eating each other's noses in doorways". He should understand that. They were *just* friends. Just very good friends, helping each other understand each other's world. She was very cool, calm, and collected.

It hadn't been easy to accept all this, and once when Jacob saw one of Bonzoni's nieces washing her hair on the pigeon-soiled roof, from a white enamel pan, he had been tempted to accept Bonzoni's offer to stifle his aches with the best the establishment had to offer. Maybe Bella was right in calling his "uptown lady" a "teaser" in several versions of the terms.

The Bonzoni had looked up at him and grinned. She was wearing a Japanese kimono, a red-and-blue-flowered affair, and she lifted her arms and the sleeves fell away and he saw the crisp, dark hair of her unshaved armpits. She stood up and the kimono opened to show a leg in black cotton stocking with a red garter around a thigh, and a great deal of plum flesh, the inside of the thigh, paler than the rest and very smooth, as smooth, Jacob thought, as her belly was, most likely. Oh, "Song of Songs"! He turned and went swiftly down to the shop, and his throat was dry a long time. He didn't go near the roof after that.

The elevated train rattled along on its steel stilts and crossed and turned and twisted through the entrails of the city, heading uptown by its own odd way. Jacob shifted and swayed with the seasick motion of the rolling train. A man was only a man. He had desires, habits to build up, love to make. Damn it, why did it have to be for him to desire the moon? Why hadn't he picked one of Mottke's odd stock, made the best bargain with the best bit of goods on hand, and settled down? No, he had to fly uptown and spend his blood and Bella's blood and Hannah's and her rancid baby's blood on taxis and hothouse fruit, and flowers, and big picture boxes of chocolates (with the centre of the box full of candied pineapple, and a little, gilt tin fork for picking up the candies in their glazes and chocolate coatings).

Later he sat with Selma in a big hall, painted a dismal, fashionable yellow, and a great mass of men on a stage sawed air, and blew wind into brass and wood, and Jacob could make no sense of it all. Bella had once called classical music "expensive noise" and tonight Jacob agreed with her. Later they sat in a marble room smelling of imported fruit, and with great baskets of canned crab and truffles; they ate ice cream out of small plates

"What's the matter, Jacob? You look as if they were drowning all your kittens."

"Selma, I can't go on like this. I'm deeply in love with you."

"I was afraid of that."

"Why afraid?" asked Jacob.

"Because I'm afraid too. I'm in love with you."

"Selma!"

"And I don't want to be. I don't want to be deeply in love. I don't want a sad love affair. I don't want to suffer and feel pain."

"But that's all nonsense. . . . Don't you see . . ."

"I see, Jacob, that nothing can be easy and simple between us. Oh, we have fun and find a lot of life amusing. But, well, I don't want to hurt you, darling, but . . ."

"You call me darling."

"I'm warmhearted and call lots of people darling. But can you really see anything serious, permanent, coming of this? How is it all going to be possible? No, Jacob. I've decided to go to Europe when my Uncle Egon goes back there."

"Damn your Uncle Egon! I don't care what he does. But you can't go."

"I'm free! I go where I please."

"You're not free. I'm not free. You can sit there, calm and cool, in a stylish white outfit, biting on that small spoon, but I think inside you're like me. It isn't maybe a nice feeling or at all neat and calm, but I think I know what's inside you."

"You've become quite a speechmaker, Jacob. Oh, darling!" She put her head on her fashionable sleeve and sighed. The waitress standing at the next, empty table looked at them indifferently, then looked away and shifted the pencil in her hair. They moaned a lot in this marble soda palace. Well, it wasn't all a slap and a tickle. You found that out soon enough.

Jacob touched Selma's hair. "I knew it was like this with you."

"Don't be kind to me, Jacob. I've been dreadful to you. I've played a game. I've been very cruel to you."

"It hasn't been pleasant sometimes. You so near and, well, so beautiful."

"Let's walk across the park. Remember the first night? Let's wallow in our foolish sentiment."

"No—not foolish."

They walked arm in arm across the dark park. Even if her talk was crisp and hard, he felt, inside it was pain, a wonderful pain, a glorious pain, choking her up as it did him, a great, gouting rush of something like fire in the veins.

He stopped under a little, looping bridge that the park path ran across. With a delightful, brutal gesture (that left her breathless with joy) he pulled her to him and swung his heavy-muscled arms around her, and he leaned over and kissed her. It was not just a kiss, it was an attack on her coolness, her small, foolish attempt to control this big, gushing thing. He forced her mouth open, their teeth grated together, and they merged deeper into the darkness under the silly little bridge. With one full-spread hand, he cupped her firm, hard breast, and it was, she thought, like that painting by Rembrandt, *The Jewish Bride*. But why fool herself? This was no ritual gesture.

She struggled free, and pushed her hat back in order, and a boy rode past them on a bicycle, whistling "Darktown Strutter's Ball".

She fought breath back into her body. "You might as well face the worst, Jacob. Dinner with the family, Friday night."

The boy had turned around on his bicycle and was looking at them. He made the swift, pumping circuit of the path, but when he came round again, they were gone.

Since the long-fought yet steep decline of the family fortunes, Egon had been coming back to the United States once, often twice a year, travelling first-class on one of the slower, smaller, and therefore cheaper boats of a good English line, bringing with him about a dozen oil paintings and some portfolios of drawings. He was now a sort of art dealer, without a gallery, offering to his friends and their friends *avant-garde* paintings. "Bonnard? Matisse? Oh dear! Who are they?"

He was staying, as usual when in New York, at a small Murray Hill hotel, in a tiny suite, with his valet Eric, and the paintings and drawings hung on the walls. He had been rather unsuccessful even with his Pissarros and a very find Seurat, a really remarkable example of pointillism. All he had been able to sell recently was a small Degas ballet dancer to Etta Sontag, who was happy to see that it matched her drapes. She had heard that the painter was a notorious anti-Semite. She hoped, in buying the painting, that somehow "he would respect the Jews just a little more". Egon's entire trip would have been a failure if he had not acted as agent for a dealer in Rome, selling at a percentage some early Ingres pencil drawings to a Pittsburgh coal baron.

In Paris, Egon was proudly American, to the amusement of his friends, but back in America he usually began to feel uncomfortable, and fell to wondering why the rush and fury of the American coming-of-age should not appeal to him. There was such an ugly disregard of taste, culture, and manners.

He had spent the afternoon talking over this feeling with Henry James, at a quiet table during tea time. Henry James, too, was in America, on one of his rare visits. They had known each other well in Europe, and both had at first begun talking rather aimlessly, and then drifted on to the subject of the United States and its problems of growing up without warping world civilization.

"It is a complex fate, being an American," Henry James said to Egon, across the table, as he put two cubes of sugar into his teacup, and began one of those long, involved sentences that were to cause such unpopularity among the readers of his later works; works that Henry James felt would not in their time be fully liked, but in some future, perhaps (if such a thing as a future to any good writing could be seen these days), for he was not writing just for today; just as his remarks were not to be taken at his full, final appraisal of his country, but rather, speaking here privately, one, just one facet of its complex aspect, its views of certain natures of its citizens. "A complex fate, being an American, my dear Egon, and one of the responsibilities it entails is fighting against a superstitious valuation of Europe. For us Americans, there are, as it were, persons to be observed, singly or in couples, bending towards objects in out-of-way corners with their hands on their knees and their heads nodding quite as if with the emphasis of an excited sense of smell. When . . ."

Egon listened to the flow of words, the smooth gliding, twisting sentences that were so full of meat, and so complex, and yet always managed to come, calmly, to a full stop and a proper, almost polite ending, like a little boy for a task well done. Egon dared not look at the watch strapped to his wrist (it was one of the first wrist watches in New York). It was Friday, late Friday afternoon, with the tea hour drawing to a close, and he was due at his father's house for the Sabbath meal. Also—Selma was bringing someone home for dinner, someone she wanted to marry. And yet Egon could not break in on this Jamesian torrent of talk. He remembered how they joked about Henry James sometimes, and the Mayfair wit who said, "There are three Jameses in English history: James the First, James the Second, and Henry James the Old Pretender."

The teacup was raised half-way to the moving, Jamesian lips. "I confess that the blaze about to come to our world soon leaves me woefully cold, thrilling with no glorious thrill or holy blood-thirst whatever. (Will you signal the waiter, Egon, for another pot of tea?) I see nothing but the madness, the passion, the hideous clumsiness of rage, of mechanical reverberation. . . ."

The cup touched the lips for one moment for a swift swallow, was lowered, and the voice went on, clear, sure, and evenly polite in tone. "I echo with all my heart any denouncement of the foul criminality of the screeching newspapers. They have long since become for me the danger that overtops all others. Thank God, however, I've no opinions —not even on the Dreyfus case. I'm more and more aware of things as merely a mad panorama, phantasmagoria and, pardon me, Egon, as a dime museum. Look at us! A boneless church, broadening itself out to be up to date; hysterical legislation over a dog with a broken leg, while society is engaged in gloating over foxes torn to pieces, the docility of classes enslaved to respectability and legislated out of all independence. American life is merely a society of women located in a world of women, the men supplying, as it were, all the canvas, and the women all the embroidery. I fear, however, I strike to excess the so-called pessimistic note. . . ."

Egon saw an opening and skilfully took it. He rose and said, "Not at all. How well you understand what Dryden meant when he wrote:

> '*All, all of a piece throughoutê*
> *Thy chase had a beast in view;*
> *Thy wars brought nothing about;*
> *Thy lovers were all untrue.*
> *'Tis well an old age is out,*
> *And time to begin a new.*' "

Henry James watched the waiter place the fresh pot of tea on the table, and as Egon finished the poem, he said, "Exactly."

Egon excused himself and spoke of a family dinner, and they juggled a little promise to attend, perhaps, a play later in the week. As Egon left, he heard Henry James address the waiter: "Tepid is not hot—neither is it warm, rather . . ."

Egon derived great pleasure from walking in the streets of large cities just after dusk. At twilight he would appear, a large man, neat, almost dainty in his dress, carrying a thin, gold-knobbed cane, and he would walk for miles through the fine residential and business districts. He enjoyed, literally craved, a feeling of being alone one dark hour, outside of life, cut off from his fellow men, walking in the gathering dark, passing lighted windows, street corners, watching the homeward trek of the office workers, the late shoppers, and the street drifters as rudderless as himself.

He imagined many odd adventures as he looked into lighted shop windows, or silently crossed great stone streets, and went on past empty buildings that were given over to business in the day. He particularly liked to be an eye-witness to brief street vignettes, a policeman coming out of an alley wiping his mouth, a pedlar sadly pushing his half-sold barrow homeward; shabby couples drifting into candle-lit restaurants, children running in panic on some late errand.

Walking now toward his father's house in the fast-falling darkness, the street lights of Fifth Avenue marching ahead of him, Egon felt that brief moment of happiness that comes not too often to anyone. The twilight and the street, the store lights all pushing him back, a shadow, a mere moving object, featureless, half-seen in the city street. Here he felt safe, walking alone, adventuresome and free from the errors of relationships and petty everyday bickering.

He walked briskly, not hurrying, but with a good, solid, steady pace. It was his only exercise, this walking, and he knew that in his middle thirties he was becoming gross. Fat was protruding down his neck, enlarging his girth; soon, in middle age, he would lose the last of that desire to move quickly, gracefully, with the limber spring of youth and excitement.

There was no use thinking of age. If youth is a fault, "we get over it quickly". It would come, old age, it would come quicker now, and he would of course accept it. After his mother's death, he could accept anything. A bum stood against a steaming iron railing fumbling his buttons. He turned toward Egon and leered. "―― ―― ――?"

Egon coolly passed him by. For a moment, he was sad. But he was happy in the thought of the dinner ahead of him, seeing the family, of being part of them, part of a tribe, a herd, a relationship. Odd, how Ralph had been able to give up all that. Egon passionately loved the family. In his youth he had felt that being a Jew was something a man should be spared, like six fingers or an extra nose, but now he was amused when he thought of this early brooding over his personal, racial predicament. A man was a man, and being born a Jew was no worse than being born an American Indian, or a Scotsman, or an Italian duke. To be born is to live and to die—it was all a common fate. If fanatic or stupid people disliked Jews, or Indians, or Italians, well, a Jew could still live with a certain grace and dignity. It was, Egon thought, pretty much a world of dupes and rogues. The dupes supported the rogues, and the rogues ruled the world. Egon felt he was a dupe; he admitted it cheerfully, and that was all there was to it. He exploited, taxed, restrained, pushed and regimented, bellowed at by the ruling rogues. He didn't mind too much. His love for beauty, art, the solid, comforting things of life, made up for being a mere dupe. He had noticed that the rogues really had the worst of it in life. They slaved, stormed, and shouted; ulcers ate holes in them; they ran and hurried, screamed and pleaded; and in the end, a friend helped them to power, and often a friend arranged for their death. No, the rogues might steal most of the good things of this world and become famous and even popular, but to Egon, being a dupe held the greater, fuller pleasure.

He walked on almost inhaling the street scene. Encased in its darkness, he was safe, unknown to the people passing. He knew this was not all there was to the town—any town. There was the section of the poor, the workhorse dupes. Slums. Ghettos. Little Italies. Hunky and Polack towns. But Egon avoided them. Selma, however, it appeared had gone down there and had found a lover among the slave dupes, among the exploited muscles and minds of the slums.

It was, in a way, just like Selma. Papa had spoiled her. She had travelled so much and been so pampered that she had no understanding of the dupe–rogue relationship. It had never been made clear to her that there were sections of lower dupedom into which one did not go. Better even to go over to the rogues, like Ralph. One could even become a fake rogue, almost pass for the genuine rogue article. He wondered what Selma's lover was like. Of course, there was no use expecting that she would accept an educating, lusty affair and enjoy it, and come out of this thing wise and just a little less happy than when she went into it. No, Selma would wait and have her love legal. Canopied and with the ritual mutterings of the tribal witch-doctors. It would be a mating for family and children and the good, solid comforts of the middle-class dupe-world. A class the rogues kept carefully, and tended like prize cattle.

He must tell Henry James his dupe-and-rogue theory. It might make a neat introduction to a short story. ("Ah, yes, that's Egon Pedlock—a Henry James character.")

Friday night dinners were always in Sam's big, bow-windowed dining room on the first floor. Sara and the cook, a Polish character called Anna, with a front tooth missing, would have spent the day in cooking and broiling and stewing; and now, at dusk, the two silver candlesticks, Rebecca's, were lit and placed on that best damask cloth. The family gathered in the living room waiting for Anna to come in and say the chopped liver and other hors d'œuvres were on the table. There was no ritual or prayer, except for the two silver candlesticks and the fact that Friday night, the eve of Sabbath, was held sacred to family gatherings.

Sam's three sons, now in their late teens, big husky youths, were away at school. Joseph sat by the few sticks of glowing fire in the black marble fireplace, leaning on his cane, while Tante Strasser read to him a long letter from some relative in need of funds. He was paying no attention to it at all. Funds were rather low.

"Arthur has the stomach *Krankheit*. My heart is not of the best . . ." she read.

Selma came down the stairs, wearing a blue gown and some small yellow violets in her belt.

"Where's Egon?" she asked.

"He'll be here," said Joseph, picking up his before-dinner glass of brandy. "Where's your Russian?"

"Let's have no jokes about Russians. Naturally, we know *we* are the salt of the earth and all others must come below us. But let's just act as if Jacob is as human as we are."

Tante Strasser folded the letter carefully. "It could have been worse. He might have been a Glitz or a Litvak."

"The snobbery and anti-Semitism of Jews!" said Sam, taking out a cigar from a leather folder. "It's worse than that of the Christians toward us. I'd rather be snubbed by a Bishop than have another Jew dislike me for my Jewishness."

"Don't smoke now, Sam," said Sara, coming out of the dining room. "Get a bottle of the good wine. Where are all the guests?"

CHAPTER IX

Deep in old walls, the doorbell gave a feeble tinkle. Selma raced to the door before Trixie, the coloured maid and day worker, who was putting down water glasses on the dining-room table, could shuffle to the door. It was Egon, smiling in the doorway, cane under his arm, peeling his gloves off carefully.

"Beware of Greeks bearing tea roses," he said, handing Selma a blue-wrapped florist's bouquet and kissing her on the nose. "Just something to brighten up the corners."

"Thank you, Egon. I hope we shall be spared your keen wit on certain subjects."

"Don't be a fool, Selma. I'm damn happy for you."

They walked into the living room arm in arm. Joseph looked up from the fire, without taking his lips from the brandy glass. "You're getting fatter than a Chicago pork-packer, Egon."

"I can't blame it on anything but well-cooked food, Papa."

"How's the art business?" asked Sam.

"I hope not as bad as the coal and timber."

"Sit down—you're shaking the house."

The doorbell tinkled again, even more feebly than before. Selma turned, but Trixie was already starting for it. She opened it and Jacob came in, his brown, curly hair plastered back wetly on his square skull, his suit, as usual, too tight across the broad shoulders. He was smiling shyly and from under one arm he held out a small box of after-dinner mints for Selma.

"The man said it's a proper dinner gift."

"Yes, Jacob dear. Come in."

Selma, straight and very taut, leaned over and kissed him on the cheek and led him into the family's view.

"This is Jacob Kozloff. Jacob, I want you to meet my family." Carefully, she introduced everyone. Jacob shook many hands.

Anna, the cook, appeared, her face wet and one loose, blonde hair tickling her nose so that she tried to blow it away and talk at the same time. "Dinner's (*poof*) ready. Better come (*poof*) eat it. . . ."

Selma completed the introductions as the family rose for dinner. The worst was over—perhaps.

* * *

Sara sat at the head of the table, Joseph at her right, and Jacob, as her guest, at her left. Selma pinched him below table level and grinned at him, and Egon settled back and peered into the candles under the mass of ceiling lights, those egg-shaped, unfrosted lights with the small glass tails of the early electric bulb.

Trixie and Anna placed *salade française* and chopped liver in front of everyone. Jacob looked around the table as everyone picked up forks. "Pardon me," he said in a husky voice, pulling a small, black cap from his pocket, "I'd like to say a prayer."

Joseph grinned. "You go right ahead, Jacob. I remember there is one that begins: *Shema Yisroel adonoi....*"

Jacob nodded. "*Shema Yisroel Adonoi Elohenu Adonoi Echod ...* Hear, O Israel, the Lord is our God, the Lord is One...."

He recited part of the prayer for Sabbath quickly and the prayer for food, and began to eat his chopped liver and salad quickly, his face flushed pink. The devil take it, he thought, what a nest of *goyim*. No covering of the head, or saying a single prayer to God in thanks for the week, or the Sabbath to come.

Selma pressed his leg from time to time with her hand to give him courage, but he was not frightened. Boldly, he decided to assert his will. He was, in a way, God's representative here tonight.

Sara received a large platter of fish from Trixie and passed it to Jacob. "You will try the fish, Mr. Kozloff?"

Jacob took the platter and said, "It's fine to find a family that still keeps kosher," he said.

A sudden emotion, almost of fear and shame, hit the table. Good lord! The man was a regular rabbi!

Egon, with a full mouth, looked up at Sam, who frowned. Sara glanced at Trixie, who looked numb; but Anna, bringing a deep-covered dish of marrow dumplings to the table, caught the desperate look in Sara's eyes and went back to the kitchen and took the floating butter balls out of the ice-filled, deep butter dish. She swore to herself in Polish. The things one did for a suitor! And him so poor-looking that his ass must be sticking bare out of his pants. Scratch a *schnorrer* (beggar) and find a holy man. (Thank God, she had decided against *kosaliena* of pigs' feet and goose jelly!)

The meal progressed through the innocent cabbage soup, the roasts of beef and chicken, the stew of fruit, and at last, after a magnificent American apple pie, to large cups of coffee, very black. Egon was about to ask for the cream when he caught himself, and looked in guilt at Jacob. Sam clipped a cigar end and put it into his mouth, but didn't light it and after a while put it away in his vest, when Jacob wasn't looking. No fire is lit on the Sabbath. Jacob stirred his coffee and Joseph leaned on an elbow and looked across at him.

"Well, Mr. Kozloff, you've impressed and cowed us all. Isn't there a prayer at the end of the meal?"

"Enough prayers," said Jacob simply smiling at Joseph. "I'll catch up some other Friday evening."

Egon nodded. "You observe all the laws and rituals?"

Jacob shook his head. "I try. But of course, you can't go too far. Like growing the beard, not carrying money on the Sabbath, not travelling."

Joseph said, "Yes. We're no longer a community of close-knit desert tribes."

"It's all out of date," said Egon, "but it has a charm, and it gives us all certain roots in a past, when on Mount Sinai God spoke to Moses. Only there is nothing worse than having nothing to turn to, even if it's only a myth, legend, or mumbo-jumbo. Some of my Catholic friends who have lost the faith suffer a lot."

Jacob said, "I lost my own faith once. It was like being dead and everyone refusing to bury you. I was much younger; it was back in a village in Russia. A poor man has to believe in God, maybe because he has so little else to believe in."

Joseph pulled on his short, square beard. "I've wondered why God made all the people who really serve him honestly, so poor. 'If he is God'—my father used to say—'he could just as well have made us all rich!' But forgive me, Mr. Kozloff, this is no time to question a guest's faith. We all believe in something, even if it's nothing; because then we believe in nothing. There is no such thing, I suppose, as a blank in one's thinking of the Godhead."

"We beat," said Egon, rolling a finger ring, "old dogmas with new sticks."

"What? *What?*" asked Tante Strasser, who was growing hard of hearing.

Sara said, "Let's stop this talk before Mr. Kozloff thinks we hold a Black Mass here."

Sam invited them all to the living room to listen to his collection of Caruso recordings, but Egon said he had to be up early, around noon, to attend an art dealers' meeting, and Jacob and Selma wanted to walk around in the park.

"Well, you see," said Selma, as they crossed to the park gates, "they don't have horns and they don't eat young Russian Jews."

"They're a very interesting family. They don't seem to take being Jewish very seriously."

"We don't carry a portable Wailing Wall for public lamenting, I admit. Oh, Jacob, I'm so happy everything is all settled."

"The truth is, Selma, nothing is settled. You see, my shop is failing. I'm closing it at the end of the month. Why should I lie? They're taking it away from me. The machines, the shop . . . everything. I've borrowed on it to get money, not that I regret it, to take you out."

"Why didn't you tell me? Ruining yourself for me. You don't know how pleased I am, darling, in a way."

"It doesn't matter. I've gotten a new, big idea. A very big idea. I can beat the Germans in the clothing trades at their own game. They're too sure of themselves, too entrenched in their ways."

"Tell me about it, Jacob. I'm damn practical at times."

"Maybe it's all a pipe dream. It would take a lot of money, for me. I'm going to talk to a private moneylender about it. Even at fifty per cent interest, I'm going to try and do it."

"No, Jacob. No more ghetto moneylenders or Mottkes. Tell me what you have in mind."

They walked on, heads together, arm in arm. Both knew there could be no victory, no real acceptance of their marriage unless the basic problem of how Jacob could keep a wife were worked out.

"It's a problem," said Selma. "Now, in the old country, I hear, you would move into my father's house, and I would get a market stand and you would spend your time with the holy men, reading the Talmud. And if you were real holy, I would shave my hair and walk with my eyes down, two steps behind you."

"Thank God, that kind of life is over."

"It would have solved everything. We'd be together. But Papa is broke, the coal business is dreadful, and all the dowry I have is some stock, beautifully printed and rather worthless, of Pedlock Coal and Iron that Mama—*olav hasholem*—left me in her will."

"Maybe I can get a loan from the moneylenders at only twenty per cent—short term."

Selma suddenly stopped and gripped his arm. "Let's stop being such giddy fools. I know where we can get the money through normal channels of business! Of course, the family must never know."

"Where? What?"

"Kiss me, Jacob, I've just discovered I've inherited a little from the side of the family that has some brains."

Sam and Sara had spent a great deal of their domestic life in sleep—in a large, black walnut bed that had once belonged to Sara's grandmother, who had brought it from Frankfort in 1849. They had managed to get it into the bedroom of the brownstone house, but it had crowded the room without mercy. Sara sat at her dressing-table, rubbing her chin, throat, and magnificent large breasts with lumps of ice. It was her beauty secret. She felt the ice treatment kept her skin young, fresh, and tight. Sam said it was like sleeping with a sherbet with legs.

Sam, in his nightshirt, was seated at a small, rosewood desk, puttering around with his stamp collection. It was the only thing of value he had salvaged out of their once prosperous past, when it had seemed they would have a great deal of money and he had been able to buy stamps that, for some foolish reason, all stamp collectors treasure. He owned a Blue Lady Macleod from Trinidad, a really rare group of Confederate States of America in fine forms (including an envelope with a return address in ink: Hefferson Davis, Richmond, Va., C.S.A.). He was now going over his British Guianas, examining the value of one error, imprinted *patimus* instead of *petimus*, and wondering why he was fool enough to enjoy this childish hobby. Yet he knew that if he were offered the famous "black on magenta", the notorious Guiana error of 1856, he would have paid thousands for it, if he had the money.

Sara was following the ice treatment with some eau-de-Cologne slapped on with vigour. She half turned toward Sam.

"What do you think?"

"What's the subject?" asked Sam, holding a stamp up to the light to see if it had been "washed" to remove a cancellation.

"Selma's young man."

"He'll do."

"He hasn't a penny. He owns a sweatshop, and I hear even that is failing."

"Selma doesn't seem to care."

"Sam, put away that nonsense with coloured scraps of paper. Do you think he's after Selma's money?"

"Can't be. She hasn't any."

"You know these ghetto types. These Russians—they have very odd customs and aren't ashamed to marry for money or room and board."

Sam closed his albums with a sigh. He went over and kissed Sara on the back of her neck. "Well, that's why I married you. For your father's ill-gotten gains, and because you were fat. I love fat girls." He pinched her. "There must be Turkish blood in the family. I could eat you with a spoon."

"Never mind the dirty remarks. What is the family going to do about Mr. Kozloff?"

"That's easy to answer. Nothing. They're in love and they're young and healthy, and most likely make love very well."

"You'll get used to my lewd ways. Selma is old enough to know her mind and certainly old enough to be passionately in love. Kozloff isn't so bad. I admire him in many ways. The way he dared to pray at our pagan table, the way he faces all of us without bending his inferior Russian backbone. It takes courage. We're rather a bunch of dragons."

"Sam! That's not nice. We're a pretty handsome family. Tante Strasser was a great and famous beauty in her day. Why, a Royal Grand Duke offered to set her up in an apartment in Vienna and . . ."

"That's an indecent and unproved family secret. Come on to bed. You've rubbed yourself long enough."

"You want a wrinkled prune for a wife?"

Sara took a last look at the mirror and patted her chin ten times more. She got into bed beside Sam and turned out the lamp. Sam relaxed against her, yawned, and took her in his arms.

Sara stiffened. "What did you mean that you liked fat women?"

"Shoot me! Can I help it if I love an upholstered behind?"

"Sam, don't talk that vulgar way to me. And I'm not fat. . . . That is *fat*."

"Fat! Who said you were fat?"

"You did. You said . . ."

"I know what I said. I'll label it 'joke' next time. Can't a man joke in his own bedroom with his own wife? Fat? You're thin like a boy. It's almost a sin to sleep with you. A regular boy I have here. And here."

"Sam!"

"Sara, honey."

"After twenty years, all these years of marriage, Sam, I don't really see what you see in me any more."

234

"I have odd tastes. 'Joke!' "

"Oh, Sam . . . you fool . . . you sweet fool."

"That's better . . . I love the way you spoil me with compliments."

"Oh, Sam."

Later.

"Sam, I suppose if Selma loves him, that's enough."

"Go to sleep, my Turkish delight."

She yawned, smiled, and in the dark, secretly patted her chin line. Not fat. Just a little plump, perhaps.

Interior decorators had again been at work on the expensive walls of the New Amsterdam–Manhattan bank. The private offices were again being done over to the taste of the holders; some new plan to make a dignified unit, a complete banking picture in light wood panelling, deep, comfortable leather furniture, and old, farmhouse kerosene lamps of brass, wired for the more modern electricity.

A small, neat office had been assigned to Ralph Manderson Perry, son-in-law of the bank's president. (Charles Pentland had gone higher than he had ever dreamed, yet fitting to a man of his abilities and background.) Ralph's office and bathroom and his secretary's fenced-in, outer empire occupied a polite corner of the bank—out of range of the ticking clatter of the book-keeping machines, and the pens scratching on paper notes, or cheques being endorsed. He had a wide, maple wood desk topped with a leatherbound blotter pad, a ship's tiller of gold a full foot across in which was set a clock, a compass, and a working weather-gauge. A bag of golf clubs in a beautiful, leather bag leaned in one corner of the room, half-hidden by pale ferns dying with curling dignity in blue ceramic pots.

On Ralph's desk were two silver-framed pictures of Alice and his son, Peter, the baby fat melting away. The firm little nose, he was happy to see, was straight as his own, or Alice's.

Ralph had few duties, but he found them pleasant. He usually left the bank at about four o'clock to catch the train back to Long Island. He was often entrusted with secret missions to Boston, to the Carolinas, to old, soot-covered castles in the Pennsylvania coal and iron hills. He was neither cunning nor conniving, and did business honestly, with leisure and tact. He was best with rather dear old ladies suffering from fashionable imported diseases, with whom he got along charmingly and who asked for "Mr. Perry" when some details of their estates became minor problems. Charles Pentland used to say, at lunch, at the Bankers' Club, when he was entertaining some Hollywood motion-picture figure, or a diamond dealer or one of the Sassoons or Lehmanns or Rothschild, that his son-in-law was a delightful chap. Only lacking "a good Jewish head for business". The motion-picture magnate or the diamond man would nod and be rather pleased that Charles Pentland could be so publicly proud of a Jewish son-in-law. Of course, there was no use carrying the thing too far, Charles Pentland felt; he never mentioned Ralph's background when lunching with Baptist oil men, Catholic stockbrokers or plain Scotch-American investors, who made six per cent interest as deadly as machine guns.

Ralph had begun to put on character. The big blond head, the trim triangle of moustache that he began to cultivate in the style of his father-in-law, gave him a beauty and style that was "wholesome and trustful to look at", as his secretary, Miss Monday, used to say.

Ralph was sitting at his desk, going through a listing of German state bonds that were beginning to give trouble, with all this 1914 war talk, and filling a handsome yellow pipe with his own mixture of Dunhill's Royal Yacht, modified to his personal needs. ("Good Virginia rough-cut, very fine Turkish strands. And a good bit of rare Irish bogy, like the string section in an orchestra," the salesman used to tell him.)

He was puffing the pipe slowly and carefully into life when Miss Monday came in with that gliding walk of hers and seemed to propel her on small wheels swiftly toward his desk, only the hiss of petticoats explaining how she stayed in motion.

"Mr. Perry, there is a Mr. Kozloff and a Miss Pedlock to see you. They have no appointment, but they say . . ."

Ralph put down the pipe carefully. "Miss Pedlock?"

"Miss Selma Pedlock."

Miss Monday glanced at the small slip of paper in her hand, to check the name.

"Oh, yes. Please send them in, Miss Monday."

"You're meeting Mr. Guntil of the Springer estate at eleven."

"Yes. Well, hold him for a few minutes out there if this takes too long."

"Yes, Mr. Perry." She wheeled out, not approving of this meeting of people without appointments; somehow she felt it hurt the bank's position to see people without making them understand how hard it was to contact an important official.

The chairs in the outer waiting room were smooth, of very hard wood and grooved for impossible, spreading buttocks shaped like flattened ducks. People waited for hours on them, trying to fit their lower anatomies into the fantastic forms of the furniture-designing joker. Selma and Jacob did not wait long on their chairs.

Ralph rose as Selma, looking very pert in black and grey, came in, followed by a wide, stocky young man with big shoulders and carefully combed, curly brown hair.

"Hello, Ralph," said Selma, as Ralph held out his hand. She took the hand and leaned over and kissed him on the cheek. "You're looking sassy and well."

"I feel fine, Selma."

"Ralph, this is Jacob Kozloff. We're engaged to be married. Jacob, this is my brother, Ralph."

They exchanged small greetings and Ralph pushed up some deep, comfortable chairs for them to sit in. He went back behind his protecting desk and relit the pipe.

"May I wish you both much happiness? It's kind of hard to believe little Selma has grown up."

"I have. However, Ralph, I didn't come here to get just your congratulations, for which we both, of course, thank you."

Ralph nodded, and was pleased at the calm grip he had of himself.

He hoped the old man wasn't dying, or that the family (he knew, of course, that they were having hard sledding) was going to ask some favour that he could not perform.

"How is everyone?" he asked.

"Everyone is fine. I don't want to fool you, Ralph. No one in the family knows I'm here. This is a business matter. Not for the family, but for Jacob, and, of course, for myself."

Jacob nodded and took out a sheet of close-written text and figures from his pocket. It was the result of weeks of hard work. "Mr. Perry, I would like to explain this whole thing right away, so you can see why I need your bank's help."

"I see. What kind of enterprise are you in, Mr. Korz——?"

"Kozloff. It used to be Kozloffsky, but you know how names get changed here in this country."

Selma cleared her throat and rubbed the end of her nose. ⌐Strike one! she said to herself. Name-changing! Ralph was busy with a pipe cleaner. Jacob seemed unaware that he had said anything either amusing or harmful.

"I'm in no business at the moment. I used to run a small shop on Division Street. But I've closed it. Mr. Perry, I've been studying American business methods for some time. And the clothing industry, naturally, most of all. Maybe because we Jews are the industry." (Strike two, thought Selma.) "The Germans practically invented the modern garment industry and the ready-made suit. They have dominated it with their methods."

Ralph nodded, showing no emotion. He looked at Peter's baby picture and inhaled a lungful of Royal Yacht slowly.

"There is no use for me," Jacob went on, "to try and compete in the men's clothing industry. But times are changing and new methods and inventions are appearing. There is a great market for cheap, ready-made, women's house-dresses, kimonos, and aprons. I want to turn them out the way Henry Ford is making cars."

"I see," said Ralph, adding a trick of Charles Pentland's—a series of key words. "Ford, mass market, women's wear."

"There has just been invented an electric cutting knife that can cut through thirty layers or even fifty layers of cotton cloth. The Germans are making vat dyes from coal tars that are wash-proof. The converting of grey goods can become a big thing, if someone were able to turn out house-dresses and kimonos and aprons on the assembly-line methods of Ford cars."

"Well, now," said Ralph. "Electric cutting, vat dye, wash-proof, grey goods."

"Ralph," said Selma. "I can see that you're impressed."

"No one has yet tried to do any of this," said Jacob. "There is at present too much hand work, too much styling and too many models. There is no real, national selling of cheap cotton goods. I feel this is something new and big, and it can't fail."

Selma nodded. "The truth is, Ralph, we want to borrow forty thousand dollars now, and establish a credit of forty thousand more."

Jacob added, "I have it all worked out here on this paper, if you'd care to inspect it." He put the paper down on Ralph's desk.

Ralph looked at it without picking it up. "Very interesting, Mr. Kozloff, but you see, this bank and its stockholders as chartered by the state . . ."

"Oh, poof," said Selma. "We know all that. I have eighty thousand shares of Pedlock Coal and Iron. I'll pledge them for the loan."

Ralph lifted his arms up, elbows bent, to show it was a little odd and beyond him. A Jewish gesture. "I don't know, at the moment, what that stock is worth, or what it will ever be worth. There's coal and iron there, of course . . . but . . ."

Selma stood up. "Ralph, I could have gone to Mr. Pentland for this. I have a feeling he'd help his relatives out. I'd rather get it from you. I wouldn't want to go to Mr. Pentland. It wouldn't seem right."

Jacob looked at Selma and smiled, a thin, small smile that he hoped was not noticed. They were an amazing family, these Pedlocks. Ralph looked at Selma, then at Jacob. He also knew that Charles Pentland would give Jacob the loan. The slick old bastard would have laughed at being called "a relative", would have slapped Jacob on the back, and mentioned a few, big, Jewish business accounts the bank handled, and most likely would have told Jacob that he certainly had an idea there; cheap cottons for women on the Ford assembly-line plan. But for Ralph to face his father-in-law alone was another problem. Ralph stood up and looked at the ship's tiller. A tiny bell in it rang three times. He didn't know just what that meant in ship's time, but the clock face showed he was ten minutes late with Mr. Guntil of the Springer estate. The weather-gauge showed a shift towards rain.

"I'll take it up with the bank. It's been nice to see you again, Selma. And to meet you, too, Mr. Kozloff. Thank you. I'll keep this paper and return it to you. Drop in any time. It will always be a pleasure to see you."

They shook hands and Selma grinned and gave him a hug and they went out. Ralph sat down and banged his pipe out into a special wooden bowl he kept for just that task. Miss Monday came in.

"Mr. Guntil has been waiting."

"Yes. Miss Monday, send him in and call Mr. Pentland and get me an appointment to see him after lunch. Around two, two-thirty. I also want to dictate a memo to him later."

Miss Monday nodded, put down a folder marked *Springer Estate Holdings*, and went out. A large, bald young man entered, the few remaining black hairs combed tight down behind his big red ears. He wore a little ceramic pig with a Harvard H hanging from it, and carried a beautiful, pebbled pigskin briefcase, its straps undone. He put the briefcase down on the desk, rubbed his brow and groaned. "Ralph, I'm as hung over as a mountain goat's rear fender. Give me a hair of the dog."

"Rye, Bourbon with branch water, or Scotch, Ed?"

"Scotch. Say, that was a nice little Hebe dish just went out of here. Wouldn't mind a little change of luck with that."

Ralph opened the cabinet set with Chinese figures in heavy black and red varnish, held up the Scotch, and poured three fingers of it into a shot glass. "You can taste the heather in this."

Guntil took the glass with shaking hand, tossed back its head, and swallowed hard. "That's better. Leave the bottle out. . . . Ralph, the lawyers are yelping about that Pacific Gas bond sale the bank has made for the estate. They say the bank keeps buying and selling just to run up expenses."

"Nonsense! Maybe we're *too* careful. That's all. I'll send you a case of this Scotch for Christmas, Ed."

"Better send the lawyers a case, too. No, better make it cigars. Those mangy old characters out of Dickens drink only port and sherry."

Ralph picked up Jacob's sheet of figures, folding it, and put it in his vest pocket.

"Boy, I'm as hung over as a burlesque queen's chest!"

Charles Pentland put down his gold-plated letter opener and laughed. He sat well back in his desk chair and howled. Ralph smiled but did not join in the laughter. Charles Pentland recovered from his mirth and repeated part of the limerick Captain Dopley of the Embassy had told him at lunch. He had just recited it to his son-in-law. . . . " 'The Vicar . . . thicker . . . slicker . . .' I tell you, Ralph, whoever says the English have no sense of humour is a fathead. Do you know the one about the hermit who lived in a cave and bent double?"

"Yes, I do. Have you read the memo I sent you on that Kozloff matter?"

Charles Pentland nodded. "Oh. Of course—give him the loan. I have a feeling that coal-and-iron project is going to pay off some day. Besides, my boy, there is nothing like family loyalties." He smiled. "The Vicar . . ."

Everyone, Ralph thought, was certainly full of humour these days.

It was to be called The J. K. Kozloff Standard Dress Company. (The first K. stood for nothing, but Selma felt it gave balance to the name, like J. P. Morgan. "Who would ever be impressed by a man called just J. Morgan or J. Rockefeller?")

The first factory was a huge, bare, whitewashed loft overlooking the East River. It had once been a warehouse. It was large; it was well lighted; and it was heated by steam. The cutting tables seemed to be a mile long, the electric knives fast little dangerous monsters that Jacob had to train his crew of cutters to use with skill and speed. The yard-goods arrived in bolts. Thousands of yards of it. The sewing machines were new and there were several dozens of them. The girls were young, fresh, earnest, and pleased by their surroundings.

Hannah and her rancid baby, the Starker Glitz, the Professor were all put in the shipping department. They were the chaff in the fields of Jacob's labour now, but he was still a little soft in his heart to his old workers. The Detroit pattern of wearing them out and throwing them away was as yet a little too brutal for him. Bella refused to have any part of his new factory. She became a cashier in a new Yiddish theatre on Second Avenue.

A cousin of Etta Sontag's, who had been to Paris and lived with a Polish stone carver and had once seen Renoir, was the designer. She was a bright, ugly girl, with heavy, black hair worn very stylish, in a tight twist on her head. She cultivated a husky-voiced English accent. She sketched the styles in the Fifth Avenue windows. She copied popular fashions from the magazines; she went to openings of the Paris houses, and brought back her loot of ideas. She and Jacob copied them into cotton housedresses to sell for a dollar. They removed a bow here, put on a simpler belt, took off a row of buttons, and by the time they were sure it could be turned out by the thousands, with semi-skilled help, they had a dress that was colourful, stylish, and yet cheap; a real bargain to the American housewife.

They made up fifty samples and discarded twenty-five of them. They threw out five more, and with a line of twenty numbers, the salesmen invaded the stores and mail-order houses and the buying combines. Jacob did no selling himself. He hired, at double the usual commission paid by anyone else, the best salesmen in the industry. They had large expense accounts and he asked no questions about parties, gifts, or bar bills.

"Standard Kozloffs" went into two great mail-order catalogues that year, and four huge department stores offered to buy a thousand dozen at special discounts and favours. Jacob, as his success expanded, began meeting the lords and kings of the department-store worlds. Men who were marketing the world to Chicago and St. Louis and Pittsburgh and Boston and Philadelphia. Kaufmans and Fields, Filenes and Rosenwalds, Levis and Marcuses, Wanamakers, Gimbels, Strauses —creators of those huge and fancy stores that served entire cities.

Jacob had never known that such American merchant families existed, such dynasties of bolts and safety-pins and ice-boxes and work-shirts and Grand Rapids furniture. "Merchant Princes", as the press called them, givers of charity and makers of speeches (and in most cases, payers of small salaries and inventors of killing sales quotas and crippling season sales and hammering down of manufacturers' profits and price lists).

In six months, the J. K. Kozloff Standard Dress Company did a million dollars' worth of business on its books and had lost eighty thousand dollars, owed the cotton mills a hundred thousand dollars, and was borrowing seventy-five thousand dollars more from the bank to keep going until the new season started. Everyone spoke of the success of this new king of the house-dress business, J. K. Kozloff. There was no doubt in anyone's mind that here was a coming man. Here was a brain. And a method that was revolutionizing the women's ready-to-wear field.

To Jacob, it was an amazing picture of the insides of the American business scene. He was more in debt than ever. He owed fortunes to banks, mills, and ribbon and button houses. He was more extended than he had ever been with his small miserable debts as a sweatshop owner. Yet he was looked upon as a great success. It was a time of rising markets, of world progress (or so everyone said), and so Jacob was not broken by a sudden depression or bankrupted by political change, or ruined by droughts or floods or animal diseases that would have destroyed the farmers' wives' desire for his pretty and cheap dresses.

He was, he admitted, in luck. When his debts were so large that a showdown was at hand, when it looked as if the banks and the mills would take over the system he had built up, along came a dreadful war in Europe, quickly converting his plant to the making of uniforms, flags, tents, bags, and stretchers. He expanded into half a dozen great plants, acquired his own cotton and converting mills, and brought out a button house. He should have emerged from the war a millionaire. He merely saw the peace of the Twenties as an owner of great factories, a surplus stock of unwanted war goods, and bigger debts than ever. He had over-produced. But by that time, he had learned how to play the game. Kozloff Standard became a Delaware corporation, recognized the garment workers' unions (among the first of the great shops to do so), and sold its stock in the future of the boll weevil and the desire of the American housewife to wear a dress in the kitchen remotely related to the Parisian fashion world.

But most of this was still in the future, when Jacob and Selma were married in the living room of the Pedlock brownstone house. He had just passed his first half-million dollars in debt; such a success could now afford marriage. They were married by a brisk young man in a business suit, with buttered hair and the accent of an English actor with a head cold.

"The success story of Jacob Kozloff," old Joseph always said, "was not an isolated incident in the American scene of its time." There were thousands of such stories, and they were to strengthen the American myth of the chance every young boy had of heading his own corporations and holding companies.

"Jacob and the rest," Joseph said, "had not produced an age—the age had produced them. The Fords, the makers of motion pictures, the canned-soup empires, the rubber and tin kings, the telephone, gramophone, motorbike, and wire toys of the new century were all produced because they were desired in a rising world power, feeling its muscles and needing the stuff of mass production to bedeck, to entertain, and to waste."

Old Joseph made many long speeches on the subject. Not that he didn't feel Jacob's real worth, but rather that he had seen the beginnings of this great march of machines that had turned the country he knew from a land of farmers and whittlers of wooden farm forms into a land of factory creatures and steel turbine designers.

"It's progress, papa," they used to say to him.

"It's speed, but is it progress? Doing it quicker and better is all right, if it's something important. Like healing the sick and housing the poor and loving your neighbour. It's not so good if used only to build racing cars and machine guns, and exploit poor blacks and Asiatics, for rubber trees and gold dust and tin."

"Papa, you admit that Jacob makes fine, cheap house dresses?"

"I like Jacob. I'm just thinking beyond that into a remade world. Ford's cars and Edison's and Lasky's and Zukor's motion pictures, and Du Pont's stinks and Judge Gary's steel hells and Hearst's and Pulitzer's way of shouting banal culture. What is all this really going to do to a world that maybe isn't going to be happy in all this so-called Progress? Progress of objects of this sort is old-fashioned. . . . It's priests and witch-doctors selling production records instead of the usual, ritual mumbo-jumbo."

But, of course, at the wedding of Jacob and Selma, no one said too much about the machine-age world. Jacob was shocked to discover that the sportsman with the buttered hair was a popular young Reform rabbi from a Fifth Avenue synagogue, and that the services were to be in English, and there was no marriage canopy. There was not even the ceremony of the wine drinking, and the rabbi putting the wine glass on the floor and inviting the bridegroom to destroy it with one crash of his heel, as is ritually expected at any good wedding of Jews.

The Colonel had come out from Butte for the wedding. Tante Strasser wept buckets in the front row. She didn't know why she wept at weddings. But she enjoyed the practice. Sam and Sara were the hosts and the boys, in new, blue suits, helped serve the wine and cake. Joseph gave the bride away, and Egon took Jacob by the arm and led him up to the sleek rabbi. There were few outsiders. The Starket Glitz and Bella (wearing actress make-up) got drunk, but even that didn't help much to make it a feast. Dr. and Mrs. Sontag gave the happy couple a Remington bronze of a bucking horse frightened by a rattlesnake, and the Colonel pointed out that one could actually "count the rattles on the snake's tail, it's that realistic!"

They went to Atlantic City for a honeymoon and Jacob came into Paradise and knew he would love no other woman as long as he lived. For three days he was happy and then he confessed to Selma that something bothered him. They were riding in a wheelchair on the boardwalk, pushed by the grandson of a Congo war chief who had once ruled an empire. They were headed into the wind, and as they passed a great green pickle with a huge, painted "57" on it, Jacob took Selma's hand in his.

"Selma, I need just one thing more to make me happy."

"That would suit me, too," said Selma, looking like a contented cat full of cream as she indicated, in steps, the size of three small children. Jacob ignored the indecent public sign language.

"I don't feel like a married Jew," he said.

"What's wrong in thinking you're living in sin, if it makes you happy?"

"Selma, I want us to be married by a real rabbi, in Hebrew. Beard, crumbs on his vest, and hungry for his fee—but I want it—very much."

She looked at him tenderly and pressed his hand. "Would that make you really happy, darling?"

They were married again, the next day, at Glickman's Golden Gardens on Arctic Avenue—a stucco building given over to Jewish weddings, burials, union meetings and loud and heart-felt services on the high holidays. They were married under a real, fly-specked canopy just vacated by a wedding couple now celebrating in the Grove of Eden Room, on the next floor. The rabbi was a small, fat man with clean, ginger-coloured whiskers, and a proud paunch, and an alpaca coat shiny with use and grease. Between weddings, he executed kosher chickens and, he admitted, dabbled in real estate.

They stood before him, Jacob with a borrowed top hat, and the rabbi and the witnesses gave them the full services with the long Hebrew phrases, and Selma aped them and repeated words she didn't know the meaning of.

The rabbi was very learned. Almost a *tsaddick*, the witnesses whispered. "Too bad he has to kill chickens for a living in this pagan land."

It took some time, and overhead they could hear the clarinets playing and the waiters running, and the rings of dancers celebrating the wedding of a popular local kosher butcher and his bride, heiress of a second-hand furniture store.

The rabbi finished his services, shook hands with them, and put the twenty-dollar bill carefully away, after a cheerful *maṛel-tov!*—good luck!

"*Nu*—how about joining me upstairs at the wedding? It doesn't seem right for you to go off now without a little *simcha*" (joy).

"We don't know them," said Jacob.

The tall, thin witness smiled on them. "It's my nephew Solly's wedding. I invite you. I insist! I command it!"

It was a fine wedding. The waiters sweated and ran skilfully, with shrill warnings, with plates of stuffed *derma* and bottles of celery tonic and wine and plum brandy. The grandmothers—the old *bubas*—puffed and fanned themselves with the fringes of their dresses, and the young folks leaped and laughed. The fiddles and the clarinets played and played with whining pleasure. Pickled green tomatoes, noodle soup, sweet-and-sour fish, baked tongue, and nuts and raisins. Everything is plenty and *more* coming. Bagel, smoked fish, salted chickspeas, roasted chickens, *gefüllte* fish. "Who has room for it all?"

Jacob and Selma were seated at the bride's table, behind a three-foot *cholla*—braided white bread—and they were forced to eat the *derma*—stuffed cow stomach—and drink the brandy, and everyone joked about the strength of the bridegrooms and the fertility of the brides. Oh, the *chuṭzpah*—the nerve—of wedding guests!

Small children ran around in their best clothes and slid across the Grove of Eden Room as if on skates. Babies with greasy mouths lay on chairs against the wall. Mothers came to feed them. A fight broke out at one table over a point of dowry, and two shrews shouted at each other. The clarinets never stopped playing. The musicians ate and drank with the guests, opened their collars, and played louder and louder. Such a pleasure, a good wedding!

On the ceiling, a great ball covered with mirrors rotated and shot shards of reflection over everyone. The butcher bridegroom grew redder and publicly more amorous. The bride answered daringly every goat-like remark addressed to her.

The music broke into "Alle Menchen Tantzendik" (Everybody's Dancing) and the bride and groom, and Jacob and Selma, were whirled on to the floor and circled by the wedding guests, who danced a *mitṛvah*, that act of piety, with them. Everybody's dancing!

The *bubas* shook their wrinkled little faces under their ritual wigs; the old men clicked their heels and store teeth; the circles formed; the dancers spun. There was joy in Zion tonight! Sing!

"Alle menchen tantzendik un shpringendik
Un lachendik un zingendik—"
(Everybody is dancing and leaping
and laughing and singing!)
"Es is schoin tsait essen tsu gehn!"
(It's time to eat the wedding feast!)

The dust rose; the gorged flies fled; the babies, smeared with chicken fat, howled; the children got underfoot. Faces were slapped. The grandmothers' teeth rattled loose. The dancers spun on.

"Es is schoin tsait schlofen tsu gehn!"
(It's time to go to bed!)

So did Jacob and Selma, in great joy and with much love, enter into the kingdom of marriage. . . .

BOOK FIVE

CHAPTER I

Several times Nicole and Peter went on visits to the big Kozloff factories with their spinning machines and cutting knives, and it was more exciting than even the bank.

Charles Pentland would agree with his grandson Peter that a factory was very exciting. "But it's we banks that make it tick. Some people make the products and some finance them. Don't fall in love with sewing machines, boy; we're saving a place for you in the bank. Nothing against us raising up a dynasty of bankers . . . eh, Ralph?"

Father would smile and the grownups would all have cocktails before dinner. Nicole said, when she grew up, they would have cocktails too and talk like the grown people about the trouble in Europe and the killing of a Grand Duke and the mobilization of Russia and England and Germany. Charles Pentland took Nicole on his lap and held up his glass of after-dinner brandy and recited for her, " 'The lights are going out all over Europe. We shall not see them relit in our time.' Like it, Nicole? A remarkable literary sentence for a mere statesman to make."

Father looked up and said, "It's more than a literary remark. I think it's true."

Mother patted Peter's fair hair back into place so that it didn't fall into his eyes. "Do you think it's really going to be a long war?"

"Six months," said Charles Pentland. "Can't last longer. The House of Morgan and the banks are backing the British, and the Russians have the most manpower. In Berlin by Christmas if the Kaiser doesn't come to his senses."

It frightened Peter and Nicole when Grandfather was proved so wrong. And the Kaiser looked so odd in the cartoons. They used to follow Father into the library every night and watch him change the coloured pins on the huge war map. The swift German advance. The Marne. The grey hordes crossing Belgium. The British "Contemptibles," and Mons. The taxi armies that saved Paris. It was the children's first touch of history. Their Troy and Ajax; their only romantic war. They remembered it always, just as they remembered that time, in 1912, when Mother and Father cancelled their sailing from London to attend a dinner with Mr. Rudyard Kipling, and so missed the tragic adventure of the *Titanic*. They remembered their first Sunday School and the battered, bloody Jew nailed to timbers in the stained-glass rose-window over their pew. It was a charming fieldstone church that smelled of peppermint drops. Episcopal, with control vested in pink, cheerful vestrymen. Their rector was a large, happy man who had baptized Peter and Nicole in a font of water from the Jordan. Peter was puzzled over it for a long time, this having the rector throw water in the faces of children. Much later, Peter's Uncle Egon told him he was lucky to be brought up under the most refined bodily manifestation of the Diety; "besides which you have retained your foreskin and saved your soul."

It was often hard to understand what Uncle Egon was talking about, but Peter and Nicole did discover that he was more tolerant of Christianity than of the Christians. They discovered that a perpetual war went on between the many Christian sects. They were not allowed to play with Catholic children because, well, they were taught by nuns and believed that all other children were damned to burn in hell forever, and that salvation was only for the papal blessed. At prep school Peter met a Baptist boy who had pimples and collected carved peachpits, who said anyone not dipped "*completely under*" during baptism was damned. Peter, who had only been sprinkled by the rector, was worried. It was pretty hard to get right through to God direct, he once told Nicole; one picked a sect and hoped it had real connections. But as they were being dressed for Easter morning, she merely whined while Katie combed her hair and set its curls. Then the whole family, neat, stylishly dressed, went on parade in the glory of the opening of the tomb of Him.

The war was at first a long way off. Something between brave little Frenchmen in long blue coats, and spike-hooded, spike-moustached Germans. There were gallant flying-men in flaming coffins who machine-gunned each other in romantic clouds high above the earth.

War could strike very close. To Peter the three sons of Sam and Sara were rather shadowy figures in the family histories. Albert was to die from shell-fire in France outside the village of Soissons, in a charge by the 6th Regiment of Marines, in 1918. Morris never recovered from the sudden, deadly flu epidemic that hit the army camp in Alabama, in 1919. Harry disappeared in the Twenties, turned up in Paris, where Egon found him starving and trying to write a great, epic poem. He went to London, fell in love with a Manderson cousin, settled down in the family business and became an Englishman and a faithful Church of England parishioner. So he, too, was lost to his family.

Uncle Egon worked for the Red Cross, in its international prisoner exchange, in Switzerland. He was too fat to be accepted in the soldiers' ranks. He used to go, evenings, to a little café, the Odeon, in Zurich—he wrote to old Joseph—to drink the Riesling and listen to two groups gather around two, bearded little men who held court there. The two groups never mixed; Egon used to move from one to the other. The short, broad, bad man who smoked many cigarettes and spoke coldly of events, with a scientific directness, who made neat little jokes, and, for all that, a sense of power about him. His charming, ugly, yellow face with its wide, deep, bald brow seemed to hold every economic problem and answer in its secret corners. The other little man, behind his thick glasses and little beard, was also an earnest speaker, with a fine tenor voice and a taste for Voltigeur cigars and a Swiss Neuchâtel. Both were very poor, both were sure of their destinies.

Later, Egon would often think of Nikolai Lenin and James Joyce (when their ideas and methods had changed the political and literary maps of the world). Seeing their fame spread in the headlines, or in the "little magazines", Egon often wondered what there was in the life force that had brought these two little bearded men out of the Odeon Café in Zurich, to amaze and jolt the world free of a lot of placid cant and humbug.

Peter and Nicole continued to collect the pictures of planes coming down in the most beautiful flames in the weekly magazines. Obscene Zeppelins and cruel, damp submarines filled their drawing lessons.

One night, very late, the phone rang at Perry Point and it was Grandfather, the Jewish one. Uncle Egon had been captured in Belgium and the Germans were going to shoot him. Charles Pentland was called, and cables were sent via Japan and then overland through Asia and over seas with odd-sounding names. It was rather ironic, Uncle Egon used to say much later, that other and do each other favours, even in wartime."

It had been very unpleasant for Uncle Egon. They kept him in a dirty schoolroom with men and women, all tied up, and every evening they took out a few men and women and shot them. Uncle Egon was very frightened, and then he was angry at the Germans' doing this to him personally. He had always loved the German culture and the German cooking and the German music and the German poets. The Germans "kept their streets so clean" and policed everything so well that "one's baggage was never stolen in German railroad stations". After they let Uncle Egon go and shipped him to Holland, Uncle

Egon told everyone there that, in time, the Germans would ravage the world and their culture was only a veneer. "They're like Pavlov's dogs," Uncle Egon used to say. "That Russian scientist trained dogs to react to bells. One bell—food; two bells—a walk; three bells—an electric shock. In time the dogs reacted instantly to the bells and ate, walked, or whined. The Germans, since Caesar found them wildly shouting in skins beyond the forests of Gaul, have been conditioned like Pavlov's dogs. One bell—Fatherland and Superman! Two bells—Earth and Power! Three bells—Teutonic *Kultur*! They react on reflexes only."

Peter saw a new Uncle Egon in a faded, slant-blue uniform with a black belt around a balloon stomach, when he came back to America. He had a lined face, his remaining hair close-cropped and grey, and bag-like wrinkles under the eyes. Later, in Asia Minor, he helped Greeks escape from Turks. A louse bit him in Salonika and he nearly died of a war-born plague.

The French made him an honorary captain. Peter and Nicole remembered him during the first Liberty Loan drive seated on the platform in front of the Forty-second Street Library. A large man with many medals on his blue military jacket, the lined face, the yellow eyeballs of his fever, and the cropped grey hair, white now over the ears. Three governments had decorated him for saving the lives of a hundred thousand Greeks (and the louse bite) and he appeared on many platforms that year for international causes.

America at war ("to make the world safe for . . .") was very exciting for Peter and Nicole. Father got into uniform and served in Italy on a minor general's staff and sent home pictures of himself against an Alp with many smartly dressed Italian officers wearing those darling tall caps. Italy was the romantic front. Mother headed a Red Cross unit and even Nicole learned to handroll bandages.

"We're the good people," said Nicole, "and they are the bad people."

"They're very bad," said Mother.

Peter had taken over the family war map. "They rape people all the time."

"Now, Peter, stick a pin in for Tannenberg."

"But the papers say it's rape, rape, rape, all the time."

"What's rape?" asked Nicole.

"It's rape," said Peter. He didn't know, but it was pretty nasty; you could be sure the Huns did things up pretty grim.

"Rape, rape," sang Nicole.

"We don't say that word indoors," said Mother.

"Why not?"

"It's not a decent word."

"*The New York Times* said it," said Peter. *The Times* was the *only* decent paper, Charles Pentland said.

"That will do, Peter, run out and get a fresh paper. I hear them calling an extra."

Peter came back with the paper. "The Huns Have Torpedoed Another Liner. A-tro-cit-ies again," he said.

"Go and play," said Mother, picking up the paper.

Nicole and Peter went into the garden. "I know what rape is," he said. "The newsboy told me."

"I'll give you my American flag, the silk one, if you'll tell me". She wasn't very impressed when she found out it was merely what Father's hunting dogs did sometimes. It had been such a pretty little flag. With an oak staff. An officer had given it to Mother after a dance. He said he was in love with her and was going off to die for her, couldn't she be kind just for one night?

Uncle Jacob Kozloff was a soldier, too, but they brought him back from France suffering from poison gas and put him back in his factories to turn out uniforms and flags and tents. "Good morning. Mr. Zip, Zip, Zip—with your hair cut just as short as—your hair cut just as short as—just as short as mine!"

It was gay in New York; the balls and parties, the Liberty Loan drives and Red Cross drives. All the gay young men in Brooks Brothers uniforms drinking at the Knickerbocker and the girls in tight skirts and feathered hats dancing, dancing to the band playing "Dardanella". There were a few war-babies out of place and time in the best families, and West Pointers were sick in the shrubbery with too much of Father's three-star brandy. Peter played "Over There" on the drums and Nicole whistled it on a comb and toilet paper.

Then the wire came from the War Department that Uncle Sam's Albert was dead. Dead in a French village and buried under a wooden cross (until they had time to replace it with a wooden Star of David).

Father came back from Italy, limping beautifully, with the aid of a lovely, bamboo cane, highly varnished. There had been a great Italian retreat brilliantly run through by the Italian general staff and Father had been hit in the knee by a fragment of an Austrian shell made by a firm Charles Pentland had floated loans for.

Peter and Nicole remembered the morning that Albert Pedlock died officially. Father came down to breakfast leaning very heavily

251

on his cane. He looked tired, but very handsome—like a jacket of a Robert W. Chambers book.

"We're going to my brother's," he said to Mother. "Albert's been killed in action."

"Yes, dear," said Mother. "We'll take the children?"

"Of course," said Ralph. And he sat down and Peter put a chair under the bad knee.

And that was the first time that Ralph (Pedlock) Perry returned to his family.

The heavy curtains had been drawn on the big windows overlooking Riverside Drive. Little wicks of fire burned in heavy, warm glasses of tallow, and trays of sponge cake and honey cake and brandy stood on buffets. The pictures of the three sons of Sam and Sara in uniform had been taken off the side table and hidden. Aunt Sara sat very tall in a big chair, holding a handkerchief to her face but not crying. Aunt Selma and Tante Strasser sat with her, and female relatives made a ring of condoling flesh around them.

Mother went over and kissed Aunt Sara, and Father took Selma in his arms and they said nothing. Then Father took Peter by the hand and they went into the next room. It was darker there and Peter felt the little glasses burning tallow were ghost souls trying to talk. Here the menfolk were sitting the ritual *shiva* for their dead. They, in humility, sat not on chairs, but on old fruit boxes. They wore no shoes and their heads were covered with little black caps. Uncle Jacob wore his prayer shawl and was reading from a small Hebrew book, shaking himself back and forth and coughing a little when the German gas in his lungs bothered him. The father and brothers of the dead man faced him. The tribe was in sad session.

Old Joseph sat on his low seat, his cane between his legs, and Ralph was shocked to see how old his father had become. The beard was thinning out, the nose had grown longer in the lean face, only the eyes were still bold. Life was destroying the old man slowly—like a discarded model.

As Ralph entered the room with Peter, Sam got up and went to his brother and the held each other in their arms in a Jewish gesture of grief.

"Ralph."

"We came as soon as we heard. I brought Peter."

"Sit down, Ralph," said Joseph. "Jacob is saying a prayer."

Ralph and Peter sat down near Harry and Morris. They were in the badly fitted army uniforms, their hair clipped short, and their sunburned arms were too long for their sleeves. Ralph and Peter were handed little black caps and they put them on carefully with numb hands. Peter sat very still, and the room smelled of the candle tallow, and he wondered if his dead cousin knew they were sitting here on low boxes offering up prayers for his soul. He had never known real death except for a puppy, a pet chicken. He remembered the battle-field pictures in the *Times Mid-Weekly Pictorial* section. Those sepia rotogravure sheets that gave all events a baked-brown look; the bodies of Serbians and Greeks and Russians and Austrians . . . and the big bearded Russian and Greek priests in their embroidery saying prayers over mass graves. And an English bishop, smartly backed up by the Horse Guards in full parade attire, reciting a last prayer over an English ace. It had all been an exciting game in the pictures—now to Peter it was real and deadly.

They sat, Peter close to his father and his kin, while Jacob Kozloff, their only student of the Hebrew language and ritual, read a prayer for Albert Pedlock, first-born of Sam and Sara in 1891, who went across a sea for his beloved country and died in a dirty French village, blown to fragments in his young manhood, all his life and dreams and desires now nothing but a floating of Hebrew in a half-dark room smelling of tallow.

"May God remember the soul of the departed, who has gone to his rest . . . may his soul enjoy eternal life with those of Abraham, Isaac, and Jacob, Sara, Rebecca, and Leah, and the rest of the righteous men and women in Paradise. We say Amen."

They all said "Amen" and Peter added a very low one of his own. This would never do to repeat in the rector's Sunday School. Old Joseph looked up and said, "There was a prayer we used to say in Richmond in the old Virginia synagogue—a Hebrew prayer for the Confederacy. Jacob, could we say it now for our present war effort?"

Jacob nodded and lowered his head. "The prayer for the nation."

A tallow flame sputtered. In the next room a woman was sobbing. The man sat bent over on their low seats. Jacob recited the prayer in Hebrew—then in English.

"May he grant victory to our chiefs, and dominion to our banners, he whose rule is everlasting, who delivered David, his servant, from the destroying sword, who makes a way through the sea, a path through great waters. May he bless, preserve and guard, aid and exalt on high the United States of America, whose glory be enhanced. May the King of Kings, in his mercy, prolong its life, protect it, deliver it from sorrow and trouble and loss, and cause its foes to fall before it . . . let us say, Amen. . . ."

*   *   *

That Sunday Ralph had the rector say a prayer for the soul of the departed. Later, when Morris died during the flu epidemic in a Southern army camp, the services for the dead became almost a habit for the family. The family had many dead. The Manderscheids lost four branches of their family tree. Uncle Louis's sister Deborah got back a one-legged son who wore so many medals that the relatives said he must have won them in army crap-games. Uncle Egon was given the red ribbon of the Legion of Honour by the French and wore it proudly on all his suits almost until the day of his death. Jacob Kozloff got his medal and a personal letter from the President.

The pictures of Albert and Morris, enlarged from snapshots, two earnest young faces in badly fitted army tunics and close-clipped hair, took their place on the walls among the Pedlock soldiers. Dr. Manderscheid who had been at Jamestown with John Smith, and the Revolutionary brothers who had followed George Washington, and Aaron Manderscheid as a Union Colonel, and old Joseph as young Captain Joseph in his Richmond tailoring just before First Manassas.

Joseph used to look up at the pictures and stamp his cane. "I have a feeling we're going to run out of walls some day."

Jacob Kozloff shook his head. "Wilson is going to Europe himself for the peace conference. His League of Nations is going to make this a new and better kind of world."

Old Joseph snorted and scowled. "As old J. E. B. Stuart used to say, 'I can't tell you how a roast pig is goin' to taste until I eat off it'. . . ."

When the war ended in 1918 Peter was a Boy Scout collecting fruit pits to be carbonized into charcoal for gas masks, and it seemed to him that the war had let him down. He had dreamed of being an air ace and shooting down leering Hun airmen who raped white virgins. He had read his way through a formidable series of books called "The Boy Allies", and had just finished, in relays, two of the series, *The Boy Allies in the Trenches*, and *The Boy Allies under the Sea*.

The end of the war meant the beginning of his prep-school years. The Pentlands had always gone to Beagle, the old prep school in the wooded New Jersey hills, and there was a Pentland Hall given to the rolling acres by the grandfather of Charles Pentland. The Pentlands usually went to Princeton from there. Peter had been entered at Beagle at his birth, just as his name had been put down for the Boston Club and the Knickerbocker Grays.

At twelve Peter was tall and thin, with blond hair just a shade toward chestnut, but looking white in a certain light. He knew he was a Pentland through Mother, and a Perry (Pedlock) through Father. He was proud of his two families, and immigrant Russian Jews were *not* called kikes by polite people.

There was such a thing as breeding, and a good Episcopalian said his prayers and was always a proper gentleman. One played the game, did not lie or cheat, and went to dancing school on Friday at Miss Malvin's, wearing white gloves and patent-leather shoes, and danced with sticky, warm little girls. One learned dirty secrets of life in the lavatories, and certain words that could be looked up in the dictionary were rather exciting. It was not true that babies came in doctors' bags, that girls became pregnant when one kissed them. There were scented vices that no adult explained when one read the fairy tales of Oscar Wilde (who looked foolish enough in his photograph).

Charles Pentland gave Peter a ten-dollar gold coin the day he left prep school.

"You're special, Peter, and don't forget it."

"Yes, Grandfather."

"Don't think I'm a snob. And don't you be one."

"I don't think I am."

"Good. It's just a man should know his worth. With a graveyard of good blood and breeding behind you, put it to some use."

"I'll try."

"It's good blood. Warriors on both sides. Solid worth and a lot of brains. Nothing to be ashamed of—brains."

"No, sir."

"We'll make you a good man and a fine banker. No nonsense in you. I can see that. Just remember where you come from and you'll have no trouble in this world."

"Beagle sounds like fun."

"It is. Fine people and they push a lot of good stuff into you young fry. Latin and stuff, not bad at all. The classics. Give a man classics and you can save a few generations in making a gentleman. Must be getting old talking like this to you. You'll be all right, I know you will."

"It's hard to leave the family, of course, Grandfather."

"Yes, I suppose it is. But family can be bad. The trouble with the Pedlocks is that Jewish family love and closeness. Not that I mean anything against them. It's a fine thing to have. But don't overdo it. In the end, boy, a man stands alone in this world. The less emotional baggage he carries the better."

"Thank you for the ten dollars."

*   *   *

Beagle (the school was proud of its odd name) stood in the middle of the grove of sacred elm trees and maples, and its sun-faded, red-brick buildings were rather cleverly hidden by ivy that covered over many of their worst features. It was a good school of crisp, old-fashioned learning and went in for "Latin and the solid classics" and good, plain wholesome food, and lots of it. "Plenty for both mind and body," the headmaster always said.

Peter liked it very much, after he got over being homesick, and he grew taller and played football and pitched on the baseball team, and learned to smoke cigarettes, after lights, in an empty fireplace with other rakehells. He drank beer sometimes but preferred pop. He had too many ice-cream sodas in town and had a fight with the class bully and lost. He hated maths and read a lot and went on nature walks with the nature teacher, who explained the local wood growths and gave the Latin names for the plants they picked and pressed between notebook pages. Beagle kept a boy's mind and bowels open.

Later when Peter read the Lawrenceville stories of Owen Johnson, he transferred their charm and oddness to Beagle, and in later years he could not remember if Beagle had really been as thrilling and exciting as he remembered it, or was he taking the Lawrenceville stories as a pattern when he talked of or remembered the old school, its unheated halls, its dusty, chalky school-rooms, the stinking drains, the smelly oilcloth-covered tables, the muddy playing fields, the scum-covered bathing pool, the dreadful infirmary where he had his sore throats, infected ears, and his toothaches.

His best friends at school were Stinky Smith, the son of a New Mexico rancher (who was half Cherokee), and Ike Sontag, the school Jew. Beagle made a point of having one Hindu, one Chinese, and one Jewish boy at the school. It could also point out with pride that its Negro servants, waiters, and gardeners were all closely related (in legal wedlock) and had been with Headmaster Crogell's family for generations. Chapel was a must, and the prayers were long and loud. Doctor and Etta Sontag used to come down once a month to take Ike and Peter and Stinky to town for the movies and a big, hotel meal of steak, French fries, and strawberry shortcake.

The boys lifted their faces from the plates like hound dogs finished with a heavy meal.

Doctor Sontag smiled. "Just one more order of strawberry short-cake?"

"No, thank you."

"No room, Papa."

"The meal was sure neato, sir."

Etta looked over the silverware. "They could use a little silver polish."

"How do you boys like the school?"

"Neato."

"Plenty of food?"

"All you can tuck in."

"Ike, you need a haircut."

"I can't cut it until football season is over."

"Everybody is wearing it pretty long this year, protects the skull, you know, in line bucks."

"Any hazing this year?"

"Just stinkers get their paddling."

"Remember when we tossed Egghead into the horse pond?"

"That's cruel."

Peter folded his hands across his tight stomach. "They used to cut a hole in the ice and drop 'em into the lake. But they stopped it."

"Children are such brutes."

One of the boys belched politely behind his hand.

Doctor Sontag said, "Well, don't overdo the studying. Nothing causes softening of the brain like too much study."

"Edward, you stop joking about such things. You were the best student in your class."

"Well, look at me."

They all laughed politely.

The teaching staff (charming unbigoted young men, but very lonely) always referred to Doctor Sontag as a "mighty white Jew". Doctor Sontag was advancing with the times. He was now a consulting psychologist, going past the boundaries of simple neurasthenia and sublimations. Etta had done over his office—lime-green walls and yellow chairs—and his fees were now in keeping with his interior decorating bills. He was the accepted authority—at least by one school of thought—on dementia praecox with catatonic reaction. His book, *The Psychology of Functional Neuroses*, was for several years the foremost authority in the field. However, Etta, always looking into the future and keeping up with the progress in her husband's field, was thinking of psychoanalysis as the real future of the up-to-date psychological field. Doctor Sontag had been twice to Vienna to sit at the feet of Herr Doktor Freud, whom he found a shrewd, wise, and exciting figure; a little calmer, he confessed, than his followers. He had also dipped into Jung, Adler and Stekel. Also into Jones, Ferenczi, and Brill. He was slowly translating Breuer and Freud's *Studien über Hysterie* into English.

"Of course they make a mystery of it," said Ike, "but it isn't so hard."

"Sure," said Stinky, "I hear if you can get them to take their shoes off, it's in."

"Girls laugh too much," said Peter.

"Can't help it. Got small minds. Girls aren't hard to understand if you want to."

"Have you ever?"

"No, but I could of. The Polish maid—what knockers!—she was real sweet to me. It's just you know how Etta talks to the servants all the time."

"Our foreman says there's nothing like sheep."

"I wouldn't care for that."

"I kissed Gertie last week, twice, of course. Gertie isn't a lady, but her legs are very good."

"Skinny."

"Well, maybe, but I don't like em fat-assed."

"The closer the bone the sweeter the meat."

"I must have Turkish blood. Fat in the right place isn't bad."

"What place?"

"Look, fellas, let's cut the bull session and crack the Latin. Etta promised me a rowboat if I pass high."

"With an outboard motor?"

"Well, maybe. But I hadda promise not to have anything to do with girls."

"The situation is in flux," Selma Kozloff used to say at meetings. "European Jewry has come out of the First World War worse off than ever. In the Soviet Republics there is no official anti-Semitism, but in Poland the 'lovers of the common man and socialism', under Pilsudski, are murdering Jews. Progroms sweep the Polish plains and lap into the Warsaw ghettos. So much for socialism as a barrier to Jewish killings. In Rumania and Hungary the Jews are no better off, and in Germany, rising again in all its foulness (helped by the soft-hearted world bankers and businessmen with their loans and post-war planning) the Jew is doomed but does not yet admit it. In Palestine the British ignore their own honour and promises to give the homeless Jews their homeland. The League mandate is merely a scrap of paper to them. When the Jews fight back in their arid hills, they face Black and Tan gangsters who had run wild in Ireland and Arabs incited to test their knives on Jewish throats!" Oh, Selma had become an impassioned speaker.

The Kozloffs did not live in New York City. Jacob had bought ten acres in the low hills beyond the Oranges, in New Jersey, and in an old house that George Washington had overlooked, they raised their family. There were four little Kozloffs now. Michael, the oldest, at ten refusing to answer to anything but Mike; Anthony, still too young to know what the final version of his name would be; Jehuda, named during a super-Zionist period on Selma's part, but who had sobered into Jed; and the youngest Miriam, born the year General Pershing landed in France.

Doctor and Mrs. Sontag, motoring north from Beagle after a weekend visit to their son Ike, stopped off at "Kozloff Corner", as the farm was called by the family and its friends. "Ridge Hill" and "River Road" had been weakly experimented with, but in the end it was to remain Kozloff Corner.

Etta drove a heavy Packard with box mud-guards, Doctor Sontag's eyes being too weak for the skilful driving needed on the country roads of the period. The Kozloff farm was ten minutes off a main highway, along a neat, dirt road past old trees and slightly rising hills, past a white church, an old iron bridge, and then up a winding, gravelled drive past pines and a tumbling stream, into a farmyard of barns, hayricks, and well-cared-for henhouses and farm tools. The main house was further along, a big, old building added to in the Eighties, stripped down in the first decades of the century, and now repaired and enlarged by the new owners. It was a placid, ugly house of no certain period, with lilac bushes, and fronted by a rough lawn cut only by the hired man's haymowing machine. It was full of daisies, and in the clover-patch borders, big fat bees buzzed and fed.

Selma, in a wide straw hat, with Miriam at her feet, was painting a rather bad watercolour, while Mike, barefooted and overalled, was experimenting with oils on canvas. A red cow, their model, looked up at them between bits of clover and shook her wet, black nose in wonder. Jacob was in a hammock tied to two small oaks, part of the Sunday *Times* covering his face. The hammock had stopped swaying and Selma knew he was asleep.

The heavy Packard came to a skilful stop and Etta pulled up the brake. Doctor Sontag polished road dust off his glasses, and they got out of the car and crossed to the lawn. Selma picked Miriam up, Mike frowned a small boy's frown at being interrupted in his work, and the cow swayed its jaw sideways and got its cud in just the right position for real, good chewing.

"Selma, how wonderful it is up here," Etta said.

"We call it 'down here'. How are you?"

"We're fine. Edward and I keep thinking we should move to the country, but it's hard for a doctor, you know."

"I wouldn't mind," said the doctor. "Do the patients good to see less of me."

"Edward, you know it would spoil your research."

"Somebody else can do it. Look at Jacob there, that's life. A hammock and asleep in the sun. 'It's his America,' as my father used to say."

Jacob removed the newspaper from his face and his feet hunted the ground. He rubbed his face, covered a yawn, and smiled. Selma still thought he had the nicest smile in the world.

"Wonderful of you to drop in. How's Ike?"

"He's fine. It's a beautiful school. We saw Ralph's Peter. He's a beautiful child. Such a *good*-looking boy."

Jacob shook his head. "At his age he better stop being beautiful and just get handsome."

"How *big* Miriam is getting."

"Her teething is bothering her. Three new teeth this week. Mike, say hello to Doctor and Mrs. Sontag."

"Hello."

Doctor Sontag came over and looked down at the picture Mike had been painting. "That's good. I like the colour of your cow."

"The horns are pretty fair."

"You going to be an artist, Mike?"

"Naw . . . I'm going to be a rancher in the West. Like Uncle Louis."

"Painting is lots of fun." Doctor Sontag picked up a brush dipped in red and began skilfully to fill in the shape of the big barn and its roof edge and the cross-beams. He did it well with a direct, bold approach, peering through his thick glasses at the distant barn. Mike cocked his head to one side.

"You're pretty good. That's neat."

"I used to be fair when I was a kid, but I haven't painted much since. I wanted to be an artist."

"Why didn't you?"

"Why, Mike?" He dipped the red brush into blue, smeared up a daring purple colour, and began to block in the shadows. "Well, my teacher said my vision wasn't right. I saw too many things the wrong way. So, if I couldn't be the best painter in the world, I didn't want to be one."

Mike said, "Why are you putting blue on my cow?"

"Well, with red and purple in the barn I just feel it ties the cow into the picture by giving it blue tones." Doctor Sontag pushed his thumb into the brown, green, and yellow ground colours and smeared them together, ridging the painting into a waving pattern.

"Hey, that looks swell, but I didn't know you could use your fingers."

"Sure you can, Mike. Now under the cow we'll put a lot of yellow dots . . . just like this . . . now a lot of blue dots . . . like this, not touching each other, just a pattern of 'em. What have we now?"

"Green!"

"See how it dances this way, like the sun on the field, instead of a solid green like the side of a wall."

"You musta been a good painter, Doc."

"Not good enough. Where's your zinc white? I'll show you a palette-knife sky."

"Boy—this is sure neat."

The rest of the party were now seated around a small, white iron table, Miriam on her father's lap, her wet, dribbling chin swabbed from time to time. Etta was removing her motoring hat and Selma was pouring lemonade into tall glasses.

"Where are Anthony and Jehuda?"

"In the hayfield watching the north ten being cut," Jacob said. "But Jehuda prefers being called Jed."

"He's not ashamed of being called Jehuda, is he?" Etta said crisply. "Jehuda, the Jew, it's a name to be proud of!"

Jacob wiped Miriam's wet chin. "He's not ashamed of it, but he's right in not going around carrying it like a sign board. After all, I was born Yakov Shmul Zbitkover Kozloffsky . . . and now I'm J. K. Kozloff. How is Ike?"

"Wonderful. He's gained six pounds and he's playing fullback on the team. You should send your Mike to Beagle."

Jacob laughed and bounced the baby. "We tried. But it seems their minority quota was filled. They have a Jew and a half, I believe, right now."

"You didn't just write in and ask?" said Etta.

"Why not?" said Selma. "We weren't asking for any favour."

"But you don't understand. It's a very exclusive school, even Christians have trouble getting in. They'd have taken Mike if they knew he was the son of J. K. Kozloff and the grandson of Joseph Pedlock."

Jacob grinned and shook his head. "*That* boy—the son and the grandson—I have no worries over. He'll do all right. But I also wanted to enter the son of Jake Kozloff, the East Side sweat-shop Jew and the grandson of Nachum Hershel who stood barefooted in a Russian ghetto market and peddled smelly herring."

Etta flared her nostrils. "That's the wrong attitude, Jacob. You must demand your special rights."

Jacob shook his head. "No. You see that's why I'm not a Zionist. For me this country, as it is, is enough. And to be proud of my country I must take it as it is. There is nothing wrong in me asking Beagle to take in Mike Kozloff, and if Beagle doesn't want him as he is—that's a kind of crazy freedom too. Maybe not in the best American spirit, but to force them to take Mike in is wrong. It's Beagle's problem and they must solve it, for in the end they will destroy something decent and American if they don't solve it."

"How?"

"By admitting Mike, and even poor, unimportant Christians. But they must see it as an American right for any boy fit to be admitted there. Pressure doesn't do any good. Charles Pentland could get Mike into Beagle for me, I know that. But it's just as well he went to a public school."

Etta looked at Selma, her long jaw set hard. "I believe in a fight, all along the line."

Selma took Miriam from Jacob's arms. "You must let Jacob tell you about some of his fights. Real ones. Is my little girl still dribbling?"

Jacob brushed his lap. "At both ends."

From across the fields came the sound of the haycutter. The bees buzzed louder and the cow stood watching them, shaking a shaggy tail at some bluetail flies, its jaws still sliding sideways.

Doctor Sontag and Mike were looking at the painting and then they looked at each other and smiled. It was a moment of shared creation between them, a mutual pleasure. Mike dipped the brush in Prussian blue and handed it to the doctor. "You sign it too, Doc."

"Thank you, Mike." Very carefully under the sprawling "M i k e" he lettered in with a steady hand (that had been cheered once for its delicate brain surgery) "E d w a r d."

"Da," said Miriam suddenly, with a bubble.

"The child talks!"

"She can say two words."

"What's the other one?"

Jacob shrugged his shoulders and smiled. "Da-da."

All the way to the city Edward thought of the painting. Dusk was colouring the great grey face of the city as the Packard slowed down toward the ferry landing. Etta steered between two huge drays, and said, "I think, Edward, that a psychoanalysis would help Jacob Kozloff get over being so afraid to push his Jewishness."

"That wasn't a bad painting Mike and I did. He's going to give it to me when it dries."

"I said . . ."

"Here's the ferry." Doctor Sontag began to hunt in his change pocket. "How much is it? I keep forgetting the rate."

Chains fell into place, the flat snout of the ferry's nose came down level with the ferry landing. Motors raced, horses' hooves sounded, and with great daring Etta swung the Packard aboard. . . .

At fifteen Peter was filling out, growing taller, his head narrower, his hair becoming more brown than blond, and he dreamed of a moustache, and large, white-fleshed women such as did not really exist on earth. Beagle had become his real home. Except for a few holidays—a rather fashionable Easter and an overdone Dickens-style Christmas— Beagle was his daily life. Summers, when the family usually travelled in Europe or went to California, he spent with old Joseph in the Berkshires at Pittsfield, or at the Kozloff farm. Nicole went on the European trips but Peter preferred woodcraft, fishing, or hitch-hiking with Ike Sontag and Stinky Smith. One Summer they went out to New Mexico as Stinky's guests and disappeared with pack animals and an old guide into the red-rocked cliff country and found what they thought was a prehistoric Indian village high up on the face of a bald cliff. Digging for shards of Indian pottery and rough, flint arrowheads, they unearthed tin cans and rusting wagon bolts and gave up in disgust.

Beagle was their monastery. They learned to live a full life in their small, panelled rooms, eat the simple food, take the required exercise, play the popular games, and study the carefully edited, dull and scientific texts of an old-fashioned, solid education. A foundation for gentlemen was laid down and they were invited to walk on it.

Their bull sessions were long, loud, and full of legends; some had had groping meetings with casual women—their mothers' maids, waitresses at the Blue Dog in town, cousins at sticky birthday parties. From afar they dreamed exalted dreams about the polite little girls who came to the twice-yearly dances at Beagle. They educated themselves in the secrets of life from a set of well-worn, dog-eared classics not on the school reading list. A Rabelais whose *Gargantua and Pantagruel* amused them in parts; naturally they owned that American schoolboy classic, *The Decameron*, and James Branch Cabell's new sensation, *Jurgen*, which bored them. In Chaucer they found, to their delight, a few lusty old four-letter words, and *Madame Bovary* had a few, well-marked passages.

They were mostly all true idealists and untried dreamers, and worshipped a tribe called women, from afar. Several of the seniors boasted of smutty trips to Trenton and Newark and their adventures with professional tarts, but most of this was bold lying, except for Tinker Evens, a tall, foul-mouthed, gangling Southerner, nephew to a big-name cigarette, who invited them to visit his home any summer, and he would "fix ya up with yella girls, homegrown on mah estate". Tinker Evens smoked cigars in secret, kept a horse of his own at the school, and shaved with an old-fashioned, long razor. He called the servants "darkies", had good public manners, and spent his weekends in Philadelphia getting drunk. He was six-foot-three and could swim under water for a minute and a half. The small toes of his feet were twisted and deformed.

Peter and Ike and Stinky were known at Beagle as a solid trio who did not grind their studies or act long-hair but got good marks and played a fine game of baseball. They liked to ride into the country, weekends, on their bikes, eat thick, cold-meat sandwiches from greasy paper packages and drink the bootleg beer of their era, when it was available to them. At first they did not like the beer.

Uncle Louis came one weekend and took them down to Trenton and bought them much beer. They stood at a pine bar and burped with earnest pleasure at their sinning.

"Yep," the Colonel said, his cowboy boots on the bar rail, his Stetson way back on his head, "the whole country ain't worth the powder it would cost to blow her sky-high. This business of drinking rot-gut behind locked doors, it's un-American."

"You're attracting attention, Uncle Louis."

"What of it? Nobody packs a gun any more except some Eyetalian hoodlums."

"Were there hoodlums on the frontier?"

"Sure, no-good characters, but they did their killin' in the open. It was a healthy way to die. More beer?"

"Thank you, sir."

"Don't sir me, Ike, there ain't no sirs here and no dukes. More beer all around."

"Tell us how Grandfather killed a man."

"Killed 'em for business reasons. Nobody was ever killed just for a notch on a gun. That's pure romance."

"Over women, sir?"

"Well, maybe sometimes. Mighty fancy women."

"Like in the movies?"

"Damn the movies. No truth in movies."

"None at all, Colonel?"

"Well, maybe a little. How's school?"

"Neato."

"Went to school a lot, myself. Went to Oxford once. Wouldn't think it, would you? Don't be ashamed to say it, I don't look like a long-haired half-brained intellectual. Like the beer?"

They didn't but they drank it because it was forbidden by the school. Later they became beer-lovers. They smoked cigarettes in secret but shunned cigars after one deadly encounter. They wrasseled each other on grassy banks and sang sad songs with changing voices.

Their secret plans were to buy an old, fifty-foot ketch and sail off to the South Seas to become black-birders, pearlers, and in the end, beachcombers. They had their secret sorrows, some of which they shared, for youth, as always, was a time of trial and error, of itch and brooding. But in the main they found life enjoyable, full, exciting, and yet slow-packed. They did not know that they were living in a child's world that did not exist for adults; that its hard knocks, its ugly truths, degrading battles, and evil forces had been all filtered out for them.

They knew their birthright and they expected to be Presidents, motion picture stars, or great lovers. "There is a brightness," old Joseph used to say, "an alertness about them which makes of youth such a wonderful thing, and which leaves people as they grow old; and it makes one sad that the progress of the human race does not keep up the effort it makes in youth."

Stinky had ten dollars sent him for his birthday by a loving sister. It was a sunny Saturday. Stinky was sixteen that day. He was oiling his hair with a popular perfumed lard (that is how got his name Stinky in the first place) and Ike and Peter were thinking of how to spend this windfall to the best effect.

Ike lay on the floor, his long, thin legs crossed, his socks falling limply into his shoes. "We could hitch-hike down to Trenton, have a steak dinner, take in a vaudeville show, and bring back a gallon of needled beer."

Peter, sitting in the mutually owned rowing-machine and pulling a steady sixteen to the minute (he had just pulled his sagging crewmen past a gasping, rugged Oxford crew and was increasing the stroke as the choppy river sent stinging spray into their faces). He leaned back on the oars. "Let's go out [row] to the kennels on [row] Sand Road and buy [row] a genuine bulldog pup [row] and call it Nero." (The last two men, their strength sapped, had caught crabs with their oars. The Oxford crew was gaining again. One after another, Peter's men slumped over their trailing oars, their brave hearts giving their last ounce of strength. Boat sirens went off. They were ten yards from the finish line, only Peter was still rowing. With a great effort, half rising from his seat, he pulled his long, heavy oar through the water . . . pulled hard and even, and as they crossed the finish line, a paint thickness ahead of the Oxford shell, he fell unconscious in victory over his oar.)

Stinky put down the military hair-brushes and inspected his big red ears and the glossy, black polished ball of his hair-coated head. Every hair was lacquered into place. "We're going to town for a movie and maybe a lobster and beer. I promised Gertie a pair of silk stockings."

Ike looked at the exhausted oarsman, Peter ("At last, you have brought the cup back to America!"), and shrugged his shoulders. Gertie was Stinky's girl, or so he claimed and she often agreed. She was a large Polish girl with red hair and hard breasts who waited on the tables at the Blue Dog. The schoolboys amused her and it gave her an idea she was accepted among the upper classes; just like Joan Crawford, mixing with "genelmin" in the movies, Gertie followed wide-eyed and sighing. She allowed a few liberties to the younger schoolboys. A wet tongue-kiss, a few minutes in their arms on the river bank, a promising leer, but like her screen dreamself, Joan (Gertie) Crawford—she was saving it for her husband, or for a rake, some dark-haired, black-eyed gambler who would rape her charmingly on a white bearskin rug in a mountain lodge. Peter and Ike envied Stinker his girl, for while their secret dreams were wilder than his, their shyness with available women kept them from acquiring anything like a girl one could give silk stockings to.

They left the school full of hopes that day. Combed, polished, nails cleaned, socks pulled up, they were inspected and permitted to take the bus into town. It was a mill town, once farm land, now company shacks, a cement-block Broadway made notorious by a best seller called *Main Street*, some old proud houses inhabited by decaying Yankee gentlefolk, and a cluttering collection of what were known to the schoolboys as Polacks, Hunkies, Micks, and Shines. Their priests spoke bad English and preached no hope of salvation for the native-born.

The boys invested in hard candies and packs of cigarettes, kidded the salesgirls at Woolworth's, and paid their admission to the temple of dreams known as the Bijou. Great flaming posters announced W. S. Hart. A rabble of town kids rioted in the cracked seats of the theatre and a thin man with small, slipping nose-glasses of gilt wire played on a piano and beat off spitballs from his thin neck. The manager, with a long ruler once used to measure yard goods, passed up and down the seats and rapped any rioting head within reach.

The three schoolboys settled themselves as near the screen as they could get and opened their bags and fed themselves cheap, strong candy and salted nuts, acid-tasting and filling. The hooting grew louder. The piano player slid into an oily series of standard piano cries and the place darkened; the screen filled with shadows and dim, leaping promises. The first few feet of film flickered and jerked with credits and then settled down to its saga.

The place smelled of unwashed mill hands, stale underclothes, cheap candy, insect spray, and a hot, iron projection machine. The piano grew bolder. A vast desert appeared. Peter settled back. A long line of waggons, oxen straining and the sand and wind stirring. Far off on a horizon, smoke. The wagons stopped. The camera wandered off into sandy space. A dot moving slowly taking shape as a man and horse. Peter was not surprised to see it was himself, Peter Manderson Perry—Two-Gun Pete, mounted on a spotted horse full of beans. His face was tanner, leaner, but Peter liked the way he looked in the saddle. A deadly killer, a man who had lived, and once, loved.

Peter leaned over the horse's dancing neck and put one brown hand to his eyes. *LONG SHOT, A RIDGE.* A rise of sand and sagebrush, then a smoking mass of painted Indians bareback on wild ponies. War-paint, tomahawks, savage faces, wild arms racing. CLOSE SHOT, Peter as he turned the paint pony and started off toward the horizon, pulling out his Winchester and firing casually over his shoulder. One, two, six, ten Indians bit the dust. All without reloading the keen, smoking weapons.

LONG SHOT, THE WAGON TRAIN as it closes up in a great circle, almost complete. Peter on his paint pony tops the rise, sees the wagon train. Innocent immigrants unused to Indian warfare. With a clap of cruel spurs in the flanks of the paint he is down and through the fast-closing gap in the wagon train. Confused war whoops. Arrows. Peter directs the defence. Here, there. Fires from hip and shoulder, hands his rifle to be reloaded. Turns. There is The Girl handing him a fresh rifle. Clean, young, every curl in place. A neat print housedress, breasts calm, unafraid under the stiff cloth. Fine hips and buttocks. Little hands and feet. A proud woman. A virgin. The Girl of a hundred thousand movies, the companion of millions of tormenting American dreams.

Peter orders her, with the other women, into the safety of the wagons. She laughs, rolls her head. A Tomboy. He scowls. An arrow hits him, digs into the shoulder. She comes to him, holds up his head. Peter shakes himself loose. It's only a three-foot Comanche war arrow. It passed between the heart and his lung. Nothing. He shouts the men into action. A counter-charge. Give it to the redskins! The men run out. The redskins break. LONG SHOT, THE RIDGE. A long blue column of horsemen, flags flapping, bugle to the charge. The U.S. Cavalry! The piano is playing "Stars and Stripes Forever", crossed with more sensual parts out of Wagner's vast pools of desire.

A charge. Troopers and Peter and the paint pony in front. The redskins turn tail. Peter smiles, faints. FADE OUT. FADE IN. The bed of a wagon train. Peter's shoulder bandaged. The Girl pouring cool water into his open mouth. He smiles, she smiles. He takes her hand. Stout Fella.

LONG SHOT, NIGHT. The wagon train in camp. A banjo melody. Peter and The Girl lying on a blanket looking up at the stars. Simple confessions of love. A kiss. (Groaning from the seated art lovers, sucking sounds and mock kissing.) Pressed against Peter's great chest, thighs rammed into his, his brown hands just above the starched buttocks, locking The Girl to him. CAMERA PANS UP to the stars. A flat black picture of a wolf howling. The piano sending shivers up damp backs. Horsemen riding in the dark. Peter leaps to his feet. Gun out, one arm around the tailored hips of The Girl. Two Mexicans ride into camp, followed by The Gambler. A leering face, a hairline moustache, a cravat with one black pearl in it.

The Gambler has come to look for his wife. Wife? The Girl hides her face. Peter is shocked, his eyes pop out on stems. The Gambler smiles, nods. Yes—The Girl is his Wife. In the eye of God, they are man and wife. No, no, says The Girl. She married him only to save her father from ruin. But she has never been his wife. She is the virgin, she loves only Peter. All this told quickly by full, played-out actions, rolling eyes, looks.

Peter is shocked. The evil that is in all women. The same simple story of all sagas. A man and a woman desired? Passion and flesh held close under God's clean sky. Then the evil ways of lust. The Girl only a woman since the Garden of Eden, a bone, a hank of hair. The other man, a monster of sexual depravity, no doubt. Ready to wreak his will on this tasty clean body. Those cherished sunkist curves from California.

The paint pony comes at a whistle. Peter leaps into the saddle, he tears off the sling. His face is scarred with suffering. He had given his love to one not worthy. The same old story of a woman's false love. A horse never let one down. Off, Paint, and away!

IRIS DOWN. He rides off into the night.

A great, tearing blurring on the screen of dreams. The film has broken. ONE MOMENT PLEASE. A stamping of feet, a groaning and shrill whistling. Left half in an opium trance, half in a groin-aching paradise, the drugged public shouts for its drug.

A miner's deserted cabin. The Gambler and The Girl alone. (Somewhere, somehow, a few hundred feet of dream are missing.) The Gambler is wrassling with The Girl. She breaks from him. He follows. His face is a signboard of lust, a mural of flesh in heat. He pants, he sweats, he leers, he mouths unheard, hot, tasty words. The Girl shakes and beats her fists on her brow. Virginity is in danger. He has her now. Backed against the table. This shall be their wedding bed. Back, back. Down, down. She has no strength left to fight it off. He pulls the starched linen from the white shoulder, his mouth drinks deep in the white throat.

ANGLE SHOT, MOUNTAIN CANYON. . . . A rock is falling, it gathers stones, trees. A landslide, and below is the small shape of the cabin. CAMERA PANS to a ridge. Peter and Paint. They look up, see the landslide. Look down, see the cabin.

INTERCUT CLOSE UP. The Girl. Naked shoulder. The Gambler snarling and chewing. Her mouth is open. She screams. Piano screams.

Peter on the ridge hears the scream. Paint hears the scream. Alert, they both know it is The girl. INTER-CUTTING. Landslide, rape. Only a moment before both are done. Maidenhead lost, cabin gone. A leap, a clatter of hoofs. The door of the cabin. A Knock. A Scream from inside. A leap through stout, locked oak door and into the cabin. Peter, Paint, shoulder to shoulder.

The Gambler turns to Peter, fear, panic on his face. A knife. Peter ducks. Fists bang. The Gambler is down. He is up. Breaks a chair on Peter's head. Peter is down. The Gambler crawls to the knife on floor. The Girl tosses the table over him. Peter is up. One blow, The Gambler is done for. Peter grabs The Girl, leaps through the window and is off, both on the back of Paint.

The Gambler pulls a hidden gun from his groin. He aims. The landslide hits him, blots out the cabin. Peter and The Girl look back. All is over. The dastard is dead. She is no longer wife, still virgin. The Girl, His Girl.

CLOSE UP, The Girl and Peter. She on the saddle before him. The look that is full of promise. LONG SHOT as they ride off into the sunset. THE END.

Peter awakened slowly. The smell and feel of the girl were still with him. An ache rode through him. He put his teeth together to keep from weeping with joy. It was the great weekly moment of his life. He had shared beauty, art, and life with millions.

The darkness, thank God, has not been broken. On the screen a large man with big feet and a big cap is making pies. Ham Hamilton is winking at the big-eyed, white-faced, fat-rumped girl who is filling the pies. He tries to kiss her and she claps a quart of flour into his face, nose, eyes, and mouth. Laughter.

Peter was paying no attention to the screen. He was still in buckskin, under a wide Stetson, riding off with the bouncing girl. Stinker and Ike did not stir either. For some reason they, too, were riding Paint, The Girl in *their* arms, riding off into the sunset and into desire. All day and during the night the nation would sit in darkness and the men would ride off with The Girl on their saddle bows and the schoolgirls and housewives would look over the shoulders at the bull-like features in buckskin and Stetson.

It seemed only fair, Peter used to feel, that at the schools and in the classroom they should teach life as the movies saw it. As he grew older he found that only this dream life existed for most people. That they worked and slept and ate and married and replenished the earth, but that only at the movies did they ever really live. There the sad truths of existence, the shoddy facts of jobs, the rancid, tired wives, the clapboard homes, the dusty interiors and installment dining-room and bedroom sets were mere makeshifts. That once in the throbbing darkness of the movie their real life began. The Girl was sweetheart, vampire, fleshpot, dream girl, mother, fairy, and spiritual comfort. The man was to the army of straining women the prize catch, the bold, clean, heroic male, the full stallion, the tender lover, the eternal mate, and the proud brother. The tiger-skin interiors, the rich facts of torrid life, the furniture and baths of Babylon and Paris and Park Avenue, *this* was the true Eden, an hour or so of heaven and drugs and dreams; the inner core of what life really should be, the dream hope. All the rest was just existence till the bill changed on Wednesdays.

It took Peter years to cure himself of this deadly, satisfying drug—whose pleasures passed too quickly.

The boys found it hard to shake off the drugged state of the movies. They walked down the sunny street close together, not talking much until the Blue Dog came into view. It was a stubby, frame building on the main street, next to the Ford agency. Its two plate-glass windows were filled with pulp magazines, plaster-of-Paris steaks and chops too realistically coloured, and some brass pots full of yellow, diseased palms very attractive to flies. Blue curtains cut off the interior from the street. The Blue Dog was out of bounds for Beagle students and so got the most daring of them.

The three boys went in through the back door and into the private dining room. The checked blue cloths covered small tables, and the yellow pine chairs held an amorous drunken couple, a salesman filling order blanks, and Tinker Evens smoking a fat, short cigar. The place smelled of needled bootleg beer, fried food, and bad plumbing. Here whatever vice, or what passed for vice, the town could produce was offered to its citizens and visitors.

"Hi," said Tinker Evens, burying his face in a mug of the notoriously bad beer.

The boys said "Hi", and whistled for Gertie. She was wearing her tight blue dress and her spike-heeled shoes, and she looked tired and somewhat strained behind her large, red-larded Joan Crawford mouth.

"The Rover Boys," she said. "How's all the students today?"

"We're feeling fine," Stinky said, "feelin' no pain."

"Yeah, I betcha. What'll be, th' usual?"

Peter shook his head. "It's Stinky's birthday."

"Many happy returns, I'm sure!"

Stinky held up the silk stockings. "For you, Gertie darling."

"Well, ain't ya got yer nerve. Real silk, huh? Fer cryin' out loud."

"Think they'll fit?"

"Who wants ta know?"

"We *can* try them on."

"Wisenheimers, ain't ya?"

"I'd hate to have them not fit. Just slip them on."

"Later, chum, later. What'll it be? Steak, chops?"

Ike looked up from the fly-loved menu. "Any caviar on ice?"

"Cav*iah*? Say, I wouldn't even trust th' ice here. This jernt ain't no Monte Crisco, ya know."

"Make it steak and beer all around. You do like the stockings, don't you, honey?"

"Sure, yer so good to me and I'm so tired of it all."

Tinker Evens from his table said, "Bulldust."

"Shut up, Tinker," said Ike. "This isn't your party."

"Come over and make me."

"Later, I'm hungry now."

"Bring your friends, I'll take 'em all on." Tinker Evens grabbed Gertie and put his arms around her breasts. "Stop robbin' the cradle, kid, and meet a well-hung man."

Gertie broke loose. "Where? Don't make me laff."

"Okay, roundheels."

The town policeman came in, pushed back his cap, and sat down. The amorous couple left, holding each other tight as if afraid to drop valuable glass. Gertie rushed in and out of the kitchen, herding flies ahead of her like geese.

The boys ate steaks and drank the ache-producing beer and speared the fried potatoes. The policeman complained about his kidneys, drank his beer, used the bad plumbing, and left.

Gertie came back wearing the new stockings. Each of the three friends had to feel and see how sheer they were and Stinky was allowed to see her garters. Hot damn! They ordered two more rounds of beers and Tinker Evens got up and went out to the front of the Blue Dog and came back reeking of Jersey lightning, a local apple brandy, pale as death and almost as satisfying. The Blue Dog sold only beer, but old customers like Tinker Evens could always beg a swig of the private stock of Jersey lightning.

Tinker Evens prided himself on his ability, as a Southern gentleman, never to show the effects of hard drinking, to be able to sleep with every girl he wanted. It was "a family tradition", he explained. Gertie was seated on Stinker's lap and he was nibbling her ear and she was screaming and laughing.

"Stop it, stop it! Why don't ya go back to kindergarten!"

Tinker Evens said, "Look, small fry, hist your tails out of here. You annoy me."

"Shut up, Evie," said Gertie, "yer drunk."

"Drunk as a pissant," said Tinker Evens proudly, "but I'm still what you need, not these pukin' kids. Come on, roundheels, let's go back upstairs."

"Shut up, ya tramp," shouted Gertie.

Stinky's face grew very pale. "Lay off, Evens. This isn't your party."

Tinker Evens came over and pushed a flat hand against Stinky's face.

"Don't talk back to me."

Ike stood up. "Last chance, Evens, to mind your own business."

"Shut up, Jewboy, this isn't your kosher neck of the woods."

Peter put his hands on the table. "Evens, his name is Ike. One more word from you and the three of us will take you on."

"Get somebody your own size. As for you, Kiky Ikey, you're lucky they let you sit down with white men. Where I come from, we don't mix with niggers or Christ-killers."

Ike stood and said simply, "I guess this is it, Evens." He drove a fist into Evens' face. Evens backhanded him a powerful blow and then drove him to the floor with a hard, short punch that snapped Ike's head back.

Gertie screamed, "Of all the lousy trouble-makers!"

Peter lifted his mug of beer and threw it at Evens. Stinky tried to bang in his fist but Evens, outweighing him, taller and more used to barroom fighting, sent him reeling after Ike. Gertie drew back, lifting her skirt to show the new stockings, the red-bowed garters, and several inches of pale thigh mottled by a series of moles. This, she felt, was like the movies (the lumber-jacks fighting over the queen of the hash-slingers).

The three boys, Ike bleeding badly from the nose, advanced on Evens. Stinky launched himself in a football tackle and got kicked in the head. Peter plunged in and got Evens around the waist. He smelled of sweat and beer and dry-cleaning fluid. Ike was punching Evens' face and Stinky, a red welt on one cheek, was pulling Evens' head around.

Evans rolled clear, kicking out, and Peter lifted a yellow chair and brought it down on the big head. The chair broke and Evens went down with a thud. They were all over him, and with fists and beer mugs they hammered on his head and shoulders.

Gertie had stopped screaming. She was staring at the blood and battle, her mouth open, some agony of pleasure on her face as she stood scratching herself absent-mindedly under one armpit.

"Murderize 'im—murderize 'im!"

Al, the owner of the Blue Dog, came in and after him two mill hands, beer mugs still in their hands.

Gertie said, very low, "They're killin' the bastar' fa me."

Al pulled a boy off and caught a fist in the nose. He yelped and stepped back, tenderly holding his hurt organ. Gertie stopped scratching herself and yelled, "Kill 'im, kill 'im dead! Tear 's arms offa 'im and beat 'im to deat' with 'em!"

Evens lay very still on the floor, blood flowing from his nose and mouth. A flap of hairy skin fell over his brow from a scalp wound made by a broken beer mug.

Al said, "He ain't dead, is he?"

"Yeah," said Gertie, "I neve' seen no one no deader. . . ."

Sam and Sara had felt for some time that the big river-front apartment was too large for just the two of them. They had never really gotten over the death of their two sons in the war. Their remaining son was now a sort of Englishman. They felt lonely, and usually listless. They had at first travelled a lot, but in the end they admitted it was more pleasant to see distant places in the movies. "Cleaner and you save the baggage". Sam expanded his stamp collection, went on inspection trips of the Tennessee lands, and took up golf. He thought this a foolish sport as he didn't get drunk or like too many dirty stories.

Sara became a letter writer. She wrote to everyone: to the relatives, to total strangers, to *The New York Times*. She sat all morning at her portable typewriter tapping out a half-dozen crisp, involved letters. In the afternoon she went walking along Riverside Drive planning more letters, or just sitting looking across at the river, the boats, and the Jersey shore. She had tried Mary Baker Eddy, but it had not helped much. She carried in her bag a small, soiled card reading: *Professor Ajor. Editor: "The Spirit Plane." Home or Studio Contacts Guaranteed with the Beyond.* She was tempted but she did not really believe that there was another world that one "passed over" to, or that the dead could come back through the help of a departed Indian chief. Or Little Joan, aged three, who came from the other world and spoke with a cold in her nose (as she had done for Sara's sister, Mrs. Gottman, and brought a message from Morris, her dead husband). Sara couldn't believe that in the next world little children still caught colds.

In a few years this grey cloud would lift a little from Sara and Sam. The depression, loss of almost all their money, would help. They would rent a small house in an unfashionable part of Florida and Sam would tinker with a cheap motorboat and become a fisherman and deep-sea hunter of the blue Gulf Stream. Sara would play low-point bridge and collect funds for a summer camp for underfed children; and in time the dead sons would fade a little. . . . But now it was very bad for them.

The windows were open and the noise and blustery air of Riverside Drive filled the room. Sam was seated under some rather over-size paintings that Egon had brought to America and never been able to sell. Heroic, slashed, and distorted examples of early cubism by Braque and Picasso. Sam's stamp collection was spread out before him and he was examining a sheet of purple monsters issued by some French colonial group. He had grown grey and a little flabby, a little careless in dress. But he was pleased that the stamps were beginning to bore him. It was a sign, he felt, that a change was coming into his life. It was, he remembered, the end of one of the seven-year periods into which he had divided his life. He firmly believed that a human being changed every seven years, stepping out like a molting grasshopper or lobster from his old shell, and had, in that period, replaced all his tissues and organs and cell structure, and nothing, or very little remained of the man of the last seven years—except for some incidental dentistry.

It was a harmless kind of thinking, and it gave him an excuse for making a change in their mode of life, a change that was slowly being planned by him. They would leave this river-front flat and move to Tennessee and he would personally look after the coal and iron and woodlands that were almost the family's entire means of living. Then an old age in Florida over the bridge tables.

He closed the stamp albums and locked them up in their rosewood desk that the dealer had sworn had once belonged to Balzac, and on which he wrote *La Cousine Bette* in six weeks. Sam walked to the windows, ignoring the cubistic paintings floating overhead. Unlike old Joseph, he paid them no mind, never knew any more that they hung on the walls. Old Joseph enjoyed them. He said it was like the Arabs and Jews sitting for hours looking into the designs of an old Persian rug and seeking there the pattern and secret of life. When asked if the secret of life was woven into a Persian rug, he said, "No one so far has discovered it, so perhaps it is also hidden in cubism." He would spend hours staring at the modern paintings. He was growing very old and people said that only senility could make one a lover of those paintings.

Sara came in carrying a tray of tea things. There was a servant problem in the land. The imported European servant girls had all married, or gone off to burlesque wheels or Minnesota farms. On the servant's day off Sara served herself.

She set down the tea tray, and Sam came over and sat down and put his hands deep in his pockets and crossed his legs and smiled.

"We need a change."

"Do we, Sam?"

"We're not so old; of course, we're not so young. We're what the insurance people call middle-aged, even if we're not prepared for it. Sara, how would you like Tennessee?"

"I could like it." She handed him a cup of tea the way he liked it— strong, two lumps of sugar, lemon, and no cream or milk. She patted his arm and smiled. "I could even get fond of it, mister."

Sam stirred his tea. "I've been thinking we better put the Tennessee lands in order. This rising market might make some money for us after all. We could use it."

"I've heard that ever since I married you. Always the family expects to get rich on that land. I was reading that Mark Twain's family also buried all their hopes in Tennessee land. All they got was debts."

"We've been a little more lucky. We've managed to scrape a living out of it. But a lawyer I was talking to suggested we divide the land into separate corporations, one for iron, one for coal, one for timber, and put some stock issues on the market and really develop the things on a big scale."

"Sam, are you in the market?"

Sam shrugged his shoulder. "With peanuts. Papa is dabbling in grains, even Tante Strasser, I hear, is plunging in radio stocks. I'm in on slim margins. I can't lose much. Even the shoeshine boy is in the market."

"I don't like it."

The front doorbell jingled and Sara got up and went to the door. Sam heard her gasp with surprise and say some hurried words, and then in marched three boys, dusty, sweaty, and flushed. Their faces were rather battered, and Sam saw that Peter had a beautiful mouse on his right eye, that Ike Sontag had skinned one side of his face. The boy with the swollen nose he didn't know.

"Sam," said Sara, "there has been trouble."

"I can see that on their maps."

"Hello, Uncle Sam," said Peter stiffly. "How are you?"

"Where's the war?"

"Sit down, boys," said Sara, "and I'll get some more cake and milk and sandwiches. You hungry, boys?"

Ike nodded. "We haven't eaten since yesterday."

Sam fingered his chin and inspected them. "What happened?"

Peter rubbed his skinned, dirty knuckles into his soiled shirt-front. "We killed a man."

Sam whistled. He sat up straight and looked at them. The Leopold and Loeb killing was still fresh in the nation's mind. "Murder for thrills" was the newest excitement to a form of journalism called the tabloids, then feeling their first youth. Sam shook his head. "What nonsense is this?"

Peter frowned. "We had a fight in a beer hall. The three of us. With Tinker Evens. He's older and bigger. We took him. Too far, I guess."

Sam nodded. At least it wasn't a thrill killing. "Go on." Peter and Ike, helped a little by Stinky, filled in the details quickly. Sara came back with food and listened and fed them. They finished their muttered, sputtered story and ate quickly and looked with sad, childish eyes on Sam and Sara.

Sam slapped his thigh. "At their age, over a woman!"

"Disgusting," said Sara. "Where do they pick such things up? Putting stockings on waitresses!"

277

"That part doesn't bother me."

The boys gulped and ate. They had carried their horror and terror long enough. They had lain in ditches and walked in rains and been chilled by morning and hitch-hiked on battered cars. They had fled senselessly from the Blue Dog, and now they had come at last and laid their burden down, as a bad hound would a dead, pet chicken, at the feet of some adults. They wanted to relieve themselves of it, let an adult carry on, to punish, scold or flog; whatever was to come, they had to unload their problem on older shoulders. And they had.

The Perrys were in California. Ike did not dare try to face his strong-willed mother. So on Sam and Sara fell the burden. The boys ate as only hungry boys can eat after a period of famine, and as only youth, relieved of grim thoughts, could at last satisfy a long fast.

Sam said, "You shouldn't run off. Better to face it. He started by calling names, didn't he?"

"We couldn't say."

"Beer mugs on a boy's face . . . hammered at him . . ." said Sara. "How can men be so brutal?"

"It was a knock-down, drag-out fight, Mrs. Pedlock," said Stinky.

Sam had decided to go into action. "Feed 'em," he said. "I'll go get Papa. Answer no doorbells, and no phone calls. Eat up, boys. Do you good to face this with a tight belly."

He went quickly through the famous doorway cut between the two apartments. The boys ate and gave details of their woe to Sara. Sam was back soon with old Joseph limping after him. The old man's eyes went darting from one face to another. He was grim but rather expressionless.

"All right, Peter," he said, sitting down at the phone. "We'll do what we can with honour. No sulking or passing blame."

"No, sir," said Peter. He felt that old Joseph understood. Hadn't he killed men and fought it out in Butte once with a killer? A man couldn't let go of his dignity, his self-respect. There had to be a time when he struck back, and hard.

Old Joseph had Charles Pentland's office on the phone. The banker was out to lunch. Joseph called two downtown clubs and got Charles Pentland at last. He was direct and cool into the phone.

"I don't call you, Charles, unless it's real trouble."

The voice on the wire said casually, "I know you don't, Joseph. Been selling the bull market short?"

"No. Peter is in bad trouble. He's with me here."

"Run off from school?"

"Yes, with two friends. They've been in a fight. Maybe killed a boy."

There was a pause at the other end of the wire. Then a colourless, cool, collected voice: "Do nothing till I get there. Admit no one. I'll bring Weatherwax with me."

Old Joseph hung up. "He's bringing his lawyer with him."

The boys had stopped eating; they felt rather ill from their gorging. They sat stuffed and logy, looking at the adults.

Benton Weatherwax (ex-judge "Picklepuss") of Bierstadt, Blakelock, Weatherwax, Weatherwax, and Raymond, was the senior partner in one of those giant Wall Street firms of lawyers whose names, like the titles of Pullman cars, create such amusement when they are repeated. It was *not* an amusing firm, and Benton Weatherwax was not a man with a sense of humour. He was a grey little man in grey clothing with thin, unsuccessful hair combed straight back. He wore rimless bifocals on a sharp Yankee nose, and was known for his pink shirts with tight narrow collars held down by a thin golden bar in prevailing Wall Street fashion. He collected Chinese bronzes to complete his father's collections.

He paced the rug in front of the boys and Charles Pentland, who smiled at Peter, wishing the damn grey rabbit would stop pacing the floor. Weatherwax turned toward the phone as it rang.

"For me, I suspect," he said as if giving unimportant evidence in an involved lawsuit.

He picked up the phone. "Yes. Well? Good. Keep me informed."

He hung up and turned to the boys, glanced over their heads, and addressed the rosewood desk. "We're sending three men into New Jersey." He spoke as if it were an expedition into Africa. "There has been no mention of the incident—of anything in the press, anywhere. Of course, Beagle is powerful enough—I'm a Groton man myself— to keep it out of the papers. Also, did it ever strike any of you the boy may *not* be dead? Youth, you know, can take a lot of punishment."

Old Joseph nodded. "I felt the same way, but I didn't want to call the school until it was decided by everyone."

Ike suddenly said, "I want to call my mother."

Weatherwax waved him off. "Sit down, boy." The phone rang, he picked it up. "Yes? Speaking. Put him on. Well? No? Good. Stand by."

Weatherwax turned and accepted a cigar from Charles Pentland's Russian-leather case. Sam and old Joseph already were lit up. Weatherwax sucked it into life and tapped his fingers on the desk.

"There are no serious hospital cases around the school, within twenty miles, that answer to this Evens. Know his uncle, great skeet shot. And now we're checking the undertakers. I wish we could be bolder and call the headmaster, but we don't want to approach them. Bad procedure; let them come to us, if they want to."

Old Joseph picked up the phone and asked for Beagle's phone number. While waiting he looked up at the men and boys and winked at Sara.

"This is a direct attack, the kind J. E. B. Stuart always advised. This is a flanking move—I used to be good at it. . . .

"Hello, Beagle Prep? Please connect me with the infirmary. Thank you. Hello, this the infirmary? Could I please speak with Tinker Evens. Yes, a friend of the family. Oh, I see. How's that?"

Everyone looked at old Joseph and leaned forward as if this buzz of phone message coming failingly to them could be of great importance.

Old Joseph nodded and rolled his cigar in his mouth. "I see. That so? Well, never mind then, I'll call again. The doctor says that? He a good doctor? Oh, I'm just a friend of the family. I'll call again. Thank you."

Old Joseph hung up and puffed on his cigar and looked grimly down his glowing cigar ash.

"Come on, Joseph," said Charles Pentland, "talk."

"Tinker Evens says he was hit by an unidentified car. Can't talk to him. He can't talk to us. Lost four teeth, and his head is cut badly. Twenty-two stitches. He's drugged and asleep. Nothing mortal, I gather."

Sam said, "We've acted like damn fools. Listening to kids' tales."

Peter gulped, "He certainly looked dead."

Ike and Stinky agreed he looked "like a dead one".

Charles Pentland grinned. "It was rather sporting of Evens, don't you think? Beagle builds gentlemen, all right."

Sara had folded her arms and was looking with great displeasure at the boys. "Silk stockings for a waitress at their age! It's disgusting, it's revolting."

"Yep," said old Joseph, giving a goat's leer, "the country and its young men is sure going to hell in a hack."

The men looked at each other and grinned, glorying in their maleness, in danger avoided and troubles sidestepped, in the deeds of the cowed but relieved boys.

Stinky went back to school with a hamper of food and some folding money. Ike Sontag went home to his mother, who was proud of him for fighting back, and she was only prevented from attacking Beagle and its "anti-Semitism" by pressure from her usually mild husband, and the fact that Ike needed the credits to get into college. Peter moved in with Charles Pentland, who warned him, laughing fit to bust, "to keep away from the second-floor maid", and could he be trusted in the village alone? There was a proud, old-fashioned girls' school in the neighbourhood.

But the more Charles Pentland thought of the whole affair, the more he frowned, and he sent a wire to Ralph at Santa Barbara, where he and Alice and Nicole were spending a fashionable season.

Lord knows, Charles Pentland thought as he sat in the library, a good drink in his hand, a dog at his feet, I'm no bigot, and I don't care what creed a man has, but I do think I owe something to my family background and all that, and to the future of my holdings. I hate to admit this, I suppose, but Peter is getting too damn Jewish. Nothing wrong in it, of course. Fine people, gave us Christ, a basic godhead, the Ten Commandments; all good family men and all that. Do the boy good as a matter of fact to have some Jewish blood. Nothing like a touch of it to give an old family some new fire. But, after all, the boy is a Pentland, of my stock. . . .

"Well," said Tante Strasser, stirring up the grate of cannel coal in the fireplace; she was always cold these days. "He's a fine boy, no doubt about it. But his Christian blood is coming out. It's all for killing and slaughter. Look how they murdered each other over just church politics. After all, it's a religion only two thousand years old. They were still in skins, carrying spears, roasting each other over slow fires, when we were the only people to know God and have a code of ethics, and have scholars and prophets. Not that Christian blood is so bad for one. It gives a touch of manners, and a little refinement to the mind; a feeling for things. But I do think we ought to do something. After all, he's one of us, a Pedlock. His forefathers were great students of learning, and doctors. I think we should take more interest in him. Be a little firmer with his parents."

The long train was running through gaunt dry cuts in the colourful earth. The smell of sage, the fine white dust of the desert came slowly, but surely, into the compartment of the transcontinental train.

"He's grown away from us, Ralph," Alice said, "that's what has happened. Boys always do. They don't become part of a family like a daughter. Sit down, Nicole, and take your face off that dirty window-pane. I suppose it's our fault, but he's always wanted schools and summer camps and woodcraft. Boys are so unthinking, and we love him so. My poor little Peter."

Ralph shook his head. "I suppose it's the frontier spirit in America. We're really only half-tamed. We still glory in saloon killings and cattle wars, rough men and wagon trains. We need a few centuries to take on a polish. Still, it's a great thing we had in that spirit. Look what it's done for us as a nation. But when it comes home to us like this, it sets one thinking."

Having been lamented as a Jew, as a Christian, as a boy, and as an American, Peter slept and dreamed of a paint pony.

CHAPTER IV

It was decided, in many mixed family meetings, that "a year abroad, with an English tutor", was just the right thing for Peter. A good solid year of the art galleries and great churches and noble cultures of the Continent was just the thing for a young man to absorb at his age. Next year, in the fall, he would enter Princeton, and the year in Europe would give him some certain advantages over those students who were still struggling in native high schools and prep schools. Charles Pentland believed in culture, "without too much book learning to make it dull". He was a well-read man himself, who had done well in Latin and Greek at Harvard, but he would much rather have his grandson excited by stained-glass windows than the inner problems of Pindar's verse. "I was twenty myself before I found out churches were not built merely to show off architectural history."

"He's so young," said Alice, hugging Nicole to her.

"The Black Prince, at his age," said her father, "had already been in battle and led an army to great victory. We start our young too late in life. I am for bringing them earlier into the fray."

They were seated in Charles Pentland's living room and the sun was beating, blood-coloured, against the calm, summer window shades. Ralph got up and walked to the table and picked up a blue sheet of paper.

"This John Warlock, the tutor, where did he come from? This report isn't very clear."

Charles Pentland smiled. "The Embassy speaks very well of him. An Oxford man and a rowing Blue. A bit of a snob of course and rather dull, but just the right thing for Peter at his age. He's a find and all he wants is his keep and expenses. Of course, we'll throw in a full outfit for travelling and perhaps present him with a leather bag. That would be fine. He's a real example of the English public-school system. That means private school, Ralph, over there."

"I knew that. Well, if he's well spoken of."

Alice said, "One hears such odd stories about public-school life. I don't mean all the young men are involved; Peter is so very young."

Charles Pentland nodded. "Nothing to fear in that direction, my dear. The Embassy assures me Warlock was shipped over here because he wanted to marry a barmaid. Normal young man, muscles like rocks, he draws, and climbs mountains. Nothing lavender there. I've drawn up the trip myself. The Derby, of course, in England and a visit to the Tower. I never forgot my own trip to the Tower. Paris, the art galleries." Charles Pentland stopped talking and looked at his carefully cared for hands. "Perhaps we better skip Paris. Full of—yes, nothing much *there* now, these days."

Ralph looked closely at his father-in-law. Paris meant Egon, and Egon meant Jew, and Jew meant something they were trying to keep Peter clear of just at that moment. He wanted to protest. Paris was the best part of any trip to Europe, but he thought better of it. After all, Peter could always go back to Paris some other time, when he was his own boss, or Charles Pentland was dead.

Peter neither liked nor disliked John Haydon Warlock. He was a thick young man with huge muscles left over from his days as a college strong-man. Those efforts had left him with a badly strained heart and, like all musclemen, once they stopped expanding their muscles, a victim of constipation. A subject on which he could talk for hours.

They had a small cabin on the good side of the ship, and they ate three tables away from the Captain's. They rose early, and after prayers, went four times around the deck. Breakfast followed, Warlock stowing away great portions of prunes and brans and other doctored fodder. They had lessons of sorts till lunch, mostly readings of Stevenson (R. L.), about whom Warlock was preparing to write one of those thin, brilliant little books. Lunch was hurried, for they were very active in deck games.

Warlock was Church of England. At night he said his prayers on his knees.

"Do you pray, Peter?"

"I don't mind to."

"You must, every night."

"Do you think God hears every prayer?"

Warlock examined his huge teeth in the glass and drank a tepid glass of water. "Oh, yes. I don't know what I'd do without prayer. Throw me that Kipling. Do you like Kipling?"

"I'm polite to him. My uncle Egon says he's a dreadful dope with mush where his brain ought to be. I liked *Kim* very much."

"Your uncle doesn't understand the Empire."

"I suppose not, but he's a very bright man. Uncle Louis says Kipling has coloured blood."

Warlock slammed the book shut. "That will *do*, Peter. Read your algebra."

Peter read and looked out of the porthole and scraped his shoes on the floor of the cabin and wondered how deep the sea was under the ship.

"Do you care for tattooing?"

"It's a vulgar habit of the lower classes. God gave us a clean body and we must keep it that way."

"The sailor that hands out the soup has a naked lady tattooed on his chest. When he wriggles she dances."

"That will do, Peter. Stick to algebra."

"I'm hungry."

"Dinner will be in an hour. Wash up and comb your hair."

"Do I have to?"

"Yes."

"I like a soap that stinks very fancy, don't you?"

Warlock dressed for dinner—naturally—and he looked beautiful in his evening clothes (although Peter noticed his underwear was frayed, his socks unwashed). He looked the proper British blood as he sat at table with Peter and some Chicagoans and South Americans and defended the records of British diplomacy and the honour of Anthony Eden. He came from a huge poor family, minor postal clerks and laundry agents, but who had descended from younger sons of almost-good families. He was honest, earnest, and full of good, solid talents. He faintly disliked children.

Peter spent an hour in the ship's reading room every night writing in his diary. He did not care for the task but he had promised Charles Pentland to keep a diary, and so, into a huge leather-bound book (with a brass lock) he put anything he could think of. For example—here is a loose sheet that still exists:

May 4, 1924

Lost two dollars betting on day's run; off by 22.81. Very fine day, but deck games out because of rough sea. Had steak for lunch and two portions of pie (apple—only fair) and read two chapters of Kidnapped by R. L. Stevenson. Ginch [his code name for Warlock] is very sad and thinks he has piles. His two front teeth come out and he keeps them in a glass of water. He can't bite into bones or chew gum.

Tom Swift and His Electric Tank

Tom Swift in the Caves of Ice

Tom Swift and His Flying Ship

May 6, 1924

Ginch was caught in the man's bath by a broken latch and missed his lunch. Smoked two cigarettes called Goldflakes and Ginch is in love with the German lady's maid of the Chicago people. She is not fat but very soft to touch and she laughs a lot when Ginch tickles her. He recites her poems. Ginch is a fool. [He suspected Warlock of reading his diary and put in such tasty items as a trap.]

We land tomorrow. I am very lonely and very homesick. Last night I cried again. I miss Mother and Father and Nicole, and of course my grandfathers. Joseph Pedlock has a hole in his neck shot there by Billy the Kid. He has killed a lot of men. Always letting them drawer [draw] first. Ate two desserts tonight. They were very bad. Like jello—but not. Ginch has piles all right.

Harlot, har-lot, 1. A lewd woman; prostitute. 2. A male servant (Ginch?); churl; anyone, male or female of low birth (yes—Ginch).

(——not in ship's Dictionary). Will try unabridged one in London. . . .

Peter always remembered the sight of London and the massive shape of St. Paul's. And the girls in the streets. The soft woman's cry, "'Ello sport—'ow about it?" and their white faces with the red, leering mouths as they held small flashlights up to their heads. The long green turf of the old, stately homes, the stink of the cheap streets, the dirt on historic stones. The dreadful cooking—everything boiled to death in steam.

The long train painted blue through France and the bottled water and the waiter spilling the soup on Ginch. Ginch very sick of physic and the trip alone to the Catacombs in Rome. So cool and chilled after the heated air of the streets. All those long-dead people on parade and the neat way the skulls were placed and the teeth knocked out. Some day he, too, would die. But that was a long, long way off. The low, blue shoreline and the bright white sun and the brown bodies of girls swimming in the Italian lake. The shouting men in black shirts with mouths like ass holes and Big Chin himself who looked as if he wore his behind as a face.

Naples with Ginch very sick of bad water and too much *pasta*. Florence and the golden hills and the silver olive trees and deep green vines. Ginch in bed with a temperature and red rubber bags with long tubes. The hell with Ginch. Let 'im die. Peter had discovered the works of Pietro Aretino, and was looking for a good English translation for comparison. He carried an unopened packet of contraceptives and dreamed of large, mellow women of thirty.

Ginch grew sicker. Peter left him in bed and crossed the square and went past the great stone David of Michelangelo which had bored him as a child in the brown print of it over his bed, and had bored him in a bad copy in plaster at Beagle. Now, when he saw it weather-naked, stained by birds and dogs, he still got no bang out of it. It was a hot Italian day and the street smelled musty, stale as goat cheese, and the full odours of close living and careless urine that filled all Italian cities. But it no longer bothered him.

He found a small bookstore full of large leather-bound copies of Dante to snare the tourist trade. In the back Peter found a tottering shelf of English translations of the lower classics and was sneezing his way through the dust and spider webs when someone touched him on the shoulder and said, "May I see your passport?"

Peter turned around, a lewd Elizabethan text in his hand, and there was Uncle Egon in white linen, a limp, palm straw hat on his head and a thin, twisted Italian cigar in his mouth. He was fatter than ever, a pale yellow vest across the expanding girth dominating the shop.

"Uncle Egon, what are you doing in Florence!"

"Looking at my nephew. But why books on such a fine day?"

"Ginch, that's my tutor, I'm travelling with him, he's sick. Dying, I guess, and it's dull in the hotel. The Palace."

"That expensive fleabag. Your folks with you?"

"No. I'm travelling only with Ginch. He's English and constipated."

"You have outlined the breed for me." He took Peter's arm. "I'm about to lunch at Virgilius Maro's. You want a book?"

"Not now."

"I have a villa full of them. But later. You like Europe?"

"It's hot."

"Habit of European summers. Come on, first lunch, and then I'll show you my mountaintop and we'll bathe in my pool. It was built by an old Roman skinflint and sinner called Crassus and I'm keeping ten war orphans up there. How are the folks?"

"Fine. I'm kinda in the doghouse. I was expelled from Beagle."

Egon shook cigar ashes off onto the marble sidewalk. "The hell you say. Why?"

Peter smiled. "Jew trouble."

Egon nodded and grinned. The kid was going to be all right. "Come on, pick up your eternal racial pack, shake out your ritual curls, and we'll go eat some unkosher antipasto, *piccioni arrosta* and a good *insolata verde*."

"That's just a green salad," said Peter.

"The boy also has the gift of languages."

In this manner were the efforts of Charles Pentland undone. Short of a world pogrom he could not, it seemed, keep Peter from his birthright.

Ginch was moved to a hospital to have his personal plumbing attended to and neither Peter nor Uncle Egon ever saw him again. He was shipped home to Surrey in luxury, with a nurse and several remedies that did not kill him, and he wrote his book on Stevenson. But Peter never read it.

Uncle Egon had a small, ugly, rose-coloured villa in the hills with marble floors and ceiling murals by a good forgotten fifteenth-century painter. And a staff of six, who got little pay but stole just enough to be happy. Uncle Egon lived an almost simple life, a life he modelled on St. Francis (with a few modifications of his own). He rose early, meditated on life and God and death and hope, while he read *The London Times*. He walked a lot, dressed simply, except for a note of colour at times. He and Eric, his valet, bathed the war orphans, salved their scabs, sated their hunger, and educated their rattled minds. He was always short of money for them but he wrote begging letters and polished his war medals and had no pride when it came to feeding his mangy group of war casualties. Egon had changed. He lived no longer for himself alone. Unlike the English ladies in Italy, he did not stop at collecting a few stray cats and putting a bird bath in his garden. He collected war orphans for years. He suffered and even wept over his charges, and when a thin one died, he bribed the proper fascist in the local office and had him buried among the lilac bushes. He always read over it some beautiful poem or some crisp quotation. He had turned to a personal God, and while he no longer mocked priests or rabbis, he could not stand them as company, except for a poor, demented little monk who worked in his garden and was carrying on a long, involved love affair with a cloud that floated pink and high over the villa at sunset every day.

Peter grew to love the Villa Egon, as it came to be called. It was ancient and dusty and very old-rose in colour in the sunlight. The goats walked the hills and gave Peter a red eye, and the old Italians, their bare brown feet square and large (like something basic out of modern art), used to bow to him and pull off ragged caps and take cigarettes from him with polite, Tuscan hisses of pleasure.

He taught the war orphans to spell, to read English, to box, and to play a frayed baseball. Evenings he sat with Uncle Egon on the terrace. They talked earnestly of life and death and art and misery. Days they often spent in town with a few other exiles. Artists, thieves, whores, saints, tourist guides, and journalists—that, anyway is what Uncle Egon called them. They usually sat, after a long, long lunch at Maro's, behind the Piazza Vecchio. Maro was a poet and once kept sixteen boxes of his poems in a small room, until his landlady burned them during a cold winter; he didn't mind, he said to Peter, because "there is too much art in the world anyway".

Uncle Egon showed Peter the city past the Via di Neri, and the Caffe della Colonnine where they drank a lot of *expressos*, which was a very good kind of un-American coffee, with the slums of Borgo di Greci and Via Pietrapiana at their backs.

Peter remembered that money was hard to get, yet they could always get good food somehow. A tasty *risotto* and *tripe alla fiorentina* and after it, a sugary, saffron cake called *schiacciata*. This went with an extra *quarto* to dip the cake in. Signora Maro said she had *un' affetto* for Peter. She was very kind to the very young far from home.

Uncle Egon and Peter used to sit at the villa drinking wine and reading Juvenal (in a fair English translation) or Lucian, Propertius, Terence, Plautus *and* Euripides.

"One must rest a great deal in Italy, Peter."

"Why?"

"Because the fools are spoiling the world."

"Are they?"

"Soon resting will be done away with. But don't take your ideas of life from me. I'm a bad example."

"Are you, Uncle Egon?"

"Yes. I didn't like myself for a long time, then I grew older and a little wiser and now I find myself bearable."

"You look happy."

"The outer shell, dipped in oil, I fear. But, Peter, I must warn you against the family. They are fine people, great people almost, but they herd together too much. One feels trapped into their patterns."

"What are their patterns?"

"Damned if I can put it into words. But personal crisis comes up and one suddenly runs for shelter to their tents."

"That's what families are for, Uncle Egon."

"Perhaps, but too much family can leave one a bystander in life. Oh, hell, let's cut the gab and just enjoy ourselves."

"There is only one trouble here."

"What's that, Peter?"

"It's so much fun you feel maybe it's wrong to be so happy."

"Oh, grim code of old Jews and early Christians. Lay off this, boy. Let's go back to reading."

"Reading was never fun in school."

"How could it be when it was a duty?"

"Never thought of it that way."

Sometimes they tried a sonnet of Petrarch, more often Manzoni's *I Promessi Sposi*, and a great deal of the time a lousy little racing sheet in gutter English that touted the flea-bitten race tracks of Italy. For Peter and Uncle Egon had become bettors of small sums on the performances of horses. Like all the good times of his life (as Peter was to find out), it could not last. When fall drew near, a vicious *tramontana*, like the mistrals of Provence, was blowing in over the villa of Uncle Egon, and now they often sat over a *scaldino*, a metal brazier of hot charcoal. Besides, the family had arranged booking, and Princeton was waiting for Peter.

"*Mamma mia!*" cried fat Pia Guicciardini, the cook, "the boy isn't ever going to stop growing." She always sent her barefooted daughter Andrea to bring him a nightly snack, some chicken on a battered, silver tray, and strong goat milk in a glass. One night they wandered out in the moonlight, into the garden, smelling of the old fertile soil and flowering herbs. Andrea was twelve and brown and big for her age. Her slim, hard young legs carried her with a poise that transformed her body into something—so Peter felt—like those solid marble goddesses balancing their curves in the foyer of the villa.

Andrea was full of erotic tricks and she had long since "lost her innocence" (as the expression went in those parts) to a Greek gardener. She was full—she admitted to Peter—of "*un' affetto*, and *una grande simpatia*." She simply took his hand and re-enacted an old game; and there, in a bed of pinks and small daisies, Peter lost his virginity in a taut, fumbling effort, a great, wonderful singing in his ears.

"You like me, Peter?"

"I love you, darling."

"Love, she is for ladies and gentlemens. You like me fine?"

"I adore you."

"You talk fine all the time. You so tender. You was virgin, I think," she said in her pidgin English.

"Andrea, you talk too much."

"Is time for talk, is time for making the loving. Some day you forget Andrea but she never forget you. You so sweet and smell so nice of English soap. I wash my feet every day for you, you like that?"

"Of course. You look so beautiful in the moonlight."

"Grass damn wet sometimes."

"Don't you feel the great beauty of it all, isn't it something beyond the mere meeting of just two people?"

"My mother say she break my neck if I get pregnant. But you good boy, you young and careful, I no get big belly and go to priest and give him a gold coin to be forgiven. You no fascist sonofabitch, you my big, strong Peter who smells so good."

"Oh, Andrea, you have made me happy."

"You bet, keed."

"Where did you learn that?"

"The cinema palace, the one with fleas in the chairs where they sell the colas. You take me to cinema?"

"Don't talk, Andrea, any more."

". . . Beautiful Peter."

"Men aren't beautiful."

"Men are hairy like goats and smell like sour wine. You are smooth all over, see? And smell like English luggage."

Peter grew to know the garden well. And nothing (as his uncle told it years later) between him and the cool ground but a beautiful native of the country.

Peter was a romantic, so, in the morning he was shocked to see Andrea serve them breakfast on the terrace with no sign that anything world-shaking or horizon-bending had happened between them. He had expected downcast eyes, warm, secret looks, or even some tears stain-ing the solid brown of her cheeks. But she appeared as usual—her beautiful, naked legs, the wide whirling skirt under which, he now knew, she wore nothing, and her light, happy chatter, all as it had always been every day before that at breakfast.

Andrea was a realist. Most women were, Peter was to find out later. Realists with a desire for *affetto*. She did whisper as she brought in the coffee that he was, this morning, *un bel giovane*, a good-looking young man.

Peter went to his room and lay on his bed and felt very sorry for himself, for he had lost that which can only be lost once, and the object of his hasty passion had not been the great, beautiful, golden woman of his secret dream life. He was growing up slowly, a little too slowly, Uncle Egon felt, for he was to retain all his life, a certain New England outlook on the pleasures of this world. "Peter is always looking for the bill to pay," his uncle said. "And if there is no bill presented, Peter will ask for one and pine until everything is paid for. It is perhaps the result of breeding stock out of the Talmudic past when 'an eye for an eye and a tooth for a tooth' was the law, with New England's frigid gentry who loved a stern puritan God and felt ashamed of their meagre, naked bodies."

For lunch they had a guest. A young German engineer and a dear friend of Egon's. A poor young man who ran, at a feeble wage, the local power plant in the village. Kurt Steinbeck was a solid enough young man, covered with a red down on the back of his hands and even on his feet slipped naked into rope slippers. He had a close-cropped head of stiff copper wires in the style of crew haircuts that were later to become popular in the better Eastern colleges in America. He was full of *Kladderradatsch*—slam-bang, heavy humour.

"This is kind of you," said Kurt to Uncle Egon as they sat down to a lunch of *crostini*, boiled capon, a traditional Sienese *panforte* of chestnut-flour dumpling and two bottles of sweet *vino santo*. "Kind of you to invite a poor German, so far from home, to a good meal. Your cook is full of *Kunst*."

"So they say," Uncle Egon laughed. "Why do you Germans always appear so humble in defeat? Germans are not *really* humble."

Kurt laughed cheerfully and speared a pear with his fruit knife. "Always you talk of a defeat. Germany was never defeated. We were betrayed by the workers, the socialists, the Jews in our rear."

"This fat, old Jew is feeding you, Kurt, so don't warp history in my face. You were defeated. Worse luck, we never disarmed you. We merely patted you on the head and let you go on. Ready to spring up again; modern dragon's teeth."

Kurt smiled, showing all his fine teeth. "It's too fine a day to talk of trouble and poverty. There must be some good Germans; why not think I am one?"

Uncle Egon waved his fork in the air. "You're all right, Kurt. You've got a good mind. And, of course, you play fine soccer, which is what interests my nephew Peter—eh, Peter?"

"It is a fine game, Herr Steinbeck."

Kurt politely wiped his mouth free of pear juice with a stiff napkin. "I envy you Americans your college days ahead. I am a graduate of a good engineering school and my English is not bad, but . . ."

"It's rather too Liverpool," said Uncle Egon, "but perfect—a little over-perfect."

"Thank you. I try hard. But you don't know what it is to grow up in a rigid pattern. My father was a woollen-cloth manufacturer and it was hard for me to break out of the mould. And always those military uniforms. On mailmen and trolley-car conductors, bath attendants, dog-catchers, hotel porters. And now that fool in Rome is putting Italy in uniform."

"You're learning to live, Kurt," said Uncle Egon. "I used to worry over you in the old days—but I can see the poetry of Italy," he waved off a covey of flies, "has gotten into your Teutonic bones. How about another bottle? This is a *festa*, Peter is leaving us tomorrow for home. Peter, you *carabiniere*, cheer up and have a half glass of wine."

"I think I will, Uncle Egon."

"Aw," said Kurt, "your uncle is a great teacher. He has brought Giotto, Mantegna, del Sarto to life for me."

Andrea came out with a bowl of white grapes, her dark hair brushed back from her forehead in the style called *alla Mascagni* in those parts. Peter lowered his head. Kurt stood up and shook their hands. He looked redder and more powerful than ever, a young, solid body with that swelling of the glands in the back of the red neck that is the sign in most Germans that they are reaching their full prime.

"I thank you again, Egon, old friend, for the lunch. We must read the fifth canto of Dante together again some day. And to you, Peter, good luck and the best of it, old chap" (he dropped into low Low Liverpool, at times, without knowing it), "and write me. I'll most likely still be here. Things are dreadful in my own country. The workers, and socialists, *and*," he stopped grinned, showing those perfect teeth, shook his head, like a puppy who remembers his nose in the last mess, "*but* everything changes."

"A fine boy," said Uncle Egon after Kurt was gone. "Proves there is hope even for a German if you catch them young enough. I found him living in a dreadful dive full of Arabs in Rome, in rags. Spent his time in front of second-hand English hotels offering to guide young Oxford men through the vice districts. He cost me a lot of money. Not that I've done much for him. He's done fine, once that first boost was given to him. Well, Peter, what shall we do on this, our last day together here?"

"Nothing, I guess, except do what we've always done."

"That's a good answer. This is one of the few spots on earth where, after a few duties, one can really just rest. You know, most people are against resting, they say because it makes one lazy; the truth is, it makes them think, and most people would rather be taken in adultery than in thought."

"I suppose so, Uncle Egon."

"Yes, it took a long time to teach Kurt—to think."

They spent the afternoon bathing the war orphans. The orphans were a mangy, evil lot of children. Thin, erotic, thieving, lying battling misfits. The true products of wars, and not at all the beautiful children that most of the aid society posters pictured them.

Uncle Egon took them for what they could become, and beat their heads with scrubbing brushes, poured coal oil into their hair for nits, and patted their thin shoulders and big, white, knobby, unhealthy heads. Peter played ball with them. But he always managed to keep facing them with a good field of escape behind him. They often ganged up on him and their bites were very dangerous; he almost lost a finger once from an infection, after one nine-year-old she-devil tried to gnaw off his middle finger in a fit of rage. Like half-grown wolves, they were only part-tamed.

Secretly, Peter was always glad to be done with them. He admired the way Uncle Egon could spend hours with these little monsters, petting them and telling them long stories (they demanded bloodshed and horror and overlooked the morals he managed to sprinkle them with). He never gave up an effort to keep them neat and well clothed. They soiled everything and amused themselves by making *pipi* in their garments and tossing mud and damp cattle pats at each other.

Peter wondered what would become of them; most of the world, as usual between wars, had lost any real interest in war orphans.

The *tramontana* did not blow on Peter's last night at the villa. They sat, he and Uncle Egon, after dinner on the terrace, the sun dying in gory splendour among the west-banked clouds. Glowing charcoal baskets were at their feet.

In the back of the villa, by the kitchen, they were singing again as they did after the few after-dinner tasks. Below, in the valley, a group of boys were marching back and forth across a goat pasture, with wooden guns, and a top-heavy young man with the beginning of a paunch, in black shirt and polished riding boots, was putting them through a military drill. They were the local fascists of pre-military age. Fat Chin in Rome was impressing a great many American tourists, but Uncle Egon said, "I don't care if the trains run on time or not in Italy. It doesn't matter if you get any place on time in this country anyway. If you're in a hurry, stay out of Italy."

"I can understand that. No one hurries here."

"We hurry fast enough to our graves. Life is very short, Peter—almost not worth the effort."

The military drilling stopped. It grew dark. A sky coloured the inner skin of a blue plum took over. The wine glass at Uncle Egon's elbow rattled on the tray as he lifted it to his lips.

"It's been fine to have you here, Peter. Perhaps life is so short because it's so good, so wonderful."

"It's lucky Ginch got sick."

"Every bit of misery has its little point of good some place, eh? Well, I hope you've had a good time and haven't learned too many good or bad habits. Too much of anything is bad. I could give you a lot of advice, but I never took my father's, so why should you take mine? You will find out, however, that, unlike the Latins, you are cursed by birth and upbringing to continue a long struggle between pleasure and duty. Happiness lies in balancing them both. My friend Henry James put it very well. 'Live life to the full, do what you want in this life, because if you don't do what you want in life, when are you going to do it?' The time is always now, eh?"

"I suppose you're right, Uncle Egon, but I don't think Princeton is the place to start anything like that."

"No, college is merely a filler—a padding out of fresh minds—no dangerous mixtures allowed."

"Certainly not original thinking."

Egon nodded in the gathering dusk. He lit a long cigarette and offered one to Peter—one of the thousand that he had manufactured that day on his little cigarette machine. He sat well back, a huge bulk in the Italian twilight, dusted with the glowing fireflies. Bats were flying among the fruit trees in the terrace below. The olive trees were silver ghosts in the rising moonlight. The clop, clop, of a tired donkey's hooves sounded far below on the bone-white ribbon of the main road. The old Roman statues dug up in the local vineyards (and not, frankly, of the first order or the highest craftsmanship) looked now noble and eternal, their defects hidden by the growing darkness.

Peter heard Andrea singing as she went out to feed the goats with the remains from the dinner table. He sat well forward and wanted to rise, but changed his mind. It was quite dark now and the cigarettes made small arcs in space. Uncle Egon's voice sounded warm and normal, but perhaps with just a little, ironic edge.

"Better get your last-minute packing done."

"Oh," said Peter, and got up and went around to the back of the villa. Andrea was on the first rail of the goat-pen looking down at the goats. Peter came up behind her and put his arms around her, just below her hips, pressing her buttocks to his chest.

"Andrea," he said tenderly, hoping he could turn her toward him with grace.

She wriggled and gave a musical giggle and faced him, grinning down at him.

In English she said, " 'Ello, keed."

She held his head in her dark hands and she kissed his mouth again and again. Then she sank back and looked up at the moon-flecked sky and kept repeating. *"Bravo, si molto bravo, paverino mio . . ."*

They met him at the pier and were proud of him, so brown in his knickers and wool socks and his little English cap.

"What did my baby do in Italy?" asked Alice.

"I studied the classics."

"Did you see the churches?"

"I saw a great many of them."

"No fun at all?" asked Ralph.

"There is a great deal to see and do in Italy."

"You didn't bring back much baggage," said Nicole.

"I have gifts for all of you."

They gave him a little party at home and Alice, weeping cheerfully, said he had grown and was a stranger. Ralph and Charles Pentland, walking in the garden after dinner, were pleased. "Fine boy. A real man. I hope he didn't get clapped up."

Ralph blushed. "He says Michelangelo's ceiling is very impressive."

CHAPTER V

When Peter was a young man just entering Princeton, his grandfather, Joseph Pedlock, said, "You must be very tolerant of your parents, Peter. You see, it is a human trait to underestimate our fathers. I did not listen to my father and I doubt if your children will listen to you."

Peter saw that it was true. He had talked a long time with his father the day before he left for college. But it had been the conversation of two people who did not understand each other. Peter felt that. "In the Twenties"—a special time on the American earth, he once said—"we were all young and bitter and the pose pleased us; in the Thirties there was a depression and we were ardent and sad; in the forties the dream of the golden weather was lost and we fought wars. Somehow three decades went by too fast."

Princeton, in Peter's youth, had the tradition of F. Scott Fitzgerald fresh in its mind and the Poes (who played such great football) shining down from every wall. The village itself, with its one dusty movie, and the red-clay, Jersey side-roads and the lake for rowing and the Triangle Club for drama, were part of an earnest, happy pattern. Peter loved the ivied buildings and the long talks about dead Elizabethans and living scientists. There were men from Lawrenceville and Groton and Rutgers Prep and Beagle at college, and they all wore a wide trouser and oiled their hair, and some drove Stutz Bearcats as was the fashion of the period. One did not strain the mind or wear tight-pointed shoes.

Peter and the members of the literary paper (three of whom had been to Paris and once seen Joyce, plain as day) grew to love the needled beer of the New Jersey bootleggers. They often went in a roaring open car up to New Brunswick, where Zellet's, on French Street, was a popular hangout. Zellet, himself, was a blond Swiss with smooth larceny in his every pore. He served strong beer in his darkened booths, and cooked well. New Brunswick was a dirty town—where Washington had once slept—full of mills on an oil-scummed canal. Here rival Rutgers stood on the banks of some song-tormented river. Johnson and Johnson factories and Carpenter's paper mills and Mack trucks were here, and many Hungarian and Polish and Irish girls worked in the mills and scented themselves cheaply on the weekends after Mass. Peter and the literary group liked to spend an evening in

297

Zellet's with three or four of the mill girls. It was almost always innocent and happy, and Mondays their heads ached and their spending money was short. Later, of course, they invented legends and came to believe they were great drinkers, and marvellous lovers of great endurance, But very little of this was true. The pale, tired girl-flesh, the cheap scents, the evil beer made poets of them.

In the fall Peter, with an eye for beauty and art (caught from his Uncle Egon), enjoyed the curling feathers of black chimney smoke over the Indian colours of New Jersey's landscapes. The flaming sugar maples, the crisp, cold blues of football weather. He ran well on the track team and played an indifferent second base. But he did not go out for football. Princeton shook with the impact of visitors when the big games came, and Peter preferred his excitement in the stands.

The town blossomed out in gay scarfs and raccoon coats of fearful streaking and striping. The derby hat and the camel-pile coat were also present. The girls were all beautiful and animated, or rich and cheerful in their felt, helmet hats over waved head shingled in back, with box dresses showing no hips and ending just above the knees. Oh, the naked, wind-blown thighs of our youth, Peter used to think, and the smell of bathroom gin and Chanel Number Five and those long legs in sheer stockings rolled at the knees. And over it all, some verses by T. S. Eliot drumming in his head.

The games were huge drinking and shouting orgies. Many deaths piled up in expensive, painted auto-steel on the steep highway curves. Virginities were lost or retained in formal shrubbery, and the lovers' lanes echoed the crisp, dismal messages in the popular jargon of Mencken and Nathan. There was a young man called Hemingway who had a hero who lost something in an odd way and didn't want to think about it any more.

Peter kept on with his reading. His Lit. Prof. was a lean, ash-blond man with tweed suits and long pipes coloured the skin of native women in travel photographs. His name was Rigby John.

One evening he came to Peter's room when he was reading Chaucer and admired Peter's taste.

"Ah, Chaucer."

"Yes."

"Nothing like Middle English! 'Whan that Aprille with his shoures sote The droghte of Marche hath perced to the rote'—and all that."

"It doesn't make much sense."

"It will, Perry, it will."

"I doubt if I'll ever go nuts about it."

Rigby John set fire to his perfumed tobacco and leaned back in the chair with the broken spring. "Ah, to be young again."

"You're young, sir."

"Touching thirty. What do you do with your spare time, Perry?"

"Not much. A little beer."

"Ah, the nut-brown October ale."

"Just needle beer in the speaks."

"Girls, I suppose?"

"Sometimes."

"Tell me about them."

"Not much to tell."

The pipe bubbled. "I'll come up this weekend and we'll go through Chaucer together, if you care."

"Well, sir, I've been through it twice with my Uncle Egon. I know it's a classic, but I think I'd rather read the moderns. Dreiser."

"Nothing worth while being done by the Americans."

The visit ended shortly after that and Peter went back to Hemingway, who was always trying to get *it*—that dream lay—in the most exotic places, in a fine style as clean and direct as a railroad lavatory. And Mr. Cabell—now read by all the new rabble—was high art.

Peter was deep in modern poets one evening (who he felt *looked* better than they read) when he was called to the boarding-house phone. It was Ike Sontag down for the game with Harvard, with his sister Rose and her husband Harry Gelhorn. And two silver hip-flasks. "Beagle, Beagle, Class of '24," and the first of the Bronx cheers.

Peter had dinner with them at the Princeton House and Rose Gelhorn took his breath away. He lost his breath with ease in those days, but Rose Gelhorn was special, being first the sister of Ike Sontag, his best friend, and secondly, a dark and wonderful beauty with fine, green eyes and something daffy and marvellous he had read in Pater and couldn't remember too well. None of his ideas of women were real or true, but he loved his personal version.

Harry Gelhorn was a little hard to take. Had he been Irish or Californian Catholic, or new Orleans planter, no one would have been very much offended by him, but as he was short and wide and already growing fat and smoked huge cigars and gestured with his hands, he was usually the kind of person people called "a loud Jew".

That he was loud and that he was a Jew was true. He sat, well back in his broad chair, and pointed his cigar, held like a hammer, at anyone he spoke to. "Take it from little ole Harry, this college stuff is the bunk. My ole man had me on the construction jobs for our apartment houses when I was fifteen, an' I was bossin' a brick crew by the time most of you punks was histin' dough outa your ole man for college capers. Not that I'm against colleges."

He took Rose's hand in his and rolled it like some valued object he owned and displayed with pleasure. "When we spawn the kid is goin' to get the best. . . . Yes sir, the best. Harvard or Yale, now, what do you think of that?"

Ike said, "I hear them well spoken of." Ike himself was at M.I.T.

"Will Princeton win?" Rose asked Peter, leaning away from her captive hand.

"Against Harvard, I would say yes."

She smiled at him, and he asked her if she wanted whisky. She said a highball of Bourbon before the game would be fine, just fine (Hemingway training . . . things were "just fine", not "really nice" any more). Harry had a flask of Scotch, of course, "just off the boat, scraped right off the bottom, ha, ha!" he said, quoting his favourite vaudeville act. "But the dame wouldn't drink it. Was the stuff any good at Princeton? was it prime? Are the beds in the bridal suite soft— did they bounce? Ha ha!"

They drove to the game the next day through traffic tight and happy, and lost only part of Harry's right front yellow fender. The Saturday air was chilly, yet sunny. State troopers on horseback cut a way with whips through the native rabble that had come to stare and shove at the quality. Peter did not remember the whips and mounted troopers in Fitzgerald's prose.

The game was good. It was "fine". Princeton won by three clean touchdowns. Between halves Harry saw some people he knew and Rose grew cold, so Ike and Peter shared a big red blanket with a huge P on it, and she held their hands under the blanket and her fingers were warm and small, but very strong, and the heart of Peter was torn to bits. When Harry came back shouting. "Boy oh boyohboyoh! What a shellacking them Harvards is gettin'!" Peter wondered why murder of certain kinds was not perfectly legal.

Later, years later, Peter wondered if he had been fair to Harry Gelhorn. Most likely Harry was not at all a bad sort, merely a product of the Twenties and a boom time. Part of a family of eager, earnest yearners for the fat, soft, material things. Harry most likely had been better educated than he claimed; he cried over the right kind of heavy German music; he liked an arty cinema; and he bowled twice a week. Ike called him "a typical mockie—a Jewish sport". Harry had married Rose in one of those sudden, furious attacks of passion, pity, and drive that often sweep a young girl off her feet. Ugly, fat, impossible men have these moments when they prey, skilfully, on young, untried emotions. They cheerfully creep into the circle of some beautiful girl, become accepted as a clown, a kindly monster, and then, once accepted, present a humble and tender side of their nature that grows stronger and more insistent until, if the object of their affection is young and kind enough, they carry off their prize, gloating and worshipping like some ogre in a fairy tale. Peter could never decide if nature was improving or degrading itself.

The second year at Princeton passed quickly, and after a summer month with the Kozloffs at their farm, Peter moved on. He left because he could not understand Jacob Kozloff. The man had become what the middle-class intellectual with his button-down, soft, shirt collar from Brooks Brothers called "a Babbitt. From that book by that fellow from someplace in the Western Swede belt." Jacob did not mind being called a Babbitt. He had his health and his family, and his business was booming. The sound of the bull market was beginning to bellow in the land.

But this was not the Uncle Jacob Peter had known as a small boy. A certain hardness (never cynical), a little too earnest, was appearing in Jacob Kozloff. Aunt Selma would laugh a little too loud when Jacob cursed the Democrats, or the Reds, the labour unions or income taxes. Jacob began to take pride in his lack of a sense of humour.

Peter went and spent two weeks with old Joseph in Pittsfield, sitting on the half-sunken barge on a weedy lake, holding fishing poles. Drinking bad beer with the old man on the leaking porch when it rained. They grew to know each other very well, and the old man told marvellous stories about the Civil War, stories not at all like the popular fiction of the moment,

Then there was a week with the Sontags in their fancy knotty-pine camp in a fashionable section (unrestricted) on the edges of Connecticut. Doctor Sontag put on a disreputable pair of faded blue shorts and sat in the sun groaning and rubbing himself with suntan oil. And reading something called *Psychoanalytische Bemerkungen über einem autobiographisch beschriebenen Fall von Paranoia*. It was a heavy book, too.

Doctor Sontag poured suntan oil into the palm of his hand and rubbed it on his thin breastbone with a studied gesture, his eyes like goldfish goggling behind his bifocals.

"Etta thinks I ought to become a psychoanalyst. I suppose she's right."

"Why, Papa?" Ike winked at Peter.

"Because Etta is always right; but the real reason is that it's a subject that attracts fools and frauds and rogues. I am a little less of a fool and fraud than most people working in psychoanalysis and I might help people. Few people ever use it properly. And damn it—it's become fashionable with the wrong people."

"Do a lot of them need help?"

"Perhaps it only seems to. I have a recurring dream. I have been living, it seems in my dream, for twenty years in the jungle, someplace, doing medical research. And one day I come home and, to my horror, I find everyone in the world has gone mad and no one has noticed it!"

"Papa, you know what Freud would say about you and your dream?"

"Respect, please," said Doctor Sontag picking up *Die Abwehr Neuropsychosen*, "respect for your old man. Seriously, I think Dostoevsky—a very pious Christian, by the way—summed up our dilemma very well when he said, 'The problem of nineteenth-century man is the problem of how to live without God.' On that profound note, I close this session. Boys, go help Etta pick blueberries."

They found Etta in slacks—broad of beam and hatted in straw against the sun—in the berry patch that ran behind their stylish acre and a half. They helped her pick a pint of wormy berries.

"Peter, you're getting real handsome. Just don't get as fat as your uncle Egon."

"I'll try."

"Isn't it wonderful up here?"

Ike ate a sour berry, and spit. "Wonderful. And only the lake is restricted."

"Now, Ike, we didn't come up here to criticize these people. They don't really dislike Jews. They just don't know any."

"They don't want to see them around either."

Peter dropped two berries in the bucket. "Where do you swim?"

"The river," said Ike, "with the rest of the sewage. The lake belongs to Cabots and the untrimmed cod-pieces."

"Ike, don't be so Elizabethan," said Etta. "I'm sure we'll be invited to the lake when they find out we're not Bronx picnickers with paper bags and loud, gaudy talk and clothes."

Ike said softly, "I think I prefer their anti-Semitism, Mama, to yours. Theirs is more honest. It means real-estate money in their pockets and no embryos with long noses in their daughters' bellies."

"*Go* to the house, Ike!" said Etta rising in wrath from the berry patch. "Papa will talk to you *later*."

302

Ike shrugged his shoulder and went slowly into the house. Etta looked at Peter and smiled. "Ike's right, you know. We grow bigoted as we grow older. But of course I can't admit it to him. How are your folks?"

"Fine. Nicole and Mother are at Lake George. Father is hunting deer in Texas with Grandfather. How is Rose?"

"Oh, just blooming. I hope to hear any day I'm a grandmother. Oh, no, she isn't pregnant yet, but it's about time. She's out on Long Island, near you. Harry is building a hundred cottages, English Tudor, out there someplace this summer. Come, let's have lunch."

"I'm hungry."

Peter decided he liked the Sontags. They were human and heirs to all the bigotry and troubles and joys and pleasures of the world. There was also a solid core of courage in them.

(The Sontags were not invited to swim at the lake that summer.)

Ralph came back from Texas with two deer heads and a sunburned nose. He sat in the garden and looked at Peter and frowned.

"I don't understand it, Peter."

"I told you, I'm in love with a married woman."

"I don't understand how you can even think of it."

"It isn't hard, I'm madly in love."

"A friend of ours, I suppose?"

"Yes, in a way."

"Don't tell me the name. I think we'd better forget the whole thing."

"It isn't that easy. Didn't you ever feel that way about someone, not give a good goddamn what anyone said or felt?"

"Your mother was not married to someone else."

"Would it have mattered?"

"Besides, this woman must be older than you are."

"Who cares?"

"It's indecent."

"Why?"

Ralph knocked out his pipe on the garden wall. "I'm not sure I know how to go on with this. Promise me nothing rash."

"I'm not going to promise anything."

Ralph put his arm around his son. "Remember who you are. Think of the family."

CHAPTER VI

The year Peter acted in one of Shaw's plays at the Triangle Club, Rose came down with her mother to see the show. He took them to dinner, and after the play Etta went to the home of a professor who was proving that the good old days were sharper, nobler, more colourful, and much more virile than the present. Peter took Rose for a ride to the lake and they parked under the willow trees.

Peter took her in his arms and he kissed her very tenderly but ardently. She lay very still in his arms; then she turned away from him and said, "Don't be a damn fool, Peter."

"You can't love anybody like Harry Gelhorn."

She looked at him, her face expressionless. "His over-Jewish look is rather distasteful to you? He's loud and vulgar in a Jewish way?"

"No, Rose. I don't put things on that basis."

"What do you base things on?"

"Let me kiss you again."

"Why?" She looked at him and leaned back and pulled him to her and he kissed her a long, hard time. He had learned kissing well.

"Peter, you're a fool. I'm a married woman."

"You love me a little?"

"A little, a lot. I'm never going to see you again."

"Oh, darling," said Peter and held her a tight time in his arms. Later they smoked four rather bent cigarettes, sitting close together, very cosy and warm. Rose wept and Peter lent her a handkerchief to wipe her big, dark eyes. They drove slowly back to town and Peter said he would write to her, even if only lists of books she could read. She said he was charming and a damn fool. Etta said it had been a wonderful night. They left the next morning and Peter sent Rose a leather-bound copy of "The Waste Land" and a long letter that made very little sense.

They saw each other twice more that year, but Peter found no chance to kiss her again. He rather enjoyed the ache of it all. The young suffer better than older people.

Like most young men, Peter, of course, did not fall in love with a real living woman but with his own personal projection of her. He fell in love with an inner vision, a woman unreal and romantically processed by his mental needs and his passionate private longings. He saw Rose Gelhorn as a beautiful thing, an object of his own imaginings. A habit of the very young in love. He gave her the unearthly grace, beauty, and allure of his dream creation. In this state she had neither natural functions, rages, fears, nor any of the normal motivations of a real person living in a real world full of shabby problems and rather small, day-to-day events. She existed only as a thing of beauty (which she was) but she ate neither coarsely nor enough, nor performed the daily functions of the human race. At least Peter never wanted to think of her as doing such things. She never, to him, had any of the blemishes of real people. Those off-moments when grace is not possible, when anger tears the throat, when the hidden weeping of feeble frustration holds one in its mean and nasty grip.

He wanted to see her always as the reflected thing of his own inventing—neither too alert nor too alive, not touched by the pleasures or vulgar ideas of the passing mob. Not, beaten back and hurt by the dreary things that spoiled so much of living. And Peter, being very young and very much in love, managed pretty successfully in keeping Rose, or his creation of her (at least at first), as he wanted to see her.

What was she really like? It was years before Peter found out. She was always really beautiful even with an attack of rash or with her dark, blue-black hair dried by sun and full of sand. She had large feet and wore good, solid shoes for them. Yet her legs were long and shaped with subtle curves. Her whole body was a wonderful thing, yet a little too full in the hips and with just the suggestion of a soft stomach, kept down by diet. When alone, she walked a little round-shouldered and her hands were long and a little too strong, almost a man's hands. She laughed a great deal and was bitter and sad when alone. She was proud of herself at times—yet ashamed of what she had done with her life. Harry was good to her and after those days of the honeymoon, she never, after a first shock, regretted giving herself to the gross hairy body—the hot aching moments, the full contact of things that are after all to a woman an illusion broken no matter how "modern" and up-to-date she may feel. Then slowly the mistake, the horror of her life crept in on her. She had been a great reader of long, classical novels. She threw them aside as false in the very important facts of life. She had loved music (not so much as Harry), but now the flow of the tone poems, the clash of brass, the deep inner thunder of the composers left her only angry, taut, and ready to rush into Harry's arms and bite his lips and hate herself.

*　　　*　　　*

305

Harry sat on the bed, naked, and rubbed his hair belly with satisfaction. Rose came out of the bathroom and went to the chair and covered her nakedness with a robe. She turned and faced her husband.

"Harry."

"Ah, honey, what is it?"

"I think we should talk."

"Who can talk at this hour?"

"Harry, how is it between us?"

"I gotta draw you diagrams?"

"Suppose I didn't love you, Harry?"

"Banana erl, baby."

"You're satisfied with our relations?"

"Ha ha! I don't even hate mother-in-laws. Look, baby doll, don't knock yourself out. You know how I feel about you. Maybe I don't always understand moods and fancy romantic things like a woman, but you're all I got or ever want. Don't worry about me, you just be you and let me look at you and hold you and there isn't anything can ever change it . . . see?"

"Harry, suppose I fell in love with someone else."

"Suppose, suppose. Stop talkin' like a lousy movie. Nize baby come and eat up all the kisses offa Harry's face."

Harry was a great admirer of the prose satire of Milt Gross.

"I'm serious, Harry."

Harry yawned and crept slowly into his night clothes. "What were we talkin' about, baby doll?"

"You weren't listening. Some day you'll come home and I'll be gone, with someone else."

"Yeah, with John Gilbert."

Rose was still too young to understand fully what had happened to her. But she knew enough to see that the basic mistake of her life had been pity. She had admired the humble, smiling Harry. She had pitied him his grossness and his ugliness. Had felt that, in this dragon, there somewhere lived beauty. She knew now that Harry, inside as well as out, was of the same arid pattern.

What another woman would have done she did not know, but being Rose Sontag there was very little she could do. There was nothing Harry did that she could find as an excuse for a separation. He was loyal, true, and madly in love with her. He had furnished for her a white Colonial house on Long Island and an apartment in the East Fifties. They had two cars, and money in the bank, and Harry had insured his life for a vast sum (after giving up cigars for two weeks to still a heart murmur), "and all in your name". They ate out in good places twice a week. They followed the football teams and saw all the Broadway "hits", which neither one of them cared for but they never admitted this to each other. They went to cheap and romantic movies and sat through two or three features a week. Glossy, simple products of the flesh that glorified the decency of mother love, the shape of women's breasts. And the nobler love of an outdoor, male type for his horse, with just a touch of homosexuality.

They slept in the middle-class morality of a single bed, a little too softly. Harry snored and his digestive processes went on all night and he exhaled a hint of rich food in gastric juices. Rose would awake often with a startling shudder and listen to him snore and sputter. She would get up and go into the living room and turn on a lamp and stare at the book-club selections they were filling their shelves with. She would weep softly till near dawn and then creep back into bed and fall into a drugged state from which she had to struggle back into life at eleven. By that time Harry was only a dent in the bed, his body having left hours ago to harass building contractors.

Life dragged till lunch. Then she went shopping with her mother or their upper-middle-class, Jewish friends. An endless walking through smart shops, of fingering luxuries, of packing into the mammoth department stores after bargains that cost too much. Sterile fumbling of expensive trash they did not really want. Then over-rich food in some over-bright tearoom run by decaying gentlewomen or smart young Lesbians out to get rich while they sneered at the customers. The upper middle class suffers stylishly to keep from being bored.

At five Rose had a second bath, viewing the long beautiful body and its crisp, secret corners and damning herself as a slut. Dinner with Harry, or the family, among able, cheerful, loud people, who knew all the scandals of the town or what had happened to the cotton market, or who were sleeping with a Hollywood star. A play, or bridge ... that dreadful game, the modern time-killing of middle-aged people waiting to die in rich surroundings ("genuine onyx base, my dear") while they held a fistful of coloured cardboard and solved simple problems in spades, cold cuts, and rather feeble cocktails.

Warm nights in the apartment, cool nights in the cottage. Harry shaving with an imported Rolls razor, his stomach pouring over his underwear shorts. Whistling a tune from the *Scandals*.

It was a cheap movie palace in the upper Fifties. The second balcony smelled of peanuts, armpits, and sweeping compound. The screen was far away, and it was a throbbing darkness close and warm.

Rose came past the legs of the old man asleep with his mouth open and Peter pulled her down in the seat next to his.

"You're late," he whispered.

"I wasn't coming."

"Don't ever say that, Rose."

"It's nasty, groping here, mashing noses in the dark."

"It's your idea."

"I don't like it any more. It's bad for us. Two hours of this and going home with a stomach full of cut glass."

"This is the last, Peter."

"Don't say that . . . listen to me . . . Oh, Rose."

"The usher is watching us."

"Rose . . ."

"Don't cry, I don't like to see men cry. Harry cries sometimes."

"It's not very satisfying, but . . ."

"I'm not crying. Rose, let's go off. I have some money. I sold some stock my grandfather gave me."

"Selling America short in a bull market?"

"Don't joke. Come to Philadelphia, I have it all planned."

She kissed him quickly and ran. He tried to follow her but he saw badly in the dark. He stumbled and the usher looked at him side-mouthed and went on humming "Life is just a bowl of cherries".

Peter felt very warm and went into the john and vomited. He had two hours till train time so he went to Jack and Eddie's and tried to get drunk very quickly, but they turned him out. . . .

Harry, Harry, Harry. Rose grew to fear him. Harry in his rumpled pyjamas that gapped at the buttons and fitted badly over his blubber. Harry stoking a cigar, listening to Wagner, his short, hard arms around her. Harry frisky as a colt yet guarding his gestures in fear of a slight hernia. Harry, Harry, Harry. Just too much of Harry, a loud Jew.

One day Rose tried a new, bloodlust-coloured lipstick that didn't fit her face and went down to Grand Central station. A man in a shabby tweed suit picked her up and they went to a grimy hotel in the West Forties. He pinched her and showed his long yellow teeth in an odd, frightened way. Nothing else happened and he collapsed sadly on the bed. She dressed and went home to bathe in very hot water. She took two sleeping pills and left a note for Harry that she was very tired and would Harry have dinner alone from the icebox.

She couldn't get drunk because whisky, after two drinks, did nothing much to her except make her sick. She began to read detective stories. Two or three a day, but they began to bore her. Murder, rape, death, degeneracy, incest, homicide, sadism, torture. It meant nothing to her. The values that she had been taught in college in a course in Greek drama on the dreadfulness of murder, of its being the great crime, meant nothing in the detective stories she was reading. They were all as damning and dull as the crossword puzzles Harry did at the breakfast table while he sucked his teeth loudly free of toast crumbs.

She did think, once or twice, of murdering Harry, of going to her death in the electric chair. But there was the family and the disgrace and the long trial and the tabloid headlines. She didn't think she had the brains for a perfect crime. Besides, she couldn't kill anything. Not Harry. Harry had a certain earnestness and charm. And it was driving her mad.

Her tragedy, Peter said, was "being trapped in Jewish, middle-class morality". And she knew it was that, and that she was wasting what could have been a very fine and interesting life. She was a woman not only beautiful, but bright, alert, and deeply honest, as her suffering showed. She had a great love of life, an interest in many things that she could not live up to in her marriage. She had a natural sexual instinct that she now found repugnant. She felt that she could make love, live marvellously, enjoy many things, live a full life someplace else, if, if, if . . .

There was a soggy track meet at Franklin Field in Philadelphia. One of those drizzly days of mist; a steady drip, drip, of rain that makes Philadelphia more dreary than ever. The rain fell, the college teams ran and jumped and swung weights. A handful of track fiends sat in the stands, newspapers, raincapes, and heavy wet felt hats over them, while the sports went on, the snap of a feeble pistol shot sending another set of legs off down the damp cinder paths. The breath of the runners was like ghosts, leaving their bodies in torn streams of white vapour.

Peter was second in the hundred-yard dash and did well in the 220, well enough to get a needed point that put Princeton up in third place. Rose was in the stands in green felt hat with a wide man's snap brim over her dark hair, a blue-green silk slicker over her rough tweed suit. She sat bent way over, feet tucked under her, smoking a chain of cigarettes and accepting a little, warming whisky from a stranger's flask. Peter had written her about the meet and hoped that she "would be visiting relatives at the time".

There was, of course, no plan to visit relatives at all, but Peter felt it would be better to word it so in case Harry should stumble across the letter. He had met Rose at the station and they had taken a taxi to the second-best hotel and registered as Mr. and Mrs. Manderson, Oyster Bay, Long Island. Rose had not eaten much breakfast and after a quick kiss he had left her for the field.

After the track meet she met him at the woven wire fence outside the dressing rooms and they went to a downtown chophouse where Rose toyed with her steak and had two Bourbons. Peter was happy, flushed with joy. He felt like the hero of a Balzac novel about to take Paris, its beauty and its wealth. He had not expected Rose to come —and she had!

It was still raining when they got back to the hotel room. There was a dismal tinkle of dripping water on the soiled window-panes. The city was half dissolved in mist below them and the bed sagged obscenely in the middle, as if too much of sleeping and loving and the passing of hundreds of bodies in transit had left it not only tired, but rather indifferent. It was a room, Rose felt, out of a sordid Russian short story—*any* Russian short story.

She took off her cape and her jacket and sat down on the bed and smiled at Peter.

"Well, darling," she said, "this is your dream."

Peter pulled up a chair and faced her and took her cold hands in his. "Darling, you understand what I feel."

"Yes, dear. I do."

"I love you, Rose. There are so many wonderful ways to say it. And I can only seem to just say it like that."

"It's enough, Peter."

It was chilly in the room. The bathroom smelled of lysol, the rug was worn in the wrong places. Rose thought of all the frightened girls who had lost their virginity in rooms like this, and she was happy that *that* could no longer happen to her. She took Peter's arm, tightly, earnestly, as if holding an oar in a shipwreck.

"Peter, I'm not like this. This room, this way. I was an honest little girl, I wanted life big and true. Let's go away, you and me. It doesn't matter how. But let's do it right." She bent over and had some inner agony, then straightened up and smiled at Peter. He saw that her face was wet with sweat. Tenderly he wiped it.

"Of course, Rose. We'll go to Mexico, or Paris. Or to Italy. I like Italy."

"Yes, yes, Peter. Any place but this grimy room."

"I'm sorry. But only about the room." He got down on his knees and buried his head in her soft belly. He let himself sink into her, his arms around her hips. He felt the beauty, the greatness of their love.

310

Now, here, this woman was his destiny. He could not make it all spiritual. He was a sensual man, he was young and ardent, and this nuzzling body was his for the taking, was to be . . . She had moaned softly.

He looked up at her. How well she foreshortened, he thought, even this close. "What is it, Rose?"

"Nothing, Peter. We'll get married some day and I'll make you a fine wife. And if we can't get married, it doesn't matter. Oh, Peter, do love me and be kind to me."

He smiled at her and stood up and leaned over her and kissed her on the brow—the wet brow—and he frowned. She was shaking so. Did all respectable married women act this way?

"You're frightened, Rose."

She bit her lower lip. "Damn, damn," she said suddenly, biting on her fists. She looked up at him, a desperate courage in her face. "Peter, can't you see I'm pregnant and pretty far gone?"

Eden was no longer Paradise. Peter expelled a lungful of air and sat back in his chair as if hurled there. College taught so little of the vital facts of life or how to face them.

"Rose!"

"It's true! Trapped, married, pregnant. Oh, yes, dear, the full works. I've wanted to tell you a long time. That's why I came to Philadelphia to see you once more. To give you what you wanted, and now I've spoiled it."

"No, dear," said Peter, wondering why women always *gave*— never *received*—"you're wonderful. You mustn't cry." He slipped off her shoes, and rubbed her feet and pushed her back on the bed. He covered her with a blanket and patted her face. His heart was tender enough to burst in his chest.

"Sleep, dear, sleep. You're tired."

"Don't go away, Peter."

"No, I'm here." He turned out the lights. From the street below came a glow of warm yellows and pale greens. Desire had drained away from him; he could only sit and pity them both.

"Come into bed, Peter. Come and take your love."

How sparse, he thought, is the language of real lovers.

"No, Rose, you rest. Just rest."

Chemistry, art, literature had a mighty language—lovers little.

She closed her eyes and her strong fingers gripped his. "Oh, Peter, what a fool you are. Don't wait, don't dream. Take life . . . hold it" (she yawned) "and don't make rules, or be polite or proper. It's a mean, crazy life and we try so hard to be strong, try to be honest. I love you, dear" (her fingers relaxed). "But in the end we do fumbling shameful things—evading truths and issues. We make a truce with existence, Peter. We get the best terms we can, like loan sharks. We keep hidden inside us the signs of honesty, the love for beauty, the . . . Peter . . ." (she tried to lift her head), "Peter, you there? I am tired. I am going to sleep. It's so peaceful with the lights out. The sordidness is blotted away. Peter, when you were a little boy, was the world a wonderful place? Nothing was dirty or smelled . . . all was castles and . . . they lived happily ever after. . . ."

So Peter came for the first time to the blind wall behind passion. He put an extra blanket over her and stood back. She looked so beautiful there on the bed. There was just the smallest bulge of the stomach, under the two, thin hotel blankets. A gilled fish, a globe of living matter. Harry's genes and generations struggling through the dark to life.

Peter spent the night on two chairs and in the morning Rose was sick in the bathroom. He put her on the New York train and they said a splendid good-bye. The last thing she said was, "You'll get over it, Peter."

"Not the first one. The first real one, old Joseph always told me, stays a long time."

"Try, try. I'm trapped, Peter. Trapped by the family, the tribe, replenishing the earth. You're not Jew enough to know what it means to bring a child into the tribe. A sacred, wonderful thing, and they'll never let me go now. Don't make this the first real one, Peter. Please. . . ."

"It happens every day—I hear, Rose."

He stood a long time in the station and looked at the still-falling rain. He should walk out and get very wet and catch some fearful death of damp and cold and die romantically. His wide reading expected it. He went, instead, to the seafood bar and had two huge oyster stews. But inside he knew he would painfully always think of her as the first big one. . . .

The dull, lead-coloured spoon beat slowly again and again on the warm china bowl of oyster stew. The waters fell across the windows of the station. It was still the rain. It ran in wet hurry across the glass, falling silver, and spread like veins in great green leaves in the mazda glow of the seafood counter. And now he could go on to something else. This weather was the ordained dress for his time and mood. It was the rain falling over the oyster beds of the Eastern Shore, the rain on the right-of-way of the train rushing through the Jersey murk, the rain on the cinders of the hundred-yard dash and the rain far off in the corners of the continent where his grandfather had dug in Butte's hills and the smelters' smog still soiled the Western skies. It was the rain coming down to meet the earth everywhere and it tasted in the stew bowl and he breathed it in the air of the fetid station, warm as the home of any fœtus in the tribal womb. The patter of its fall drummed in his ears and his blood and was a brake to some of the hopes and illusions of a very young man in a very old world. All eternity was in one drop of rain, and the shiny bottom of the bowl, under his fixed stare, was all the universe in miniature.

BOOK SIX

As Peter came to maturity another member of the family was slipping away. It was apparent now that the old man was going, this year, next year—soon. Old Joseph, who had seemed eternal, was slowly drifting away from life's stage. There was no sudden sign, no giving up quickly the functions of living. But there was a lazy indifference to the things of everyday living, a gradual breaking down of old habit, a sloughing off of the elaborate symbols and details of existing.

He was an old man, not so old as his sister, but his sister was "one of those old women"—Egon said—"who, once they reach a certain age, can only be killed by an axe". Tante Strasser went on, as usual, behind her drawn, blood-red drapes, dusting her old pictures, feeding her dreadful birds, and trying to encourage her brother to drink the fearful broths she concocted for him.

It was ironic, Sam used to think, of his father, old Joseph, so much of once splendid forces lost, reclining under a thin blanket in the great sunroom overlooking the Hudson, the bird cages glittering in the sunlight. When he no longer cared or could remember the many details of business, the Pedlock companies for the first time were solid and rich and making money, as what company was not in those days of the great bull market. Yes, ironic in many ways. Stocks and bonds were advancing in a mad flurry of speculation, holding companies grew, and even the man in the street held his few shares on margin. Hoover, with a head like a jelly apple, was in the White House, and the nation in its respect for an engineer was going insane with joy on Wall Street. Hoover didn't seem to understand his late success.

Old Joseph let Sam light a long cigar for him, and he held it in his wrinkled hand and looked down across the river.

"Papa, about the coal companies. I'll explain again. We're splitting the stock six for one. It's being gobbled up on the market. Your Civil War holdings have come into their own."

The old man said, "A land of fever and pine trees. The Tennessee lands. We recruited there in '63. When could you get planters who lived off rice and indigo to support coal and iron mining? There were wonderful horses and I owned a bay with white feet. Charleston was a fine, white town and everybody—almost everyone—kept a yellow

315

girl with pointed breasts." The old man looked up, took a puff of his cigar and grinned. "Been wandering, Sam, been wandering. What did you say?"

"We're putting new issues of the companies on the market."

"The market? I can't believe it. Is it really such a bull market? Or was I dreaming I read it someplace?"

"It's true."

"Can't they stop the upward trend? It isn't healthy. The stocks aren't worth what they're getting in a run-away market."

Sam grinned. "Can't sell America short."

"Morgan, it's some scheme of his. No, he's dead. Everybody seems to be dead. Well, don't let it bother you, Sam. Try and protect yourself. Don't go too far on margin. Keep a good cash balance. Hold on to true things. Coal, iron, mills. Not paper."

"We're part of a stream, Papa. It's hard to pull back."

"It's solid, this country, way down. Under it all is the earth. What does a man need? The Russian Tolstoy has the right answer. Just six feet of it. Sam, I want to see Louis. And Peter is in trouble, some scandal. What?"

"Wild oats—nothing to worry over."

"Good. Don't draw the shade. When you're as old as I am the sun is a life force. It bites into you and feels fine, fine."

Sam took the drooping cigar from his father's mouth, put it in an ashtray, and went out. The old man was not asleep. He lay with his eyes closed. Relaxed. It was odd to be suddenly so old, be so ancient and tired and yet somehow feel that life has slipped by before one could grab it by the tail and swing it over one's shoulder like a victory. He had always been so ready to leap onto everything and mould it to his own desires. To make something, to hew out something enduring— well, not a dynasty, but at least something of value as a way of life. Now he was very old and the sun felt good on his eyelids. And Peter was in trouble. Wild oats. In woman we meet the mystery, the in-going and out-going of our agony and joy on earth. Through her we plunge into the dark, the mystery, touch the hem of the eternal, wallow in a desperate quest.

And all the rest—the hard work and effort had been in vain. For all that was happening was one of those boom times and it was coming too easy. The old man let the sun beat direct on his face. Boom times. Boom times in the South with the tobacco markets, and the rice fields green. Boom times on the frontier with the lawyers and the land-grabbers stealing it all back as usual from the pioneers. Boom times and the panic of 1907 with the Robber Barons turning the nation on its

316

head so its pockets could be emptied quicker. He yawned and he half slipped off into a state of fantasy.

He was young again and had an arch to his back and his chin was firm and arms hard and manhood was in his loins. He was riding a wild horse and his sword rattled and he was in a bitter war. It was always the same dream now. The same moment of youth, strength and fire in the vigour of his youth. Odd how for one old Jew, the rest of his life did not seem to matter or have any moments worth recalling. Even Rebecca was drifting away. He would forget her face for days at a time.

The market went on rising. Great times, said the people, and the streets were full of dreamers. Egon could not understand such a time or a place. He no longer had trouble selling his collections of paintings. The modern school of Paris was fashionable. Solid as T & T or Goldman Sachs. Its frauds and witch doctors were crowding out the firmer members of the group. Picasso still managed to keep his true place. Art had become an object of value like a stock issue. Etta Sontag was bullish on Bonnard, and dabbling in Van Gogh.

Egon would have given up the art business but he needed money for his projects, his children's camps, his refugee settlements, his ideas of starting new communities in Palestine, in Australia, in the Argentine, for displaced people. No one thought much, any more, of the forgotten wanderers in the cracks and corners of the cage of Europe. Egon had become a fanatic on the subject. Vast numbers of people travelling on the Nansen passports of the League of Nations were in misery, even as the stock market went up, as tourists and artists and writers poured into Europe to make American colonies of sections of Paris, of Nice, of Vienna and Budapest and Mayfair.

Egon was the only member of the family who agreed with his father that conditions were unhealthy. The Kozloffs—that is, Jacob—felt it was rather un-American to doubt that Radio Common and U.S. Steel were not a bargain at their new listings.

Egon went down for a weekend to the Kozloff farm. He rose late and washed his great body carefully and came down to breakfast with a small Guys drawing, a gift for Mike Kozloff, who was secretly painting at college while studying business law, a subject that was as sacred to Harvard now as Greek and the more recondite aspects of physics.

Jacob was reading the stock-market reports in the *Times*. Mike, in shorts and a yellow sweatshirt, was spreading wine-coloured jam on a roll. Selma was stirring her coffee and complaining about the servant problem, a popular upper-middle-class subject. In the barn-yard the sounds of the other children taking a riding lesson were heard.

Egon sighed. "I couldn't sleep much. Too silent. I agree with a character of Chekhov's who said, 'The country is only a collection of trees.'"

Selma grinned. "You don't fool me, Egon. I've seen your villa. It's full of beautiful trees."

"Yes, I suppose it is. The American trees are too tall and proud. They need to be bent to the landscape, be humbled a little. Tormented by a few centuries."

Jacob rattled his paper. He had grown bald and round and seemed shorter, harder and just a little remote from anything but business and a rather bad game of golf.

"American Tobacco . . . I don't see the value for those prices."

"I don't own much any more," said Egon. "And that little, on margin."

Mike said, "Thank you for the drawing, Uncle Egon, it's wonderful. Just a few lines and some wash tones. It's like magic."

"Guys could do more with a pen scratch than Jacob's entire stable of outhouse Americana and talented sign painters."

Jacob frowned and looked up at his Grant Wood and his Benton. He had bought them as investments. The dealer, a sharp Fifty-Seventh Street con man, had explained that art was real and of value. "Unlike stocks and bonds, it always has some value". Jacob buttered a roll.

"I smell a dealer talking," Egon said to his coffee cup.

"Mike, don't be foolish enough to get involved in art". Jacob rattled his copy of the *Times*. "It's a heart-breaking business. The good ones struggle all their life; and when you're dead, a lot of good it does you that they hang you in a museum. Live on solid earth—not in the clouds."

"Art is as solid as house-dresses, Jacob," Egon said.

Egon sipped his coffee, and Jacob didn't look up. It was hard to believe that this was the Jacob who had suffered for his youthful hopes, been beaten and tormented by honest doubts and joys. Felt the great-ness of a godhead and the glory of a vision on tattered rolls of old Talmudic texts. That dreamer was gone now. Here was the hard, little ritual-following Jew and businessman, the good family man, the Re-publican committee man, the chairman of prosperous chilly charities, the solid citizen talking, like any fool, of artists starving in attics—and "solid" values.

But Mike was used to his father's ideas. Youth learns easily to ignore its past. "I'm not good enough a painter, Father." (Was the word *Papa*, Egon wondered, a little too much of the ghetto to be fashionable?) "Not good enough to suffer for my art. I only paint because I enjoy it. I don't think I have the great touch, yet."

Egon rolled his head. "Who knows, Mike? Goya was a pretty bad painter till he was forty. Cézanne, between you and me, found himself pretty late. I don't trust too much the bright young men, who had a style of their own at birth. Skyrockets burned out by thirty."

Jacob made a throat noise.

"How's Father?" asked Selma, looking at Egon with a frown.

"Papa"—Egon poured honey on the word—"Papa is the same. Nothing wrong with him. Just tired and very old."

"We'll lose him soon," said Jacob, snapping the newspaper shut. "So goes the world. A little time to struggle, a long time to rest."

"I hope not," said Egon. "I'm old-fashioned enough to depend on my parents. The truth is, we all know how to die well these days. That's easy . . . but we don't know how to live. There was a time when we really were shocked by death, and carved skulls on our tombstones, put black plumes on our graveyard horses and saw death as it is— all bones and decay. Today it's been made a pleasure to die, an expensive pleasure. It's all silver coffin handles and real-silk linings and chapels full of sweet, sad artwork on the beauty of going off to feed the worms, or the furnace. But we don't live to make a good death any more, we exist at the end of long tubes that feed us pleasure and thrills and insurance money and Early American cottages. We can't any longer face life as it exists."

Jacob laughed. "It's not such a bad world. Our factories in Europe are giving people real values at prices they never heard of. Our Hamburg plant alone is the finest machine plant on the Continent. The fancy stuff you call life, Egon, is translated by us old bores into a better, easier life."

Egon nodded. "You have a fancy board of directors. Prussian Junkers, anti-Semites, and the blackguards of the clerical-fascist groups."

"Oh, go read the *Daily Worker*," Jacob said, smiling at the ceiling. "Everybody who isn't out in Union Square on May Day is killing Jews, according to you intellectuals."

"Now, Jacob——"

"How is Peter?" Egon asked, knowing that Jacob had reached his favourite subject, the execution or deporting or exiling of every intellectual, Marxist, socialist, reformer, civil-liberties believer or defender of minorities who had not been able to become as American as Jacob, or able to merge a little with the old Yankee stock.

"Peter?" asked Selma. "Well. Oh, Mike, go hang your picture in your room."

Mike shrugged and got up and left the table.

"Peter," said Selma, "is having an affair with a married woman."

Jacob frowned. "A Jewish woman. It's hard to believe it. A *shiksa* or those fancy, Westchester debutantes you expect these things from. But Rose Sontag. She just has no shame."

"Rose Gelhorn," Selma corrected him. "Etta's girl who married Harry Gelhorn, the builder's son."

"I hadn't heard about it". Egon said.

"It's a real scandal in Rabbi Wise's congregation. A regular scandal," Jacob said, taking out his after breakfast cigarette. He was permitted six a day now that his blood pressure was acting up.

Selma rose from the table and frowned on the farm girl who removed the plates from the wrong side. "Etta acts as if it weren't true. And poor Harry, he doesn't notice a thing. Of course, not one of his friends would dare tell him. He'd kill himself."

"And his family building half of the new apartment houses in the Sixties. Women are certainly odd people," Jacob said as he got out of his chair and kissed Selma on the cheek. "I'm sure Selma is carrying on with an Argentine tango dancer on the side."

"Go water your strawberries," Selma said, grinning, and pushing Jacob out of the room. "More coffee, Egon?"

"No, thanks. You and Jacob seem to hit it off all right, all these years of marriage."

Selma patted one of Egon's huge arms. "You know you think he's a middle-class slave-driver with no more idea of beauty and taste than this cup and saucer and as bigoted as they come. But I do love him."

"Sure," said Egon. "I'm not knocking love," and he thought of Peter. "One is always in love one's self—or knows someone who is."

It was a bad time to be a college graduate, Peter felt, and the world agreed with him. There was excitement and talk of the wonders of the market, but everyone looked worried.

Old Joseph never left his bed now in the big, dark room with the blood-red drapes. No more did he summer in the Berkshires. He lay back calm and lonely and looked a great deal at the ceiling and slept a great deal and often never knew when he was sleeping and when he was awake.

Peter, Nicole, and Ralph crossed the rich, worn rug and stood by the bedside. Ralph was pale and well dressed, and he carried himself with a tightness that showed in his too casual stance, his wetting of his full lips under the trim moustache showing grey now among its golden hairs. Nicole was big-eyed with awe and fear. Peter trembled.

The old man opened his eyes. Nicole smiled quickly.

"Ralph," the old man said. "I must be pretty bad if they sent for you."

"No, Papa, I've wanted to come a long time."

"Yes, I knew it. Hello, Nicole, Peter. How's fishing this year?"

"I haven't been," Peter said.

"Sit me up, put some pillows behind me."

Ralph shook his head. "I don't think we should. The nurse said we weren't to stay long."

"Don't disturb the corpse. That's right," the old man said.

Nicole smiled wider. "We used to have such good times when we were children, on our visits here."

The old man nodded. His breath had trouble climbing out of his throat. "A long time, a good time. What's all the noise outside, Ralph? Everybody talking and planning?"

"Things at the moment are going badly on the market. I don't think it's much, just a period of adjustment. The market will hold."

"You in trouble, Ralph? Or Charles?"

Ralph shrugged his shoulders. "Oh, we're a solid bank."

"Bankers don't look well in jail," the old man said. He grinned, showing the strong but worn teeth, the thin red lips, cracked and wrinkled. "But no time for jokes. You've come home, Ralph . . . home with your children. They're fine children . . . fine, fine."

"We'll go now," said Nicole, kissing him on a dry hot cheek. She felt thrilled to be so close to death.

Ralph bent over and gripped the old man's shoulders and kissed his cheek. "We'll be back, Papa."

"Yes . . . yes . . . the Union guns are planted on the rise and the brush is very thick."

"What?"

Peter tried hard not to weep and said, "I'll come and read to you, Grandpa . . . any time at all."

"Let us cross the river," the old man said, "and rest in the shade of the trees."

They walked softly out of the room and Tante Strasser sat in her deep red chair and nodded to them. Sam and Jacob Kozloff were in the living room. Ralph said, "Does he want a rabbi?"

Sam shook his head. "Papa is pretty firm about that. He says he can find the way himself."

Uncle Louis came in, his eyes red, his white moustache a tangle stained by tobacco juice. "It's hard to believe he's going. Solid he was, always. Hard to think it's happening to us. Remember the time he shotgunned Pontdue and fought the Copper Combines?"

"How's the market?" Jacob Kozloff asked.

Uncle Louis and Peter went to a speakeasy and invited Ralph. They stood at the bar and drank bathtub gin and colouring.

"The old man isn't scared to die."

"I wonder, Uncle Louis."

"Not him, Peter. He's died a lot. In the war, in Butte."

"Papa is very tired."

"Hell, yes. I'm tired myself. But I wanta go fast with my boots on."

"Let's not talk about it, Uncle Louis."

"Old men can only talk about death and whores. There isn't much more to life. Oh, you dress it up in romance and money and art and living fat off the hog, but in the end it's all death and whores."

Ralph looked at his watch. "I must get back to the bank."

Uncle Louis watched Ralph go and turned back to Peter. "I talk too much. Always have."

"I like it. It's better than talking about the market."

"That's whoring too, with your fly closed."

A blonde at the end of the bar began to weep about a guy in Newark who had gone back to his wife.

Peter, years later, reading about the great stock-market crash, felt one got the idea it came suddenly one day and by nightfall we were all ruined. That is not true, Peter used to think I saw it happen. Maybe I missed Waterloo, Gettysburg, the flight at Kittyhawk—but I saw the bull market lay the big egg.

The world was not well. Money and credit were hard to come by even at the great New Amsterdam–Manhattan Bank. The corporations were hard hit, but still the owners supported them on the Stock Exchange. Call and commercial loans and the rediscount rates of the . New York Reserve Bank made night reading for bankers. Prime bankers' acceptances, eligible for purchase or rediscount by the Federal Reserve Bank, were too high. Charles Pentland gave optimistic interviews to the press.

Gold bullion was pouring into the country, but even with the prices on the open London market and the low, bar-silver rates, the banks did not care to encourage the corporations to ask for future loans. Ralph Perry assured rich old ladies this was the best of all worlds.

Panic gripped business. Foreign exchange showed sterling and the franc lower, the guilder and the belga being driven down. Grains rotted, sprouted, in storage. Freight lading was off. Miles of rust-coloured cars filled the way stations. Idle railroad systems ate up dividends. Lard, butter, cotton were lower. Sugar, cocoa, silk, hides —irregular. Copper, rubber went lower. Pedlock Coal and Iron began to sag.

Ralph Perry went to see a doctor. "Nerves."

The dollar sold down, and the franc was too many to the pound.

(The old man muttered in his sleep and smiled. Was he dreaming or was he far away and a long way back in time?)

"Give us a tune, Sweeney."

"Give you a crackerjack tune, General."

The fat man in Confederate grey took a battered banjo from a nail and without much introduction began to plunk it with those loose, dirty fingers, with the fastest fingers Captain Pedlock had ever seen. And he sang:

> "*It rained all night*
> *The day I left*
> *The weather it was dry.*
> *The sun so hot, I froze to death. . . ."*

"Couldn't fight this war without Banjo Sweeney."

"He plays well," Joseph said.

"Best banjo player in the whole goddamn army. Jackson wants him for hymn singing at his prayer meetings. But Banjo, he isn't that kind of a player. He's a real, cork-faced, nigger minstrel man. Real as Jim Crow."

> "*Hangtown gals are lovely creatures,*
> *Think they'll marry Mormon preachers,*
> *Heads thrown back to show their features,*
> *Ha, ha, ha! Hangtown gals!*
>
> *Shocked to hear 'em say 'goddamn it,'*
> *Tried to blush but cannot come it,*
> *Ha, ha, ha! Hangtown gals!"*

The franc fell deeper into the well of foreign exchange. A large outflux of foreign capital was reported. Bank of France was down; Suez was down; Rio Tinto was down; Royal Dutch was scraping bottom. *Rentes* closed, with the three per cents 40.20. Amortizables, 40.20. Sterling closed at 120 francs and the dollar at 23.35 francs.

Egon closed his Paris art gallery.

Americans on the Left Bank began to pack and hunt for addresses of relatives in the States. The painted ladies moved back to smaller apartments. The French peasant buried his rancid sock deeper under his fireplace and piled his manure heap higher. Franco-Americans, on the day of fortnightly settlement, went down from the mid-month 3½ to 2 per cent. Wires across the Atlantic to New York went unanswered.

In Berlin paper marks flew from fist to fist like snow—and worth little more. Forty stocks failed to qualify for official quotations. Out of the beer halls came Nazi street hoodlums and gutter brawlers to smash the windows of poor Jewish tailor shops and curse the Rothschilds. Red counter-riots broke out. The Second Reich sat twirling its thumbs and told the boys to behave. The Kozloff German plants closed down.

Commodities went down, Wheat No. 2, Red; Rye No. 2, Western; Cocoa No. 4, Superior Bahia. Flour, barrelled, stayed in warehouses or under mouldy canvas. Steel bullets, Pittsburg; antimony, Chinese in bond; copper, electrolytic; tin, Straits Settlements, no longer moved up the private spur to the Jersey plants.

A whole crew of gutter brokers sprang up to join the old-timers in the slaughter. The Pedlock companies sank and stumbled and no one told the old man, sleeping in the wide, family bed, upstairs. (If he slept, he dreamed—if he didn't dream, then he was having a vision. . . .)

Night . . . The Union troops, their back well set against a steep hill, and Jackson did not care to count his dead after the Union artillery stopped its fire.

Chancellorsville, the night of the first day. Major Pedlock at Lee's headquarters . . . a simple, slab house lit by oil lamps. Lee and his staff crowded the black, horsehair parlour. Union guns hammering at the Confederate rear. Voices came out for a retreat. Lee and Jackson bent bearded heads together and Major Pedlock slept standing up against a rose-pattern, papered wall. The door opened and Stuart came in whistling Banjo Sweeney's version of "Jine the Cavalry".

Major Pedlock came alert. Stuart reported to Lee, "I've ridden all day."

"Where have you been?" asked Lee.

"Riding back from Gordonsville. I've found something. The road west of Chancellorsville. Their whole right flank is unprotected."

Lee moved his white beard slightly. He turned to Jackson. Jackson faced him with a face all hair and mind. Lee spoke. "What do you think? Could you take your whole force, all three divisions, and make a wide circuit? Attack the open flank?"

"It can be done." The old lamps sputtered, the creak of leather, the jangle of spurs filled the little room.

Jackson hit hard at noon, coming out of the tunnel in the brush and cutting away whole Union regiments. Joseph went forward and slashed away until his arm ached, and he saw the village of Chancellorsville. They all went for it with a whirl of dust and a shout. But just then the Union artillery, unfortunately in reserve at the spot, swung around and gave them canister and ball fire (the old man on the bed moved his lips). The Rebel columns and Major Pedlock's horse rode hard in a charge. They were flung back and again they went in and Joseph felt fear and dread that he would die here in this futile flank attack. But sudden disaster among his men took his mind away from

325

his personal survival and he rallied them. Jackson's flanking attack was stopped dead in its tracks.

The men all took cover and Joseph, suffering like most of the army from dysentery, got off his horse and waited for orders. Stuart was some place on his right. The Union attack came on and Joseph fought his men on foot all through a dreadful evening, while his dead piled up, and the Union never stopped its guns and attacks. Jackson rode up in person, shouting, "Press them! Press them!" in his God-filled voice.

But Joseph knew that nothing could move the men in the darkness (the old man was breathing regular and even).

WALL STREET STEMS PANIC
HOOVER SEES CONDITIONS AS NORMAL

The men in tattered battle grey were tired after a hard day of marching and fighting and they sank back into the brush to wait for morning. The shelling still went on.

Joseph mounted and rode back to a barn where the staff was gathered in the light of farm lamps. A staff officer, dusty and sweat-stained, came toward Joseph. "Can you go on, Major?"

"Not tonight."

"That's what I told Jackson. It's sure hell out there."

"Shells still falling among the Thirty-third North Carolina."

"Will they break?"

"I don't think so."

Jackson came over. "Let's ride out and see if we can find a spot for the morning attack. Major Pedlock, show me your front."

Joseph and the staff mounted and they rode off after Jackson. The shells were still falling. As they rode, the tired horses tried to catch passing leaves in their teeth, but they were sternly pulled back to the centre of the path. They crossed a rise and Joseph said, "We're too close."

A Southern voice came up from near a board shanty in the tangled shrub. "Hey there!"

"It's Stonewall," shouted Joseph. "Don't shoot!" A shot was fired.

"Cease firing!" yelled Joseph.

"Who's thar?"

"You're firing at your own men!" Joseph shouted.

Someone answered from near the shanty, "It's a lie! Pour it into them, boys!"

Jackson was hit by the sudden volley that cut into the night. He lost his bridle rein. The sorrel he was riding started for the Union lines. Joseph reached it as a branch almost swept Jackson from the saddle. Joseph jerked the rein on Jackson's horse and they got the sorrel turned around.

"You hurt, sir?" asked Joseph.

Jackson didn't answer. Another officer rode up and between them they held Jackson steady in the saddle. His arm felt broken. "Can you move your fingers?" Joseph asked.

Jackson said in a low, stern voice, "You had better take me down." He fell into their arms and they got him to lie down under a tree. Suddenly many men crowded round. Joseph got out the small flask of whisky he carried. Jackson was not a drinker, but Joseph asked, "Will you have a sip of whisky?"

Doubt filled Jackson's face, but he nodded, "Just a little spirit," and took a swallow of the whisky. He was in great pain and a staff officer told Jackson they had sent for a good surgeon. Jackson did not trust the army surgeons.

"Is he a good one?" he asked.

"A very good one."

Jackson's mind seemed to wander and Joseph saw he was in great pain. Jackson said, "Let us cross the river, and sit in the shade of the trees." Then he fainted. (The old man opened his eyes. Someone was spooning hot milk into his mouth. They wiped his lips and went away.)

STOCK EXCHANGES MAY NOT OPEN IN MORNING
HOOVER SEES NO FURTHER DROP IN MARKET

"If we can hold a while longer we can attack," Stuart said, standing in the direct sun.

"Yes, General," said Major Pedlock. "I hear Jackson died."

"Yes. Get a little rest and be prepared. We're advancing on both sides of Hazel Grove. Good luck."

They shook hands and Joseph went off to find a fresh horse. They went into the fight shouting, "Remember Jackson!"

The Union pulled back to a series of ragged ravines and the Rebel hosts ran like braying hounds toward them, into deadly fire, and spent the day in attack after attack. (The Angel of Death came into the room. Joseph saw it was his father, Aaron.)

Stuart never let up, and Joseph, himself, led two charges. He had found a wild stallion with wonderful, black-leather fittings and chain reins. The horse was very angry and very strong. Joseph had a great deal of trouble mastering him. At last the stallion settled down to obeying, and it was already dark when he led a brigade into attack,

327

for one last effort to turn the Union retreat into a rout. There were Vermont troops ahead, and they held, and as the black horse cleared a log trench, Joseph felt the animal shake, and he put the spurs in hard. The whole horse, every nerve and every muscle, seemed to protest in a sudden, great explosion of flame. A soot cave of darkness closed in. He felt nothing, heard nothing.

(. . . The old man on the bed was far from the Dow Jones ticker reports and brokers putting down their gold-banded cigars, their gold-rimmed bifocals, their copies of world market news from *The* London *Times, Zukunft, L'Echo de Paris, Vossische Zeitung, Le Temps, Deutsche Tageszeitung,* and other sheets.) Major Joseph Pedlock was dead on horseback. ("I'm ready, Papa.")

The President of the United States sent a long personal telegram. The New Amsterdam–Manhattan Bank sent a huge blanket of roses and lilies which couldn't be used, for Hebrew ritual forbids flowers at Jewish burials. Charles Pentland and Ralph Perry (out on bail and awaiting trial) were there in neat, banker's pinstripe, black pearls in their black ties. The little Jewish graveyard in Philadelphia was packed with people. They lowered old Joseph in his plain unvarnished pine box, as is the burial habit for Jews, into the good, brown earth by the side of his wife. Sam had invited a rabbi, who did not speak at the graveside, but stood on the path, for the old man had made it clear he wanted no ritual mumbling over his head. And Tante Strasser was there, grim and silent, to see he was obeyed.

Peter and Nicole and all the Kozloffs and all the relatives stood sadly by while the clods thudded against the coffin. It was an old-fashioned burial that made death real, not exterior decorating. No grass matting to hide the earth, no silent machine to lower the coffin, no canvas shields to keep the thud of the earth hitting the wood from the ears of the family.

The tired rabbi on the path in the hot sun closed his eyes and earnestly chanted:

> "*May he come*
> *Back to us*
> *And soon*
> *With the Messiah*
> *Son of David. . . ."*

For a week the three sons of Joseph Pedlock sat the ritual *shiva* for the dead. They sat in stockinged feet on low boxes and repeated the *Kaddish*, a son's prayer for his dead father. Two repeated it every day for eleven months, and Egon said it once a year on *Yahrtseit*, the anniversary of the death. They said it in a sing-song Hebrew, learned by ear, and they put their own personal meaning into the words.

"*Yisgadal veyiskadash sh'mei rabbo. . . .*" said Ralph Pedlock, Long Island gentleman, member of the fashionable clubs, owner of hound dogs, a silver-mounted, hand-made shotgun and a collection of Early American furniture; a banker, indicted for his father-in-law's misuse of funds entrusted to the big bank.

"*Y'hei sh'mei rabbo me'vorach,*" said Egon Pedlock, beauty lover, dealer in modern art, supporter of a boys' home and a girls' home in Europe, traveller, lover of good food, ballet, and advance-guard music; a large, expanding balloon of a man with exotic habits, seated now on an old fruit box swaying and praying for the soul of his dead father gone from him.

"*Oseh sholom bimromov hu ya'as eh sholom oleinu ve'al kol Yisroel ve imru, omein,*" said Sam Pedlock, industrialist, stamp collector, hard-working man with good intentions, now a newly made bankrupt by the crash of the market.

Ruined, grieved, numb, they recited all together:

"*Y'hei schlomo. . . .*"

Charles Pentland walked with Peter down the windy street.

"I shall miss Joseph. He was a fine man, Peter."

"Yes, he was."

"He saw through me. The veneer, the culture, and the manners. He saw I was really soft and rather frightened by the world. He saw I was a kind man and rather weak. The pose didn't mean anything to him. He never had a pose. He was direct and honest as my people, our people, Peter, used to be in New England. Well, I'm talking too much. I'll be rather sorry later. But I want you to know something, Peter: I was never ashamed of the Pedlocks—oh, I don't have to tell you what Jews have to go through, but I admired the old man. And the family. Mine was rather cold and stiff. We never kissed, you know. Well, to see the Pedlocks, so warm and so kind to each other . . . I'd better stop talking about it."

BOOK SEVEN

CHAPTER I

Charles Pentland was not a dishonest man. He had a rigid set of ethics, an honest core bred into him by a long line of good people who took perhaps too much pride in their honour. He did not open the vaults of the bank and fill a sack with gold coins or packets of bills. He did not juggle books, gamble, or spend his money unwisely on women and personal pleasures. He became involved in a system which he did not invent and which he neither disliked nor enjoyed. He acted like a banker and was caught during a panic.

Like all bankers with vast funds and credits ("for real money," as he used to say, "does not exist; it is merely slips of credits—taking from one to credit to another, something that doesn't exist except in book-keeping"), Charles Pentland had to keep the phantom credits moving, to mark up interests on fairy gold. He supported large, private building projects and poured vast funds into apartment houses and amusement centres. There were certain legal rules . . . rules about security and assets. He loaned millions to firms which, he admitted, "held paper values in certain stocks that depended on rents as yet uncollected in certain building not yet built".

All banks did the same. At first the only real sufferer was a Jewish group, The Bank of the United Nation, which was crushed, left to die by the Morgan, Rockefeller banks. Its president and his staff were sent to jail. The bank closed its hundred branches, and years later it was found to be fully solvent and its cadaver paid off almost ninety-nine cents on the dollar. But the Jewish bank was gone. The other banks had, however, sent a bank president to jail and so, by knocking down one bank, the public began to suspect that the rest, too, were not stainless steel saints. Trouble came to the banking system. Charles Pentland and his son-in-law, Ralph Perry, were indicted for misuse of their bank's funds. They had company. Many other great men in the world of finance saw prison stripes staring at them as they tied their cravats in the morning.

Everything moved toward the final crash. U.S. Steel had dropped from a high of $261\frac{1}{4}$ to a low of 204. American Can, General Electric were more than fifty points below certain highs. People took a trimming on Radio when it slid from $114\frac{1}{2}$ in a mad break to $82\frac{1}{4}$. Charles Pentland shook his head. His personal fortune was now involved. That too? The world was really ending.

Professor Irving Fisher had no fears. He felt stocks were on "what looks like a permanently high plateau". Charles E. Mitchell of the National City Bank, Charles Pentland's friend, was glad to see the press. "... Absolutely sound. Our credit situation is in no way critical."

Then one morning, as Sam Pedlock and the Colonel sat in a broker's office, the ticker tape began to fall behind the trading on the floor. Down went prices. How far? The ticker was late.

Later than it had ever been.

"Sell! Sell! For the love of God, sell!" voices kept shouting all day. . . .

Sell Kennecott.

Sell General Motors.

Seven o'clock. Jacob Kozloff doesn't go home. "All the fancy holding companies gone. I'm wiped out. I'm back in the dress business running a sweatshop, where I belong."

Eleven speculators have committed suicide. Buffalo and Chicago exchanges have locked the doors.

They may have troops guarding Wall Street tomorrow.

President Hoover made a headline: "*The fundamental business of this country . . . is on a sound and prosperous basis. . . .*"

Kozloff Standard and Kosloff Industries were no longer on the board. Jacob Kozloff went home and Selma put him to bed and fed him hot broth and listened to him moan. She did not tell him that his son Mike, that morning, had packed a few things into a paper bag and gone out on the highway and thumbed a ride west. She did not weep, she just sat by the bed of her husband and wondered why she felt no pain.

Sam Pedlock slept soundly for the first time in months. The Pedlock companies were now all in the hands of receivers. His own private investments had been sold out. They would have to get out of the apartment by the first of the month. Sara wept in her mirror and decided to sell the furniture and move into a hotel. Hungry days were ahead.

Louis combed his white moustache with his fingers and smoked long cigars (not yet paid for) as he walked the floor in his high-heeled, cowboy boots. His mind was already active, busy hunting here and there in his now lost interests for some crumb to use, some forgotten plan or hope to set up and begin all over again.

He had been through a hell of a lot of bad times. Boom days would come again. He was sure of that: "never been let down yet by the country." But how was he to start? He was getting old, no doubt about it. A big, bald patch in the middle of his long white hair, the knee he hurt in Cuba acting up. And he had trouble waking up now after a night of helling and bending the ole elbow. Joseph Pedlock was what they needed. The old man was a solid wall; one could sit in his shade and watch things start to hum again, no matter how hard the fall. Well, just as well the old man was dead and buried. Let 'im rest. He had earned it.

The damn boots were bothering his corns again. He sat down on the crumpled bed, the stub of a cigar smouldering in his face, and pulled off the boots with a tired, grunting effort. Tomorrow was another day, as the fella said . . .

Harry Gelhorn had tried to kill himself. They watched him retch on the bed and toss like a new-caught trout. He hadn't gone about it very well. A few drops of iodine, a slight slash on his wrist with the razor Rose used for her armpits, and then a wailing, moaning drop onto the bathroom tiles. They had pumped milk into him, and retched him, and rolled him, and tied up his wrist. Two unfinished hotels, their iron skeletons rusting over Park Avenue, were to remain for years as Gelhorn's Follies.

Rose looked at the whining object on the bed, turned and went into the baby's room. The baby was sleeping on its stomach, its face in the pillow and its tiny rump up in the air, supported by chubby knees crossed under it. The father of the child moaned again in the next room. Rose did not go back to him . . .

Alice Perry and her daughter Nicole came down to breakfast, their hair in close-worn nets to protect their settings, which they would comb out in time for the horse show they were attending that day. It was no use going into a panic. One must, of course, act as if all were right with the world. Breeding and manners demanded that much.

The breakfast table looked cheerful in the sun. How old Father was getting. Alice hadn't noticed before, but now, looking at Charles Pentland put jam on toast with the morning *Times* propped in front of him, she saw how white and bent he had become. She kissed his cheek and sat down across from Ralph, who, pale and still, wearing a dark tie in memory of his father, was not eating—he only drank his coffee.

"Where's Peter?" Ralph asked.

"Staying at the Sontags'. Harry Gelhorn," she looked at Nicole spooning up corn flakes, "well . . ."

Nicole grinned, nodded. "Tried to do himself in, as they say in English novels."

Charles Pentland put down his coffee cup and laughed grimly. "Harry would. No spine. A gentleman doesn't make *that* mess of things. It . . ."

Alice took her father's hand in hers and gripped it hard. "Father."

Ralph looked up from the end of the table. "You were about to say it wasn't Christian, I suppose."

Ralph was grinning. They stared at him, surprised. He looked at his plate. "The toast is cold. I've decided on something, and to do it, I fear, I've lost my Christian virtues."

Alice bit her lips together. "Ralph, you didn't sleep very well last night, did you?"

"No, of course not."

Nicole said, "Can I get you some aspirin, Father?"

"No, thank you, Nicole." He turned to Charles Pentland. "I've been thinking. I owe a lot to you. My family, my happiness for many years, my position . . . what is left of it. Last night I decided to become a Jew again."

Nicole giggled, "Really, Father."

Alice pulled on her napkin until her fingers went white. "Ralph, *what* a time to be a Jew."

Charles Pentland merely carefully dabbed a bit of toast with jam (it was cold, damn it).

Ralph put his elbows carefully, solidly (the way old Joseph did) on the table. "I decided last night that there was no need for Charles Pentland to go to prison."

"Please, Ralph."

"That's all right, my dear—must get used to it," said the old man.

"The loans, unsecured loans, were made through my department. The trusts and estates that were depleted were in my charge. I am going to take all the blame and clear Charles Pentland."

"Nonsense—I ran the bank my way, Ralph."

Nicole began to weep and her mother put an arm around her. Charles Pentland put down the silver jam knife and looked up at Ralph.

"Am I that old, Ralph?"

Ralph did not answer. He got up, kissed his wife cheerfully on the mouth, and went out into the garden. He whistled for his favourite dog. They heard him cross the garden, the steady tramp of his well-made English shoes.

Charles Pentland covered his eyes with his lean, graceful hand. His shoulders shook. He wept silently, then without looking up he said, "I'm sorry to have lost control of myself like this."

Nicole looked from her mother to her grandfather, as if waiting for some clue to the next move. Charles Pentland slowly folded his napkin together. "You two better hurry or you'll miss the horse show."

Alice refilled her coffee cup and looked off toward the garden. "I don't think we'll go. The club, I seem to remember, doesn't exactly approve of Jews."

See him then, Peter Manderson Perry, in the years the locust ate, the years his father was a model prisoner in Sing Sing, the years he wandered and stood in lines and held little jobs while the depression wore itself out. He and Ike Sontag—and millions, it seemed, like them—went from house to house with unwanted vacuum cleaners. They stood, one foot jammed in the door, peddling a set of books that told of everything in man's knowledge, they dug WPA ditches, they sat one night (and just one night) on a bootlegger's beer truck and saw officers of the law paid off.

By 1933 they had done many things and were tired of being children of disaster. They were no longer children but young men who could not afford to marry, dusty, unfashionable young men. Ike went off, at last, to repair motors in Greek fishing vessels off a Florida Key. Peter sat in a speakeasy, known (of course) as Tony's, and waited for the Colonel to meet him. Old Colonel Louis, two years older than God and never giving up. Repeal was due soon, but the speakeasy still flourished before it became a legal nightclub or a dance hall.

It is hard to see Peter clearly during these years of turmoil. He once kept a sort of diary, and part of it still exists. His sister Nicole, who had married quietly (when her father left for prison) one Ned Bowren, a polo player and chicken rancher on Long Island, found it one day stuffed into an old package of college text books. Just a few sheets that ended suddenly as if Peter had become bored with it.

It was written in pencil on that cheap yellow paper one finds in failing newspaper offices, so that perhaps he wrote it while wandering and attempting to work on one of those sodden weeklies that sound so romantic to old newspapermen and prove such failures in practice.

It begins with a quotation from a book Peter never really finished, but a book he struggled with for years, and read into, the way a mouse tunnels into a cheese . . .

June 6. I read this [Peter's diary begins] the other day and I feel it's so right and true that I wonder why I didn't think of it before . . .

A man lives not only his personal life, as an individual, but also, consciously or unconsciously, the life of his epoch and his contemporaries . . .

It's in Thomas Mann's *The Magic Mountain*. I like to kid myself that makes me more important than I am. I've never really looked at myself closely. Here goes.

I am entirely a simple, over-exerted child of the twentieth century, with enough freedom in whatever kind of mind I have and a certain satisfaction in the work I do, to now and again escape from the vexations and immediate activities (and the disasters that I fear doom my world) to look over my shoulder at my puppyhood.

I came into existence when the world, as my Uncle Egon said, was manufacturing more history than it could consume, but I have never regretted being born—and being born in the time I was.

Man, the college experts told me, is the only mammal successfully engaged in the extermination of his own species. So that, perhaps, the person sitting down to write something of his past is helping to destroy a legend of man's fine purpose on earth.

The first two decades of the century in America (its martyrs and miracles) strikes me as being one of the most amazing periods in world history—perhaps only because I was young and alive and coming of age during that time. Egotism is pretty dreadful—in other people—but when we ourselves look back at the past, we are using an intervening generation as a pad against too much shock—just as the fork makes us forget that meat is eating meat.

To think with the heart instead of the head is an old disease and I shall here try to blend the memories of both organs honestly. It makes me wonder if such a world once existed; it did . . . I sometimes meet fellow travellers who once saw the Twenties with me. To the . . . [a page is missing here].

We did travel—all us young men. In the Twenties, wearing horn-rimmed glasses, tweed plus-fours, and carrying the Holy Trinity of Freud, Marx, and Joyce, we were everywhere. We met ourselves sunburned in Capri, drunk in Mayfair, and broke but rowdy in Paris. We showed our muscles by going up the Amazon, bought bad bronze art in Peking, and yet always we came back home to howl down the barbarians and demand that we begin a culture. For as someone said (I don't recall who)—'*Il faut vivre, combattre et finir avec les siens*'—one must live, struggle and die among one's own."

It may appear that I met only freaks, odd characters, madmen, eccentrics, and misfits. The truth is that I knew hundreds of thousands of normal people, and nothing they did or said, or very little, anyway, is worth remembering.

I will not tamper with history. I did not, believe me, invent the

337

Charleston, Herbert Hoover, the great bull market, the Model T, bobbed hair, the raccoon coat, James Joyce, Freud, or the hip flask.

Some writers (again to quote Uncle Egon) have the habit of catching humanity napping and nailing it to paper before it struggles out of position. If the Twenties tried a deliberate exodus from sanity, if we attemped to pursue aesthetic concerns in a period of decadence, well, our present day is no daisy either.

June 21. Pawned my winter overcoat. Promised a job in an advertising agency.

July 3. Very low. Owe Tony $23.45.

It is important to understand the mores, morals, and manners of the last ten years and not to confuse them with our own sad times. We peer almost across centuries when we look back at the gay days of the Flying Fool, Jimmie Walker, rolled stockings, Clara Bow, plus-fours for golf, and the proper way to seat a flapper against the floorboards of a Stutz Bearcat.

The advertising job fell through. Owe Tony $47.15. Without idiots the world would be a very unfashionable place but I didn't really care for the advertising business.

Aug. 2. Letter from the Colonel. Has a great scheme to make us all rich. Wants to see me next trip to town.

Aug. 10. Am rolling in money. Made twenty dollars washing cars and ran it up to seventy-three bucks in a crap game in a Greenwich Village apartment. Met Mike Kozloff, who is painting post-office murals on the Federal Art Project. Who says art doesn't pay off these days? If I could spell, I'd try and get the Federal Writers' Project.

Aug. 18. Tony's is calm and normal this morning. Am hung over but cheerful.

Ah, now to be a casual observer, and sit at a good table and never feel indigestion, and remember only beauty. I had hoped to write of the world as if it were a pond filled with clear water, in which certain odd waterbugs and wonderful cell forms and proud minnows (and other denizens of the pond) dart about and live out their cycles. Yes, I was only going to be the observer of the human spirit, the student, but I see now, as I begin to pin together these notes, that I have fallen into the pond and must swim along with its inhabitants, my eyes hanging out on stems. Met Mike's girl last night. A little Polish Jewess. . . .

Mike is becoming a madman—all art and hair and his painting strong, ugly, and powerful. I feel I am only going to be a bystander in life—not a creative artist.

Aug. 21. Mike's girl is a bore.

All speakeasies seem to be called Tony's these days, unless they are called Jack's and Charlie's. I like it here. Tony's is behind a rusting, grille door, a small opening through which a bloodshot eye protrudes. Inside it is knee-deep in cigarette smoke; a real Model-T speakeasy out of an early Warner Brothers movie. The usual mural of the Bay of Naples, painted by Mike Kozloff for for food; the usual paper grape leaves; the usual pine bar; the usual drunk at one end counting sticky pennies; the usual crying woman sniffing up gin at the other; the usual phone booth full of the usual hoodlum talking out of both sides of his mouth into a battered phone. It is strange what a pattern all these places have.

At the bar there is a reporter talking of his unwritten novel, and two girls—or rather tomatoes, as they are called here.

"Girls, meet Peter. Peter, meet Emily—that's for you—and meet Jennie Joy—that's for me," said the reporter.

"Old fashion," said Emily.

"Whisky sour," said Jennie Joy.

Emily, big and blonde, as beautiful as a punch by Jack Dempsey, and built like a drawing by a French painter of the King's second-best mistress. Jennie Joy thin and bobbed, and smoking cigarettes in a jade holder; her talk that afternoon consisted of saying, "I wish I had a dollar for every glass of Bollinger champagne I drank last night. Just a dollar for every glass—that's all."

"Well," said the reporter, shivering after our fourth drink of what passed for pleasure at the bar. "How you doing, Peter?"

Emily shook back her head of taffy-coloured hair which was sagging into a fashionable Garbo hairdo. "I'm on a diet. You like fat girls?" She looked at me.

"I'm not going as far as some Dutch painters, but I like the padded woman."

"I'm so happy," said Emily, giving me her hand.

"Boy oh boy, I should have a dollar for every glass of champagne I put away last night. Just a dollar."

Tony came over to us. A soft, spreading native of Little Italy; made almost of stale bread and olive oil moulded into a man; a wonderful way of smiling; a habit of shaking cigar ash over himself.

"I cook, myself. The drinking I leave to the Irish barman. It is cold as death. No?"

The reporter grinned. "This Wop is much given to brooding over death. Dante in a speakeasy."

Tony rolled his eyes (in pure butter, I swear). "Always the living

339

is with the death. Yesterday an Elk from Westchester leaves here, the first time in three days. I worry he drink himself to death. So he walk home, take bath, slip—tomorrow I send lily."

Emily looked at the slate Tony held up, and rerolled her stockings. Stockings rolled below the knees, the girdle is unknown among the younger set, and the complete wearing apparel of a lady of fashion—right down to the skin—as the advertisements said, "would fit neatly into a large brandy glass" (if you left off the shoes, of course).

"I'll have another old-fashion, first."

"Bollinger and guinea hen."

Tony sighed. He pointed a hangnailed finger at something written on his slate. "Potage Madeira à la Speakeasy."

Every Tony in every speakeasy in New York City that prided itself on its cooking serves the potage. A drunk can eat well all across the country and *always* get his potage.

"It's made with Madeira?" asked the reporter.

Tony sighed, "They call it that."

"If I had a buck for . . ."

"And drinks?" said Tony.

"The same as we've been having, but don't space them so far apart," said Emily. "You only—" [The diary ends here.]

The Colonel wasn't wearing well. He was so very old now, Peter was shocked to see, a wide, tired, old man with his hair the soiled yellow-white of neglect, his chin loose, his jaw wobbly, and the moustache thinning out in spots. He looked like a neglected drunk. But the eyes, for all their surrounding areas of wrinkles, were still alive, as if they would be the last things in this man to give up hope and slide into decay.

The Colonel crossed the speakeasy and came up to Peter and wrung his arm Western style. "Well, my boy, you sure have grown up big and sassy. Yes sir, old Joseph looked mighty like you when I first saw him. Hell and high water, boy, it must be a long, long time ago . . . back in '65 or '66. What kind of drinkin' they serve here?"

Peter ordered whisky sours and they sat and drank and the Colonel hunted up some tattered ten-dollar bills in his dust-filled pockets, and swallowed a lot of whisky.

"How's your family, Peter?"

"Pa is up for parole soon. Ma is with Nicole—she married, you know, and is expecting a baby. Things are about the same. We've sold Perry Point, of course. But mortgages and law fees got most of it. Uncle Sam is in Tennessee. You look pretty full of ginger, Colonel. What's new in the West?"

340

"Nothin'. The dust storms carryin' off the topsoil, the cattle are thin as mangy cats, and the damn government is steppin' in and killin' off any effort by solid citizens."

"Also keeping them from starving."

The Colonel snorted into his glass. "Skip it, boy. I'm no man to take orders from Washington. Listen, I've got something and it's big. What do you think about oil?"

"I don't think about it."

"I've figured out a virgin field. I'm goin' to wildcat and I need some young blood for the hard work. I need you—you know money and bankin' and that foolishness. And Ike Sontag knows engineerin'. We're goin' to hit it so hard we'll wear nose rings of solid gold."

"Costs money, doesn't it? Leases, rigs, crews, all that?"

"In Louisiana they've hit oil and hit it good. But they don't know what they have in their front yard. Listen, Peter, there's oil in the Gulf of Mexico! That's where I'm goin' to drill!"

"The Gulf, under water?"

"Sure. It's a brand-new trick. As slick as your grandfather's first copper smelter. The shoal water out there in spots is only a mile or two from shore. Fifty or sixty feet deep. We'll sink piers, build a rig on it and drill through a cement retaining well . . . right through the Gulf, right down to the oil."

"Sounds fantastic."

"That's why we can do it cheap. I've got an old pirate called Gates to lend us his rigs for shares. Old Joseph once did him a favour. As for the water rights, well, that's in a state where you can buy whatever you need from ole Huey Long."

Peter looked at the Colonel and grinned. "It sounds crazy. But anything is better than sitting here rotting away at Tony's. Ike will like it. The sponge fishers in Florida aren't paying their bills. Oil from the bottom of the Gulf of Mexico? Colonel, in a way you're a kind of genius, even if you flop."

"Can't afford to flop. I'm an old tired bronc. My plumbing and wind machine isn't none too good. It's gotta be this time for a killin' or I don't make it. I'm slowin' up. Been punishin' the old frame a long time." The Colonel shook his head. "You never believe you're goin' to die when you're young, and you're never sure of tomorrow when you're old. It's a sad state of affairs. Let's have another drink and toast somethin' we could both use, a little *mazel*—Jewish for luck. To oil, Peter."

Peter signalled for two more whisky sours. "Hello, *mazel* . . ."

The sun came up glazed and hot across the Gulf and hit the drill rigs and barges with a current of deadening heat. It reflected in the yellow waters and bounced off the tin hut on the barge with the letters OFF SHORE OIL CO. A long mile behind the barges, and the rig standing on its stilts, the bayou country was a faint, violet fringe topped by decaying green. The smoke of the fishing villages singed a sky already too hot for comfort. Dead fish, white bellies up, floated in the soiled Gulf around the rig.

They had already been three months on the Gulf. Ike Sontag wore a rag around his middle in the direct sun and was the colour of a Moor. The Colonel stayed on shore, on the porch of a termite-eaten general store, where he whittled soft pine and set up cold beer for the fever-shaking natives. Peter lived in the tin hut on the barge and kept books, hustled supplies from the mainland, and tinkered nights with the outboard motor. Except for the heat and bad sleeping conditions, he felt this was all a change for the better.

Ike came away from the rig and crossed the cleated board to the barge. He went to the ice chest, took out a can of beer, punched a hole in it, and sat down facing Peter.

"It's a hell of a hard job. I wish the Colonel had dreamed up something better to make us some cash."

"The drilling has stopped."

"We fouled the Kelly bar for a little while. How's the cash on hand?"

Peter shook his head and wiped his face with his sleeve. "Not so good."

"Well, you better go up to New Orleans and get Gates to shell out that five thousand dollars he promised us when we were ready to drill."

"He's stalling."

Ike threw the empty beer can out of the hut window. It bobbed and drifted and then began slowly to sink as it filled.

Ike stood up. "What a time of the year to drill. The crew is just about melted down."

Peter put on a wide felt hat that was supposed to help keep the sun out and went across to the derrick. They were drilling in three shifts, twenty-four hours around the clock. They didn't dare stop drilling for fear the cutting would settle in the mud of the Gulf bottom. They were pumping mud out of an old brick barge down the hole to keep the drilling cool. Nothing seemed to work right.

The crew under red composition hats grunted over their tools, and stark naked, except for rags around their hips and necks, greeted Peter and shook their heads. The rotary table was turning again in the middle of the derrick floor.

Kinny the foreman said, "We're going down slower."

The cable spool began to wind up overhead and the bit came out of the hole and the crew broke the joint with a cat-head and attached a new length of pipe and the bit went back into the hole.

"Any signs?" Peter asked.

"Sure signs, but not of oil yet."

The travelling blocks creaked as the bit hit bottom. Everything was so complicated and so clever about well-drilling, Peter felt.

Kinny shaded his eyes and looked up at the sky. "No storm in sight, anyway. We do need a new bit. One with three pinions with teeth in 'em that rolls around. Old Gates promised us one. Make him pony up. Also get that Christmas tree from him."

"What the hell is a Christmas tree?"

"It's a big hunk of stuff with valves and gauges that you attach when you think the flow is about to begin. All the valves are painted different colours. So I guess that's why they call it a Christmas tree."

"How far down are we?"

"About eight hundred feet. The crown blocks aren't going to hold much beyond fifteen hundred. The rig builder didn't work too hard on this job."

"I'm going up to New Orleans to see Gates. Give me a list of what you want."

Kinny nodded and went over and spit on the rotary table. "I got a feeling we're running in new kinds of sand."

"That mean anything?"

"Don't know."

Peter went back to his tin hut. Ike was under the rain-barrel shower, lathering himself. A hoot came from the Gulf and a small dirty motor-boat came alongside and the Colonel, in crumpled soiled white, got out, a bottle of brandy under each arm.

"Certainly is cooler here than on shore."

"Like hell it is," said Ike, getting into shorts. "Any news from Gates?"

"Don't answer my wires. I guess Peter will have to go up and get the cash from him."

"Thanks," said Peter.

"Cheer up, boys. I got the whole country interested in this well. Going to raise us some cash for a little cracking plant. Yes, sir, our own little refinery. What they call a teapot with about three stills running gas fires, pipes to flash towers, bubble towers, storage towers. And our own brand on gas stations: Off Shore Gas. Need a good slogan for it."

"Stop dreaming," said Ike. "Seen oil prices lately?"

The Colonel opened a bottle of brandy. The heat was like a sticky aspic under the tin roof. The smell of brandy and the rancid mud they were pumping back and the hot tin and the dreadful yellow light of the Gulf all made Peter's head spin. He had been sleeping very badly and he was running some kind of fever.

Kinny came in, his hands soiled with sand and some discoloration. "*This* is the baby!"

"What is?" asked the Colonel.

"Oil signs."

They grouped around Kinny. Ike nodded. "Looks like it."

"We're down about nine hundred. . . . If we'll hit before we go a thousand, the rig will hold. You'll be pumping oil from the Gulf through fifty feet of water! A hell of a note."

The Colonel filled the sticky glasses. "This calls for a drink all around."

Kinny swallowed his drink. "Gates is certainly a lucky crud. He's got peanuts in this set-up and he's going to get oil for it."

The Colonel's hand shook. "It's like the first run of old Joseph's copper vat. A big moment."

A mucker came in wiping his face with an oily rag. "Musta hit a rock down there. Bent the Kelly bar."

"Have a drink," said the Colonel, "we're bending horizons today."

Peter found New Orleans not much cooler than the Gulf. His head ached but he decided to plunge right into talks with Gates. He called him on the phone and the fat voice on the other end said it was pleased to hear of the signs of oil. Of course Peter could have the money and the tools. Just drop over to his office. Yes, it was hot. There was always, it seemed, something wrong with the climate in New Orleans.

Gates Enterprises did not look impressive. The office of Gates himself held an old green file, a stuffed owl leaking sawdust, and a signed picture of a bishop. Gates sat well back in a polished swivel chair, scarred with time and jabs of a letter opener.

He was called "Sugarlips" Gates because he neither drank nor smoked the burley-leaf stogies, but chewed on raw sugar-cane instead. His dusty office was just around the corner from his great warehouses. He rubbed the fringe of fat around a round, cunning face that neither disarmed nor repelled. He nodded piously at Peter.

"Perry, we're doing the Lord's work down here and the oil will civilize these people. Huey Long is no man's fool."

Peter looked up at the lazy flies droning in mid-air, with just enough stir to their wings to keep them afloat.

"Can you fellas rush the drilling?"

"We could with more help," Peter said.

"Get more help—get niggers."

"All right."

"I don't hold for the way they treat niggers here—and white men fornicating with them. Look at the octoroons, griffes, and redbones among us. It's bad. But hire more niggers."

"I'll try. We'll rush the drilling if you'll send tools and pay us what was agreed on."

"Good. Come over to the house for evening prayers and dinner."

"I will when I'm settled. Now, about our first payment . . ."

"Sugarlips" Gates kicked his heavy cowhide boots down the splintered, dusty floor, got up, went to a small rosewood and steel safe, much scarred by wear and tear, and took out a roll of bills and counted off a fistful.

"I pay on the nose in cash and I'm a hard man in a deal. God-fearing. I don't hold with these people down here. They gamble and go dishonestly after profits. They're lazy and worthless, like a blind hound dog. Good day, Perry."

"Good day, Mr. Gates."

"Keep away from the town chippies. Marry, young man, marry. Better to marry than to burn."

Peter tried not to smile. He put away his money carefully and went down to the Delta House to get three fingers of good Bourbon whisky and branch water inside himself for a starter, and thought about Gates, their partner.

"Sugarlips" Gates had appeared ten years before, driving a new wagon loaded with cheap, shiny tinware. He traded it for old copper pots, brass clocks, pewter pitchers, or anything a farmhouse was likely to have on hand. He had a love for metal in any form, and his tinware was

345

shiny and durable (for at least six months). From the wagon he took to a river barge, taking in whatever the river boats had to trade in the years of the depression. He hated to do anything but trade. A deal in cash had no bite for him. Trade was his harlot, his Bourbon, his orgy. He did not gamble or whore. All his time was given to trading. He got control, in the bad years, of some leaking river boats and the wheezing railroad. He bought up leaning river houses on their last cypress pilings. He grew rich.

Not all of New Orleans was like "Sugarlips" Gates, Peter found out. The true Creole and Cajun civilization was gone. Great levees hemmed it in and, as the river was in flood, he saw the ships were a good ten feet above the town. He could look in over the levee and see the surrounding country spread out below him. It gave him a feeling of living with disaster during the years of depression dust bowls and shack towns.

He grew to like the town. Long plank wharves led to the big, brick warehouses of "Sugarlips" Gates. A thundering din of Negroes, horses, trucks—wagon and steamboat sounds—filled the day and night.

The Jews were the only people who were permitted to be buried underground, not a very pleasant privilege, Peter felt, in the soggy soil.

Little chameleons, darting little lizards, lived under cisterns and in the burying grounds. Peter kept a dozen of them in his room under brandy glasses until the yellow girl refused to have anything to do with his cleaning. Then he let them scamper away and disappear into the green corners of the small garden behind his boardinghouse.

A week after Gates paid off they hit a gusher out on the Gulf. They capped it and cheered. Oil dropped seven cents a barrel.

The Cathedral led Peter into its towers and he looked out miles across canals and little houses and great waterwheels draining the boggy land and the cows standing in groups against bright green landscapes. He waited in New Orleans to sign oil contracts. The cypress trees were every place. With the dried moss in their branches, they made him sad and feel near death, as if their jaws were slowly chewing the dead stuff while waiting for the end of the world.

After a splendid dinner on devilled whitebait and soft-shell crabs Peter loaded up on juleps and Bourbon. He grew used to speaking an English as soft as pillow down and as mellow as the corn whisky that was often allowed to age in charred oak kegs. He had "dinnah" and swore on his "honah" it was very fine. He learned the habit of giving *lagniappe*, that extra gift for any service.

Peter visited the sugar crushers and the great blackstrap mills, the waste and plenty of vast acres; marching plantations that seemed to Peter to disappear at last at the watery edge of the world, only because they had to end somewhere. There was a great deal of this muddy land, fertilized by the flooding river. The sinews and loins of the black men and women (it appeared) would go on bending and breeding for all time.

He went hunting while the oil market took another drop.

Fiddler crabs lived in the drainage ditches. River fish swam under the jetties. Ducks and doves filled the skies over the fields. Not all men were polite and lazy on their white, plantation porches. The depression was fearful here. Peter found cabins and huts and a hardy breed of men, who still pegged a long, six-foot rifle to their chimneys; a hard-drinking, tobacco-chewing race, with tired, washed blonde women and many children—almost as many children as hound dogs. Hound dogs cost more, too. He saw these people—their independence, their sudden angers, their hard-fighting and stomping rages. They took to leaning on WPA shovels. In their dirt, ignorance, and poverty, they had a force and vitality that even swamp fevers, hunger and river diseases could not take from them. The "miseries", as they called their illnesses, only preserved them.

Peter went once a week to dinner at Gates' house.

A mean table, three silent daughters, a washed-out wife with a shy tic. Gates carving the stringy roast.

"They eat too much down here, Peter."

"They eat well."

"Stomach juices all pus and wine. Have some more roast?"

"No thank you."

"Be lean, young man, in your youth. Save your cash."

"Haven't any to save."

"Lucy, bring in the pie. Use my daughters for cooks, Peter; it brings 'em up proper. Saves 'em from the movies and the dirty pleasures of this town. I don't allow local young men in the place."

Peter nodded. The pie came in, crisp, brown, hot, and wet.

"Too much sugar, Lucy. But you can afford it. I didn't have a rich father like you have."

"Just two spoonfuls, Father."

"Stuff the stomach and deny the mind, Peter. You a church man?"

"I was."

"Hell-fire, hell-fire and terrible trouble. Better marry, young man. Disease and terror waits the single man. More pie?"

347

"No thank you, I've had more than enough."

"You can smoke if you want to. I don't hold for it myself."

"Tobacco doesn't seem a vice."

"All pleasure is evil, Peter. I keep telling the girls that, but they prim and fuss over hats and feathers. Mother, you too."

"Yes, dear. I like a hat."

Peter was invited to bring the Colonel next time. The Colonel, up for a day, said, "Depresses me like a kick in the ass. No, thanks."

Gates lived in a grey world with his daughters and wife, in a large white house, and he grew vegetables instead of flowers in his front garden. He kept two near-white servants and read the Bible out loud for twenty minutes every day. Before each meal, too. None of the daughters was married. His dogs and cats did not mate. He gelded everything but himself.

Peter caught malaria, a disease that didn't exist in America, he was told. He lay in black vomit and died every night and feebly came back to life in the morning. After three weeks in the hospital he went back to his hotel.

Lucy, the eldest Gates daughter, discovered him one morning. Ike and the Colonel were busy at the wells. He did not bother them. She cleaned him, and washed him, and prayed for him. He was too weak to protest. In time he recovered enough to wish he were really dead.

Lucy came at dawn every day. She bathed him and fed him, cleaned out his mouth, and washed out his eyes. Peter was too tired to protest. In the Gulf they were drilling two new wells.

Lucy was tall, a girl with small, hard breasts in her tight housedress. And so expressionless as to seem almost numb to life. No man had ever touched her. She had a fine, long nose. Like those Greek statues Peter had seen in museums in Europe. Her eyes were a brown-green turning to gold when she was on her knees, bent over on her shapely hams, earnestly in prayer. She prayed a great deal, dryly, directly to God. Even for that, her expression never changed.

The wells continued to cause trouble but oil flowed and prices dropped.

When interest returned to Peter, he sat on the small, iron balcony of the hotel room and looked down over the town. Lucy stopped coming and he was almost thankful. He knew he was ungrateful. But a man had to admit that good women with a habit of continual prayer were hard to take. Her long graceful hands were kind, but just a little too strong. When she rubbed his brow or bathed his naked body, she was awkward and a little too powerful to be really tender. He sent her a note of thanks. And a turtle-shell comb for her blue-black hair that she screwed up into a ball and tied down by some secret pins to her long, artistic-looking skull. He thought of Rose bitterly, then kindly —then not at all.

It was the season of the rains. A great, grey cloud hung like a lead bowl over the low, wet city. The cracks in the Prussian-blue ceiling of the room filled with moisture. The spiders were less active and stopped printing their etchings. The rank, pervasive smell of river mud and old silvered wood was very strong. Peter's last letter from home was three months old. Times were hard. He lacked the energy to answer. He sat very still in his room and smoked the first pipe since his illness. When it grew very dark he went to bed and lay looking up at the ceiling growing darker and the cracks wider. Outside the rain hammered on the wooden shingles of the hotel roof like a circus drum he remembered. He felt an energy in his toes and entrails that made him feel very good at being once more alive. He stretched and read a little from one of the cherished volumes of Pepys' *Diary* which had belonged to old Joseph.

> Up after talking with my wife with pleasure about her learning on the flageolet a month or two again this winter, and all the rest of the year her painting, which I do love, and so to the office, where sat all the morning and here Lord Anglesey tells me again that a fleet is to be set out; and that it is generally, he hears said, that it is but a Spanish rodomontado; and that he, saying . . .

He enjoyed—as old Joseph always had—Samuel Pepys' ramblings. He blew out the cheap dollar lamp with the rose-painted shade (a valuable bit of Early Americana, he was sure). He had been sleeping for some time when he felt, rather than heard, the rattle of a loose shutter. It sounded like a rat in the stables at Perry Point long ago. He lay very still and drowsy. His door opened. He turned, as a flash of river lightning, somewhere miles away, lit up the room like a stage set.

He knew the woman was half-insane as soon as he saw her wide eyes and heard the hiss and intake of her laboured breath. It was only a moment later that he realized that she had taken off her clothes. Her face was covered with mud and blood.

"Lucy!" If it was Lucy, Peter thought.

"Lucy," he said again, sitting up, powerless to lift his limbs. She was suddenly all over him, her long arms around him, and he could smell the hot, hard flesh and the mud in which she had rolled. She kissed him and tore his cheek with her small, sharp teeth, and he fought her. And again called her, for the last time.

"Lucy!"

She did not answer. He took her arms and twisted them but she did not scream. He saw to his horror she was smiling. Then somehow, in the rain-sounding night, something in him clicked and he laughed. He laughed because he did not want to be afraid. He laughed because he didn't know what else to do. He was, in a dreadful way, enjoying this. There was such a mad, animal surge in him that he was suddenly as crazy with something warm and burning as she was. He let go her arms and they clung together. He took her with a brutal directness, a fierce energy like a release to an odd, thrusting, sensual power that had been damned by fever and control for too long a time.

There was nothing romantic or tender about it. Yet it had a perverse satisfaction to it . . . a climax of tremendous, draining tautness . . . that ended with a suddenly satisfied return to normality and spent endeavour. . . .

They were married in a plain, white church at the end of the rainy season. Peter could not believe the thing was real and not part of his fever dreams. Ike was best man and the Colonel got drunk and smashed up his new sports car and spent a night in jail.

Oil prices fell.

CHAPTER IV

The blue Warsaw Express was rushing along in the damp night across the endless Prussian plains. It had long since left the winding Oder. They were approaching Breslau and the tall, belching factory chimneys never stopped setting the horizon on fire. Doctor Sontag came out of the dining car, happy that it was night, that he could no longer see the drilling troops, the marching, happy German population with their bent cross on its blood-red circle. The whole mad parade of the cheerful Germans following their leader and sure they were the salt of the earth depressed him. If only Germans had a sense of humour.

The waiter had been surly, a new thing for German waiters, who are a race apart, faithful as hound dogs and usually as slobberly eager to please. Of course Doctor Sontag knew it was because the Jews were no longer part of the human race. He opened his compartment door and looked down at Egon, his huge bulk crushed into a corner of the compartment trying to read a French art magazine. Egon looked up and pulled down the shades halfway. Doctor Sontag bit off the end of his after-dinner cigar and lit it slowly, as if in no hurry to talk.

"Not going to have any dinner, Egon?" he said at last.

"No. We'll be in Warsaw by morning."

"The poles are bigger anti-Semites than the Germans."

Egon closed his magazine, tossed it into a corner. "It's hard to believe all this. Even the English and French selling out the Czechs at Munich seems like a bad dream."

"The evening papers are quoting Mr. Chamberlain: 'Peace in our time!' Egon, let's go home."

"I can't. I must see about buying the art collection for that museum. My cut will just about take care of my children in Italy."

"How many have you now?"

"Twenty-one."

"I never expected to see you the father of such a family, Egon. I'm turning back. I'm getting out at Breslau and getting a train to Paris and then a boat for home."

"And miss the medical meeting in Prague?"

"It isn't going to be much of a meeting, I feel. Come with me, Egon. Europe has become a rat race in a jungle."

"No, and don't nag at me. I'm dying of hunger."

"Too proud to be insulted by a German waiter, you'd rather gnaw on yourself than on *Fleisch und Fischüberreste und Knochen?*"

Egon sat up straight and lit a long paper-tubed cigarette. "Style is important to me, Edward. I believe a man has to live or die with a certain style. Dignity is about all we can truly have in this world. Everything else is decay and death."

"Hunger is making you morbid."

"Or thoughtful. . . ."

The train was running now under massed, hanging wires and past great brick factories working full blast in the night. A city was near. The mounds of brick and rubble began to show signs of life. Faces, poverty, and debris cluttered up each side of the right-of-way. Soon came better, stronger buildings and massed people moving off into the darkness, the bark of trucks, the passage of traffic. They were in the city. Doctor Sontag pulled down his two bags and tested their straps.

"I'm getting off, Egon. I guess I'll have to carry these myself. No German would carry a Jew's bags."

Egon yawned and picked up the French art magazine again. "I see Mike Kozloff is having an art show in Holland."

Doctor Sontag grinned and took his umbrella and hat from the rack. "I don't know if Mike is a good painter, but he's a loud one."

"His work baffles me," said Egon. "It's so ugly and strong. But then I suppose I'm old enough now to be old-fashioned. I don't know much about art any more beyond that old man, Picasso."

German trains stopped without a jar, carefully and with a polite hiss. The station began to walk past the compartment windows. The train became rigid and men in SS uniforms lined the platform, their faces under their hooded caps green in the station lights. An *Arbeitsdienst* regiment of young boys, with cropped heads, marched past them carrying polished shovels on their strong shoulders under a banner labelled *Kraft durch Freude.*

"Good-bye, Egon," said Doctor Sontag.

"Take care and hold on to your passport."

They shook hands and Doctor Sontag staggered out. Egon sat awhile and then closed the magazine and lit another cigarette. A lorry had backed up to the station platform, and bowed, chilled men in worn clothing were being crisply moved into it by the SS men. The shabby men numb and hopeless, the SS men splendid and tall. There was no visible brutality, just the hunted and the hunters. A little man with a busy moustache, looking like Charlie Chaplin, came along the train, tapping the train wheels with a long-handled hammer.

352

Under a banner reading *Bolschewismus ist Juden Radikale Herr-schaft* a fat, warm woman was handing out plates of blood sausage to farm boys in army uniforms. They ate quickly, their wet, blue eyes stealing a glance of admiration at the SS men from time to time.

An old newspaper fluttered across the station floor. *Deutsches Selbstbestimmungsrecht!* (German Right of Self-determination), shouted the headline. A uniformed station master picked up the newspaper, shocked at this soiling of a clean railroad station. Doctor Sontag passed, carrying his bags; round-shouldered, slow-moving, he disappeared into the steaming waiting room. The lorry rattled off and the SS men went to eat blood sausage and *Bauernwurstl.*

Egon felt ill. He wondered if only from hunger. The door opened and a lean man under the cap of the élite *Schwarze Korps* came in and sat down, asking politely if the place was empty. He had two books with him. Egon read their titles: Heine's *Poems* and a new book labelled *Schicksalsgemeinschaft* (Fate by Horror). . . .

East of Lexington Avenue in new York City the art galleries take on a shabby look. They are not on the ground floor. One must walk up some chipped, brown-stone steps, or pass through a paint-supply store, or go around a dank, dark tearoom. The Nu World Gallery was a flight up, two rooms back, and lit from a bank of windows made with the wire glass badly cracked in spots. The one-sheet catalogue merely said "Paintings by Mike Kozloff. Oils. Watercolours. Drawings."

It was eleven o'clock in the morning. A thin, pretty girl, with black hair cut away from her long, slim neck, sat in a green silk robe at a modern plywood desk, folding the catalogue. The paintings were huge, strong, and oddly coloured, but powerful with a wide range of peculiar tones. There was no direct moulding in the figures, no effort to see them in the round. They were powerfully drawn with merging planes of remarkable, yet somewhat odd colour. There was no technical trickery or polished good taste and charm. It was a new kind of art. And, of course, as yet, neglected.

Mike Kozloff came into the gallery. He needed a haircut, sleep, and a little money. He was dressed, as usual, in workingmen's clothes, like a paperhanger or house painter. He looked over the gallery and grinned, hands in pockets.

"Turning them away I see, Olga?"

"We did have two people at nine . . . thought it was a second-hand furniture sale."

"It is, kid, it is. Furniture for the inner man, the human animal. Look at these walls and shake in terror at man. Look at these forms and pity us . . . pity us all."

"Have you had breakfast, Mike?"

"No." He sat down suddenly and chewed on a finger-nail. "Don't pay any attention to me. I've been playing one-night stands, talking like Van Gogh and Gauguin. Playing the rebel artist with the biting tongue. I'm scared, Olga . . . scared as hell. Suppose I paint and paint and no one ever knows it?"

Olga pushed the folded pile of catalogues aside. She tenderly took his hand in hers. "I'll always love you, Mike."

"I don't want love, just like a stud bulldog. I want to paint. I want to paint and I want to show them the world as they've never seen it before. I want to go out with sunlight on my fingers and smear it on their faces. Can't they see it?"

"No, baby," she said, kissing him on the mouth. "They can't because they never have. No original talent was ever seen for what it was. Fifty years from now a Kozloff will be properly cheered."

"A hell of a note. Don't be good to me, Olga. I'm a heel. I'll only let you down. Again."

"Let's close shop and I'll buy you a breakfast."

Mike said, "At least a blind man once came to feel Cézanne's paintings when no one else would. All right, let's go find some blind and crippled people. Let's invite some of the neighbourhood whores in . . . give 'em free use of the place for their trade if they bring in anybody who also wants to look at a painting. Hell. I'll even sketch 'em in action as an added attraction."

"Oh, shut up, Mike—for whining out loud."

Olga combed her hair quickly. A little man with a derby hat and a small, paper-wrapped package came timidly in, cleared his throat, and looked up at the paintings. He glanced at Mike, then at Olga, and went over to the other wall. He looked quickly at the paintings and started for the door.

Mike faced him. "Well?"

The little man grinned weakly in self-defence. "Hm, interesting."

He went out quickly. Mike looked at Olga and began to laugh.

"Interesting! I'll paint him just like that. The face of Norman Corwin's lousy little, timid man—that fake—looking for something." Mike was excited and happy again, all his troubles and doubts suddenly forgotten. "Sure, the shabby half-oval shape of the derby, the face in off-reds like a primitive, half-wit Indian painting, and the feeble little

354

hands, like tired roots in sterile sand. Half horse-manure—half Walt Whitman. Come on, kid. I'll take the breakfast now."

In Westchester live people called by local newspapers "the young married set". One house is a great deal like another. Peter's was one of those timbered fieldstone houses in the better part of the newest section, "Paradise Estates", on the outskirts of Larchmont. A house with a bit of garden, a bit of style, and a large portion of modern built-in comfort. And a tendency to become unfashionable after ten or fifteen years. Peter left this house every weekday morning at nine, was at the station by nine-ten. He caught the nine-twelve, a copy of the *Herald Tribune* under his arm, and was in New York at his desk at the Off Shore Oil Company by ten. A breakfast of orange juice, toast, two eggs, and very strong coffee churned in his stomach, tasting for some reason of the strong toothpaste he used. The office was in the Graybar Building on Lexington Avenue—the furniture had once cost a great deal.

For some years now he had done the same thing every weekday morning, except for the month he and Lucy spent in Florida, the two weeks' vacation in Maine and those huge weekends that made the liquor bill a major problem on the first of every month. *Life* magazine once modestly photographed him as a "typical, middle-class American reader".

The Off Shore Oil Company was one of those small holding companies, part of the great Gates business and industrial empire. Peter, as president of the company, had little to do but mark up the wide-edged proofs of its advertising—the words "clean rest rooms"—with a big blue pencil. He also listened for hours to singing jingles for their radio spot announcements:

> *"Off Shore Oil is at a boil*
> *To drive you away from strife and toil!*
> *Say Off Shore clearly*
> *Your car loves it dearly . . .*
> *Off Shore, Off Shore, Off Shore!"*

When Ike Sontag—vice-president and company engineer—was in town, they had lunch and smoked cigars till two, and went to an art show or a motorboat exhibit. But Ike was usually off somewhere exploring oil shale or leasing drilling rights.

"How do you stand it?" Ike asked, picking up his drink.
"Stand what?"

"The office routine, the trains every morning and night."

"I don't mind it."

"Those crumbly fashionable people trying to look like ads in the *Saturday Evening Post.*"

"You're wrong—they're trying to look like ads in the *New Yorker.*"

"All right. I need another drink. Peter, I guess it's all right for you. It would stink for me."

"You expect too much, Ike."

"From what?"

"From life."

"This is worse than a bull session in prep school."

"My turn. Bourbon again?"

"Bourbon."

"Waiter, two more, the same."

"Let's stay in town, Peter. Call Lucy and I'll dig up a dame. Let's get stinking and see some fun in Harlem."

"Lucy hates Harlem and she's on the wagon this week, I think."

Ike set down his glass carefully. "Habits, that's all you've got—good, solid habits."

"I suppose so. Wait until I get some money together. I'll buy a fifty-foot ketch and put Lucy and Joey in it and sail off down the coast to Florida."

"Sell out your stock now and do it."

"Can't, its down. Gates doesn't let it make any money."

"Another?"

"I don't want to miss the five-twenty."

Once a week Peter lunched with his father over near Third Avenue. The rest of the time he ate in a timbered cellar with dress-manufacture and department-store buyers. He usually left his office at four-fifteen, bought all the evening papers, and caught the four-twenty-seven to Larchmont. He usually sat in the third car, fifth seat, near the window, on the right. He felt angry, exploited, and lost, if this seat was taken by a stranger. The first few years of their marriage Lucy had delivered and picked him up at the station. But now, after five years, the third-best car, a protesting, lazy Ford, was left in a parking lot till his train came in (the maroon Caddy roadster and the big black Buick were house cars, and Lucy was thinking of a cute station wagon).

On the way home he read the papers, at least those parts of them that related to the radio news he had heard at noon, and refolded them carefully for Joey, his son, who was an avid comic-strip reader. Peter always wore a hat, a fresh shirt every day—but in summer he wore no vest.

Joey went to a private school that delivered him at his front gate about the same time Peter got home. Joey was six and raised hamsters and had a liking for Western movies. Peter usually took him to the morning show Saturdays, and they sat through old Disneys and Bugs Bunnies and Buck Joneses and Hopalong Cassidys while they both got sticky hands from a vile popcorn. Joey was a happy, rather silent child. He grinned as if amused a great deal.

Dinner was at seven, after Joey was in bed, and Peter had gone out to silence Roger, the small, copper-coloured hound who lived in the yard. Dinner was formal, no black tie of course, but full settings and the best glass and china, served by a coloured girl who, as Lucy often said, "was either earning enough to pay for her degree at Hunter, or a moron secretly smoking reefers in her room". They all adored Lucy but they never lasted long enough to get properly fitted for their uniforms. Lucy treated them with a high hand. "Being a Southern girl, I know *all* about *them*."

Lucy herself never appeared until dinner, for she usually spent the afternoon at their club—the second-best Larchmont club—or on the course, or at the bridge table. The first year or so of their marriage Peter had gone up to their bedroom (they shared a master bed) on getting home. But she often had a headache or the sun had affected her eyes and she needed a "nice quiet little ole hour or so". The truth was, Peter now knew, that she was usually drunk before dinner. For clubs, golf links, and bridge parties were near bars.

"Hello, hon," said Lucy, dropping her bags of golf clubs in the hall. "Great little day in the office?"

"No. How was golf?"

"Banged my best iron on a rock."

"Too bad."

"You mix the cocktails?"

"All right, Lucy."

"Easy on that grenadine. I think we're gettin' bad liquor."

"How would you know? You never had any in your father's house."

"——," said Lucy.

"Anything for tonight?"

"Ask me after dinner. I'm tired, powerful tired."

"Joey in his room?"

"Let 'im stay there, Peter. I'm in no condition to hear him scream cheerfully over the evening comics."

"Didn't you ever read *The Captain and the Kids* once?"

"Who can read? I'm just pore white trash."

Peter got the shaker and mixed the new drinks up very strong. They sat down facing each other and drank quickly to get the bite fast. Peter always promised himself he'd drink them slower, but somehow he never did.

"Got a dividend there, mister?"

"It's the heel, mostly ice."

"Where the hell is dinner? Servants aren't worth the powder to blow 'em up these days."

Peter began to mix another batch. Lucy waited and drank the refilled glass and took off her shoes and rubbed her silk toes together.

"I'm givin' her five more minutes and then I'm goin' in there. What is she doing, roastin' an elephant?"

Dinner was a ritual with Lucy. Tanned, classically beautiful, large, skilfully healthy, she sat at Peter's table like a processed goddess and goddamned the cook who couldn't make a good, wilted lettuce salad "Any old darkie down home can beat sixteen of these Harlem shines sassin' back their betters."

Peter had long since given up trying to correct Lucy's powerfully bigoted ideas. He blamed them on her rigid upbringing, the early suppression of her natural sexual impulses for so long a time, her powerful golf strokes, and those assorted endowed bums, the people she lived with all day in barrooms, club porches, and cocktail parties. Their feeble Noll Card (Noel Coward) chatter, their low boiling point made them, Peter felt, poor excuses for human beings.

Dinner, usually a colourful array of tasteless food copied out of the better camera angles in women's magazines, was as slick and characterless as the publications themselves. Dinner was soon over with. They both had big balloons of brandy. Movies saw them twice a month. Big, glorious Hollywood projects, rich in detail, sensually glib and full of good tunes and paced so fast no one could bother even to dislike them. They forgot them as soon as they left the theatre. Once or twice they had tried French and Italian pictures. But Lucy had been bored and left in the middle, muttering, "Those lousy, Red bastards and their arty crap, honey. I don't think it smart to go to a picture to just read titles." He found her later in a bar, a sailor out of a New London submarine base eyeing her breasts with delight and trying to buy her all the Bourbon in the joint. They saw all the "hit" Broadway plays. They admitted the theatre was pretty dull.

They played bridge on Tuesdays, bowled on Fridays, and twice a year gave Joey a party, either on the lawn under their own oaks or indoors, in winter, in his battered, happy blue room, with the stupid, old-fashioned wallpaper full of giants, witches, pink rabbits, and cows leaping over the moon. Joey tacked cowboys and animals over the fairyland figures. The children Joey met were as carefully screened by Lucy as if the job were an FBI project. Greeks and Italians, naturally, even with money, were kept out. Irish need not even attempt to enter. Their development was restricted, in some clever way, to "Caucasians not of Oriental migration", so there was no danger of Jews. Joey was a fine child and an active, bright one. Lucy retired from every party for him early and pulled down her shade and swallowed a little brandy, and lay down with a wet cloth over her head. She was a good mother and believed one should not baby a child but leave it on its own a great deal.

The Perrys were well off. As well off as their set, a group of smart, well-combed, barbered Americans in advertising, bonds, yachts, chain stores, publishing, management or even (ah, these artists) industrial designing. No one made less than twenty thousand dollars a year, or spent less than twenty-five. Almost all were in debt, behind in alimony, thinking of embezzling, committing suicide, or running off with a large-boned blonde. Of such stuff were their dreams made.

Peter was a sort of outsider among them. He was not considered fully white, Protestant, or American. One grandfather, after all, was tarred with either Italian or Jewish blood and his father had done time. Peter himself was not always the full, true Republican on many natural, manly, and conservative issues ("that crippled s.o.b. in the White House"). But Lucy, being the daughter of the old man Gates, made up for everything. There was the Gates money (lots of it), the Gates holdings, and the Gates press agents who held "Sugarlips" Gates up to the world as the wisest, bravest, most kindly example of free-wheeling, rugged individualism the world had ever seen. Fair to everyone he paid his son-in-law no more than any of his other presidents. Of course, Peter did hold ten per cent of the stock in the company. And some day Gates would allow a real dividend. "Just wait," he would say, in his Sunday School voice. "I think of your future."

It took Peter several years to come secretly around to the idea that his marriage was not, perhaps, a romantic cloudbed, and this, his life, was not, in all details, the fulfilment of his boyhood dreams. Yet he could see no way where he had gone wrong, no place where he had sold out to anything sordid and dishonest.

They had been fifty miles away at a dance. Now they were home and Peter's arms ached from the long drive. Lucy stepped out of her evening gown, left it obscene and glittering on the floor. She kicked off her silver slippers, shrunk herself out of her slip and girdle, and stood there in her stockings, scratching the girdle marks on her white hips, the rest of her very tanned and smooth.

"Great little band."

"Too loud for me."

"Your samba, Peter, could stand a little dry-docking."

She pulled off her stockings and folded her arms over her breasts and frowned. "Gained half a pound last week. Getting to be an old bag."

"Put out the light."

"I oughta put on some skin cream."

Peter dozed off the light in his eyes. He came awake as she sank into the bed. The light switched out.

"Not a bad dance."

"Um."

"Peter!"

"Great little dance."

"You got Eskimo blood?"

"Great little dance."

"Huh? Oh."

"That's better."

"Want a light?"

"No."

"No what?"

"You're the talkingest man."

Later he felt almost tender and ashamed of himself. He wanted something; he didn't know what to ask for. He groped as if begging human contact. . . .

"I better put that skin cream on."

He was, he admitted to himself, beyond the faddy, childish nonsense about passionate love. True love, eternal—that was all right for a puking college boy in love with Rose Gelhorn. But the real thing was neither as spiritual nor, frankly, as painful. Lucy was, within the limitations of the female sex, a good wife.

Sensual, heavily earnest, the first few years of their life together had been like a powerful drug to him. She certainly (he hoped) had been faithful to him. They looked good together—tall, tanned, muscled people—and danced well and never went out of their way to get on each other's nerves. It was, of course, to be expected that, once free of her father's pious home, Lucy would broaden her interests, gain new horizons. She cut her hair and shingled it like a boy at first. She bought too sheer clothes and flimsy, tight underwear. She liked to roam the house, naked and brown, her powerful shoulders, tight stomach, and fine legs as beautiful as a Greek art object of the best period.

She told everyone how wildly she had broken with her puritan past; and, of course, no frenzy, no orgy of energy left her anything but a puritan. She dressed smartly, daringly, with colour and dash. She drank. but then, Peter felt, wasn't it true all Southerners drank. Tiny red lines were appearing around her nose. Her hand was not as steady as it had once been, but her golf game did not let her down. She became a gobbler of sleeping pills and a user of much, scented lard from Fifth Avenue shops at twenty dollars an ounce. People at the Colony knew her. She served God at St. Thomas', in the city, twice a year.

Joey had been the result of an unsanitary Maine vacation far from the luxuries and the scientific care of their normal life. Lucy had, she admitted, had a dreadful time of it. Tied to her porch, or deep, soft chair, a measured two drinks a day, a fancy doctor (much beyond Peter's means) and a quick delivery at Doctor's Hospital. Peter had loved the boy from the first sight of the thin, black-topped baby twenty minutes old, yawning a red, toothless face up from behind two layers of vita-rayed plate glass. Lucy had fought to call him Beauregard, but Peter had insisted on Joseph, and, naturally, Joseph Beauregard Perry it had been. The idea of any more children drove Lucy to cursing. She used to parade naked before Peter, her firm hands on her hard belly, pushing at her flesh, pulling at the little slack, and shouting, "I'm no goddamn niggrah mammy filling a cabin full of pickaninnies, or a filthy shoat littering all over the town. I'll never get these wrinkles out of mah belly. I'm as loose as a bitch hound after sixteen pups! You want any more children you just go adopt yourself some little ole babies someplace!"

Lucy did not have one of those professional "honey chile" voices. To Peter, sometimes, it seemed odd to hear this powerful, husky voice using the phrases of a limp, Southern belle out of popular fiction. She had not spoken like that, he remembered, in her father's house, but had acquired this practical, working Southern accent from the golf pro at their club (a gentleman, Peter found out later, from Ohio who had spent five years on a Georgia chain gang).

Peter himself was under the impression that he was a very lucky man in this century's turmoil.

The tall, shabby man crossed to the fat German waiter. Ralph was not really badly dressed. He wore his old sports jacket and his baggy, grey flannel pants and once very good tie with a dignity that matched his greying hair and his ageing, still handsome features. He came out of the dark entry of the little chophouse and looked over the few white-covered tables. Peter, at the bar, saw his father and rose, a Martini in his hand, and came over to him carrying his glass.

"Hello, Pa. I got here a little early."

Ralph laughed, his weathered face crinkly with wrinkles, and put his arm around his son. "Little trouble with the truck. Tires going."

"Let me have Off Shore Oil send you a set of tires on the cuff."

"Thanks, but I'm running the budget my own way."

"How's Mother?"

"Fine. And Joey, and Lucy?"

Peter grinned at his father. "Dandy. Here's our table. Otto, Mr. Perry's usual gin and tonic, right?"

They met once a week for this lunch in a little rundown chophouse that Ralph had known in his youth. Peter admired his father. He thought him one of the best of all living people. Prison had mellowed Ralph, perhaps even given him a fuller understanding of life. Prison had left certain of its marks, of course. There was a mood about Ralph now. He had, for some reason, perhaps of penance (who knows these things?), kept his hair close-cropped. But now it was more white than blond.

Sons-in-law of bank presidents, who have to go to jail, find new jobs open to them. Ralph had taken the little left to him and retreated to Blue Point, Long Island, with Alice. They bought a run-down, little house on the edge of Great South Bay. Ralph, having little to do but smoke his pipe, had rebuilt a small motorboat and gone into the oyster-shipping business. Perry Bluepoint Oysters at first were unknown, but as Ralph put down his own beds and studied the art of oyster culture and imported a good Maryland spawn, in time, by hard work, driving his own truck, and laughing at the need of more than four hours of sleep a night, he had a small business. Anyway, it kept him out of doors and busy fighting off the starfish. Alice helped in the dredging boat and got the idea of canning their best oysters in a big blue-and-gold can: Perry's Premier Bluepoints. The more snobbish shops carried them now and *Gourmet* magazine spoke of their extra price with a certain pride.

Ralph looked across at his smartly dressed son—the fine blue tailoring befitting the president of an oil company, the school tie, the faint cerulean-blue shirt with the thin, navy-blue stripes. Ralph secretly missed his old tailor.

The old German waiter, scowling as usual, put down a dozen opened oysters on ice at each place. Peter grinned and Ralph looked at the mollusks with pride. "Prime, extra-big Perrys."

Peter dipped one up from its bed on the pearly shell on his tiny fork and bathed it in the proper sauces and juices as called for, his father watching him closely. Peter swallowed the spicy glob and smiled and flexed his throat muscles.

"I'd know a Perry oyster any place."

Ralph said, "It's foolish to get so worked up over oysters, but I suppose you feel that way about oil."

"Peter shook his head. "No. All I see is the advertising copy now and our damn radio scripts. The truth is I'm afraid to admit I hate it."

"I never hated the banking business. I guess for a Jew I was a real snob, still am a little bit. I liked the game of it. The big polished bank, the private offices. You remember my office, Peter? You used to come there as a little boy and press all the buttons and write with a big, gold pen. . . ."

"Of course I remember your office. How is Grandfather?"

"Old, very old. In a way, he's happy now he's living with us. But he fought coming to us. He's a little odd at times. Still think's he's a bank president and living at Pentland and it's still 1928. The bank let him go with a pat and a small pension."

Peter watched the waiter remove the empty shells. "A lot has happened in the last eleven years. Grandfather seems to have slept through them. In his way Charles Pentland was a great man. He outlived his time. Maybe I have his faults."

"Nonsense. Nicole comes over from Port Washington with the kids. He likes being a grandfather. But his memory is bad. Nicole adores him."

"Must have Nicole and Tom out for dinner sometime. You and Mother, too. But Lucy is so involved in this damn golf tournament. Well, later in the fall—we'll all go down to Princeton for the football games. The Colonel is coming east for the season. He's been selling his stock in the company. I hope he doesn't go broke again."

"Louis?" Ralph smiled. "Papa loved him so. Sam tried to get him to settle down with him but the Colonel said, 'Damn farming.' He was a cattleman and in oil."

"He dislikes the New Deal, a regular Roosevelt-hater."

They ate their way through the roast and the potato pancakes and had black coffee and pie. And after lunch, brandy. They talked of the family and talked of each other; wondered about Egon in Poland with the war talk in the air. They refused to talk too much about Hitler. He was something filthy and insane and rather comic and not to be brought up at a friendly family lunch. Let the menace with the Charlie Chaplin moustache remain just beyond the horizon.

After lunch Peter ordered two large Havana cigars and they sat smoking until two o'clock. They parted, talked of their meeting next week, and Ralph went off to get his truck, a tall, lean and ageing man in well-worn, well-cut clothes.

Peter stood at the curb looking down at his smouldering cigar. He threw it into the gutter, ignored the come-on signs of a pink taxi, and decided to see a French picture. Raimu perhaps. He sat through *The Baker's Wife* twice, missed his train, of course, and got home ten minutes before seven.

He let himself into his house, worried by what explanation he would have to give that would be acceptable. He hung his hat and coat up carefully in the hall closet and put the bundle of newspapers down where Joey would find them in the morning. The coloured girl of the the moment was placing crystal water glasses on the table.

"Mrs. Perry down yet?"

"No, sir, she hasn't come down yet."

Peter went up the softly carpeted steps past the framed prints of American barns and wheat fields by a school of "artists" he rather disliked. Wedding gifts. He tapped on their bedroom door. "Lucy?"

There was no answer. He opened the door and went into the dark bedroom. The black sleeping shades were down and little light leaked into the room except from the hall. He tripped over something and found the light button. At his feet was an empty Bourbon bottle. For some reason he thought, this isn't at all like the cheerful whisky advertising in *Life*. There was another empty bottle on the big, crumpled rosewood bed, next to Lucy, who, in only her sheer slip, was lying on her back, snoring, her hair tangled in her face. The room smelled of whisky, and a close, warm personal odour—the male smell of an animal in rut? Peter opened one of the windows wide and returned to the bed. He called, "Lucy," but she only licked her lips and turned over on her side. Then she groaned.

Peter wet a towel and put it on her head. She moaned again and mumbled something. Peter looked over the room. He sniffed the air. He knew he lacked the courage to ask the maid if Lucy had come home from the tournament alone. Perhaps he didn't want to know.

Lucy kept to her room the next day—"a little ole sick headache." Peter emptied the liquor cabinet, the bar in the den, and put the bottles in his car, where they rattled for weeks. Lucy stayed in bed for two days, then sat in the sun porch for an afternoon, and said her eyes were hurting her. Perhaps she needed glasses.

364

At dinner that night she asked for a cocktail. Peter ignored her. Later she became very mean and ironic, and Peter listened without saying anything. Two days later the golf pro drove her home very late, explaining to Peter she couldn't really be trusted to drive the Caddy on those sharp turns. "Quite a bun on."

Peter called in Doctor Bruden, who had been their doctor since Joey had had a bad ear one summer. Lucy left the next day for an expensive milk farm near New Canaan that had been photographed in *Vogue*. In a month she was back, thinner, browner, more active, and with a great dislike of Larchmont. She talked of moving to California. "Bel Aire and Brentwood have fine golf courses. I had an aunt in Pasadena."

One afternoon during the football season Peter got a call from the Mountain View cabins outside of New Haven. The owner of the cabins explained to Peter that the lady was hung over and didn't make much sense, but they had found Peter's office address in her bag. The Caddy and her luggage were gone for good. This time they tried a small, well-recommended place on West One-Hundred-and-third Street for two months. Bland diet, bathrobes, and locks on the doors.

CHAPTER V

It was a peculiarly luminous, yellow landscape. Rigidly Teutonic. One of those Munich factory buildings, in that ugly modern style so much favoured by the Munich school of piano-box forms. A huge wedge-shaped affair that looked like an art gallery or a motion-picture studio. It had once been used to manufacture modern furniture, and its vast work rooms were now busy with desks. Many minor officials of the Gestapo did tons of paper work under its huge plate-glass windows and stark, off-grey walls. In the cellars where the timber-drying and paint rooms had been, several very efficient torture chambers with sensitive perceptions to moods had been set up, and after a while a bear-pit odour drifted up from them; a stinking, choking odour that the building never got rid of. The *Obergruppenführers* under the roof grew to hate it.

Only prisoners of importance were kept and tortured and interviewed at the factory: the highest Communists, Catholics, Jews who still had foreign exchange, and German military men suspected of loving the Kaiser's son or denounced as planning an attempt on the Leader's life.

The horror, the skilled evil, the remarkable breaking and grinding that went on in this factory was a satisfying, scientific thing, neatly trimmed with a personal sadism and devilish ingenuity that made it the most ghastly spot on earth. The guards sang "Endkampf gegen England" and shrugged their shoulders.

The high-ranking officers of the Gestapo lived in the beautiful club rooms and steam baths that a once trusting owner had built on the roof of his factory. They were well lit, with great sheets of plate glass looking down ten stories to the well-kept courtyard and the flanking workshops. The building must have pleased its former owner (he died of being dipped first in ice-cold water, then in boiling water . . . for only six hours at a concentration camp). He like to look down at his busy factory, and it always gave him satisfaction to know that he could put machine guns up on the roof garden and fire down on the socialist swine, the workers. He had overlooked, it seemed, the shape of his grandmother's nose.

The big teak and rosewood desk had been moved nearer to the great bank of windows and Kurt Steinbeck, drawn, dried out, his head like an old turtle's under his cobra-like police cap, sat well back in his chair looking over a file of reports. He had changed since those lunches at Egon's villa in Italy. Two naked Jews, a stripped priest, and a Communist with one eye hanging bloody and staring out of its socket faced him at attention. Their dirty flesh sweated, their teeth chattered in battered jaws. They did not dare move. A fly buzzed around them and settled on a goose-pimpled chest scarred with old cigar burns. Not one of the naked men moved. Steinbeck looked up at them but he did not really see them or the *Lustknaben* in uniform behind them. The feeling had long since gone out of it. The emotions, the hate or pity, the pleasure or contempt, had quickly evaporated. He merely functioned now as part of a nation, as a true German. If they had money or information, he screwed the last drop out of them before they were (elsewhere, naturally) flogged to death, scientifically drowned, burned alive, or allowed to scream their way to death from slow and subtle methods—like camphor injected into their testicles. He no longer hated or was interested in them. He wished there were no more of them. Yes, if only they could all evaporate and leave him alone.

He motioned a slim, blond Bavarian in tight, black uniform to the desk. "Why was the transport of Herr Pedlock delayed?"

"He wasn't in our division. Berlin didn't want to give him up. You know, office politics."

"He is here now?"

"Yes."

"Bring him up."

"He hasn't been softened yet," said the Bavarian with a simper. He knew the ropes and wanted to show every detail was taken care of at all times. A flight of Focke-Wolf Furies over the factory made talk impossible for a few moments.

Steinbeck waved the Bavarian off. "Get him."

He looked up at the naked men. How dreadful they were. Such sorry excuses for the divine human form he and Egon had once admired in art. Drawn, sagging, limp, veined, hairy. Pimply, too—what could happen to the sensual flesh—and they smelled so. He waved at them. "Crawl to the other wall and back a hundred times on your stomachs. Go."

There were no whips. No brutal gestures or oaths. They had been well "softened" in some lower hell. Yet, Steinbeck wondered, were the *Lumpn-proltariat* shouting "Horst Wessel" any better?

The naked men fell to the stained rugs quickly and with a thud.

Torture is a dreadful thing, Steinbeck felt. No strong man can hope to come out of it whole. The naked men knew that too, for they had been through the procedure. They obeyed quickly and as alertly as they could. They began to crawl with obscene gestures, on their stomachs, to the far wall. They panted but did not groan. They would go on automatically now, obeying all orders, stirring and moving Steinbeck to thought like those laboratory lobsters in the Roman school with their heads cut off, obeying by instinct after everything else had been blotted out of their minds. How far away were those old days with Egon.

The door opened and Egon Pedlock came in, followed by two guards and the Bavarian. He was a naked monster, great hurt sacks of him, globes of flesh, grossly marked now by skin-cutting whips and deep-festering burns. Blood caked one side of his face. Sharp stumps of teeth cut into his lips. He tried to keep his mouth in a position that would avoid painful contact. His face was expressionless.

He stood there with a certain dignity, a certain strength. It told Steinbeck at once that Egon had not been really softened up. Merely formally beaten to a pulp at arrest as the *Reichskanzler* expected.

Egon stood very still. Steinbeck waved to a chair, wondering if Egon was thinking of those golden Italian times.

"Sit down."

Egon sat down, slowly. Raw, half-rotting skin covered his back and flanks. Steinbeck held out a cigarette.

Egon took it to his painful mouth with broken fingers and the Bavarian politely lit it. The naked men had made one round of their tortured race and were again off in their fearful journey. Egon did not look at them. He smoked slowly, taking down full lungs of tobacco.

"I sent for you," said Steinbeck, "when I saw the report that you had been captured during the fighting in Poland."

Egon said slowly and calmly, "I have only one statement to make. I am an American. I want to contact the American Embassy. We are not at war with the Third Reich."

"You are no longer in Berlin. There is no embassy here. Jews have no nation."

"I have no other statement to make."

"We have, I fear, treated you badly, Pedlock."

Egon smoked his cigarette and carefully tore it loose from a bloody lip cut and looked down on the smouldering tobacco. It was a very bad cigarette. Germans never could like anything but a very stinking leaf. He had been badly battered over the eyes, but now he was focusing his sight again. Poor Kurt. How dreadful he looked. He must hate this kind of work. All the tender moments of the past must hamper the evil of the present.

"You were in charge of an art commission to buy certain paintings for an American museum group, weren't you?"

"Yes, of course."

"Where are these paintings?"

"I have said before they were burned in a bombing raid. They were. A Rembrandt, two Cézannes, and a very fine Goya. Others."

The Bavarian said, "*Verdammte Dummkopf!*"

"Göring wants that very fine Rubens," said Steinbeck, motioning the Bavarian to keep out of it.

"I didn't buy the Rubens. I think it a modern fraud. However, you don't believe that either."

"I am sorry our methods seem so brutal to you. Actually, man is a creature that understands only fear, hunger, and hate. We must get results quickly."

"I'm in no mood to talk of principles."

The Bavarian lifted a hand to slap Egon. Steinbeck shook his head and the Bavarian stepped back. Steamroom scum, thought Steinbeck. The Bavarian was going to cause trouble.

"We must have those paintings."

"Have you ever known me to lie, Kurt? These paintings are of value only in what they once were. They were coloured mud on stale linen. They are destroyed now by your Stukas. Other artists will paint better ones some day. I am not assuming any noble pose. You could have the paintings if I had them hidden. They're ashes."

"I believe you. But what am I to do with you?"

"Shoot me. I would be very thankful. I am tired and I have been very humiliated. It's indecent for man to do this to man."

"That was the wrong thing to say," simpered the Bavarian.

Steinbeck rubbed his left ear. "I could shoot you, but it would be a bad example for them." He pointed to the naked racers, now much slower and groaning out loud. They still crawled, the fearful eye touching the rug, dragging.

"Our enemies must expect fearful deaths or they would no longer dread us. Life is hard, but death must not be too easy. No, I can't shoot you, Egon. You will receive the same treatment as all Gestapo prisoners in your category. You see, we do have a class system, even among prisoners. I do not, cannot, interfere in our normal procedures."

The Bavarian took the cigarette stub from Egon's mouth and put it out in a big, ceramic tray on the desk. One of the naked men on the floor had fainted. The eye dragging from its socket looked wildly across the room. A guard kicked the fallen man. His heavy boots thudded into the thin ribs again and again. The man did not move. The Bavarian shook his head. (He was the only German in the room to come through the war alive, to become governor of an American Zone.)

"He's dead, Lingberg. Up here, we don't get so rough."

Egon was very tired. He looked over the room. That bad German modern, that dreadful, Munich cigar-box art. Even that bank of windows, just sheer blank sheets of plate glass. Making its point by mere bulk alone.

He had just shut his eyes when the door opened and a Gestapo general and his staff came in, tunics unbuttoned, carrying wine bottles and glasses. Egon noticed one carried a book: *Von Winde Verweht*, by Margaret Mitchell.

"*Heil Hitler!*" shouted the General. "My dear Kurt, it is all over. It is reported we have taken Moscow!"

"Good!"

The General and his staff fell into chairs, laughed, and poured champagne for everyone—but everyone. Even the scum! Egon got a slopped tumbler of it.

"To victory," shouted the General. "Everyone drink!" Egon drank. It was vile wine of a bad year. Corked and slightly soured.

The General was making stallion sounds. Steinbeck frowned. "You're sure we've taken Moscow, General?"

The General said crisply, "I said so. Our radio from Hitler's headquarters says so. Let's have a wheelbarrow race. One prisoner on his hands is the wheelbarrow; two prisoners, one to lift each leg, to be the gardeners. You fat one. You're a *real* wheelbarrow. You can have *two* men on each leg!"

Egon stood up. The pain in his eyes was back and he could no longer see details on faces, just shapes. Steinbeck was looking at him, but Egon no longer could make out his expressions. Was he dead-pan, horrified (not likely), sorry, or indifferent? *The villa, those warm nights, the string music from the olive groves, the white linen suits, the red beach at Capri, the dim, blue lights of the grottoes.* Egon cleared his head.

"No," he said. "No, it's not human dignity. . . . No."

The General opened his mouth very wide. "What! Who is this Jew bastard, this circumcised pig! He'll dance and sing, he'll crawl on his belly, he'll whimper and kiss our big toes, one by one! Kurt!"

Egon lunged suddenly at the General but missed. Great red fists hammered on him. Steel fingers clutched at him. He flung them off, panting, the great bulk of the man muscled in dreadful effort. For a moment he was clear. Then he leaped at the glass bank of windows. He came on them hard, even, steady, sure of what he was doing. He went through into the dropping night, huge shards of glass kniving at him. The last thing he remembered was . . . *dignity . . . dignity . . . a man couldn't do . . . it somehow, and lose it . . . that is a man had to go out like a man . . . die . . .*

They took the body away in the morning and burned it in a furnace they had designed to burn human beings scientifically. The Germans used all their furnace ashes then to fertilize little cabbage plants.

Westchester has a special autumn weather. The day was damp and a gritty grey. Chilly. Peter turned on the car heater and the miles of the Parkway dropped behind him, dropped, he felt, as swiftly as the years. And as dully. He was returning home from the memorial service for Egon Pedlock, Egon dead and disposed of in some horrible manner in Germany. The world did not shake with rage—no stranger was roused to fury.

Odd. He had never been in a synagogue before. One of those fumed oak and grey stone vaults supposed to be modelled on the Temple. The Art with its worn Torahs throwing faded red and gold flames in the half-moaning dark, the old men in their fringed payer shawls. And the family and friends in the splintering front pews. His father and mother, dreadfully hurt by the death and its mangling horror. The Sontags. The doctor smaller, whiter, more bent than ever. Etta, big, and sobbing with a gasping, controlled breathing. Ike bent very low and looking at his big fist. The Middle Ages was returned to the Jews.

No, Rose Gelhorn hadn't been there. He hadn't dared ask where she was. Or how. Poor Louis, the Colonel—a dazed collection of tough old joints—not knowing much of what was going on or caring. Wandering, very old. The Kozloffs. A whole tribe almost. With Mike sitting by himself, dressed in working clothes (like a paperhanger or house painter), the full rebel artist, his hair black, uncut, his eyes hunting every movement, every speck of colour. To be a genuine artist and genuine Jew at the same time was almost too much!

Tante Strasser. Over a hundred years old, they said. Eternal. Nothing seemed to change about her. Dried, wrinkled, tall, stern, not talking much any more. Just sitting as if in judgment on them all. And some strangers. Friends of Egon's. Very few.

The little rabbi in his failing chant had said the prayers in Hebrew, and added a few ill-chosen words for the dear departed (whom he had never met). Peter felt a little out of it. This gathering of Jews to which he was connected seemed already a condemned race. The Germans were on the move. This rattle of Hebrew banged over their hurt heads like a warning of worse to come. How he loved them. How great Egon had been in the end, if all the rumours were true. Egon, how his jewel-spotted life had twisted and travelled, how odd and bold it had become. How lost it had once seemed. And something good and fine had come to it. He had worked and been exploited, gone down into the dirt, cared for his lost children, the wild, the filthy, and the mutilated, and had in the end given his life for them. Trying to the last, to collect enough for their bread and rags and thin blankets. Peter remembered the glowing charcoal-heated nights at the villa, the smell of olive oil and *pasta*, the sunsets and the sunrises out of bad art, the rustle of skirts on brown legs in the tall grass, the dew in the garden on hot bodies, even the wisdom and slow talks over the delighful dinner tables. Everything wiped out, blotted out. Egon, a short struggle between two gloomy sleeps, was no more. Cold hate—a hot flow of words and blood-red thinking—had broken him and finished him. There was no poetry in this dying, Peter felt. Words, thoughts, prayers, all expressed to make us forget the horror of the gravecloth, the sharp, slow bite of the grave worm.

They were chanting again in Hebrew. His father bent over him and said, "It's from the Lamentations." Yes, Peter nodded, he remembered the Lamentations. He had read them in Sunday School a long time ago. The King James version, of course. They hadn't sounded like the Hebrew now bubbling up around him. Was he cut off from them so much? Was his merely the world of Larchmont, and Lucy and Joey? Oil, radio advertising, and meals cooked for colour alone?

Mine enemies chased me sore, like a bird, without cause.
They have cut off my life in the dungeon, and cast a stone upon me.
Waters flowed over mine head; then I said, I am cut off.

Remember, O Lord, what is come upon us: consider, and behold our reproach.
Our inheritance is turned to strangers, our houses to aliens.
We are orphans and fatherless, our mothers are as widows.
. . . Our necks are under persecution: we labour, and have no rest. . . .

When it was all over, they stood for a moment in uncomfortable, pressed black on the sidewalk; stood grouped as if for an official picture, in the pitiless light of a grey, New York day. Uncle Sam, his face red with weeping, stood at the curb, head down. Peter went up to him and took his arm.

"How's everything with you, Uncle Sam?"

"It could be worse. Worse. Farming agrees with me. No money, not much of a living in it. But I'm expanding." Sam stopped talking as if he were about to mention Egon and thought better of it. "Yes, we like it. I'm taking over three hundred more acres. Had to get a loan on the family pictures to buy 'em. But a few good seasons and maybe I'll be able to build a gallery for them. You look fine, Peter. Yes, fine."

Uncle Sam began to weep softly to himself and Peter pressed his arm and said good-bye to his mother and father and all the rest and went to find his car in the parking lot. Long ago the Sunday School had smelled of furniture polish and girls' bath powder.

Turn thou us unto thee, O Lord, and we shall be turned; renew our days as of old.

But thou hast utterly rejected us; thou art very wroth against us.

He drove through the shoddy housing of the lower part of the town, crossing to the Hudson River Parkway. The Jews in the street looked depressed and frightened. Peter felt very sorry for them. The tabloids thundered threats from Berchtesgaden. He drove, the wind in his face, until it grew so cold he closed the windows and snapped on the car heater. He turned off toward his house and crossed a fine, neat section of timbered housing, good green lawns—solid bank risks —and children bundled against the chill of fall, playing in the driveways.

He let himself into the house. It was very still. Joey was at school. Lucy was not in the bedroom. He went down to find the nurse, and the cook waved a half-peeled onion at him.

"Nurse's day off. Very fancy she is, too. She left for town at ten o'clock after eatin' a good, fat breakfast. Mrs. Perry? Oh, I tried to keep her upstairs but she got out her golf clubs, and went off. Yes, sir, went off in a hurry."

Peter frowned and the cook frowned back at him. "Golf in the rain?"

They both wondered if Mrs. Perry had gone to a bar someplace, but neither put it into words. It was one of those Larchmont secrets that everyone knew and pretended not to.

"I'm going out," Peter said, re-buttoning his top-coat. "Keep Joey indoors when he comes home."

"Will you be back for dinner?"

373

"I'll be back—we'll have dinner on time."

The cook lifted one corner of her mouth for an answer.

Peter went out and looked over the grey day: a wetter, colder rain with a steady patter. Objects far off were merged and patterned into flat values as in the Japanese prints Uncle Egon had once owned. Peter drove slowly to the club. There were no players on the sodden course. The flags drooped sadly. The rain was coming in on a slant, Knifing the over-green turf and washing against the tan brick walls of the club. Peter went into the bar and had a shockingly bad Martini from the coloured man listening to a muddy track on the radio. He came out and stood rubbing his chin, looking across at the little white house up a lilac-lined lane where the golf pro lived.

He walked up the path and knocked on the scarred white door. He knocked a long time. The door opened and the golf pro stood there, his half-bald, sunburned head staring at Peter, the slopping highball glass in his hand drooling onto the floor. The pro was wearing a T shirt of gay red and yellow striping, and nothing else. He was very drunk.

Peter pushed in past the cup-cluttered hallway and the sporting prints and the warm smell of an oil heater. He walked into the bedroom. Lucy was there on the wide, low studio bed, pouring herself a drink out of a fifth of pinch-bottle. She said, without looking up, "Honey, I've killed the heel of this bottle," and then saw Peter. She tried to cover herself with the sheet, fumbled, and looking up, she suddenly grew angry in self-protection.

"You spying son-of-a-bitch! You no-good, crawling, nasty-minded bastard. Spying on your wife dying of thirst, hunting up just a drink, a little ole drink."

She tried to hide more of her nakedness and made a mess of it. Peter just stood in the doorway of the room staring at her; numb, filled with bitter bile, his throat as tight as a hangman's knot.

Lucy lurched to her feet, dropping all cover.

"That's right, stand there and feel full of virtue, you dirty Jew!"

Something went tight in Peter, some cord that kept him taut and numb, and he suddenly felt a flooding of terror and horror, like a nightmare out of his childhood.

"Only a filthy bastard would break in here like this!"

The golf pro, his face very red, his T shirt crammed now into a pair of soiled tennis flannels, was standing by the cup-crowded fireplace, a steel golf club within reach. He stood swinging the ice cubes in his glass back and forth. Peter paid no attention to him at all. He turned and went slowly out of the house.

"Jewboy!" came in mocking tones from the bedroom.

Jewboy. Jewboy. He stood in the rain. *Dirty Jew bastard.*

He went home in the now raging rainstorm. Joey came home from school. They packed some bags and left. Joey was very happy to go visiting Grandpa on Long Island, and could he, could he go out in the boat and help pull up the oysters?

"We'll see," said Peter calmly in the car, and he pressed his foot down on the gas pedal and hurried more quickly back to the shelter of his childhood.

The shock of being called a Jew, and a dirty one at that, never let up hitting him. Peter Manderson Perry had never thought of himself as a Jew, and here it was close held, like a spiny fish. He was the son of Ralph Perry and Alice Pentland, those Pentlands whose sacred name was part of Boston's glorious history, whose family, in their dignified, holy way, went back into the roots of a great New England culture.

All the way to his father's house he brooded over it. Was he a coward to run and hide? What else could he do? Joey looked at him and Peter ran a hand through his hair and smiled weakly at him.

"Can I go out and help pull up oysters at Grandfather's?"

"Of course."

The real-estate agent opened the front door and let the fat Greek and his wife in ahead of him.

"Yes sir, the old Perry place. Not that it's so old. Solid timbers. Jump on this floor."

The Greek sucked his fat lips and looked over the place. "Toilet downstairs?"

"Four bedrooms upstairs. A great little buy. First mortgage held by a good bank. Feel them drapes."

"Not bad," said the Greek, "but small. I don't know."

"Look, it's a steal. Man and wife broke up. They aren't going to hold out for a real price. Make a fast offer and it's yours."

"All the way upstairs to the toilet, I don't know."

"Mr. Vassilios, let's talk man to man. This is pretty restricted stuff. Of course, we're proud to have the owner of the Better Bargain Stores with us, but it isn't every place that's available in Paradise Estates."

"Well . . ."

"Offer half what it cost to build, you'll get it."

"All right, for half, I'll walk upstairs."

CHAPTER VI

It was a time when anything could happen. Dunkirk. Fireside chats. Bund meetings. And then a shocked realization it would have to be brought to an end.

The Colonel died the day America entered the war. He passed unnoticed except for a few lines in the back pages. Everything else in the newspapers was reserved for pictures of the sunken fleet resting, burnt out and torn, in the mud at Pearl Harbour. The Colonel died at two in the morning on the sidewalk in front of a disorderly house in the better section of Denver, his heart stopping suddenly after a night of visits and pleasures. Someone had found him and pulled off his boots. They were handstitched cowboy boots of good leather with solid-silver trimmings, and so he died, unfortunately with his boots off, shattering a Western tradition he was so very proud of.

Mike Kozloff volunteered and joined the Air Force and spent the war in an English field painting large, nude women and Mickey Mouses on the noses of Flying Fortresses (named *Dirty Gertie* or *Minnie*). In between he flew twenty-two missions and got a fragment of flak in his right elbow. He switched his paint brush to his left hand and confused the art critics even more.

Ike Sontag joined up and fought in North Africa and Sicily and all through the murder and mismanagement of the Italian campaign. He wore the Purple Heart, and was busted as a top kick for breaking into an officers' mess when his squad had been for two days in the cold mud and had gone hungry for a week. Peter found him reading the *Stars and Stripes* the day they all entered Rome.

They found a nearly clean café and drank bad red wine.

"It's a great war," said Ike. "Only I don't like great wars."

"What kind do you like?"

"Old ones in history books."

"It's been pretty hard."

"Stupid stuff, this climbing up the boot of Italy," said Ike. "Who dreamed it up? This isn't the main battleground."

"Oh, forget the war."

"All right. How's the old Beagle crowd taking it?"

Peter grinned. "Stinky is a major. All brass and pink tailoring. Been wounded twice. Married, some cowgirl from a rodeo, and has a kid. Named him after me. Peter Smith. You been naming any kids?"

Ike shook his head. "Hell, no. You ever smell any of them Arab girls in North Africa? No, I'm just serving time. Just serving time. Funny, war isn't like the novelists say, is it? All that grim grace under pressure that they talk about. Do you think they were all lying?"

"I don't think so, Ike. They're simple souls. It's nice for them to see it through the eyes of Marx or an erection, but I guess this is a tougher war. How's the family?"

"Fine. Etta is driving a Red Cross car. The rest stay busy. Pretty busy."

Peter wanted to ask about the rest. He didn't. He ordered more red wine and they sat, very tired, and watched the jeeps pass and the dirty kids beg for cigarettes and chewing gum. Far off some guns boomed and sun shone down on the old stone street. They sat and drank wine and looked at each other's cropped heads and muddy uniforms. They sat there until the MP's with their casual, brutal faces drove them off the main streets as being improperly clothed in battle dress.

Peter went to London, where an old headmaster from Beagle was on the invasion staff, and he remembered Peter and put him in charge of a daffy crew that was turning out German newspapers with startling news items, to be dropped over German cities. For some reason Peter was supposed to be an expert on the Germans. Later he found out that the advertising agency head that handled the Off Shore Oil account was also on the staff and was merely trying to butter up a client.

Peter used to grin when he thought of it. He was well out of Off Shore Oil, with no money and no future. A divorced man with a son growing up fast and not much chance of finding a decent job. He knew almost nothing about anything practical.

The war had not impressed Peter as anything but organized murder. He had been wounded twice and suffered in three bungled assaults in which the heroic action of the troops and the hugeness of their supplies had atoned for the bad staff work. He knew now this was a war like all wars, cluttered up with good, solid reason for fighting it. He never admitted to himself how he really felt about it. He was an American and he was with other Americans and he hoped it was a war to settle everything, and keep the Germans tied down for a long time. Peace would be just ahead, a fine, golden peace with no worries and no problems. Oh, dreamer in the Italian mud!

War didn't mean as much to him as it had meant to his grandfather, or his father. They were both men who had often been old-fashioned romantics in their way and had suffered blood and fever and dirt and horror because of the values of their world and the results of the wars, and their rewards had seemed clear. Peter felt none of this. War had become the grinding up of tired men and the managing of complex machines. As he rose from Lieutenant to Captain, from Captain to Major, he saw that, in the end, the men with the guns in their hands would, at the last moment as usual, have to go in and win it, for all the machines. His chest was filled with ribbons and he had a dandy scar on his leg.

He used to lie in the Italian mire on his rubber sheets and two thin blankets and think about it all, and get no place. He was thinking again of Rose Gelhorn, and that was bad after all these years, now in his middle age. This fixation was a foolish thing that should have worn out a long time ago. Lucy he never thought of any more. She was married to a Carolina fox hunter, now a full Colonel with the Signal Corps, and between bad benders and hasty cures and D.A.R. conventions she was beating big, social drums as a Washington hostess.

When the German 88's fired all night, and the mud near Rome was like ice, Peter used to shiver and feel lonely and lost. Being alone is a madness for which there is nothing to take or say, he used to think. You are blood brother to all these tired shapes around you and when you have gone into battle with someone, always after, you will feel you need them. And they made you lonely now, thinking of how, later, it will be without them. You taste the bitter brownness of fast living in this discordant pandemonium of muddled horror. Almost, as Uncle Egon used to say, the everything of nothing, the nothing of everything. It's the dark, it's the enemy army in the abbey above us. Morning will change it all. Maybe it will. For good, quickly.

You rise before dawn, and stand leaning on your jeep, wiping tears of dew from the yellow steel. . . . You run a hand across it and the machine-gun belts—and you have found something out. Something they didn't say in the churches or the books at Princeton full of yolky optimism. I show you loneliness and the end of loneliness. The Germans have booby-trapped the village.

The pickets are beginning to drift in, firing as they fall back. The world awakens after a night of restlessness into an exotic coarseness. The mouth is full of terror. The helmet is torn and frayed.

The war went on. The men lost tents. It never looked like the end of the war in Italy. Years seemed to pass. Peter let his hair grow long over his tanned ears and a full square beard appeared on his face, like Willie's in *Stars and Stripes*. He was wounded at a river, sitting by a fire eating soggy griddlecakes and brandy. The bullet hit his right shoulder and stayed there. Three days later they removed it, but he no longer cared, and spent a month in a hospital at Naples.

He went back into battle and saw the mountains and lay at night again, thinking.

When you were a child you were often lonely and you said wait until you grew up and got a girl. That would end it, but it didn't. . . . Being in the army and seeing places and many faces . . . that didn't end it, and you damned well knew, like most soldiers, you're going to be very lonely, at times, till you die. With maybe some good times and songs and fun in between. Suddenly you know you've learned something about life's diplomatic subtlety. So you smile and to-morrow maybe you meet the panzers on your flank; they have been coming in all night across the creek near the stone village full of ghosts.

Yes, with an army at your back and an army spread before you in the night, you are still lonely. Singularly contradictory, isn't it? You know now perhaps no one can creep inside you and warm you and you know what you feel and how you feel it. The lonely are those men who think, and the sad ones are all men who feel. Who said that in one of Old Joseph's books? And the drink is good for an hour, the battle will carry you along with its terror and speed for a day or more. But when it is over and done with, when the drinking doesn't bite, when the fighting does not hold you facing a German, you will settle down and sit in the grass and park your gun carriers with the others, and rub your tired, dirty toes and feel lonely again.

Sleeping here on your side on the ground, staring from the row of helmets to the deep pool of darkness out there, you will be alone. And when the marching and gunning are over, you will go someplace and call it home, and there the lonely feeling will engulf you. Later Peter was ashamed of this thinking and tried not to remember. But it was very real to him—much realer than the bitched-up war.

Now that I've been there, Peter used to say to himself marching up, it's all a lot of talk, what they say about it. Battle is nothing but trying to stay alive and getting the other mug; and for all you see of the whole battle, you might just as well be seeing a river from the moon. Only, you remember the morning dew on the ox-churned fields. It wet your pants legs and you slept damply in a barn smelling of wine vats.

A battle is one field and a hillside and a tank coming at you, and you run around in circles and then you pant and when it's near you, you come up fast and push in the hand bombs in a lecherous toss. If that doesn't stop it, you go low and somebody comes up with a half company of bazookas and blasts away. Then you puke in a ditch when the stink of burning flesh comes your way from the Tiger tank and maybe Germans come out of the weeds with short grey jackets carrying Tommy guns. Your loins are writhing erratically, so you pick off one and it's funny but you never knew it was so easy to murder like that. . . . And while you're thinking, they toss death at you, so you duck and signal more mortar shells and you've got them down. . . . Yes, but first they got Conners and Warlowski out there on the road by the white oak tree. So you try not to feel bad and ride ahead, and it's a battle. You're sublimely pleased you came out whole. . . . It isn't at all like Stephen Crane or Tolstoy to you.

You are in a fresh-dug ditch-trench as wide as the General's behind for two days, and you almost never get out. You stink and you ache and you always find the guns going, the big stuff overhead. You hug that hole and smell the dead, and when it's over you come out. All around the jeeps and trucks are burning, the walking wounded are hugging their broken arms as if they were very valuable to them . . . and very susceptible to pain. That's a battle, too, Peter felt. Yet later, the Italian war was nothing much to anyone.

He talked about the Italian war one night in London. The big V-2's were falling in the East End and he had a long time to wait for the All Clear. It was a cellar pub near Old Bailey, deep down and its walls sand-bagged. Peter sat with Mike Kozloff, drinking a warm, bitter ale, "weak as cat breath", as Mike said. Mike was rather natty in uniform, his hair close-cropped, his face tanned, and his eyes alive.

"Sure, Italy was bad. I took a whole crew of bombers down there to help set out the Rumanian oil-field bombings. But it's been rough here too. I don't shive a git about the high-nosed brass and the Colonel's daughters keeping their tails up in uniform by the royal tailors, but think of the people in the poor shelters and the ruins and the tube stations. It's pretty amazing."

"Of course it is, Mike. War is no longer safe for civilians."

"Oh, well, nobody asks 'em to be heroes. The French weren't, the English are. What's new with you, Peter?"

"I think I've found myself. I'm a bystander. I guess that's a good job. I just stand on the sidelines and everything happens around me. I can touch it but can't feel it any more."

"Too much of this bad ale."

Mike laughed. From the street came the shrill urge of sirens and the aching thud of debris falling. "Why don't you get married and suffer?"

"Too easy. Anyway, even in passion, I just stand and watch . . . others."

"Ike's sister, huh? You never got over it—"

"No. It started that way, maybe. But something else is lacking. Think how lucky you are, Mike—you never have to admit to anyone you're half-gentile."

"Snobbery, Peter. You should say, half-Jew. Ike's the boy to teach you the proper respect for your tribe. He's off to Palestine, he said, as soon as the shooting is over here."

"There's no answer for me. Old Joseph and Charles Pentland have pretty much salted my bones down as an American. Could you ever be anything but an American, Mike?"

"Hell, no—could El Greco be anything but a Greek, or Rowlandson anything but an Englishman, or that mug who signed himself 'old man mad about drawing', could he be anything but a Jap? No, a real artist grows from his roots up, not from painting what the Fifty-Seventh Street galleries want."

The All Clear went off. The barman polished his bar pump. "There it is, lads. All Clear. Must 'ave been fearful tonight near the Helephant and Castle."

Mike got up, pushed his tin hat on, and hiked his gas mask over his shoulder. "Care for a bit of slap and tickle? Found a lousy art colony near Kensington. Broads with long cigarette-holders and hand-blocked linen drapes. But they strip down like Degas pastels."

"No, thanks, Mike. I'm briefing a crew of propaganda writers in an hour. 'Don't let's be beastly to the Germans' is the new tune we're planning to drop in our leaflets."

Mike said a very dirty word and left. Peter finished his ale and went out. His heels echoed sharply on the pavements as he crossed to his hotel. It was damp and chilly and he turtled down his head into his trench coat. A tart flashed her light in her pale face for just a moment, a soft, pretty face with ash-blonde hair peeking from under a white turban. She quoted him (without knowing it) a line from Chaucer's "Wife of Bath". He thanked her, no, and went on. The barrage balloons were coming down like elephants hurrying to their keepers.

He wondered if Rose Gelhorn had become a fat, fortyish bag. The kind that street corner anti-Semites shouted after, "Hey, you fat old Jewish mama."

It was over so quickly that Peter felt almost cheated. He was wearing his Purple Heart and his silver medal and there had been a big review of the base personnel. The General sat smoking his pipe as Peter came with the reports.

"Peter, I hear it's over. Secret meeting to sign a let-up."

"All over?"

"Looks that way."

Peter sat down and took out his pipe, and he and the General sat smoking.

"Worried, Peter?"

"Hell, yes! What am I going to do now?"

CHAPTER VII

THE ENTIRE PICTURE COLLECTION
OF A WELL-KNOWN AMERICAN FAMILY
TO BE SOLD AT AUCTION
AT THE PARK AVENUE GALLERIES OF
CHADEN-BLENHEIM, INC.

The collection of family portraits, still lifes and landscapes, consisting of some of the best examples of the works of Gilbert Stuart, John Copley, John Singer Sargent, J. M. Whistler, Frederic Remington, Degas, Lautrec, Renoir, Pissarro, Picasso, and many others. Including several fine examples of Early American portraiture and American primitives by unknown artists.
Thursday, May 9th, 1947, at 10 A.M.
Catalogue: One Dollar

Peter saw the notice in the morning *Times* as he lit his old Italian briar with the bent stem, the pipe he called his Sherlock Holmes pipe. He puffed it into life and reread the notice carefully. Of course he should have been prepared for it. Uncle Sam had never been able to repay the loan against the family paintings, and the banks had sent several fine legal notices that they were going to sell the pictures. Too bad, Peter felt, none of the family could afford to keep the paintings; the collection was now worth a lot of money, but at that moment none of the family was in a position to take the paintings, as Sam put it, "out of hock".

Peter walked slowly to the window of the rather second-rate hotel overlooking overcrowded streets, and glanced out at the early morning traffic in the cross-streets. Perhaps it was just as well the paintings were going. A bunch of old Jews already forgotten, long since dust in American graveyards. The important thing was that their seeds still spawned in the "well-known American family", still replenished the earth.

One of the seeds turned away from the window and knocked out the heel of his pipe into a chipped-glass ashtray. A hell of a lot of replenishing he had been doing. Drifting, brooding, no base, no home. Even the war seemed lost in history, was far away, belonged to another century of his life. He would like to see the old faces again. It seemed his whole life had been built around the old family pictures; all the monthly visits he and Nicole had made to "the Jews", as children, became now the most important events of his youth. He smiled. The psychoanalytical boys were so sure that childhood was the only real stage in the development of a human being.

The phone rang with the shrill, unabashed ring of a second-rate hotel. It was Di. Her voice was soft, close and husky. He had forgotten something, most likely; a date to have breakfast and a visit to the museums, or early tennis in borrowed pants.

"Hello, Peter, have I dragged you out of the hay?"

"No, Di, I was brooding over a fairly ill-spent life."

"Buck up. Dinner?"

He did not answer at once. Did he want to go on with it? Then he said, "Where will you be this afternoon?"

"Writing copy about the fit of milady's girdle or rustproof bananas, as usual."

"Can I call about four, or is that too late?"

There was a crackle of laughter on the other end of the connection. "It's only in popular novels that the gal is coy. I'm ready as usual with vine leaves and half-burnt offerings."

"Save that prose for advertising copy. I'll call you at four."

" 'Bye, darling. Has it been very good for you?"

"You know it's been wonderful, Di."

"Make me a kissing sound, Peter."

He made the sound and hung up and hunted out his least frayed necktie. A man who had dug three dry holes in Oklahoma in the last year is not very well dressed at any time, and Peter was at low ebb. His partners were trying to raise money for one more try in Dalton County for a gusher, but Peter had another, bigger problem on his mind. Dinah ("hate that name darling—call me Di—it's short and easy"). Di Selwin, then, as one of those beautiful, tall, red-haired girls who are well known as copy chiefs in the better advertising agencies and swankier publications. They are all smartly, even slickly dressed, keep their bodies as keen as their minds (and all, secretly, Di confessed, "dread the day they will reach thirty, hard, efficient, successful, and pretty lonely in bed"). Di had found Peter in the rain outside of the Music Hall one sad matinee—his Oklahoma tailoring looking worse than ever, the big limp Stetson (he wore it because he had no other) pulled down over an unshaved face. She had offered him part of her taxi, and he had accepted because the rain was getting worse and he hated the city street filled with muck and odours and cold dampness.

"This is a pickup," the girl in the sheer silk raincoat had said, her red hair escaping from under the oilskin hood. "An old-fashioned pickup out of Faith Baldwin."

"Thanks, I'm flattered." He beat his Stetson on a wet knee.

"You don't remember me, do you, Mr. Perry?"

"No." He was puzzled: this scene was just like the movie he had just seen. Life is such trite melodrama.

"Lord and Thomas Advertising Company, the Off Shore Oil account. The little eager beaver a year out of Smith who rushed the copy to you."

Peter wiped the rain off his unshaved face. "Those god-damn radio jingles."

"To quote a wit—how about slipping out of your wet coat into a dry Martini?"

It was warm and cozy in the cab, the rain beat, beat, and turned to sleet, the cab skidded, the sky turned into a heavy lead bowl. He took her out to dinner after buying a clean shirt and spending two dollars in a scented barber shop that dug the just-lived past of Oklahoma oil fields out of his fingernails. He felt tired but game, a lousy mood, he admitted, but the best he could do.

He spent the night in her small little apartment off Fifth Avenue with a white piano, a small bar, Miró and Rouault on the walls, and in the morning he found her gone to business, a lipstick smudge on his left pap. He felt weak, lazy, and characterless, and slightly happy. He read her Heritage Club books and found a bottle of Scotch and mixed himself some stiff drinks that bit like old times. . . .

That had been two weeks ago. He made effortless love to her and borrowed two hundred dollars on the old furniture and silver old Joseph had left to him, and which had mellowed in storage since the Larchmont days. Poor Joey, his father had spent his heirlooms on a copy writer.

They were very good for each other and very tender and neither was in the first romantic glow of an early, eager love of illusions and demands, at least not at first. They rattled around in the nights and lay side by side smoking cigarettes in the warm dark and talked about their ideas and their hopes. They locked fingers and begged each other not to take this seriously. Ha, ha.

It was only because he did not want to hurt her that Peter decided to bring the thing to a quick close. Like all women, she was deeply serious after all. He wired his partners he was coming back, there was no money for wildcatting in the town. It had dawned on Di she wanted to get married. All women did, he suspected, but the ash inside him (as he romantically called it) was cold and had no spark of that kind in it. He could not see himself again the dutiful husband, the settled-down male with the marching diet of little duties and casual household tasks. Di was wonderful, of course, and earnest, and under the glossy chatter, a full and honest person of deep integrity. No, he thought, as he brushed the cheap suit that was only a week old, no, he would not take her out to dinner. Let her marry a vice-president and see Scarsdale plain.

The middle-aged Peter in the hotel mirror looked back at him and agreed. The blond hair was thinning deeply on the sides. Soon he would have a Shakespeare brow. There was grey in it now, too, and he was putting on weight. The back of the head was filling out.

There was a hint of coming snow in the air as Peter walked over to Park Avenue, but the day was still crystal clear and sharp and full of detail. He felt almost a morbid pleasure in his sad heaviness over the family pictures.

The gallery had a white, sedate front, and a doorman dressed with dignity and with a face that would have made his fortune in Hollywood playing honest bankers. A dim, holy light, skilfully arranged, filled the gallery walls. And on them hung the family. The Manderscheids, the Pedlocks. All the tribe that could afford either a fashionable painter, or a travelling sign dauber with not too much talent. Rows of comfortable chairs had been placed before a kind of plush pulpit, and a fat young man with an old face was peering like a popular minister over his wing collar and plum-coloured, ascot tie at the well-filled gallery while he picked at his right ear. A crisp young woman, unhealthily pale, sat at a table selling a thin catalogue. Two men in neat overalls were moving Uncle Sam's favourite Remington of madly dramatic cowboys from a raised platform toward a back room. The sale had already started. People held cigarettes in their fingers and comfortably watched the sale.

The two men in overalls were back and were moving a heavy, ornately framed picture onto the platform. It was a very heavy dark canvas; one could just make out a long head, a handsome thin beard, great, goggling eyes, and pale, high forehead.

The young-old man nodded at it.

"Item 10. Of the school of El Greco. Said to be a portrait of the Duke of Escalona. Don Diego Lopez [Peter noticed the Levi had been skipped] Pacheco Cabrera y Bobadilla."

Peter looked up at the dim "New Christian." Around him several men talked to each other, and one of them held up a finger crooked in some signal. The man on the pulpit nodded, and the bidding went on in that half code, half ritual of professional dealers and buyers bidding for private parties. Peter felt a buzzing in his ears. Was it the past in some odd way signalling good-bye to him, or was it only the fact that he had forgotten to eat any breakfast?

"Notice this hand-carved sixteenth-century frame."

Tante Strasser sat all day in a deep chair, her claw-like hands folded in her lap. She did not talk much any more, but the Kahn-Wassermans were very proud of her, and took special visitors to her room in their big house and whispered she was over a hundred and three years old, perhaps even more, and as bright as they come. "Hello, Tante Strasser." The old face peered "*Morgenstunde hat Gold im Munde.*" Wonderful.

Tante Strasser saw them only dimly and heard them not at all. Deep in her, memory stirred, like lazy seaweed in a long, stagnant pool. Sometimes she could start the old, long-lost visions moving in her mind—heavy, clotted pictures of Vienna long, long ago. A childhood in red velvet and the old man who had known Prince Metternich and Franz Josef Haydn. There was that rake Count Coudenhove and the carriage on their way to Schönbrunn. Those warm afternoons in the little bedroom with the green hussar's jacket flung onto the chair by the deep, deep bed and music far away. The golden gulden being thrown at the gipsy fiddler. . . . The colours of the Hapsburg-Lothringen and singing in the woods, picnics with sunshades over the ladies' heads. Herr Strasser she never saw too clearly. They had been married too long a time. A heavy man with a clever beard for prayer and a wise eye for business and with comfortable shoes on his tired feet and the fish just right on Friday nights. All *gestorben*.

But mostly she just sat and waited. They fed her three times a day. She was very greedy and ate with great, slobbering relish. They never gave her enough. She dreamed at times of a great roast goose and *Rebhuhner mit Sauerkraut, Westphalischer frischer Obstkuchen mit Schlagsahne*. She waited now for her midday bowl of gruel, her acid and ancient juices stirring impatiently. . . .

"This sale to continue until all the paintings are sold. Next. Item 12 . . ."

Mike Kozloff sat in a mean, little room on Post Street, in San Francisco, bent over a kitchen table of unpainted pine. His uncut, black hair fell over his eyes, and he brushed it back when he reached for a soiled glass, grimy with fingerprints, from which he took a gulp of raw gin from time to time. Stacks of unsold paintings, their canvas faces glazed with odd colours, stood against the wall. He was writing quickly with a large pen, tracing with India ink quick lines of text to his series of drawings, "The Fifth World War".

Mike had spent six frenzied months on the series of drawings, and had tinted them with watercolours, and now he was finishing the text to go with them. He had forgotten everything else; the world outside, its people, his family, his few friends, his poor little art dealer; everything, to finish in one creative surge the series of drawings depicting an era of the future. The world smashed flat by the last great atomic bluster and the error of one of the major world wars. Albert Einstein's remark had inspired the series: "I don't know what the weapons of the Third World War will be, but the Fifth will be fought with stones. . . ." He finished the glass of gin, scratched a dirty hand with vigour through his heavy head of hair, grinned to himself, and drove the pen across the paper. . . .

Then something happened [he wrote]. They never found out just what. Someplace someone in a scientist's rat nest pressed a wrong button? Or the hangover was a little strong and a flask was dropped? Maybe a wall of lead gave way, or a tool broke. Anyway it happened. The Big Bang!

When it happened it must have happened very fast. So fast no one could do anything. Perhaps they screamed or just stood there. Anyway it was very quick, wherever it happened.

The atom split and something in the next atom gave way and suddenly there was such a chain reaction that atoms were popping like vest buttons off a fat man running, and the thing was done.

Once done—well, there was no stopping it. It looked big and fearful, something that sent up steam and smoke and a lot of solid things, or rather things once solid, and as it spread it went on eating its way along, like a rash. . . .

In space—the great all-space that has no end, no beginning, no top, no bottom—the matted matter and asteroids followed the great, sober laws of routine as laid out along the ecliptic paths of their routes. If anyone noticed the plight of the little crumb of earth far down in the corner of a corner's corner, no one did anything about it.

The tides were running amuck, spewing in over the lands in long, sweeping waves of bottle-green fury, topped with white spume, boiling mad, and carrying everything before them. The very atoms of things clashed apart.

A wind had risen—after the great fires—that blew with a steady, whirling note—like a giant violin string being plucked by an idiot with steady, nerve-shattering regularity. In Asia and over what had once been called Africa, it blew northwest, a tangling skein of blasts ruffling the palms and fronds like the tail feathers of a broad-beamed hen. Trees were the first great sufferers. After a few hours in the wilting grip of the winds, they would bend over and expose the belly surfaces of their leaves.

The blowing never let up, never stopped sounding its note of despair.

Birds of beak, birds of feathers, rainbow-coloured, birds of cruel claws and birds of sweet songs all flew swiftly in the maw of winds with a flapping of wing tips and the gutteral peep of open beaks.

No winged creature could battle against the wind. Even the insects of the field were shattered as the toss of currents smashed their delicate wing surfaces. The weaker birds dropped out first, to plunge with smashed hearts in a long drop from the skies. Then the heavy, creaking birds with their black wings spread, sped on alone, growing weaker and slower in their tossing flight until they went down, too, around in their last smashing thud to the ground.

The great luxury liner Rex was driven far inland by a great sea and her cargo of people and crew screwed up their white, pop-eyed faces into the driving rain and waited for the end. For three days she drove on, her prow cutting water that covered land thousands of miles from any charted sea. Like a huge ghost she moved in the boiling sea, her giant motors ruptured in the fight against the lashing waves and only the pouring sea slapping her ahead into the dark wetness of nothing.

The third day saw a pale dawn and the heaving seas calmer but the wind still blowing. The Rex lay on a new-made shore and shaggy horsemen in heavy, dirty furs rode down along the hissing surf and shook long spears at the monster liner floating over their submerged village.

They attacked her with heavy torches soaked in oil, shot from giant bows, and set her on fire in three places. With their long spears they killed all who tried to land. All were shoved back into the blazing liner while they lashed their ponies and sent up their savage cries against the backdrop of the hills.

For two days the Totentanz of the Rex went on until she was but a charred, twisted steel hulk, and when, at last, like a gutted whale, she slowly smoked out her life, the horsemen turned with a last snarling look and rode off into the vast fastness of central Asia—all that had survived of the mighty far-flung land of the East.

In Paris and London the fires died out. A great silence came down like a pall. The reactions died out. . . .

The young-old gentleman was again reaming his ear with a thin finger. He watched the overalled men place a fresh painting on the platform.

"We have here four prime Copleys. Rare examples of this master's work. I doubt if you will find anything as good outside of the Boston Museum. The first one we offer, Item 17 in your catalogue, is 'A Colonial Gentleman', now before you. Move it forward, please."

Peter watched The Colonial Gentleman become Moses Samuel Manderscheid. It was the last afternoon he would be Moses Manderscheid. After this he would grace some New England mansion, or some Greek's Brentwood hilltop house in California. He would become a bit of well-painted American history. Good-bye, Moses Samuel, Peter said to himself.

"We have a great many fine paintings to sell today. May we start the bidding?"

Captain Tom Manderson of the Black Guard on a tour of duty in the Near East wiped his damp neck again and looked out of the armoured car, across the wide, ugly wadi they were slowly passing. He looked over the sun-baked interior, the iron roof and the iron walls and the machine guns mounted at the slits. The train was slowly puffing past Arab olive groves and Zionist settlements. It would be hours before this bloody train would reach Jaffa. It was a bloody, bloody bore, but served him right for getting involved in that gambling debt and being shipped out here. He looked over the sweating gun crews. A nasty lot of buggers; old Black and Tan ruffians that had done murder (and worse) in Ireland in their time, and had now been sent out here to murder and kill. Either Jews or Arabs, it didn't matter which, as long as they kept the place in bloody turmoil. Those Foreign Office bastards set a policy and someone had to keep it going. "No Mandate, no Hebrew State, just keep the swine stirred up." The Black and Tan knew their trade. Had failed in Ireland of course, but Jews don't fight back, you know. "Blasted cowards the lot," old Aleface, the top-kick, had said, "ain't enough guts in 'em to fill an 'erring."

Captain Manderson sat on a box of machine-gun belts and half-closed his eyes as they passed another wadi, the slopes of this one spotted with goats. Behind him the rails clattered, the freight train, heavy and slow, its wagons loaded with barbed wire and riot gear.

And all that Barclay Bank stuff. Captain Manderson didn't approve of the way the country was being run. Damned Labour chaps had no idea of Empire. But then, unlike Captain Manderson, they didn't go back (at least on one side of the family) to the Norman Barons.

Aleface rubbed his red-scarred face and spit from between where two huge front teeth should have been.

"Don't like that rise ahead, Captain. Bloody sure to be a band of them muckin' Irgun or Stern chaps out to snipe at us. I better 'ad get the muckin' bombs out."

"Do what you think best, Bailey."

"Right, sir."

"This is a fine example of Copley's American period. His early solid style which is so rare now, a style that he later modified in London when he began to compete with the English portrait school of Gainsborough, Reynolds, and Lawrence. Notice the brush work on the sleeves. Are you bidding, Mr. Fenning?"

Joey Perry lay on his stomach in the school gym finishing the large poster in front of him. He got up to admire it. It showed a large schmoo with a lot of little schmoos as a borner. The red letters read: "For school president we schmoos vote for Joe Perry."

Ed Wright came in scuffing his black canvas sneakers on the polished gym floor. He folded his arms and closed one eye and nodded.

"We'll make fifty of them, Joey, and knock the election for a goal. That's a poster we can't lose with."

"What are Kramer's bunch plannin' to do?" Joey asked, painting in the whiskers of the big schmoo.

"The ole intellectual yap. The high school needs bandstands for the band. And the hundred best books as picked by some jerkwater college in Maryland. But don't you worry, Joey, you're in. We're not going to let a Yid like Kramer beat us."

Joey put down the brush and wiped his thumbs carefully on the seams of his jeans. He was already six feet tall but very lean and the character in his face kept shifting from month to month; first it was in his deep dark eyes, then in his thin mouth; just now his jaw lines were forming.

"Kramer is a very good man, Ed. Maybe even better for the school than our side."

Ed Wright put his hands in his pockets and sang in a low voice, "Papa, won't you dance with me." "Hell, Joey, I didn't mean nothin'. Kramer isn't a bad guy. Come on, let's have a coke."

"I gotta get back to the cannery. See you later. What's playin' at the Empire?"

Ed gave a wolf cry and ran his hands tenderly over his torso. "Lana Turner! Pick you up at seven."

Joey put the poster on the leather gym horse and went out and lit the last cigarette in his pack. He started the hot rod at the curb by kicking the starter button and putting the car into gear at once. He was proud of the cutdown flivver and its silver exhausts but he did not open it up between Tatchogue and Blue Point. He drove with little effort in skilful spins on the course and sat on his spine frowning.

Charles Pentland, his great-grandfather, was deep in his wheelchair on the wharf, a blanket across his legs.

"Hi, Gramp," said Joey, "getting a noseful of sea air?"

Charles Pentland lifted one eyelid and smiled at his great-grandson. "Fine day. Very fine day. The Pentlands, you know, were a seafaring race once. Owned their own clippers and sent them to China and I fear to Africa for black cargo. The counting house caught us. Sad. Remind me, I want to call a meeting of the board of directors at two. Very important."

"Sure, Gramp." Joey tucked the robe around the thin old man and crossed the beach to the cannery. He put on long white rubber boots and went into the steam room. His grandfather Ralph was washing the cement floor with a scalding stream of hot water. The great clam kettles were beginning to churn and bubble. The odour of Perry's Prime Clam Chowder (Boston style) filled the shed. Joey hated the taste of the stuff and of all fish products.

He took the hose from his grandfather and finished washing the floor and dumped two wheelbarrows of clam shell onto the growing mountain behind the shed. He came back to watch his grandfather tinker with the canning machine. A long line of open tin cans, shining new, waited to begin their march to the soup-canning pipes. Joey refilled the labelling machine with the bright blue-and-gold labels.

"How's the election going, Joey?"

"I'm withdrawing."

"I thought you were keen on it."

"Takes up too much of my time. Wanta calk that old ketch I bought. Anyway, Sol Kramer is a better man than I am. Deep thinker. Has all the facts and a sense of humour. A real hep guy."

Ralph wiped his hands and spun a valve. The canning tools leaped into life. Ralph turned on the labelling machine. The soup kettles made bubbling, belching sounds. The odour of clam and spices filled the shed.

"Let 'er go," said Joey.

"Be sure the glue pots for the labels are filled."

"This fashionable group was painted when Sargent was painting a great many of the European families of importance. We have here some portraits of the Perry family who are connected, I believe, to the Pentlands of Boston. No Sargent of this size has been on the market in the last three decades."

Peter brushed his eyes to make sure there were no damn teardrops there. How young Joseph looked with the dark beard cut square across, the strong hands holding the glowing cigar. And Aunt Rebecca and those three small boys, their naked knees, the big blue bows around their necks and the Eton collars. Hard to believe that Sam and his father and Egon had once been bare-kneed boys in Eton collars. He remembered his own baby picture, the one his father used to keep on his desk in the bank. It seemed even longer ago than the smart brush work on the platform.

Ike Sontag pulled the belt around so that the hand grenades did not dig into his stomach. They were all lying in a clump of camel bush and the rails burned like ribbons of fire below them. They had been here for two days now and were going a little mad from sun and nerves. Ithamar pushed the nose of his Bren gun a little ahead of him and cocked one sunburned ear to the ground—the holy ground of Israel (Ike thought). Ithamar held up his hand. He spoke Hebrew with a Russian overtone. None of them spoke Hebrew well but none spoke anything else.

"I hear the train."

Lazlo shrugged his shoulders. "Wrong train, I'm sure. And if it's the right train, the bastards in the Agency have sold us over to the British again."

Ike asked, "The dynamite well hidden?"

"Deep under the roadbed. Don't worry, they'll splash all over the landscape. Dirty bastards. They tortured my brother to death in Acre Prison and beat me last year for six days without reason before they let me go."

Ike said, "They'll have reason enough after this. Remember, after the blast goes off, fire at all men in uniform that try to leave the train. We're outnumbered badly so don't waste any bullets or bombs. Set fire to the coaches. We'll meet at Abe's place in two days."

Ike picked up the loose wires and fastened them in the plunger box and put his hand on the firing lever. The train was puffing up the rise

393

now. They were on the alert in there—the noses of the machine guns moved back and forth through the gun slits on the armoured car. . . .

Ike closed his eyes to keep them clear for the last exact moment when he set the charge off under the steel-clad car. Odd he should be here with a group of outlaw patriots blowing up British soldiers when all he had wanted was a place on one of the farms, repairing their tractors. Odd how he had turned against the waiting, bootlicking policy of the Agency, and had found the one group that was willing to attack the British and drive them out of the land. Odd he had found that the whole people were behind the outlaws and hid them and fed them and buried them neatly when they died. Only the Agency was against them and turned them over to the British. Some day when the country was free and belonged to them they, the underground, would be forgotten and the others made the heroes of the resistance. Odd . . . but enough of odd. The train was close now, its steamy cough beating at the bushes. The engine crossed the wooden tie marked with a brown cross, then the tender, then the mail car, then . . . Here it was, the great iron car, its black noses of death still fanning the landscape. . . .

Ike leaned on the firing lever. "Let it go," said Ithamar.

"Let's hope," Lazlo said, "the dynamite was well made."

"Confederate Major in full uniform, painted by Johnson of Charleston, dated 1864. Also an unsigned painting of General Jeb Stuart. . . ."

Peter smiled. The damn fool didn't know it was J. E. B. Stuart, never Jeb. He stood up and walked slowly to the back of the gallery. It had become boring watching the family paintings being sold. Some how the kick was missing. He felt free of the past. The feeling of being a bystander was also gone.

"Notice the detail on the uniforms. Confederate officers do not wear shoulder straps. The sleeve detail is remarkably fine, and . . ."

"Was it a hard day, Jacob?"

"Like any other day in the dress business."

"I have tickets for the Bowl tonight; Rubinstein, but if you're tired . . ."

"Who's tired?"

Jacob Kozloff brushed off the idea with a gesture and opened his copy of the *Los Angeles Daily News*. "Trouble, trouble all over the world." Selma skilfully drove her way through the five-o'clock traffic and turned up Beverly Drive. Close on the right rose the dark-brown hills of Hollywood and beyond them, the snow-topped Bernardinos. She never got over the excitement of California. Even after the war years when Jacob's business went into a slump and they had to take out a mortgage on the Westwood bungalow. Time had thinned Selma and whitened her hair, which she wore in ordered, beauty-shop waves now. She shopped in the supermarkets and kept the house clean and hoped Jacob would have a good season in Famous Hollywood Sport Fashions. Even here in the sun people had to struggle for a living.

Jacob rattled his paper in anger. "The Irgun scum blew up another British train. Seventeen dead. Gives us good Jews a bad name. . . ."

Doctor Edward Sontag, certainly the most famous of living psycho-analysts, listened to the old men chant.

מִזְמוֹר לְדָוִד יְיָ רֹעִי לֹא אֶחְסָר: בִּנְאוֹת דֶּשֶׁא יַרְבִּיצֵנִי עַל מֵי מְנָחוֹת יְנַהֲלֵנִי: נַפְשִׁי יְשׁוֹבֵב יַנְחַנִי בְּמַעְגְּלֵי צֶדֶק לְמַעַן שְׁמוֹ: גַּם כִּי אֵלֵךְ בְּגֵיא צַלְמָוֶת לֹא אִירָא רָע כִּי אַתָּה עִמָּדִי שִׁבְטְךָ וּמִשְׁעַנְתֶּךָ הֵמָּה יְנַחֲמֻנִי: תַּעֲרֹךְ לְפָנַי שֻׁלְחָן נֶגֶד צֹרְרָי דִּשַּׁנְתָּ בַשֶּׁמֶן רֹאשִׁי כּוֹסִי רְוָיָה: אַךְ טוֹב וָחֶסֶד יִרְדְּפוּנִי כָּל יְמֵי חַיָּי וְשַׁבְתִּי בְּבֵית יְיָ לְאֹרֶךְ יָמִים:

It turned out to be an old friend:

The Lord is my Shepherd; I shall not want.
He maketh me to lie down in green pastures: he leadeth me beside the still
*   waters.*
He restoreth my soul:
He leadeth me in the paths of righteousness for his name's sake.
Yea, though I walk through the valley of the shadow of death,
I will fear no evil: for thou art with me; thy rod and thy staff, they comfort
*   me.*
Thou preparest a table before me in the presence of mine enemies: thou
*   anointest my head with oil; my cup runneth over. . . .*

As a village lad, Doctor Sontag thought, Christ, too, had recited this psalm. . . .

Nicole's parties were always such fun. Not too longhair and not too much polo pony talk. Just right and the right people. Pansy song-writers with a hit show on Broadway full of delightfully dirty double meanings, Hollywood glamour boys who were accused daily of being fellow-travellers, poets who carried Parker 51's and wrote for tele-vision, cameramen from *Life* and a reformed book reviewer or two from *The New Republic*. Nicole felt that the fashion designer from Lord and Taylor was just the right company for Doctor Wymer, who had done something fearfully clever with biological warfare. Still secret, of course—"only Drew Pearson knows all the details".

The party had spread out.

The tray was empty and Doctor Wymer hugged his drink, too lazy to go to the bar for a new glass. The fashion designer rubbed her lips together and said in a voice carefully moderated to a husky imitation of a popular Southern actress. "Doctor Wymer, I hear you are an admirer of D. H. Lawrence."

"He's interesting but it's difficult to separate the nonsense from the sense."

"Too daring for you, Doctor?"

"Listen to the simple Lawrence bragging:

> '. . . Then willy nilly
> A lower me gets up and greets me;
> Homunculus stirs from his roots. . . .
> He stands, and I tremble before him.
> —Who then art thou?—
> He is wordless, but sultry and vast . . .
> How beautiful he is! Without sound,
> Without eyes, without hands;
> Yet, flame of the living ground
> He stands, the column of fire by night.
> . . . . I salute thee
> But to deflower the . . .
> Pardon me!' "

Peter stood in front of the drugstore phone booth waiting for the large woman to finish her talk with someone in Rye, New York. He held the warm coin in his hand and smiled. He was a free man suddenly. Somehow the sale of the family pictures had freed him from the Pedlocks, their problems and their powerful hold on his mind and body.

He felt now that Peter Manderson Perry could do what he wanted, love whom he wanted, and that no shadow of family or ritual would again ever bring him into to its orbit. The family was dead or scattered, the old, sacred faces sold. A prisoner since birth, he was now free.

Peter spun the coin in his hand. Yes, he had always been afraid to love properly. His fantastic love for Rose Gelhorn had perhaps been only a tribute to the Pedlocks, "the Jews" he and Nicole had visited as a child. The whole thing had been wrongly begun and lamely ended because the pull and the example of the Pedlocks held him.

His father had been braver. Ralph had broken away and done what had to be done. Ralph was a free citizen in a free country.

"She's the one who drinks," said the phone booth voice, "and married that retired General in Pasadena."

Peter looked at his wrist watch. His marriage with Lucy had been doomed from the start. He had spent the years of wedlock just waiting patiently for the day she would call him a dirty Jew. And Lucy had at last delivered. But now he was neither afraid nor unhappy. He was a middle-aged man standing with a hot coin in his hand waiting to make a call. It didn't matter if he were Hindu, Jew, or Hottentot, or a Cabot or a First Family of Virginia now. The family was sold up, dead, or dusting away. He was just an American of the twentieth century; he was alive and kicking and his days of bystanding were over. Life stirred deeply inside him.

The woman came out of the phone booth popping a pink candy drop into her rust-coloured mouth. Peter shut himself up in the airless coffin and dialled.

Of that aimless, gruff, murdering little creature Homo sapiens, there was little sign. It was a still world; cracked, empty—the silence broken now and then by the caw of birds of rapine which had passed slim months and were now pecking on nasty morsels snagged on exposed rocks.

The land reeked with a fishy odour and the white crust of sea salt caked everything like a leopard's pelt. In the sunlight, the glazed whiteness of the reflected salt streaks were blinding. The fields, the vineyards, and the gardens were bone-barren and sterile under the salt. Only after long rains would they produce again but many washings would be needed before the fields would be scrubbed clean enough to cherish in darkness the sprouting seed and send it forth to the sunlight alive and pale green, with roots nourished in healthy ground. Only when the saltiness was gone from Earth would the seed shells open and send out the whiter feeler roots into the mould of the underearth.

The first land to see the sea depart completely was in the hills high beyond India. Here, far northeast of the Arabian Sea, in the stronghold of the Himalayas, beyond even the lands of the Waziris and Afridis, the long-cliffed valleys first saw Sun and felt the glow of its touch.

There were faint grey lines that might be Africa and, on the north shore, stretched a few hundred miles of deadly fever swamps, knee-deep in muck and populated by knife-bearing insects that zoomed like bombing planes in hunger at any animal whose flesh they could feed on.

Broken columns, rusting, high-speed autos, and tangled wires dotted the bug-buzzing landscape. Under strong moonlight Rome was a lovely ruin, like a long-forgotten page of old history now read only by the flitting moths and the long, lean wolves that came down from the seven hills to sniff at the rubbish and howl to the sky.

To the westward, one came to many islands.

Peter remembered now some lines in a book of letters of Anton Chekhov's that he had read in Italy: "Remember that in our day every cultured man, even the most healthy, is most irritable among his family, because the discord between the present and the past is first apparent in the family. It is an irritation which is chronic, which has no pathos, and does not end in catastrophic consequences. . . ."

A far-off voice on the other end of limbo came out of the phone. "What number did you dial, please?"

He discovered he had dialled C-H-E-K-H-O-V. He hung up and dialled again. Yes, some day he would fall really in love again. Not with a Lucy, or with a sleek bit of magazine bait like Di. His days of innocent bystanding were over.

"Hello," said a changing youth's voice on the other end. "Perry Packing Plant."

"Hello, Joey, it's Dad."

There was genuine pleasure on the other end. "Hello, Pop, how are you?"

"Pretty good. Just wanted to talk to you, and maybe see you tonight."

"We're running a batch of sea secrets, but I'll be finished soon."

"Joey, how about dinner, and a night baseball game?"

"Sure, give three to one on the Yankees."

The earphone was damp with Peter's grip. "Joey, how would you like to come west with me?"

"You mean it?"

"The two of us. I have some work to do there. It's big and it's lots of fun. We could sort of rough it."

Joey's voice reached a new pitch of excitement. "Like old Joseph, huh? Like the time he went west to Butte and got shot in the neck and killed a man?"

"I can't promise any gunplay. Meet me in front of my hotel at seven. Give my best to Papa and the rest."

"You bet."

The wire died as the click cut them off. Peter smiled and hung up. *Like old Joseph, huh?* Odd, he was as excited as a raw kid, like Joey.

There were smoke columns once in a great while and there were washed-up tree branches showing recent axe work and glass balls from fishnet floats.

The great American cities were almost all levelled to the ground; the water turned all foundations to mudholes. A few places like New York presented a better class of ruins because of being built on solid rock, but even here, on close inspection, the streets were head-high in debris. Many buildings had proved their faith in building inspectors by folding up and much of the tall town's former pride was now trespassing on neighbouring boroughs.

Of human beings, even a new pithecanthropus erectus, there were at first no signs. As the world shook itself like a wet collie and the water drained away, man—shivering and damp—did appear from the highlands and on some of the floating wreckage. But he was not in great numbers and seemed too weak to do much to stay alive.

Around the world only a few smoke columns went up (where some shelters had been thrown up) and a little digging in reeking rubbish was being done. Not many lived after the coming back of the land. Chills, fevers, starvation and low spirits took their toll. Only the strongest, the toughest, remained to walk around. They hunted for food, seized stray women, burrowed for shelter, dressed in rags, when they were lucky enough to have them—and shivered when they thought of the life ahead.

There was no way of telling how many people had come out, no way of knowing how many people the world now held. The atoms, very tired now, rested. . . .

"How many dozen cans is that?"

"Three gross of the clam chowder and half a kettle of the oyster stew still to go."

"Be sure the labels aren't sticking together, Joey."

"Good Jews? To most people, Jacob, they're like Indians—the good Jews are dead Jews."

"Don't make me jokes."

"The last car is beginning to burn."

"Good. Keep firing. A group of them are hidden in that gully beyond the signal block. Have Lazlo crawl in there with some bombs."

"Lazlo is dead. Got it the first blast."

"Painted in 1913, during Picasso's best cubistic period. 'Egon's

Room in Blue and Yellow.' Signed and dated. Notice that the flat-patterned treatment is . . ."

. . . As Tante Strasser spooned gruel into her mouth and the Captain looked where his right leg had been and already, in the sky, the big dark birds were gathering and the smell of the burning train gagged him, two of them walking very fast and carrying Lazlo, but Ike made them put him down; as the last can rattled through the machine Joey began to seal the brown cartons . . . from the tall buildings the workers were piling out and later she would cry, when she was all alone and he gone back to Oklahoma . . . the leg stopped hurting when he died as the car crossed Wilshire Boulevard and turned toward the high pylons of the Westwood shopping district . . . Ike vomited in the ditch . . . the men removed the Renoir from the platform. . . .

Peter came out of the hotel and the doorman put away his racing form and asked about a taxi. Peter shook his head. He put his hands in his pockets and grinned. People would think he was drunk. A middle-aged man waiting to take his son to dinner. His son and Ralph's grandson and Joseph's great-grandson, and the genes of the Mander-scheids and a lot of Pentland history all walking toward him in the shape of one lean young man with a sunburned nose, his arms growing out of his jacket and his pants showing too much sock.

Joey waved and grinned and Peter started toward him. All around him the streets of the Republic were full of people moving towards their evening meal. The weather remained fine.